NO MAN'S LAND

A NOVEL

PAPER FOREST PRESS

C. K. MCADAM

Contents

To Clay Reynolds who believed in this story
and encouraged me to finish it.
May you rest in peace.

And to my dad who defected
but came back.
And then tried again ...

"Is freedom anything else than the right to live as we wish? Nothing else." ~Epictetus

Part I

1972

Chapter 1

The woods and fields west of Wallhausen were watched. East German border guards maintained a restless vigil over the land. In the stillness of the night, a deer might wander into that country, but caught in the watchmen's gaze escaped the silence that nature itself was cowed into.

Breaking through the stillness, a couple staggered through the dark, ignoring the turrets, those dusky sentinels in the distance, which towered over the scene with dread.

Though branches clawed at their faces and thorns tore their clothes, they didn't seem to notice. The woman stumbled and fell, and at once, the man was at her side, helping her to her feet and pulling her with him while she pathetically brushed away the dirt and leaves.

It was a moonless night, just as he had hoped. Now and then, he threw a wary glance over his shoulder, even though in that total blackness his eyes might as well have been made of glass. His senses were alert, tuned to the highest frequency of animal instinct, and with uncanny awareness he sensed his way through the wild overgrowth and dewy fern. As they reached the edge of the woods, the woman pulled him to a stop. With a look of urgency, he caught her shadow by the arm and whispered, "We need to hurry."

Winded and pulsing with fear, she leaned against a tree and placed a cradling hand upon her stomach. He moved closer to her, again scanning the dark forest behind them while gently pulling leaves from her now disheveled brown curls and rubbing away a smudge of dirt from her cheek.

"You're sure we can do this?" she asked between breaths.

He put his hand on hers, and she stopped stroking her stomach. "If you have second thoughts, you need to tell me," he said, searching her face, which shone ghastly pale like chiseled marble.

Scarcely able to move, she could only manage a weary smile, and with a faint half-voice muttered, "I don't. Really. Just catching my breath."

At this assurance, a look of relief shot through his face. "We've almost made it. The river is close. Once we've crossed, we're there."

He took her hand and led her out of the forest into an open field overgrown with thistles. Pausing for a moment, both cast their eyes to the vast sky above, which shone dark and cold and glistened like an obsidian knife. They crossed the field more slowly and more carefully than they had the forest. Both now scanned their surroundings as they made it to a group of trees beyond, from where the gurgling of a river could be heard.

"We better stay low from now on," he whispered.

She nodded in agreement and they both crouched down and crept forward toward the river bank. As they reached it, they both stared toward the other side, which was hard to make out in the dark. He looked at her, took her right hand, and rubbed it. "It will be very cold. Let's get across as quickly as possible." She only nodded. Her eyes were fixed on the dark waters that flowed by. He followed her gaze and swallowed hard. The water would be freezing cold. After all, this was November. He looked back at her, and their eyes met. He managed a smile and squeezed her hand.

As they slid down the steep riverbank and stepped into the dark cold, they both gasped. She covered her mouth with her hands to muffle a scream. The cold water stung like needles and stole the breath from his lungs. If they had been spotted, all that could be discerned were the grey wisps of breath, which now and then appeared like spirits escaping upon the water. They strode steadily forward in the dark, waist-deep, silently streaming water, breathing hard. The current was strong and they constantly had to steady each other not to lose their footing.

"I can't feel my legs anymore." Her voice was barely audible over the rushing of the river. But he had heard her. "We've almost made it. Look. A few more steps. I'll pull you up," he said between short breaths.

He was at the other side first and feebly attempted to pull himself up onto the grassy riverbank, but slipped and slid back down into the water, cursing under his breath. Shivering, he pulled himself up again. His wet clothes on the steep bank made him slip again, but he clawed at the grass and was up at last. Flat on his stomach, he faced the river and reached down. "Give me your hand. I'll pull you up."

She obliged. He pulled hard, but her feet found no hold. "With your other hand ... hang on to the grass," he urged, tugging hard on her right hand as she tried to get a hold on the grass with her left. He kept pulling until she reached the top and collapsed upon the ground next to him, a breathless heap of nerves and frenzied exhaustion.

This had been harder than he had expected. He looked back toward the other side of the river, now engulfed in darkness. They had made it across their second toughest obstacle. He felt a surge of exhilaration. No one had discovered them, or at least, no one had made it known that they had been discovered. He moved close to her, sat her upright, and embraced her. She silently shivered in his arms. He brushed the curls out of her face and kissed her softly on the mouth. Her lips were surprisingly warm. He felt guilt wash over him. It was something he had gotten so accustomed to in the past few weeks. They had agreed that now was the best time to defect, but still he felt selfish putting her through this, especially now. If something were to go wrong, he would never forgive himself.

"We better get going," he said.

She wriggled free of his grasp and got up, still shivering. Her clothes clung to her body like a death shroud.

After he finished wringing the water out of his pants, he took her hand, and staying low, they left the river behind and made their way through shrubs and bushes until they came to a wide-open field. This was no man's land, a barren wasteland where nothing green grew anymore, and where the only signs of life were seen in the tire treads of military vehicles which crisscrossed the area. *Todesstreifen.*

"We're nearly there," he breathed, trying to ignore the large warning sign ahead of them. Nothing could be seen in the pitch dark, and briefly exchanging worried glances with her, he thought it best to keep silent from then on. Around them, the night, in one chorused breath, seemed to hush itself into an unknowing act of solidarity with the trespassers.

The inner German border was an extensive system of fortifications that ran along the entire length of the state line between East and West Germany, from the shores of the Baltic Sea to the mountains of the Bavarian Forest. He had heard rumors that their government intended to further secure the border by using mines, as well as raising the fence even higher. They couldn't possibly wait for better times. He knew there wouldn't be any. Brezhnev was ruling Russia with an iron fist, which was felt throughout all member states of the Warsaw Pact. The East German border to

West Germany was the last frontier of communism, and Russia was eager to see that frontier further secured. He looked at her. "Let's run for it." He took her hand, and together they started running, their wet clothes flapping against their chilled bodies. A tall metal fence appeared out of the dark in front of them, and he stopped short, pulling her to a halt as well.

He had researched and scouted this area every time they had visited his mother these past two months. Luckily, the border patrol had not discovered him on his scouting trips. He had been careful. Very careful. But one time he had come so close to being discovered. He had to lie flat on his stomach in the forest for over an hour while border guards with their German shepherds combed the woods. He had wondered if they were looking for him. On that same day, he had gotten a first look at the fence through his binoculars. If they had caught him with those binoculars ...

He had discovered that the border was less secure here. The next watchtower was a mile upstream, and there was only one fence instead of two. The border guards were counting on the river to do the job for them. This part of the border seemed their best shot. And they would only get one shot.

He reached into his pocket and pulled out a small curette. He felt the metal between his fingers, wondering when he would get the next chance to hold one. His fist closed around the instrument and he drew his arm back and hurled it at the metal mesh fence. Nothing happened. No sparks. No voltage. The propaganda had worked. Fewer people had tried to defect in fear of high voltage fences. But it had all been a lie. *But they can't keep us away*, he thought, and took her hand to pull her with him. For a split second he thought about the possibility of mines again, but he brushed aside the thought and kept running.

They sprinted the last few meters. He was at the fence first. She came up next to him only seconds later. She was breathing hard and looked around. Her eyes were anxious. He followed her gaze. They were still alone. He pulled the small backpack he was carrying from his back and opened it. He handed her what looked like a pair of large metal hooks found in slaughterhouses. He took his own pair of hooks out and cast the backpack aside.

"Come on. Now or never." He stuck his hooks through the holes in the fence above his head and pulled himself up. It worked but the muscles in his arms burned. His feet couldn't support him as much as he had hoped. The holes of the meshed metal were too small. He placed his hooks again, one after another, and pulled himself further up. He knew that this wouldn't be easy for her.

Just like him, she stuck her pair of hooks through the tiny openings of the fence above her head and pulled herself up. He heard her breathe hard. The fence seemed higher than before. He placed his hooks again and kept pulling upward, his feet struggling to find footing. He hoped that her pointed shoes would give her more support than his shoes gave him.

He couldn't believe it when he finally reached the top of the fence, which was crowned with barbed wire. The last obstacle. Hastily scanning his surroundings, he reached over it to place one of his hooks on the other side of the metal mesh, the wires cutting through his shirt and leather jacket. He cringed at the pain. Slowly, he distributed his weight to the other side. Then he carefully lifted one leg over the fence. With short breaths and wincing in pain, he searched for footing. In a swift movement that ripped his leather jacket, he placed the second hook on the other side and flung his second leg over the barbed wire. I'm on the other side, he thought, we've almost made it. Exhilaration washed over him. With short hysterical laughs of relief, he hung onto to his hooks, his eyes eagerly searching for her through the meshed metal fence.

Her hooks were only a few centimeters below his. On the other side. She looked up at him, her face jubilant and strained at the same time. With what looked like renewed determination, she placed one of her hooks again, above his. He watched her pull herself up, her arms shaking. They would make it, he thought, trying to suppress the overwhelming relief. And no one had discovered them.

He looked down on the ground below him. There was no need to climb down carefully. With a thud, he landed on both feet on the other side of the fence. I made it, he thought. Unbelievable. I made it. "I made it! Can you believe it? Come on! Oh, I can't believe it was that easy. Come on, now! You have to hurry!" He was now almost shouting, looking up at her.

She glanced over her shoulder. He followed her gaze. Would they have heard? He saw no one. He turned back toward her, urging her on. And then she slipped. Or she couldn't hold on any longer. He wasn't sure. She fell to the ground.

He rushed toward her, but they were now separated by the fence. He tried to reach through the meshed metal, but of course couldn't. "Are you hurt?"

"No," she said, clambering to her feet with her hand pressed against her hip.

He bit his lip, seeing she was in pain, but he knew that she had to start climbing the fence again. Right away. "You need to hurry now. Come on. There is no time." He stepped back, and she looked up at the fence. He saw the doubt in her eyes and felt panic. The hooks were hanging on the fence three and a half meters above her. She jumped to grab them and missed. She jumped again and caught one of them, but couldn't hang on with only one hand. She looked at him, and he knew she was close to giving up.

"Try again," he urged her, struggling to keep the panic out of his voice. Why had he just jumped down and not taken his hooks with him? He could have thrown them over the fence to her.

She looked up and jumped again. A cry escaped her mouth, but he saw her hanging on to the lower hook with both hands. With what seemed her last bit of strength, she reached the second hook higher up and began placing them again. He felt relief wash over him, but urged her on while pacing back and forth, looking in all directions. Then he heard them approach from behind him. He turned and faced the West German border guards.

"What are you doing there, man?" Their voices echoed in the night. "Come away from there. They'll shoot you." The West German border police grabbed his arms and tried to pull him away, but he wrestled free and ran back to the fence, now shouting at the woman. "Now or never! Now or never! Come on. You can do it. Climb up! Please! You need to hurry." He was panicked.

She was now almost to the top of the fence as two East German border guards appeared out of the dark from behind her, a German shepherd at their side and their Kalashnikovs pointing up the fence at her.

"No!" The man lunged forward and tore at the fence. He was now screaming at the woman. "Please!" He looked around wildly, trying to shake off the West German border guards now trying to pull him away with more vehemence.

She looked over her shoulder at the Kalashnikovs.

"Come down from there. We'll shoot. Come down! Now!" The East German border guards were yelling at the woman, but so was the man on the other side who was now being pulled away from the fence by four West German guards. "No! Leave me. Let me go!" He threw punches and landed one. One of the guards held his nose. The three others kept trying to pull him away while he was kicking wildly and screaming at the woman.

Then a shot split the air. Everyone froze. The sudden silence was only broken when the man began screaming again, though now his screams were farther off.

The woman looked at the man on the other side being pulled farther and farther away from her. With a shot in the air, the East German border guards below her had made it clear that they would shoot if she were to keep climbing. She knew it had to be over. She felt her heart stop. She had no choice. There was no way out. Slowly, she climbed down the fence. The Kalashnikovs were still pointing at her, but she didn't look at them. Through the fence, she looked at the man who was pulled away from her into the dark, still yelling, and what she now thought was wailing. And then he was gone. And there was silence.

Her feet hadn't even touched the ground when the guards grabbed her, pulled her down from the fence, and threw her against the metal mesh. They started kicking her. Frantically, she tried to shield not her head but her stomach from those military boots. As she was pulled up and dragged off, she tried to make out any yells in the night. But there were none. They were gone. He was gone.

The guards pulled her with them for a good mile until they reached the watchtower upstream. It seemed the longest, yet the shortest mile ever. The guards pushed her inside and threw her onto a wooden chair. She didn't look up or around, just stared at her reddened hands in her lap. He was gone. He had made it. She hadn't. The thoughts were hammering in her head and she closed her eyes. She licked her lips and tasted blood. It didn't matter. Nothing mattered now. She swallowed hard and tried to fight back the tears. She took deep breaths to calm herself. Just as she looked up, two of the three guards left the tower. What did that mean?

A white light was pointed at her and she squinted.

"Name?" It came out so matter-of-fact that she had to look up at the guard who had asked this most common question in the world, only that his tone was harsher. The guard was writing something down on his clipboard. *I'm not the first they're questioning in here*, she thought. It seemed much too routine. She scanned the little room around her. There was a table in the corner with three chairs. It looked as if the border guards were killing a lot of time there. Cards, a newspaper, a few bottles of beer, and a pack of cigarettes beside an ashtray were on the table. The cards were strewn across the table in total disarray, which told her that they had been put down in a hurry.

"Name!" the guard repeated in an even harsher tone of voice.

She looked at him. His face was smooth and boyish. He could have been her younger brother if she had had one. Only his uniform made him look beyond his years. His eyes, however, showed impatience and arrogance. It was better to cooperate.

"Susanne Schmidt," she said.

The guard looked down at his clipboard, biting his lower lip and scribbling down what she thought was her name.

"The other?" The guard looked at her again. Susanne didn't answer. The guard's brows furrowed. "His name!"

They would find out anyway that it was her husband who had made it across the border. She had no doubt about that. Once Dieter didn't show up for work at the Berlin Zoo, they would know. "Dieter ... Schmidt," she said softly.

The guard was smirking at her. "So, the bastard not only deserted his country, but also his wife. Fine husband you have." Susanne swallowed hard, still tasting the blood from her lips.

"Place of residency?" he asked.

She glanced out the small window. But only darkness stared back at her. "Berlin."

"So, you're not a resident of Wallhausen or any other village in the Restricted Zone?" he asked.

Susanne didn't answer. There was no need.

"Do you know anyone in the Restricted Zone? Has anyone from around here helped you enter the Restricted Zone?"

Susanne looked up at him. She hesitated for a moment. "No ... no one helped us," she said, and looked away.

The guard searched her face and then wrote something on his clipboard. Then he put it aside. He went over to the table and took a cigarette out of the pack. He lit it and looked up and down at her. "You know the law. Trying to flee the republic carries severe punishment." He exhaled. "You're lucky we didn't shoot you."

Susanne didn't respond. There was no use. She felt as if someone had hit her over the head. This couldn't be happening. She had never thought they would get separated. They had talked about getting caught and what would happen to them, but never about the possibility of one of them getting caught and the other one making it. She swallowed. Tears were welling up in her eyes now as the cold reality settled over her. He was gone. He had made it. What was she going to do?

Susanne was left to her thoughts when the guard stepped outside. She hoped that he had believed her. No one had helped them enter the Restricted Zone, so she had answered truthfully. But Dieter's mother lived in Wallhausen two miles down the river. Dieter had grown up there. But the village was in the Restricted Zone and they had not gotten permission to enter it, nor had they sought permission, as they always had to do if they wanted to visit Dieter's mother. Their connection to Wallhausen and one of its residents would soon be discovered. Her mother-in-law would be questioned. Susanne had no doubt about that. It had been wise not to let anyone know about their plans to defect to the West. That would now protect Dieter's mother, but the thought of how her mother-in-law would learn about what had happened made her sick.

The door opened and all three guards came in. The one who had been questioning her grabbed her roughly by the arm. "Move it."

As she was pulled up and out of the watchtower, back into the open, she tried to get a glimpse of the West and its new citizen, but the grounds on the other side lay still and deserted. As she was pushed toward a military off-road vehicle, the sun broke through in the East, igniting the fence and the West that lay beyond with an orange glow. The houses and fields on the other side lay peaceful and still in the breaking dawn.

As Susanne took her seat in the back of the Horch P3, she put her left hand on her stomach. Tears flowed freely now as the vehicle pulled away from the border. When the car entered the *autobahn* minutes later, she knew in an instant where they were going. *Berlin.*

Chapter 2

There was a loud knock on the office door of Walter Fleischer. He looked up from the file that lay on the desk before him. "Come in."

"Prisoner 3/1, Comrade." A prison guard was leading in a woman in her early twenties. She looked around the spartan room in which Fleischer held interrogations. The desk, behind which Fleischer was sitting, another chair in the middle of the room, as well as a small filing cabinet in the corner, presented the only furniture. There was a phone on the desk and a typewriter was sitting on the filing cabinet. A picture of Erich Honecker, Party Chairman and the leader of their country, hung on one of the walls.

Fleischer was glad to see that the woman's demeanor was calm. He hated nothing more than prisoners making a scene. But he thought he detected a hint of desperation behind the calm demeanor. She was quite pretty. Her hair was in disarray, wild brown curls that reminded Walter Fleischer of a barbaric woman or perhaps an Amazon, a stark contrast to her fine clothes, torn and soiled at places, but fine clothes nevertheless. Not the kind of clothes one would wear to make a run for it, Fleischer thought. He had expected no less from what he had read in her file.

He scrutinized her face further. There was dried blood on her lip. They had ruffled the chicken's feathers, he thought.

Walter Fleischer cleared his throat. "Sit down."

She stared at the wooden chair in the middle of the room and didn't move until the guard gave her a little push. For a moment, as she sat down in front of him, Fleischer took his eyes off her. "You may leave," he said to the guard.

The guard clicked his heels and disappeared through the door.

Again, Walter Fleischer cleared his throat in a rather obvious manner. "I'm Walter Fleischer. I'll be handling your case."

The woman in front of him looked up. For the first time, their eyes met.

———

Susanne looked at the man behind the desk. He seemed to be in his early forties. His graying hair matched his gray uniform, which blended in with the plainness of the room. *Stasi*, she thought. Of course. Her case was now a matter of national security.

"Do you know where you are?" The man across from her examined her from head to toe. Susanne chose not to answer. They wouldn't get anything out of her.

"You are in a prison of the State Security Office. Those who have tried to defect or have caused our beloved republic grief of any sort are held here until they do not pose a threat anymore. Do you understand that, Frau Schmidt?" The man peered at her. "Your file tells me that you have been a model citizen. You're an accomplished violinist and you've made a name for yourself in this country and abroad. You've been a great ambassador for your country."

They had kept a file on her? Susanne tried to keep her face expressionless, but her jaw clenched anyway.

He leaned forward. "Frau Schmidt, what I don't understand is why you didn't just stay abroad when you traveled there for your performances. Why this risky undertaking? You could have been shot. Those imperialist West German border guards take any chance they get to do harm to our beloved republic and its citizens. You're very fortunate to sit here in front of me."

Susanne couldn't believe what she was hearing. He couldn't seriously believe that. She stared at him, but he didn't seem to notice and simply continued his little speech.

"The Minister of Culture is aware of the situation you find yourself in. Since he's a fan of yours, he has asked me to do everything in my power to... let's say, avoid the full punishment that would await anyone who tried defecting to the West."

Susanne was still silent and stared ahead, right through the man in front of her.

"I see. You don't wish to cooperate," he said, closing the file in front of him.

Still, Susanne didn't react. The man leaned back in his chair and folded his hands as if to pray. His gaze was penetrating. And then his eyes wandered down to her stomach, where they rested for a moment. He cleared his throat for the third time. "I am told you are pregnant," he said matter-of-factly.

Susanne stared at him. She opened her mouth. How could he possibly know?

"You wish to speak, Frau Schmidt?" Susanne closed her mouth again. There was no use.

Fleischer looked at her with disdain. "We know what's going on in our republic and with its citizens, Frau Schmidt. Since we find you in this delicate state and the minister wishes to expedite your case, I'm pleased to inform you that your trial will be held within weeks. You don't need to wait for months, as is usually the case."

With that, Fleischer got up from his chair, only to sit down again on the edge of the desk. He leaned in toward her. He was so close that Susanne could make out the color of his eyes. They were gray, like his hair and his uniform.

"Frau Schmidt," he said in a sort of fatherly tone, "I recommend you find your voice. We will have to meet again tomorrow and the day after that and so on." He was waving his hand around. "I will need to hear from you what your intentions were. You need to cooperate, Frau Schmidt."

Susanne looked at him in defiance. So, this was how it was handled. Well, she didn't get kicked again or beaten. Quite civilized, actually. She was sure her name had saved her from that kind of treatment.

The Stasi officer got up and stepped around his desk. He picked up the phone.

"You may take prisoner 3/1 back to her cell, comrade."

As soon as Fleischer hung up, the door swung open and the guard appeared. At Fleischer's nod, the guard pulled Susanne up and out of the room.

Chapter 3

Susanne was led to another room where a female guard waited for her. The woman looked like a stuffed sausage in her uniform. Her hair was tied back, but it didn't hide the grease. "Undress," the guard commanded. Susanne obeyed reluctantly. She was too slow for the woman in uniform, who yelled at her to hurry up. When she stood there in only her panties and bra, the guard smirked at her. "All of it," she ordered. Only when the woman stepped toward her did Susanne start to undress completely. She swallowed, trying hard to keep her composure.

What happened next was even more humiliating. Every opening of her body was inspected. Susanne hugged herself, and with clenched teeth tried to swallow down the rising tears. Why wasn't she waking up from this nightmare? Why had everything gone so wrong? She wanted to scream.

At last, the guard threw some prison clothes at her. Susanne put them on and found they were too big. Again, the woman smirked at her and then started to record Susanne's personal items. When she was done, the guard pushed a paper toward Susanne.

"Sign," she commanded. After Susanne had signed, the other guard picked her up again and brought her to a cell. She was led into cell number three, and the heavy door was pulled shut behind her.

Susanne looked around. There was a plank-bed screwed to the wall, a small table in the corner, a stool, a toilet without a seat cover, and a small sink. Glass bricks at the end of the cell provided some light. She stared at the glass bricks as if she could see the outside through the milky haze. But she couldn't, no matter how hard she strained her eyes.

For what seemed like minutes, Susanne could do nothing but stand there and stare at the outside that she couldn't see. When the cold crept up her body, Susanne finally forced her eyes off the glass bricks and slowly walked over to the bed. She felt the rough fabric of the blanket as she sat down. The worst would be the loneliness and all this time to think.

There was a loud bang on the door. "No sitting on the bed during the day," the guard yelled. Susanne looked at the stool. She couldn't imagine having to sit on that all day. So instead, she started pacing back and forth in the cell until a guard pushed what looked like soup through the small opening of the cell door. Susanne ignored it. She couldn't eat. She knew she had to, but she couldn't. She would try tonight.

What seemed like an hour later, she was picked up again and led into Fleischer's office for a second time. He asked her about Dieter's and her plan to defect. Susanne was silent. She wouldn't tell him anything.

"It must have been your mother-in-law then who helped you," Fleischer said.

"No," Susanne said, instantly regretting that she had allowed him to get to her. But she had to make sure they didn't accuse her mother-in-law.

"So ... you *do* have a voice, Frau Schmidt."

"My mother-in-law had no idea about our plans," Susanne repeated. "Dieter scouted the border on our many trips to Wallhausen." She could blame it all on Dieter. He was safe in the West, and after all, this was true.

For the next four hours, Fleischer asked her about her trips to West Germany and the West Germans she had been in contact with. The same questions, over and over again. Susanne only gave minimal answers. She was certain the Stasi was already aware of it all. At the end of the interrogation, Fleischer got his typewriter down from the filing cabinet and started typing up his notes. She had nothing to do but to watch him. When he was finally done, he presented the typescript to her. "Sign here," he said. She scanned the document. He had recorded what she had said, but it sounded so different. The tone was accusatory, and her words had been turned around.

"I'm not signing this," she said.

Fleischer's cold gray eyes penetrated hers. "You'll need to sign," he insisted.

"I didn't say that. Not like that."

"It's the truth, Frau Schmidt. Out of your own mouth. Is it not? Are you telling me that you lied to me?"

Susanne couldn't believe the man. There was no use in reasoning with the Stasi. Only their truths counted. She was so tired. Her body ached. So, she took the pen and signed. What was the use in resisting? She had never felt so powerless in her life. She was completely at their mercy.

The interrogations went on daily. Susanne was almost looking forward to them. That was better than the isolation of her cell. At the end of each interview, Susanne signed whatever Fleischer had typed. She suspected it would be used against her during the trial, but she had no strength to resist. Nothing mattered to her anymore.

Finally, the day of the trial came. She met her assigned lawyer only a week before. Since they weren't allowed to discuss her defense, he only inquired after her health and told her that the minister was doing everything in his power to get her the minimum jail time. But she would receive jail time. After a month in the Stasi prison, she couldn't imagine spending many more, or even years, there. The worst was the loneliness. She wasn't allowed to have any visitors or mail. How she longed to have word about Dieter, but she was completely cut off from everyone and everything.

On the morning of the trial, she got her clothes back. She was put on a prison transport and soon sat in a courtroom. The trial only lasted a couple of hours. She wasn't allowed to speak in her defense, and her lawyer was resigned to listening rather than speaking up for her. At the end, Susanne received a milder sentence than the usual three years. Nine months. And because of her pregnancy, she would spend that time in the hospital wing of the prison. Her lawyer seemed satisfied and even congratulated her. She didn't care. After the initial despair of the first days in prison, she had gone numb. It was as if she couldn't feel anything anymore or would ever again.

After the conclusion of the trial, she got her prison clothes back. They assigned her to a cell in the hospital wing of the prison, which she would be calling home now for the months ahead. This time, however, she shared her cell. Susanne wasn't sure if she liked it. The woman she had to share the cell with had welcomed her warmly, but Susanne kept to herself for the first few days. She didn't feel like talking, but slept almost constantly. Sleep took her away from the harsh reality of the nightmare she was living. She felt utterly alone and forgotten.

After a few days, Susanne was no longer able to sleep much, and a great boredom settled over her.

"Can't sleep anymore, can you?" Her cellmate peered at her from the bed across the room. The woman, whose left leg was in a cast, usually sat on her plank-bed all day, reading or playing cards, and so it was today when she looked over at Susanne who had sighed one too many times in the past hour.

"You're bored. Let's play cards." The woman looked at her in anticipation.

To her own surprise, Susanne managed to get up. She sat down on the woman's bed next to a stack of cards.

"Brigitte." The woman stretched out her hand and smiled at Susanne.

Susanne took her hand, shook it, and returned the smile. "Susanne."

Brigitte started shuffling the cards, and Susanne had time to get a good look at her. Brigitte seemed to be her age with a bony body and short blonde hair.

"Why are you here?" Susanne could no longer wait to ask. In the back of her head, she had wondered about it since she had come here.

Brigitte looked up at her, amused. "I assume for the same reason you're here."

"You got caught as well?"

"Yes," Brigitte said casually.

"I didn't make it, but my husband did," Susanne said, realizing it felt surprisingly good to say it out loud.

Brigitte, who had just dealt the cards, looked up in a mixture of confusion and shock. "You actually tried to defect?"

"Yes," Susanne said, with some confusion of her own.

Brigitte put down the cards, scooted closer, and with a look at the cell door whispered, "Did you just say you tried to cross the border?"

"Yes," Susanne repeated, "Is that not what you're in for?"

"Oh, no. Goodness, no. I helped a friend cover up her plans to flee to the West.

I'm considered an accomplice. Most in here are. I wouldn't dare try to –" Brigitte broke off and stared at Susanne. "Your husband made it?"

Susanne only nodded.

"Good grief!" Brigitte seemed to have forgotten all about the cards. "He made it. Unbelievable. I mean, that's awful. He's over there, and you're –" Brigitte looked at her pitifully, and then put an arm around her.

Susanne felt herself go stiff in the embrace of this woman she barely knew. She couldn't cry any more tears or feel anything. Not even a compassionate hug could trigger anything in her. Susanne was relieved when Brigitte let finally go of her.

"How long did they give you?" Brigitte asked, wiping at the corners of her eyes. "Nine months."

"Me too," Brigitte said with a hint of contempt in her voice. "They must like you to let you off that easily after pulling something like that."

Susanne didn't reply, but looked down at the cards. "Should we play, then?"

Brigitte still eyed her and made no attempt to pick up the cards. "What will you do when you get out of here?"

Susanne looked up at her. She had been so lost in her misery that she had given no thought to what would happen then. There was only one thing that mattered now. The baby growing inside of her. It was her only connection to Dieter.

"I'm pregnant."

"Mother, have mercy!" Brigitte quickly covered her mouth with her hand to muffle her outcry.

"It's the child I have to worry about now," Susanne said quietly.

"Does he know?" Brigitte asked.

"Dieter? Oh yes. He knows. That was one of the reasons why we didn't want to wait any longer to defect."

Brigitte looked at her thoughtfully. "Maybe they'll let you out early."

"Yeah, maybe."

"Here in the hospital, it's much better. We're allowed to use our beds all day. We can have books and visits once a month."

"Visits?" Her mother-in-law must know by now where she was. Would she come to see her? She needed to hear how Dieter was doing. She couldn't bear not knowing.

"What will you do when you get out?" Brigitte asked.

"Find a way to be with Dieter, of course," Susanne said with some vehemence. Brigitte's brows furrowed and shot the door a concerned look. "There must be another way..." Susanne continued. "I can't stay in this country. Especially after what happened."

"Maybe your family can help you," Brigitte said.

"I don't have any family left. My father was captured somewhere in Poland at the end of the war. The last letter my mother had from him was sent from a POW camp in Siberia. He never came home. My mother died ten years ago. Cancer." Susanne looked at the glass bricks that made up the window as if she could see the outside. "I was at a summer camp when she died."

"They probably sent you away because they wanted to spare you seeing her dying like that." Brigitte's voice was soft and comforting.

"My mother's employer insisted I attend the camp. All the kids whose parents worked at the factory were shipped off for a two-week vacation. It's not that she could refuse. She had to send me." Susanne made no effort at hiding the bitterness she felt every time she thought of that summer. "My grandma raised me after ... my mother's death. She died a year ago."

"What about your in-laws?" Brigitte asked.

"I don't know. Dieter's mother didn't know we wanted to leave. We didn't tell her."

"I'm sure she knows now," Brigitte said unnecessarily.

"I can't believe we're not even allowed any mail," Susanne said.

"Yes. We're completely at their mercy." Brigitte started picking up the cards.

Yes, I'm completely at their mercy now, Susanne thought bitterly. She yearned to have news from Dieter. Any news. She swallowed. How she missed him. He had been ripped away from her

24

just as her mother had been ripped away from her. Her only hope now rested with her mother-in-law. A visit from her was all that mattered to Susanne at present. She would be able to tell her about Dieter. But the waiting would kill her. She had never had much patience. She wanted to scream. But who would hear her? Who would care? She had never felt so utterly alone, and she had been certain that she was acquainted with loneliness before.

Every day, Brigitte was picked up by a guard. After about an hour, she would return. Susanne noticed that Brigitte was unusually quiet when she returned. She would lie down on her bed, turn her face toward the wall, and sleep.

One day, when Brigitte had been picked up, Susanne got up from her bed, though with some effort. Her belly had grown and she started to get uncomfortable on the hard plank-bed. She walked over to Brigitte's bed. Susanne knew that her cellmate kept her things in a small shoebox underneath her bed. Holding her belly, Susanne went down on her knees and then bent down to fish for the box.

Susanne pulled out the box and then opened its lid. A card game, a comb, and some sanitary napkins were in it. Nothing else. Susanne closed it and slid it back in its former hiding place. She held on to Brigitte's sheet and pulled herself up with some effort but the sheet gave way. Out of the corner of her eye, she saw an envelope slide to the floor.

Susanne looked down at the envelope. A letter? They weren't allowed any mail.

Susanne bent down and picked it up. It bore Brigitte's name. Susanne turned the envelope over and looked at the return address. The same name as Brigitte's last name. Her mother? So, Brigitte did receive letters. Why had she lied?

Susanne heard someone come down the hallway and quickly shoved the envelope back under Brigitte's sheet. She wasn't sure if she should confront her cellmate with her findings. Brigitte would know that she had been through her stuff. Susanne listened intently. Whoever had come down the hallway had passed her cell. She went back over to her bed and picked up the book she had been reading. With the prison library so well stocked with German classics, she would leave this place well-read.

Susanne woke up with a start. There was a sharp pain shooting through her abdomen. She sat up and felt wetness between her legs. What was happening? She looked around frantically in the semi-dark cell and tried to make out Brigitte's form on the bed across from her.

"Brigitte?"

Brigitte gave a small grunt, but didn't stir.

"Brigitte!" Susanne said loudly. She could see her cellmate turn around and then sit up.

"What?" Brigitte rubbed her eyes sleepily.

"Something's wrong," Susanne said, trying to keep the rising panic out of her voice.

"What's wrong?" Brigitte yawned.

"Could you call for the guard?"

"What for?"

"Never mind," Susanne said angrily. She didn't feel like having a lengthy discussion. The pain was becoming unbearable.

Ignoring Brigitte, Susanne threw back the blanket and sat up. She felt a great gush of fluid escape her and drew in her breath sharply.

"What's wrong, Susanne?" Brigitte had jumped up and was now by her side.

"Susanne! I think there is blood. Everywhere!" Brigitte looked down at Susanne's bed and then the floor. With two steps, Brigitte was at the door, hammering and yelling at the top of her lungs.

After a minute, Brigitte pressed her ear against the door and listened intently. She turned around to Susanne, who stood there, shivering and holding her belly. "I think someone's coming," Brigitte said.

Susanne could hear steps. Brigitte started yelling again and only stopped when the light came on. The key rattled open the lock, and the door opened. A female guard stepped inside. She was rather young and looked around angrily until her eyes fell on Susanne. For a moment, the guard just stared at her. Then she stumbled backward and out of the cell. They heard her run down the hallway. To get a doctor, Susanne hoped. She was breathing hard now and shivering violently. She felt so cold.

"It's too early, Brigitte. Too early. Something's wrong," Susanne said feebly.

Brigitte came over to her, put the blanket on the wet bed sheet, and helped Susanne lie down. "The doctor will be right here. Try to breathe steadily. It will be fine, Susanne," Brigitte said rather unconvincingly.

Brigitte looked in the direction of the door. The guard had left it open.

"I'll check and see if they're coming," Brigitte said, leaving Susanne's side and then stepping outside the cell.

Everything was quiet now. Susanne listened but couldn't hear anything. They had just left her here. Alone. Was no one going to help her? She pulled herself up and slowly got up from the bed. Her head was spinning, and the sharp pain made her feel winded. Taking small steps, she headed for the open cell door and then stepped outside. At the end of the hallway, she saw Brigitte hurrying toward her with the guard and nurse in tow.

Susanne stood there, in the middle of the hallway, still shivering. She was hugging her belly and a mixture of fluids and blood was running down her legs.

When the women got to her, the guard and the nurse each took one of Susanne's arms and dragged her back inside the cell, leaving a puddle of fluid in the hallway. Brigitte tried to calm her, but Susanne was beside herself now. The pain was so intense that Susanne thought she was surely going to die. She was crying now. The nurse ripped the sheet off the bed with one hand and both guard and nurse put Susanne down on the plank-bed.

"Get it wet in the sink." The nurse threw the sheet at the guard.

While the nurse was gently pushing down on Susanne's tummy and examining her, the guard went to the tiny sink in the corner and tried to get the sheet wet.

"There is only cold water. Don't you need hot —"

"Of course, it's cold. How long have you been here?" The nurse threw the guard an impatient look. "Just get it wet."

It was no easy undertaking to get a sheet of that size thoroughly wet in a sink of that size and just a trickle of water coming from the faucet. But that seemed to be the least of the nurse's concerns at the moment.

"We need to get her to a hospital," the nurse said.

"But isn't this a hospital?" The guard looked dubious.

"A real hospital." The nurse was trying to sit Susanne up as she screamed out in pain. The guard came over to help her.

"You need to run to the captain and inform him what's happening. This woman can't deliver these babies in the hospital wing of the prison. She must be transported to an outside hospital immediately," the nurse said.

"Babies?" The guard staggered backward and out the door.

"Babies?" Brigitte repeated dumbly.

Susanne was still screaming out in pain. The nurse tried to calm her, to no avail.

Susanne clawed at the nurse's arm. Between screams, she turned to her, sounding very weak. "Twins?"

Susanne saw the nurse open her mouth, but then everything went black.

Chapter 4

Susanne Schmidt stared out the small window of her hospital room. She wore a nightgown and lay in a white metal bed next to the window. Did they not fear she would escape through the open window? She sighed. They knew she wouldn't. What new mother would?

She kept staring out the window. The sky outside was a pale blue. It was spring now. Through the open window, Susanne could feel a warm breeze and wished she could be outside, strolling the walkways that wound around the hospital and feeling the warm sun on her face. But the antiseptic stench of the room told her that she was still inside.

Two more beds stood next to hers in the white-washed hospital room. One was occupied by another woman, asleep with her back to her, and the other one was empty. The woman had gone for a walk outside with her visitors.

There was a knock on the door, and a doctor, followed by Walter Fleischer, walked in. They stood by the door and whispered to each other while looking in her direction. Then the doctor went out, leaving Susanne alone with Fleischer, who came over to her and pulled up a chair next to her bed. With a side-glance at the sleeping woman, he sat down and cleared his throat.

"You seem to be doing well," he said.

Susanne didn't answer, but stared out the window.

He seemed to assume that she had heard him because he went on. "I was told the babies could be discharged in a week. They seem to be doing quite well for being born early. What did you name them?" Susanne turned to him and looked at him as if he were a mad man. "What did you name them?" he asked again in a way someone would ask a child.

"What do you care what I named them?" Fleischer looked offended. "What will happen to my children?" That was all that mattered to her now. Susanne knew she was still at their mercy. She had months left until her release.

"That's why I'm here, Frau Schmidt."

She swallowed hard. They wouldn't do that to her, would they? They wouldn't take her children away and lock them up in some state institution. *My children are not orphans,* she thought. *They have a mother and a father.*

Fleischer glanced at the sleeping woman in the next bed. "It's time we re-evaluated your loyalty to your country, Frau Schmidt. In light of your circumstances, it has been agreed that it would be wise to pardon you. You don't need to serve the rest of your sentence."

"And my babies?" She held her breath and clawed at the duvet, every muscle in her body tensed up.

"They will be going home with you, of course."

Susanne exhaled and fell back into her pillow, tears of relief running down her cheeks. She didn't care about crying in front of him now.

"However," he went on, "you'll have to prove where your loyalties lie."

Susanne didn't hear him. Her ears were ringing, and she felt the first real joy since the birth of the twins. The babies would go home with her. She would be released. And they wouldn't take the children away from her. Susanne didn't care about what was coming, what Fleischer wanted from her. Relief washed over her like a hot shower, and she finally felt the desire to sleep, which had escaped her since she had delivered her little girl and boy, two healthy, beautiful little babies.

"You will be an informant for the Office of State Security now," she heard him say, bringing her back to reality.

"You want me to work for the Stasi?" She laughed hysterically.

Fleischer's brows furrowed, and he glanced at the sleeping woman in the other bed. "You receive a great opportunity, Frau Schmidt, to pay off some debt, if I may say so."

How she hated this man, this state.

"Your country has done a lot for you. The state has furthered your education and has provided you with great opportunities for your professional advancement. It's time to give back," he said.

"Berlin is full of Stasi. I don't see that there is anything left for me to do," she snapped back, anger building up in her. They had not only trapped her in this country, now they wanted to keep controlling her life and make her one of them. She felt like screaming. Everything was so wrong. She felt as if she was racing down a road she didn't want to take, but couldn't do anything about it. She had nothing and no one that could make it stop.

"You won't be living in Berlin," he said.

Susanne looked at him, flabbergasted. She opened her mouth, but he went on.

"Your mother-in-law has agreed to take you in. We have arranged for a job in the local carton factory." He searched her eyes. "You didn't expect us to let you perform again, did you? Frau Schmidt ... you must see that we can't allow that. What message would that send? Your fellow musicians, the entire orchestra, and the conductor himself have been quite disappointed with your decision to abandon them and our republic. They wouldn't welcome you back with open arms. You must see that."

Susanne only stared ahead at the white-washed walls of her hospital room. Never had she been treated like this. She could only venture a guess as to how much more cruelty lay ahead of her. Something told her that this wasn't the end of it. They would make sure she got what they thought she deserved. This was a blow. But her children were now her sole concern.

Fleischer wasn't done. "You're to keep us informed about what's happening in Wallhausen and with its people. I want you to report any suspicious activities and any strangers that appear in the village. Since the village is in the Restricted Zone, strangers in that area are always a cause for alarm."

"And I will be allowed to leave the hospital... with my children?" she asked.

"If you agree to our little deal, yes. In one week, after your full recovery, of course." He looked at her intently, the gray in his eyes shimmering darkly. "Do we have an agreement, then?" he asked.

Susanne only nodded. No words were needed.

Fleischer gave a satisfied nod and got up. At the door, he turned around to her one more time. "You can consider yourself very lucky, Frau Schmidt." With that, he left the room.

As soon as Fleischer was gone, the woman in the bed next to Susanne's turned around, sat up, and looked at her. "Bastards!"

Susanne smiled sadly and then turned back toward the window. Red streaks ran across the blue of the sky now. She closed her eyes, letting the warm breeze brush her face.

She thought of Dieter. The last thing she remembered before dozing off was seeing him on the other side of the fence, holding the hand of a boy who looked just like him and a girl who looked like her. She looked at the three of them through the fence, her hands clawing at the metal until they were bleeding, screaming for them until a dark mist began to rise and swallowed them up completely.

Chapter 5

The little white Trabant swerved down the winding cobblestone road. Gisela Schmidt tried to avoid the badly
patched-up mud holes, not only because of her precious cargo
but also because she had just washed her white Trabant, which
she did every Saturday morning meticulously. Today was only
Monday, and she had already driven more kilometers on this day
than she usually did in a whole month. Today she had been forced
to take her car on the Autobahn, something she had tried to avoid
since owning a car. Driving on the Autobahn scared her, not only
because it was in virtually the same condition as it was in 1945, but
also because of the higher speed, as well as the difficulty of getting
on and off.

Gisela had ordered a car ten long years ago, and when she
had finally been informed that there was one ready for her to
be purchased, she had not hesitated. Since the day Gisela had
become the proud owner of a Trabant, she had taken every chance
she could get to drive it, although only around the village or to
the nearby town. And only another shut-down of the only gas
station in their village could prevent her from hammering down
the cobble-stoned Main Street of Wallhausen to show off her
white Trabant.

While she was driving along the poplar-lined road, Gisela off and on checked her rear-view mirror. Susanne sat in the back seat, her two babies in her arms, and staring out the window. Her daughter-in-law looked tired; the sheen from her hair was gone. She had changed. She didn't look like the Susanne Gisela had last seen about six months ago. She was dressed in sweats and her hair was pulled back. She wore no make-up. Gisela couldn't remember a time she had seen Susanne like this. Her daughter-in-law was a musician and had always looked very sophisticated.

Susanne could feel Gisela's gaze in the rear mirror. She had waited for an accusatory speech, tears, or ridicule since they had left the hospital, but Gisela had not confronted her about what had happened. At the hospital, she had been greeted by her mother-in-law with an emotional hug. And only after Gisela had tearfully welcomed her two grandchildren and they were walking to the car, did Gisela simply state that she had been informed about what had happened. One sentence. Nothing more. It had been a relief to Susanne. Apparently, the Stasi hadn't suspected Gisela had any knowledge of Dieter and her plans to defect to the West. They had left her alone. Susanne was glad. What she couldn't understand was why her mother-in-law hadn't visited her in prison.

Susanne was still holding the letter Gisela had given her the minute Susanne stepped outside the hospital. Eagerly, as soon as they were sitting in the car, Susanne had read Dieter's letter. How she had longed to hear from him all these months. Gisela had told her that the letter had probably been opened and read by the Stasi and that this had been the only one so far that had made it through to her.

Dieter had heard from his mother what had happened to Susanne after they were separated. He wrote about how much he

35

missed her and what he went through after they had been separated. He was staying with Susanne's musician friends in Hamburg, as they had planned. Susanne had met Wolfgang and Anna Borowski when she had traveled to Hamburg to perform with the city's orchestra. Susanne had never befriended any West Germans on her performance trips before, but Anna, who played in the Hamburg orchestra, and her husband Wolfgang had been so welcoming, taking her out to dinner and shopping, and introducing her to their friends and family. Now she was glad that they had still welcomed Dieter, even though it had gone so wrong for her. She was glad to know Dieter was in good hands. He was just as much alone as she was, and he had lost just as much as she had.

In his letter, Dieter had written that they had a good chance that the West German government would help them secure her and the babies' freedom because of their special circumstances. He promised he would do everything in his power to bring them together again as soon as possible. These lines had instantly uplifted her. She would play along with the Stasi, work those hours in the factory, and get through those few months in Wallhausen. This would only take a few months, wouldn't it? While she pondered that question, she looked out the window at the scenery that flew by. It was so good to be out of prison, but this wasn't the freedom she had envisioned. She could be patient for a few more months. What were a few months compared to the many years that still lay ahead of them?

If the Stasi had read Dieter's letter, they knew now of his plans to collaborate with the West German government. Would that make a difference for her and the babies? Susanne looked at the back of the envelope lying next to her on the seat. She couldn't see any traces that the letter had been opened previously. Gisela had slit open the envelope, and the flap was still neatly glued to the paper. It would all work out. It had to work out this time.

She stared at Dieter's handwriting on the paper in her hand and started to read the letter again, as if to find more meaning behind every word. She still felt Gisela's eyes on her and let the letter glide down next to her on the seat without waking either of the babies still deeply asleep in her arms. She had long gotten used to the aching in her arms from holding two infants for several hours every day. It probably helped that her arms were well trained from holding up a violin and a bow for hours at a time.

Susanne glanced at the rear mirror and caught Gisela's eye. Her mother-in-law looked over her shoulder and gave her a faint smile. "Hungry?"

Susanne nodded and looked back out the window. Below lay a village, spread out between fields, meadows, and forests. Train tracks ran along the north side of it. Susanne took in the familiar scenery, the poplar trees lining the road, and the fields and the meadows that lay beyond. She had loved this place. Dieter and she had visited his mother at least one weekend a month. They had to get a pass for entering the Restricted Zone every time, which was rather tedious, but they hadn't minded. Wallhausen was quiet, secluded, and peaceful. Here they had felt worlds away from their busy lives in Berlin, enjoyed Gisela's cooking, and spent so much time outside that Susanne had started to feel quite at home in the place where Dieter had grown up.

There had been those weekends and holidays, of course, when she had to perform and stayed behind in Berlin or traveled across the country or abroad. Before she met Dieter she had enjoyed traveling immensely, but since the day she had met him, it had caused her pain to be separated from him, even just for a weekend. It had been love at first sight. She had instantly fallen in love with his boyish face, the blond hair that he wore below his ears, and his laid-back and caring nature. Susanne swallowed down the tears that tried to well up again. Only one thing mattered now, to find a way to be with him again, to be a family, to have him hold his children, she reminded herself.

"Here we are," Gisela said, interrupting Susanne's thoughts.

Susanne looked outside. They had finally reached the first houses of Wallhausen.

"Everything still looks the same," she said, taking in the familiar sight.

Her mother-in-law laughed. "Susanne, you know change doesn't come easily to this corner of the world. Nothing will ever change here."

As they pulled up to Gisela's house, Susanne took in the familiar sight of the paint peeling off the stucco and the meticulously kept garden that shone brightly with a colorful array of spring flowers. When they pulled into the driveway, Susanne noticed two older women on the sidewalk, staring at them.

"Ignore them," Gisela said, motioning in their direction. "They finally have something new to gossip about."

Susanne knew that nothing ever stayed private in a village. Someone would find out the most intimate secrets, and then word would spread like a ravenous wildfire, destroying truth and reputation, with the story changing from day to day. While one was struck down with the flu at one end of the village, the next day he was pronounced dead on the other side of town. Gisela had told her that one time, flowers and condolences were brought to someone's house, and the "dead" person opening the door was alive and well and shocked to hear the news that he was dead. That was one of the reasons why Susanne had always preferred living in the city, even though she enjoyed coming out here on weekends and for the holidays. Now she would spend months here. Susanne sighed as her mother-in-law drove around the house to park the car in the back.

Gisela got out and came around to the other side of the car to open the door and hold back the seat for her. Susanne carefully handed one of the twins to Gisela and then pulled herself out of the car with her free arm, clenching her teeth while doing so. She still felt pain from the C-section when she had to use her stomach muscles.

Susanne breathed in the air as she looked up at the house. The familiarity of it stung her. She was here alone, without Dieter.

"Let's put those babies down while they're still asleep, don't you think?" Gisela said, pushing Susanne gently toward the house. "I was able to get a crib at the second-hand store in the city and convinced Frau Friedrich down the street to give hers up by telling her that she will never have any grandkids of her own, anyway, but could borrow mine if she felt she needed to spoil someone. Each has their own crib. They don't need to share. I put the cribs up in the room next to Dieter's old room."

Gisela led the way in and up the stairs. They passed Dieter's room and Susanne felt the all too familiar sadness wash over her again. This was where Dieter and she had stayed when they had come to visit his mother. They had slept close together in his old narrow bed, with stuffed animals looking on when they made love, and the sound of trains waking them up at the crack of dawn.

Gisela had opened the door of the room next to Dieter's, and Susanne followed her inside.

"Oh, Gisela." Susanne was touched. Two cribs stood against the wall on either side of the room. Some of Dieter's old stuffed animals sat on a small chest of drawers next to the window. Light blue curtains cast the room into a washed out watery light. It looked like a nursery. Susanne turned around to her mother-in-law and mouthed a "thank you" in her direction. Gisela smiled back, looking pleased with Susanne's reaction. They carefully put the sleeping babies down in their cribs. Before leaving the room, Susanne bent over each crib and gave her children a gentle peck on the cheek.

After Gisela had closed the door carefully, she turned around to Susanne, looking worried. "I wasn't able to get a lot of formula."

Susanne had also worried if she would be able to get all the necessities for her babies. Formula was hard to come by and baby clothes were scarce. There was only one grocery and one clothing store in the village, and she probably would have to go to the nearby city or even ask her friends up in Berlin to buy what they could get their hands on. The capital was always better off than the rest of the country.

"We'll be fine, I think. Don't worry." Susanne said, trying to sound upbeat. It was time to call in favors from her friends in Berlin. She looked at the closed door of her children's room and the familiar feeling of separation began to overwhelm her again. "Should we leave the door open just a crack?" Susanne asked with her hand on the door handle.

"I never left the door open when Dieter was a baby," Gisela said, but Susanne had already opened the door again. She peeked inside and then left the door ajar. "The room is beautiful. Thank you," Susanne said.

"Well ... don't mention it, dear," Gisela said. "You forget ... those two are my only grandchildren. They'll be spoiled rotten while living under my roof." This was the mother-in-law Susanne re-membered. "Well, I'll be downstairs. I'm sure you're hungry. Go get settled in and then we'll eat." Gisela said, motioning toward Dieter's room. Susanne looked at her with raised eyebrows. "I thought you might like to be in Dieter's room, and it is right next door to the twins," her mother-in-law said with a contemplative look in Susanne's direction.

"Yes ... thank you," Susanne managed to say.

Gisela gave her a quick smile and went downstairs. Susanne stared at the closed door for a minute and then entered the room that had belonged to her husband.

Everything still looked the way Susanne remembered. The way Dieter's room had always looked when they had visited for weekends and holidays. Today, fresh sheets lay on the bed, and Gisela had even put some flowers on her nightstand. There had never been any flowers in this room while it had been Dieter's. She breathed in deeply. It still smelled like Dieter in here. Susanne swallowed down the lump in her throat.

She went over to the phonograph on Dieter's desk and looked through several records until she found what she was looking for. Oh, how she had missed music. There hadn't been any in prison, no records, no violin.

Susanne took the record out of the case, blew the little specks of dust off, and placed it on the phonograph. She lifted the tone arm and placed its needle carefully on the outside of the record. Then she closed her eyes and for a minute concentrated on the familiar notes. Remembering that the babies were sleeping next door, she found the volume control and turned it down. Looking around the room, she went over to the bed and sat down. She grabbed Dieter's old pillow, took it in her arms, and rested her cheek on it. Only then did she see the four suitcases behind the stove. She recognized the two fine leather suitcases as hers. The two old ones were Dieter's. *Our clothes*, she thought.

She contemplated getting up and opening them when someone knocked on the door. Without waiting for Susanne's reply, Gisela stepped in, carrying a violin case.

"I thought you might want to have it now," she said.

Susanne took the case from Gisela and set it down on the bed. "Thank you," she whispered, wiping the dust off the black case.

"I kept it inside. Your clothes, too." Gisela pointed to the suitcases that were partially hidden by the stove. "Your other things are outside in the carport." At Susanne's worried look, Gisela added, "I put blankets over your furniture. The boxes should be fine.

It hasn't rained too much this spring."

Susanne could only imagine what six months of being stored outside in changing weather had done to her expensive brown leather sofa or her many records.

Gisela seemed to have read her thoughts. "They just brought all of yours and Dieter's things one day, unloaded it right in front of my house, on the side of the street. Fortunately, Georg was so kind to come over and help me move it all." When Susanne didn't reply, Gisela said defensively, "I didn't know where else to put it."

Susanne waved it off wearily. "It doesn't matter. Really." She turned her attention to the violin case, and Gisela left without another word.

Susanne opened the case and looked at her instrument. How she had missed playing. She ran her fingers across the wood. Feeling the texture of the stained wood and smelling the rosin, she felt the same sense of loss she had been feeling every time she was thinking of Dieter. She wouldn't be able to perform anymore. *Only for a few months*, she repeated to herself and closed the case. She put it on the floor beside the bed and then lay down. With the pillow in her arms, she curled up and listened to the soothing music.

Susanne woke up with a start. She didn't realize she had dozed off. She listened intently. Had the twins woken up? How long had she been asleep? She listened again and heard someone come up the stairs. Then there was a knock on the door, but no one entered.

Susanne went over and opened the door. "Georg!" She threw her arms around the tall man's neck and he hugged her back. "It's so good to see you." Georg was not only Gisela's next-door neighbor but also Dieter's best friend. They had grown up together. And when Dieter had introduced Georg to her, she had instantly liked his quiet and serious nature. He was a lot like her, as Dieter had pointed out. And Dieter had been right. They had become good friends instantly.

"It's good to see you, too." He looked at her while running his hand through his dark hair and pushing up his dark-rimmed glasses. "Well, Gisela's cooking should get you back to your old self." She playfully hit his arm. "Care for a walk?" he asked.

Susanne hesitated. While the babies seemed to still be asleep, she felt uncomfortable just leaving them. "I don't know, Georg." He looked puzzled, so she pulled him with her to the room next door. "I want you to meet someone." Carefully, Susanne opened the door wide. The babies were indeed still asleep in their cribs. So she hadn't been asleep for long. Susanne put her finger to her lips and Georg followed her quietly into the nursery. She smiled at Georg. As she went over to each crib to pull the blanket back over their little bodies, Georg watched her thoughtfully.

She looked at him. "What?" she whispered.

"Seeing you like this ... You're a mother," he said quietly, shaking his head.

"Aren't they beautiful?"

He nodded, smiling at her expression of motherly affection.

With another look at the babies, Susanne ushered Georg out of the room, leaving the door ajar. She beamed at him and Georg smiled but then his expression turned serious. "What about that walk?" he asked.

Susanne looked at the door. "Let's walk, then," she said earnestly. Susanne knew that it wasn't the walk Georg was interested in, but hearing her account of what had happened.

They went downstairs. Susanne asked Gisela to keep an eye on the babies and said that they would be back in half an hour, so she could be there when they awoke.

For the first few minutes Susanne and Georg walked in silence, side by side. When they had left the houses behind and were walking toward a small forest of oak trees, Georg broke the silence. "What happened, Susanne?"

She didn't answer right away, but kept walking on.

Georg didn't want to push her. He knew that this was probably painful for her to talk about. He had heard about their attempt to flee to the West from the Stasi who had shown up at his house the day after to question him about his involvement. His reaction had told them that he had known nothing. He accused the Stasi officers of lying and repeated over and over again that Dieter and Susanne would be the last people to do something so foolish. He was sure he had behaved like a lunatic. At least until they told him that Dieter was now in the West and Susanne in their custody. That revelation had stopped short his outbursts of lunacy. The officers continued to bombard him with questions, but he did not hear them. He stood there silently in the middle of his living room, while the Stasi men circled around him, too numb with shock to react to their questions or the feelings of disbelief, worry, and betrayal that raged within him.

For weeks, Georg had raked through his memory to find clues or any hints about their plans to defect. In his mind, he repeatedly went over conversations, phone calls, and get-togethers with Dieter and Susanne for answers. What had he missed? Dieter had been his best friend all his life. They had grown up together, even studied together at the university up in Berlin. Why hadn't he sensed anything? After weeks, Georg had finally accepted that Dieter was gone. Dieter had left them. What remained was his worry for Susanne. Georg had felt sick when he heard that she was serving time in a Stasi prison and that she was pregnant on top of that. Fortunately, he had gotten regular updates about Susanne from Gisela, who was his next-door neighbor.

As they walked silently, Georg tried to shake the feelings of disbelief, betrayal, and worry. Out of the corner of his eye, he was relieved to see that she looked well. Too thin for just having had twins, but well.

"We made a run for it," Susanne said suddenly.

Georg glanced at her from the side. He didn't want to interrupt now that she was talking.

"Dieter and I had planned it out very well. For months we'd been talking about it and planning it. We knew that there was a chance we might fail."

"He made it, though," Georg said.

Susanne fell silent and he could see that tears were rolling down her face. She wiped them away angrily.

"What happened? How did you get separated?" Georg could no longer hold back. He needed to know.

"We just did. I wasn't fast enough. I slipped and had to climb the fence a second time. All of a sudden, the border guards appeared. Dieter had just made it across..." Her voice broke off.

"You two never told me that you wanted to leave." Georg could no longer hide his disappointment.

"We didn't want to drag anyone into this. Not even Gisela knew. It was too dangerous. Don't you see?"

"But to just leave us like that? Without any goodbyes?" He shook his head, trying to keep the anger out of his voice.

Georg didn't feel like reproaching Susanne. He would rather have this talk with Dieter. How could he have been so irresponsible? Trying to flee across the border with his pregnant wife?

Susanne knew that Georg was right. It had been the most difficult decision of their lives to leave everything behind. Family, friends, their careers. Dieter had called Georg's house the day before their attempt to talk to his mother, who lived next door. Susanne had owned a telephone in Berlin, a special privilege only a few citizens of the GDR enjoyed, but Gisela had never been able to own one. Georg, on the other hand, was allowed to have one because he was a veterinarian. And he had always been willing to let other people use his old black dial phone.

Susanne remembered that Dieter had just wanted to hear his mother's voice that morning. And Susanne herself had felt she needed to talk to the only mother she had known since her grandmother had died. They had both spoken to Gisela, and Georg as well, and Susanne had considered that their goodbye. Who would have known that she would see them both again so soon?

It was Georg who broke the silence this time. "You could have just stayed abroad when you had one of your performances, you know. It would have been less dangerous." He took her by the arm and stopped her from walking on. "You could have been killed, Susanne. And your children ... People who try to flee the republic get shot at and killed.

You've heard the stories."

Susanne didn't appreciate his serious and almost stern demeanor. Without a word, she pulled free from his grasp and started walking again. He followed her.

Now Susanne's voice was full of bitterness as she turned around to face him. "Do you think I could just leave Dieter behind? We're married, Georg. I love him."

"So it was Dieter's idea, then." It wasn't a question.

Susanne answered it anyway. "No it wasn't, Georg, it was mine, just so you know." With that, she turned around and headed back to the house. The babies would wake up any minute. They needed her. Georg didn't follow her, but Susanne felt his eyes on her back as she walked away. She could only imagine the shock and pain he no doubt felt. Her only hope was that Georg wouldn't share with Gisela that it had been her idea.

Chapter 6

S usanne hit the alarm clock blindly, and the ringing ceased. Dawn had just broken outside and there was already a stir next door. She turned over in her bed. *One more minute, just one more minute*, she thought, and pulled her down blanket back over her bare shoulders. She still hadn't gotten used to having to go to work so early in the morning, especially after getting up with the babies during the night. Moreover, as a musician she had been used to sleeping in after her concert performances the previous night. "Only a few more moments," she mumbled to herself, and dozed off again.

Crying broke the silence. Susanne was awake in an instant. While work was no motivator to get up in the morning, the babies were. She needed those few minutes with them in the morning, even if it was only changing a soiled diaper or wiping spit-up off their chins. She would not see them all day. It was a long time to be separated from them.

Susanne kicked back the blanket and got up. She still couldn't distinguish if it was Jana's or Hendrik's crying. Gisela, on the other hand, insisted that she knew which of her grandchildren was crying. Susanne believed her. Her mother-in-law spent all day with the children while she worked long hours in the factory, a cruel reminder that she was still being punished for trying to flee to the West. Whenever she was gone, she missed the babies terribly. To some extent, Fleischer had succeeded in keeping her separated from her children.

The work at the factory was monotonous and mindless. She and other workers, mostly women, stood along an assembly line and folded cartons all day. Her female co-workers were mostly friendly to her but kept their distance. She was an outsider. How Fleischer expected her to spy on these people baffled her. He had to know that the villagers wouldn't easily trust her, especially since they probably all knew what had happened to her. No one would want to openly associate with someone who had tried to defect to the West. She was an outcast. A traitor to her country. A criminal who had served time in jail. No one would want to associate with her.

While the women folded cartons all day, the men at the factory worked the forklifts and were mostly responsible for loading and unloading the trucks that brought in tons of newspapers that were turned into cartons. The men had tried to harass her on a few occasions. They taunted her every time she passed them, and to her disgust had even tried to grab her. Each time though, her boss, a tall, fat man a few years her senior, had come to her rescue by threatening to report them to the Stasi for stealing from the factory. Each time, they would scatter instantly like scared chickens, leaving her alone for a few days until the game started all over again.

With a sigh, Susanne threw on her work overalls and headed to the nursery next door. Dieter would be shocked to see her like this. She hadn't worn any make-up for weeks, her wardrobe had changed completely, and she now wore her hair in a ponytail most of the time. Her friends in Berlin would be just as shocked to see her like this. But things had changed. She wasn't living in the capital anymore, nor did she travel or perform at prestigious opera houses or concert halls any longer. Her new life in Wallhausen and her new line of work didn't require formal dresses and make-up.

It was Jana who had been crying and, of course, she had woken up her brother too. Susanne put a sling around one of her shoulders, picked up Jana, and placed her in it. She instantly stopped crying. Susanne wiped the wet little cheeks and kissed her softly, breathing in deeply. She loved how they smelled. Next, Susanne picked up Henry, as she called him, and cradled him in her arm. She took them downstairs where she found her mother-in-law, wearing a robe over her nightgown, already in the kitchen preparing the bottles. Together they fed and diapered the babies and then it was time for Susanne to leave for work. She took a few bites of her toast and kissed the babies goodbye. She laughed at the crumbs she left on their cheeks and wiped them away. With some effort, she tore herself away from them and hurried off to work.

Rain or shine, Susanne took the old bike that once had belonged to Dieter to work. She had never owned a bike. Growing up in Berlin, she had used buses and trams to get around. Later, Dieter and she had owned a 1960 Wartburg 311, but that, of course, had been confiscated by the Stasi, along with most of their other valuables.

The factory was located outside the village. It took Susanne less than fifteen minutes to get there. Her first week, she had been late for work almost every day. She had not cared and to her surprise, her boss hadn't been upset about it, either. He treated her respectfully and seemed to take pity on her and her situation. Now she was only occasionally late. As she pulled into the yard where the men were already unloading old newspapers from a truck, Susanne saw her boss waiting by the bike stand. Was he waiting for her?

"You're late, Fräulein Schmidt."

"*Frau* Schmidt, Herr Hauser." Susanne said, before she realized that her boss seemed rather displeased.

"I want to see you in my office immediately," he said abruptly.

Susanne stared after him as he made his way back into the building. *What could he possibly want, and why is he like this today?* she wondered as she followed him into the building.

The door to Hauser's office was closed, so Susanne knocked and waited for a reply from inside. But no reply came. Instead, the door opened and Susanne saw Fleischer sitting inside her boss's office. She swallowed hard and stepped inside.

Hauser didn't offer her a chair, so she just stood there, waiting for one of them to speak.

"Leave us alone, Herr Hauser," Fleischer said.

Susanne could see that her boss wasn't pleased to be sent out of his own office, but he complied, leaving the door open behind him. Fleischer got up and closed it.

"Please sit, Frau Schmidt." Susanne didn't want to sit on the chair behind her boss's desk, so she took the one that Fleischer had occupied just a minute ago.

"How are you doing?" he asked.

"Fine."

He looked at her carefully. "How does work at the factory suit you?" Fleischer seemed to notice the changes in her outward appearance because he examined her with raised eyebrows.

"It's work," Susanne said simply. She wouldn't give him the pleasure of letting him know how miserable she was working here.

"I'm told you don't take the work here very seriously."

Susanne just stared at him. What had Hauser told Fleischer about her? She was late off and on, but she had always done her work to Hauser's satisfaction.

"You know that every worker in our republic shares the responsibility of increasing the productivity for the welfare of all citizens." He paused for a moment to sit down behind Hauser's desk. "But this is not why I'm here today, Frau Schmidt. I'm here to see what you were able to find out about the people here that could be of interest to the Office of State Security. You must have expected me to follow up on our little deal."

"I need more time."

"You had time," Fleischer said, his eyes scrutinizing her.

"I'm not one of them. You can't truly expect me to know everyone and everything in just a couple of months," Susanne said. What did he expect her to accomplish in such a short amount of time?

"Over three months, Frau Schmidt," he corrected her. "You see the people here at the factory every day. You must have befriended them by now. What about your boss? Herr Hauser seems to favor you, so your co-workers tell me. Anything on him?"

"No." She understood now why Fleischer was really here. This was just another interrogation. They wanted to demoralize her. Fleischer would harass her until she gave him what he wanted.

"I suggest you start fulfilling your part of the deal, Frau Schmidt." Fleischer got up and went over to the door. He looked back at her. "I hope you'll have something to report the next time I pay you a visit." He left.

Susanne stared at the open doorway through which Fleischer had just disappeared. She needed to get out of there as soon as possible. Fleischer's surprise visit indicated that they wouldn't leave her alone.

As she left the office, her boss came down the hallway toward her. He didn't smile. "Get to it," was all he said when he passed her, slamming the door of his office shut once he was inside. No day was good that she had to come to the factory and work. She hated every morning. But today? Today she wanted to run. She dragged herself to the big hall of the factory, through which an enormous assembly line ran. Women, their hair held back by bandanas, stood at regular intervals along the assembly line, taking up cardboard, folding it, and placing the finished box back on the conveyor belt.

When she came closer, the happy chatter that had made work so much more bearable ceased. No one spoke. They pretended not to see her, but here and there someone glanced up at her. Susanne found an open spot, pulled a pair of gloves from her overalls, and started to work. After a while, the conversations around her started up again, but no one spoke to her.

She thought of Jana and Henry and swallowed hard. For them, she had to get through this. She looked up and out of the tall factory windows. Gray clouds were moving swiftly across the pale late summer sky. Fall was almost here, she realized. It would be one year in November. Almost one year since Dieter was gone. She couldn't wait for him to get her and the babies out. She, too, had to find a way to try again. If Dieter failed, or took too long, she would have to have another plan, or she would be stuck in this country. Alone with her children and without Dieter.

Gisela was just preparing dinner when Susanne came home, more exhausted than usual. She had pedaled home like a maniac. Especially after today, she longed to hold her babies. The twins were lying on a blanket on the living room rug, sucking happily on their little fists. Susanne went to each of them, picking them up and holding them. Henry cooed happily, drool all over his mouth and chin. "Has the tooth come out yet?" He only cooed, sticking his little fist in his mouth to chew on it. She kissed his forehead and checked his diaper. Gisela was on top of things. What would she do without that woman? Susanne promised herself that she would launder and boil the soiled cloth diapers tonight. She couldn't possibly leave it all to Gisela. She already felt a huge amount of guilt as it was. Just a little rest, and then she'd do it. With a sigh, she fell into the cushy old armchair next to the twins and put her feet up. She felt utterly exhausted and drained.

Gisela came in and brought her a plate full of bread, sausage, and pickles. "You better eat and then head off to bed. You look awful. I can take care of the babies tonight."

Susanne wanted to protest, but Gisela shook her head. *Well, then*, Susanne thought, looking longingly at the babies but with no strength left to protest. *I will take them out for an extra-long walk tomorrow. And I'll wash the diapers after that.* She fell back in the chair, plate in her lap, and started eating. She looked at Gisela who was wiping the drool off Jana's cheeks.

"Thanks, Gisela. For everything."

"Don't mention it. I enjoy taking care of the little ones more than you think. Besides ... I'm their grandmother."

"Any mail today?" Susanne asked.

Gisela just shook her head sadly. They hadn't heard from Dieter since that one letter in which he had promised to get her and the babies out of the country with the help of the West German government, but nothing had happened. It had been two months without any word from him. *Three months,* Susanne reminded herself.

She had written Dieter almost every week. How many of her letters had made it into his hands, she didn't know, but none had come from him. Was that Fleischer's doing? She needed to give Fleischer what he wanted and play along. There was no other way. She would start by taking Fleischer's advice and make an effort to befriend the people in this village, and maybe there would be even something to report after all. Not everyone embraced communism and was a model citizen. And while most professed their loyalty to communist ideas and state publicly, many were not looking for the state's permission or approval in their private matters.

Suddenly, Susanne felt a surge of confidence and swung herself out of the big chair. She would find something or someone to report. She had to think of herself and the children now. And giving Fleischer what he wanted would maybe leave some room for her to find a way out if Dieter's plan failed. She picked up the twins and went upstairs and put them to bed. She even washed the heap of soiled diapers while Gisela protested.

Chapter 7

Susanne parked her bike in front of the butcher's and then waited in line with others for him to unlock his store. She knew that the sought-after meats and sausages would be sold out within an hour, so she had ordered a big roast and different kinds of sausages in advance for the family get-together they would have tomorrow after the babies' christening.

To ensure they would have a proper feast, Gisela had also stood in line this week, at the only grocery store in the village. Every second Tuesday of the month, fresh fruit was delivered, which would sell out in minutes, particularly on the rare occasion that bananas and oranges made it to Wallhausen's tiny store. They would be sold right out of the boxes, never even making it to the shelves. On Thursdays, fresh dairy products arrived in Wallhausen. Yogurts and cheeses in particular were in high demand. Gisela's persistence in standing in line on both days had paid off. They would have a proper feast to celebrate the twins' christening on Sunday.

Susanne wanted it to be a special day. She would see some of Dieter's relatives and family friends again, some of whom she hadn't seen since their wedding. They had let her know that they were eager to see the babies, but she knew they were all hoping to hear her story about what had happened.

She sighed so loud at that thought that the woman in front of her turned around in surprise. She smiled at the elderly woman, who turned back around without returning Susanne's smile.

Susanne looked up into the gray sky and felt the light drizzle hit her face. Bad weather was always blamed for the surliness of people and did make them moody and depressed. And this was November. The grayest of all months. Deep down though, Susanne knew that it wasn't the bad weather that had prevented the woman from being friendly to her.

Susanne's thoughts were interrupted when the people around her began to move forward, elbowing their way inside the store that had just opened. The stocky-looking butcher with his red face and his little round wife were serving at the counter. Susanne was glad that there were only five people ahead of her. While she waited, she looked around the almost bare shop. No sausages were hanging from hooks, and only a few jars of aspic stood lined up on the otherwise empty shelves. Some of the trays behind the glass counters were also empty. Susanne was glad she had planned ahead and preordered the meats she needed.

Finally, it was Susanne's turn. She just looked at the butcher. Surely, he would remember her special order from three days ago. A special occasion like a christening was always talked about in the village. But the butcher just stared at her impatiently. "And? What do you want?" he grumbled.

Susanne stared back at him. "I came in three days ago and ordered a roast and sausages. I'm here to pick them up." She tried to keep the rising anger out of her voice.

"Your order couldn't be filled. You can buy whatever you see here in the store."

"But you said I could pick up everything today. You did not mention that ..."

A woman behind her sighed with impatience. "Are you going to buy anything, or not?"

Susanne ignored her. "You could have told me that three days ago," Susanne said to the butcher, her voice trembling with anger.

"Next!" The butcher had just dismissed her. The woman behind her had stepped forward eagerly and was already ordering. For a moment, Susanne just stood there staring at the butcher and the woman. Then she felt a tug on her sleeve. She looked right into the face of the butcher's wife, who smiled kindly at her. "Come with me, I can help you over there." She pointed to the other end of the counter.

Susanne followed her, tight-lipped. The butcher's wife was already packing sausages and pork chops on a piece of paper. "I don't have a roast. How many sausages and pork chops would you need?"

"Ten of each." And then she added "Please!"

The butcher's wife smiled at her. "Anything else?"

Susanne just shook her head, smiling back now. The woman rolled up the sausages and meat in the papers and handed it all to Susanne, who put it in her bag. "That makes 5 marks and 25 pennies, then," the butcher's wife said with a smile.

Susanne put the money on the counter. "Thank you."

The butcher's wife gave her a friendly nod and moved on to the next customer.

Outside, the drizzle had turned into rain. Susanne got on the old bike and on the way back home she swore to herself that she would never, ever set a foot into the butcher's shop again.

Chapter 8

I t was early Sunday morning when Georg Hoffmann heard someone knock on his front door. Half of the village was still asleep, and he hadn't even heard the church bells yet, which rang out in vain every Sunday. It could be that someone's cat at home or a cow at the collective farm was in labor, he reminded himself as he stretched and tried to roll out of bed. Besides, people would have called first. Out of politeness. But then again, only a few people owned a phone. He shook his head as if to try to disperse the fog that clouded his mind during these early morning hours. It wasn't unusual that someone came knocking on his door in case of an emergency at any hour.

Georg put on his glasses, threw his sweatpants on over his boxers, and grumpily went for the front door, the dog at his side. He opened the door, rubbing the last little bit of sleep from his tired eyes. Outside, a man in a gray overcoat stared him down. Stasi? There was no mistake. The man was definitely Stasi. The haircut, the penetrating gray eyes, and an aura of self-importance were unmistakably Stasi. What could the Stasi want from him? Remembering their last visit the day after Dieter and Susanne's attempt to defect, he fought down the feeling of trepidation. Georg swallowed. Rudi, his dog, growled.

"Georg Hoffmann, yes?"

"What do you want?" Georg asked, unwilling to acknowledge the Stasi officer's authority. The man in front of him didn't look familiar. He hadn't been with those questioning him about Susanne and Dieter a year ago.

"To come inside, for a start," the Stasi officer replied curtly.

For a moment Georg hesitated, but then held open the door, and the man stepped inside. There was no use fending the Stasi off. He knew that. Rudi was still growling as the officer followed Georg into the living room. The man walked casually around the room, scanning the titles of books on the shelf and lifting up an old figurine that his father had left him. Georg had no idea why he still hadn't gotten rid of it.

Georg watched the Stasi officer with apprehension and folded arms until he saw him finally take a seat on the old couch. "It seems the Stasi doesn't even take Sundays off. A shame, really," Georg said.

"I'm not here for small talk, Herr Hoffmann."

"I see. I can't remember doing anything that would give me the pleasure of your visit, though."

"Our republic is in need of your services," the officer said.

"Is it."

"It's about your neighbor. Susanne Schmidt. You two are still friends, I presume?" The officer wasn't waiting for an answer. "You will inform me of any suspicious activity that involves Frau Schmidt."

"You want me to do what?" They couldn't be serious. Susanne? Suspicious activities? "You can't possibly think I'd be willing to spy on her. And what for? What did she do?"

"This is not about what she did but what she will do."

"What do you mean?" Did the man know something he didn't?

"We are taking all the precautions, Herr Hoffmann. We know Frau Schmidt plans another defection."

"She wouldn't. The children ..." Georg couldn't believe what he was hearing. Without thinking, he went over to the window. The shutters on Gisela's bedroom window were still closed.

"She would. We have reliable information that warrants our concern for her and her children's safety."

"You seem well informed," Georg said, still staring out the window, "I don't see why you would need another informant. Besides, you can't possibly think I'm willing to spy on my friends and neighbors," Georg said, looking over his shoulder at the man on his old couch.

"You're willing, believe me, Herr Hoffmann."

Georg turned around slowly. "I beg your pardon?"

"You're a veterinarian?"

Georg knew this wasn't a question. His brows furrowed. What was the officer getting at?

"You're invaluable to the local LPG, the collectivized farms and their cows, and your private practice is going well, too. Let me put it this way, Herr Hoffmann. It would be quite easy to call down a veterinarian fresh from the university, eager to start practicing right here in your village."

"The locals don't trust strangers," Georg said, his countenance darkening.

"That might be true, but they would trust an informant of the Stasi less, if word got out that you performed such services for your government. I believe your fellow villagers would have a hard time entrusting their dachshunds and kittens to you. And besides, you don't want to end up like your father, do you?"

"How dare you?" Georg stepped forward, clenching his fists. His dog was growling again. But then Georg heard the church bells, and it hit him. His face fell. How could he have forgotten? He hadn't received a formal invitation, but this was open to the public and part of the Sunday worship. Even though he had tried to avoid setting foot in a church for most of his life, he knew he had to go today.

"You must excuse me now. I have to go to church."

The man on the couch looked at him as though he had just escaped from a mental hospital.

"Herr Hoffmann, you don't seem to understand–"

Georg cut the man off with his hand. "I'll do it."

———

"Don't you dare put your dirty paws on me, Rudi. Not right now. Not while I'm wearing this." Georg tried to ward off his dog, a full-grown German shepherd, with his knee while trying to fold the collar over his tie. He looked in the mirror of the old bedroom wardrobe he had inherited, together with the house and everything else in it, from his father. What he saw in the mirror both surprised and shocked him. What he saw was not the tall and dark-haired man he was, but his father, except for the glasses he wore. Georg looked down at the suit. He certainly looked presentable and would make quite the impression in this suit, but at the same time he looked too much like the man who had worn it last. Only a few years younger, in fact. The picture of a man wearing the same suit flashed into his mind. He was standing next to him at the side of an open grave into which a casket was lowered. That had been the last time his father had worn this suit. He shook his head as if to disperse the dark thoughts that had entered his mind. *I'm not like him*, he thought, and with another look in the mirror, running his hand through his dark hair one more time, he left the room, followed by Rudi who seemed to think he could come along.

Georg was walking briskly down the sidewalk of the cobble-stoned Main Street. The half-timbered houses on either side of the street lay peaceful and still. Here and there someone leaned out of a window, but except for him and a few other pedestrians, there was nothing interesting for them to see on a Sunday morning. Even during the week, the main road running through their border-land village wouldn't have much traffic. No one could just simply pass through here. Their village was the end of the world–a dead end, as his father had always emphasized. What lay beyond their village was only no man's land.

Georg hurried across an intersection, glancing at the street sign bolted to the side of a house. Here Main Street turned into Karl-Marx-Street. His father had referred to it as Adolf-Hitler-Street, which it had been called under the Nazis. Georg sighed. The street that split their village in half had changed names too often. He thought back to this morning's rude wake-up call and felt his fists clench again. At times, living in the GDR bore too many similarities to living in Nazi Germany. He still couldn't believe he had agreed to spy on Susanne. How could he? But then, what choice did he have? He would find out whether she really planned to try to defect again and if she did, as they claimed, he would talk her out of it. Then he would have nothing to report. Georg felt better instantly.

After days of rain, the skies looked friendlier today. The air was mild and the few people out on their Sunday morning strolls greeted Georg as he passed. He merely nodded back in acknowledgement. No one but he seemed to be in a hurry. As he approached the corner that led down the alley to the village's church and parsonage, the church bells began to ring again. Georg hurried his step, but he knew there was no use. He had missed it. So much for a good impression.

Down the alley, a small square opened up in front of him, and the church finally came into sight. Next to the weather-beaten old church stood the parsonage with its neat little garden, well kept by the pastor's wife. Across the square from the church, two men entered a little half-timbered house, which seemed to be

61

leaning toward the church, looking almost hunched-over. The weathered aluminum sign that dangled above the door displaying a beer barrel could not be mistaken. This was where most men from the village "worshipped" Sunday mornings.

Georg turned his attention back to the church. He slowed his step. People were already exiting through the old wooden doors, among them Susanne who wore a light blue suit. He noticed that her hair was up, and that she looked radiant, smiling at the few people around her. She held one of the babies, all dressed in white, in her arms while a woman about Susanne's age stood next to her holding the other baby. Georg took a deep breath and made his way toward the group. Susanne had avoided him since their walk when she had revealed that it had been all her idea to leave. He had been furious at first, but it had quickly turned into a sense of loss. He had lost his best friend, and he hadn't been there for Susanne when she had needed him. They had seen each other, of course. After all, they lived next door to each other. But they hadn't exchanged more than a nod or a superficial greeting. And now he was late to the christening of her children he hadn't even been invited to. As he approached the group, the pastor stepped out of the church and shook everyone's hands. Georg couldn't avoid another sigh.

"It's Georg. Look," Gisela said. Susanne looked in the direction Gisela was pointing and saw Georg coming toward them. Georg in a suit. Susanne could hardly believe it. She tried to think of a time when she had seen him in a suit. She couldn't remember. Not even at Dieter's and her wedding had he worn one. She handed little Jana to her mother-in-law and met him at the steps of the church.

"I thought you never go to church." Susanne positioned herself in front of Georg, as if to block his way.

"I see I won't today." He looked past her and up the stairs, where people were still gathering. "I'm sorry I missed it," he said.

Shrugging, Susanne replied, "I didn't expect you to show up anyway."

Georg looked hurt. Susanne swallowed. That had sounded too harsh, but she was still mad at him. It hadn't been his place to lecture her about trying to defect to the West.

Susanne stepped back and examined Georg from head to toe. He looked quite presentable. Dieter and Georg were both nature boys. The only time she had seen Dieter in a suit was at their wedding. And now, for the first time, she saw Georg wearing one. She wished Dieter could be here, as she had all day, to witness it. He would never believe her if she told him.

"I'm really sorry," he said again, searching her face.

That he had come, wearing a suit and all, was more than Susanne had ever expected of him. They hadn't spoken for what seemed like an eternity, and she was tired of being mad at him. It was Gisela and her house, as well as Georg next door, that helped her to feel close to Dieter. When she looked at them, she felt as if Dieter was with her, as if he had just stepped outside to return in an instant. But he wouldn't. She was especially aware of that reality today.

"Well ... I better get going then. Rudi was already disappointed that I didn't allow him to come along. I'll need to take him on a walk." With that, Georg turned and started walking away.

"You can make up for missing my children's baptism and babysit for me some time," Susanne said hurriedly.

Georg turned back around, looking dubious. "Babysit? Me? I mean ... both of them?" His eyebrows raised.

For a moment Susanne thought Georg looked as if he wished he could vanish on the spot. She couldn't help but grin.

"I guess I ... could. Shouldn't be any worse than watching a litter of kittens learning how to walk," he said slowly, with a hint of humor in his voice.

Susanne eyed Georg curiously. It sounded as if he would truly consider babysitting the twins.

"Well, then you better come and say hello to Henry and Jana. And the family would love to say hello to you, too, I'm sure. Look, Dieter's uncle can't wait to remind you again how to properly woo a woman." Susanne saw Georg roll his eyes at that and laughed. "Yes, he has complained to me how he has unsuccessfully tried to teach you his way with women. He really insists on being of assistance to you, Georg," she said teasingly.

"I guess I could always use some help with that." Georg now grinned from ear to ear.

With another laugh, Susanne pulled Georg with her up the stone stairs. "You can start by meeting my dear friend Diana from Berlin. She is the babies' godmother. And you're in luck. She's staying for a few days. Lots of time to practice wooing a woman."

———

Their little procession left the church square, walked up the alley, and moved along Main Street to make it home for the festive lunch Susanne and Gisela had been preparing all week.

Finally, there was something for the people of the village to see. More and more heads appeared in the windows, looking at the small group of people all dressed in their Sunday best passing by. Off and on well-wishes were extended, while others chose not to show any solidarity. Susanne knew too well that religion was frowned upon by most who had chosen communism as their new ideology, even in their remote little village where old traditions, some reaching back to the Middle Ages, were observed without fail.

When their little procession had made it to Gisela's house, Georg excused himself to take Rudi for a walk. He promised to be back in a hurry to practice feeding the babies so they wouldn't starve to death when he babysat them. With a sigh of relief, Susanne realized that their friendship had not suffered. Georg was still her friend, one of the few she had left.

"How did you get your hands on all this food?" Dieter's uncle asked Susanne, while taking in a deep breath through his nostrils and scanning the heavily-laden table displaying an array of delicious, steaming-hot dishes. Sausages and pork chops, cabbages, dumplings, potatoes, carrots, beans, and peas. In the center of the table stood a platter with a crisp brown-baked rabbit.

Gisela answered for Susanne, who was busy taking a squirming Henry from her friend Diana. "Susanne and I stood in line all week," Gisela said, scanning the table proudly.

Susanne nodded in agreement. "And we'll have fruit salad for dessert."

"Fruit salad? What kind of fruit besides apples and pears have you got? It's November," Uncle Heinrich said.

"We really got lucky this week. With Gisela's connection, we got our hands on some oranges, believe it or not," Susanne said proudly.

Uncle Heinrich looked dumbfounded. He surely hadn't expected a treat like that.

With a look at the table Susanne said, "Now all we need is Georg. He better get here before everything gets cold." She craned her neck to look out the window, but there was no sight of him.

"And Henry is squirming like a hungry little caterpillar,"

Susanne said, winking at her friend. She then glanced over to Jana, still peacefully cradled in Uncle Heinrich's arms. Susanne knew that little Jana wouldn't be that content for much longer.

"Well, Georg insisted on feeding the babies. I can't wait to see that," Gisela said.

Just as Susanne was about to announce that they should start eating, Georg burst in the door, panting heavily.

"Right on time, G—" Susanne stopped herself when she saw Georg's face.

As she was about to speak again, Georg interrupted her. "Dieter!" Georg stared at her imploringly, but she already knew. She hurriedly placed Henry in Georg's arms and ran past him, out of the house and next door into the dark hallway, where she found the handset lying next to the phone that was sitting on a small table next to Georg's wardrobe. She stopped for a moment and just stared at the handset, panting. Then slowly Susanne picked it up and put it to her ear.

"Dieter?" Her voice was barely audible. She wasn't sure he had heard her.

Just as she was about to say his name again, he spoke.

"Oh, thank goodness you're there," Dieter said.

At the sound of Dieter's voice, Susanne felt her tears well up.

"Susanne? Are you still there?"

"I am. I am, Dieter." She tried to think of all the things she wanted to tell and ask him, but her mind was blank.

"How are you?" he asked, his voice full of love.

"I miss you. Dieter, it's been so long." She swallowed hard. "There haven't been any letters. Nothing," she said, the words tumbling out now.

"I've written. I have," Dieter said.

"Did you get my letters?" Susanne asked, slowly sitting down on the bench next to the wardrobe.

"I have. Some. And the pictures. Thank you... they... both are so beautiful," Dieter said, his voice breaking.

Tears were streaming down Susanne's cheeks now. She didn't care. She was alone. Alone in this dark hallway in Georg's house. Alone with Dieter. His voice so clear, as if he was standing next to her. She closed her eyes, picturing his boyish face.

"Susanne?"

"I had the babies christened today," she said, sniffing back the tears.

"I know. I got your letter... I thought I'd at least try to call," Dieter said quietly. "I'm glad I got through."

"Dieter, what's going to happen?" She could no longer hold back the question.

She assumed *they* were listening, but she had to ask him.

"I'll get word to you," he said in a hushed voice.

"How, Dieter? Your letters don't get here. How? Tell me!" Susanne said.

"I promise I'll get word to you ... Do you believe me, Susanne? Do you?"

"I do, Dieter. I do. You know I do," she said. "When?" she added.

"Soon. Soon we'll be together."

She heard him breathe and closed her eyes. She was afraid for the call to end. She didn't want to let it end. She needed to talk to him, tell him all the things she had yearned to tell him for months. She needed him. "We shouldn't have done it," she heard herself say, and started sobbing, to her dismay. "I don't want to be without you. I can't. I can't do it."

Suddenly Susanne felt an arm around her shoulder and looked up into Gisela's face. Her mother-in-law was crying as well. Behind her was Georg, his eyes full of pity.

Susanne couldn't bear what she saw written on their faces.

"Your mama. She wants to talk to you," Susanne said, wiping angrily at the tears on her cheeks.

"Don't go yet, Susanne. Not yet. Please," Dieter said. His voice was pleading with her.

"They'll cut you off soon. You should talk to your mother." As much as Susanne didn't want to let go of Dieter, she couldn't talk in front of Gisela and Georg. It had been good to hear Dieter's voice, but they couldn't discuss any plans for the future over the phone anyway. *They* were listening in, waiting for any indication that they were up to something. She had to trust Dieter to get word to her. How he would do that, she had no idea. It would take time, she knew that. But she trusted him. He would find a way.

Susanne hadn't lied. The *Stasi* would certainly end the call for them in only a few minutes. Calls from the West didn't last too long, and Gisela was waiting anxiously beside her.

"I have to go," Susanne said gently. "When will you call again?"

"As soon as I can." Dieter paused. "I love you."

Susanne swallowed hard. "I love you, too." Susanne let the handset slowly sink down. Gisela took it gently from her and started to talk to Dieter. Her mother-in-law was still crying. The words came tumbling out of her, and she clung to the handset as if it were Dieter himself.

As if in a daze, Susanne looked at Gisela for a minute, her eyes hanging on her mother-in-law's lips. She tried to understand what Dieter's mother was saying, but couldn't comprehend the words. Her mind was racing, again and again returning to the few words they had exchanged.

She turned to leave, only to find herself looking into Georg's face. He searched her eyes, but she cast them down and walked past him toward the front door.

Closing the door behind her, Susanne leaned against it. Her eyes were shut. She tried to picture Dieter in her friends' living room, talking on the phone. She realized that she didn't even know how he was living now or if he worked. She knew nothing. She hadn't asked. It really didn't matter. Soon she would be with him.

They would catch up then. All that mattered was that he still loved her and hadn't given up on them.

Georg waited discreetly in his living room, so Gisela could talk to Dieter in private. He sat on his couch and thought of Susanne. She had been so upset. He had never seen her like this. For the first time, he realized how hard it still was for her to be separated from Dieter. Why didn't he just come back? Georg was aware that it wouldn't be that simple and easy, but there had to be a way.

Gisela came in. "He wants to talk to you," she said simply before sitting down on a chair across from Georg.

He got up and hurried out of the living room. "Dieter?"

"Georg! Sorry that I had to cut you off earlier. I had to talk to Susanne first."

"Of course," was all Georg could reply. "How are you?" Georg asked. He had wondered all this time how things had gone for Dieter in the West.

"They'll cut the line soon, Georg. Listen," Dieter said, without answering his question.

"Did you–" Georg wanted to ask, but Dieter interrupted him.

"You need to make sure she's all right, Georg. And the babies. Please!" Dieter said hastily. "How is she? Is she well?"

"It hasn't been easy for her. She's been through a lot. She needs you, Dieter," Georg said. Dieter didn't reply. "Why don't you come back?" Georg couldn't hold back the question.

"I can't," Dieter said simply. "Susanne wouldn't let me do that. And *they* wouldn't. And if I did, they'd arrest me."

"I'm sure there's a way. Maybe you can cut a deal with them," Georg suggested carefully.

"Are you mad? Seriously, Georg. Who in their right mind would go back?"

"Susanne, your children. You must be ..." Georg stopped talking. There was no doubt. He had heard the click. They had cut the line. Dieter would no longer hear him. Georg cursed and slammed the handset back on the phone. He ran his hand through his hair. *There must be something I can do*, he thought.

Georg and Gisela returned to the party next door together. Neither of them spoke on the short trip there. At Gisela's house, they were greeted with a gloomy silence. No one was talking when they walked in. Georg was certain they wanted to know about the call, but it wouldn't be his place to talk about it. He would leave that to Gisela.

Everyone had already eaten. Susanne was nowhere to be seen. Georg knew that it was best to give her some time alone. No one would be able to comfort her now, at least not anyone on this side of the border fence.

Georg chose to interrupt the gloomy silence that seemed to have settled over everyone by announcing that he needed to keep his promise and feed the babies, who sat on Diana's and Dieter's aunt's lap, bibs around their necks, and a bowl of mashed carrots in front of them. Both women had already started to feed them.

Georg took little Henry from Diana, who smiled encouragingly, and sat down opposite her. He told himself that it couldn't be any harder than trying to bottle-feed an abandoned young kitten whose mother had strayed too far west and never returned.

So Georg took up the spoon, dipped it in the carrot puree and carefully put it into

Henry's mouth. He eagerly sucked the carrots off the spoon. Georg smiled to himself.

This turned out to be far easier than he had thought.

"You feed him like an old pro," Diana said admiringly.

"Well, in my day, feeding babies was a woman's job," countered Uncle Heinrich, but fell quiet again when he saw his wife's face.

"You should try it sometime. See, it's quite easy. Any man can do it," said Georg, scraping around in the now almost empty bowl. He put what carrots were left into Henry's mouth, but the baby sputtered and orange pieces flew all over Georg's suit.

"I see. Any man can do it," mocked Dieter's uncle. His wife hit his arm and threw him a nasty look while handing Georg her napkin.

"Well, I can feed Jana, if you like. You haven't even eaten yet. It's all cold now," Gisela said. She had sat quietly with a forlorn look in her eyes since their return from Georg's house.

Georg looked at her as if she had asked him to sell the babies. "A promise is a promise. I'll feed Jana, too. My suit is a mess anyway, and besides, I can warm up the food later. I'm not as hungry as she is." Georg was pointing at little Jana with Henry's spoon. Then he handed a now satisfied Henry back to Diana. With another look at his suit, he got up and took off his jacket.

Little Jana proved far more difficult than her brother. Whatever amount Georg placed in her mouth, half of it always came back out. It took him twice as long to feed her. After what seemed like an eternity, he was done. Gisela insisted that the babies had to be put down for a nap. So Georg took it upon himself to take Jana upstairs, followed by Diana, who carried Henry.

Georg entered the nursery, Jana in his arms. He looked around, not sure what to do next.

Diana walked in after him. "We should probably change their diapers, first," she said.

"Yeah. You're right," Georg said, feeling completely out of place. He looked on while Diana changed Henry's diaper. She seemed to know what she was doing. He had seen her at Dieter's and Susanne's wedding, but they hadn't had more than a few courteous exchanges. She was a tall woman and bore the same sophistication as Susanne. They appeared to be around the same age as well. Her hair was dark and fell below her shoulders. He couldn't deny that she was attractive. He wondered if she already was with someone, but then Susanne wouldn't have dropped hints at the church if she were already taken.

"It's your turn," Diana said suddenly.

"I ... I can't," Georg said, trying to collect his thoughts.

"Well ... you've watched closely. You should be able to," Diana said teasingly.

She stepped aside to make room for him.

"Would you show me one more time?" he asked.

Diana put Henry in his crib and then faced Georg, her hands at her sides. "If you're really going to babysit those two, you need to know how to change a diaper. Feeding is only part of it. What goes in must also come out, right?" She patted his shoulder. "Learning by doing, Georg," she said with a grin, and left.

For ten minutes, Georg struggled to fasten a new diaper around Jana's waist. It was still somewhat loose when he got her dressed again. He hoped it would hold whatever it needed to hold. He put Jana down in her crib and checked on Henry. He lay wide awake in his bed, flapping his arms wildly at the sight of Georg. "You only like me because I fed you," Georg said. "What a day," he mumbled to himself as he left the nursery.

In the hallway, Georg listened intently. The babies were quiet. He went up to Susanne's door. Everything beyond her door lay still. He wondered if she was asleep, or even in her room. Georg knocked carefully. There was no response. He knocked again, more forcefully this time. Again, there came no reply. He slowly creaked open the door to the room that had once belonged to his best friend.

Susanne was lying still on the bed, and only because he heard her sniff up the tears did he know that she wasn't sleeping.

"Susanne?" Georg walked quietly over to her bed and sat down on its edge. "Susanne?" he asked again.

She turned around to face him. Her eyes were red and puffy, and her face looked almost swollen. He placed a hand on her arm. "Are you all right?"

Susanne nodded, wiping at the tears.

"I fed Henry and Jana, you know." He smiled at her, hoping to get a smile out of her.

Susanne raised her eyebrows. "You did? How did it go?"

"Well, let's put it this way—whatever didn't land on my suit, should have ended up in their bellies."

Susanne chuckled and looked at his pants, which still had traces of carrots on them. "Thank you, Georg. You'll make a fine babysitter," she said, pulling herself up into a sitting position. "Has Gisela put them down for a nap?"

"Diana and I did."

Susanne's eyebrows rose again, but she didn't say anything.

"I spoke to Dieter," he said suddenly. She didn't react. "We need to find a way for him to come back," he said, wondering if she ever considered that.

Susanne looked at him in surprise. "He can't, Georg. How? They would arrest him as soon as he puts a foot on this soil. Or they won't let him back in at all. Who knows what they would do?"

"There must be something that can be done," he said. Someone that had the power to do something. Fleischer? Georg pushed the thought aside.

"Dieter will work something out," Susanne said. "He'll get word to me."

Georg looked at her for a moment. Dieter would get word to her. How? Georg shook his head. "Don't you know people, Susanne? High up, I mean?" Georg knew Susanne had admirers, among them party functionaries.

But Susanne just shook her head. "I certainly don't have any admirers left after what happened."

Georg nodded knowingly. And then his thoughts turned again to Fleischer. He might be the key. If he were to give Fleischer what he wanted, maybe the Stasi officer would be willing to consider doing something for him. Georg grew determined to ask Fleischer to help him to get Dieter back over here. That was the only way. Georg was sure of it.

"If Dieter's plan doesn't work out, I'll have to think of something," Susanne said suddenly and got up.

"Like what?" Georg asked, doubtful she had meant it.

"Try again."

Georg got up with a start. "There's no way, Susanne. How? The babies!" He couldn't believe what he was hearing.

"I'll find a way. There must be a way," she said determinedly and walked over to the mirror. "I look awful. Goodness." Georg just stared at her. "This is my babies' big day. We should go back down," she said, trying to wipe away the mascara that had run down her cheeks.

"You're right," Georg said simply, following her out of the room. His mind was racing. Susanne couldn't possibly attempt another escape. Was she out of her mind? He had to act fast before Susanne did anything that would make this worse than it was. He needed to talk to Fleischer tomorrow.

Susanne made her way downstairs. Georg followed her. She could hear the sound of voices and the soft clinking of glass from the living room and wanted to turn around to go back to her room. But she reminded herself of the reason everyone was here and celebrating. Still, she didn't feel ready to face everyone. They would bombard her with questions about Dieter's phone call. She turned to Georg. "Go on ahead without me. I need to get some fresh air before facing everyone," she said. Georg wanted to protest, but Susanne just turned around and left him standing there in the hallway.

As she opened the front door, the fresh, cold autumn air hit her. It felt like morning dew on her face. Susanne closed her eyes and breathed in deeply. The cold air would definitely help with her red and puffy eyes. A short stroll through the garden should do it, she decided, and opened her eyes. As she closed the door and hurried down the steps, she saw Gisela at the bottom of the stairs, smoking. Susanne was stunned. She had never seen Dieter's mother smoke. Never. As she went down the stairs, Gisela looked up at her, blowing out the smoke.

"You look as if you've always smoked," said Susanne, sitting down on the cold stone steps next to her mother-in-law.

"I have, dear," came the matter-of-fact reply. Susanne raised her eyebrows in surprise, wondering for a moment if her mother-in-law had ever smoked around the babies. "Want one?" Gisela held out the pack of cigarettes to her. The writing on them was Russian. Susanne just shook her head. Dieter had smoked, and it had always bothered her, especially because he had also smoked in their little apartment. She had not, and yet her clothes and hair had smelled as well. But Gisela had never smelled of smoke. How did she do it?

"You should go inside and eat. There's a lot left," Gisela said between puffs.

"I'm really not hungry."

"Then at least go inside and make your guests feel welcome, Susanne." Gisela said, not looking at her.

Susanne looked at her mother-in-law as if she had been slapped. "Is something wrong? If there is, you need to let me know," she said.

Gisela turned toward her. "You're not the only one this has been hard on, you know," she said.

"I know you're his mother and you miss him and all, but I'm his wife, the mother of his children. Don't you think that—"

"I wasn't talking about me, Susanne. I was talking about Dieter," Gisela said, cutting her off. Susanne just stared at her. She swallowed. Had Dieter told his mother that it had been her idea to defect to the West? After all, it was she who had convinced him to leave, although it hadn't been difficult to persuade him. He was fed up with the state as well. He was ridiculed for his longer hair and the way he dressed. He yearned for the freedom to travel, dreaming about going to Africa and Asia, knowing that it would only remain a dream if they stayed. It had pained Dieter to stay behind when she got to travel to the West with her orchestra. And once they had found out she was pregnant, they knew they had to act quickly. Dieter had planned how to cross the border all on his own. Susanne had let him. Had Georg said anything to Gisela? She hoped not. Georg was a sensitive man and would know better than to hurt Gisela's feelings and cause a rift between Susanne and her mother-in-law. But what, then, had gotten into Gisela? Dieter's phone call?

Gisela got up. Without another word, she walked off into the garden, leaving Susanne staring after her. For the first time since coming out here, Susanne could feel the cold of the stone steps creep up from underneath her. Susanne looked up at the now overcast sky. Even though it was only late afternoon, it was already starting to get dark.

Susanne shivered. She wasn't sure if it was because of the cold or because she was mad. Mad at Gisela and mad at herself. But at the same time, a feeling of shame crept up, just like the cold. Gisela was right. It was just as hard on Dieter as on her. She knew that. She might not have said it out loud, but Gisela must surely believe that she knew that.

Susanne rested her chin on her knees and stared out into the garden. She felt miserable. Was she really so absorbed in her own self-pity? She thought of Dieter day and night. She missed him terribly.

Susanne searched the garden, over which the gray darkness now slowly settled. Was Gisela coming back? Susanne could make out Gisela's shape in the far-off corner of the garden near the fence.

Off and on she could see a small red gleam appear near Gisela's shape. Susanne imagined Gisela leaning on the fence and smoking.

She sighed and got up. There was no use waiting around out here in the cold for Gisela. Susanne felt her face. The cold had done the trick. She didn't feel her eyes were still red and puffy. Time to go inside.

When Susanne entered the living room, everyone fell silent. She tried to avoid looking at anyone. Straightening her skirt, she put on a smile and resisted the urge to turn around and run upstairs. Instead, she went over to the phonograph. Still no one talked. Susanne could feel everyone's eyes on her back. With an album in her hand, she turned back around and looked into their concerned faces. "Even in our part of the world people find occasion to celebrate, right?" She turned, put the album on the phonograph, and then walked over to the couch to sit down next to Dieter's uncle. Susanne had always liked him. Heinrich just looked so much like Dieter, even though he was decades older. But looking at him tonight gave her unexpected comfort. Susanne patted his knee and Heinrich put an arm around her and placed a drink in her hand.

"Even under Hitler we had a few reasons to celebrate," he said. "They were very few, of course." He looked endearingly at his wife who was putting dessert in front of Georg. Dieter's aunt was a little plump woman who always wore flowery dresses. The dimples in her face flashed every time she smiled. "Marrying her had been a good reason to celebrate, even then, even in those dark years," Heinrich said quietly, looking thoughtfully at the beer bottle in his hand. Then he looked up and smiled at Susanne encouragingly. She managed to return the smile, certain it was only a distorted grimace.

As the evening wore on, Susanne caught herself smiling and even laughing on occasion. She finally ate, together with Georg, some of the food Gisela and she had prepared. It tasted even better warmed up. Susanne had to smile to herself when Georg had gotten up to reload his plate for the third time. Susanne knew that Georg seized every moment to get a great home-cooked meal. He cooked himself, but his cooking lacked variety. And Susanne had to admit to herself that nothing could outdo Gisela's cooking.

By the time midnight approached, everyone seemed tired, but no one left yet. It was the familiar atmosphere Susanne had always appreciated when Dieter's family had gotten together. At this hour, everyone sat quietly around the room, talking and eating a light late night meal, consisting of cake and cheese. This would go on until the early morning hours.

───

Fortunately, Susanne had listened to Gisela's earlier advice and taken Monday off. She was dead tired and there were heaps of dishes from yesterday's party that needed to be washed. The living room was a disaster and would need some special attention. There were bottles everywhere. Dieter's family used any family gathering to consume as much beer as they could. When Dieter had introduced her to the family at his mother's birthday party, it had surprised Susanne how much everyone drank, but how little it seemed to affect them.

Susanne didn't mind the lingering smell of beer in the living room or having to collect the sticky bottles. She was home today, and that was all that mattered. She was looking forward to spending some extra time with Henry and Jana. True, restoring the living room to its former state would take a couple of hours, but what was a couple of hours of cleaning compared to a whole day's work at the factory.

Susanne pushed against the coffee table, but the heavy piece with the glass top didn't budge. She would need help putting the furniture back where it belonged. The coffee table, the couch, and the two heavy armchairs had been pushed out of the way when Dieter's uncle decided it was time to dance after midnight. They had all danced and, to Susanne's surprise, she had actually enjoyed herself and no longer had to pretend to be cheerful. Susanne knew the dancing had helped her to forget the many things she didn't get to tell Dieter on the phone. And even Georg, who had been quite somber for most of the night, had finally given in to Uncle Heinrich's nagging and danced with Diana. Gisela, however, had been distant all night, and even this morning, she still didn't look at her.

It was already afternoon when Susanne finally got to vacuum the living room. She had spent the early morning hours with the babies, glad not to have to leave them and rush away to work. While Jana and Henry had taken their morning nap, Susanne had gotten started on the living room while Gisela was in the kitchen, washing the mountain of dishes. After the babies had their lunch, she had put them down for a nap and then continued to clean the living room. Now, already well into the afternoon, Susanne was vacuuming and actually enjoying it. A year ago, she could not have imagined that this was something she would take pleasure in. Staying home had never been for her. But since the birth of the babies, it was all she wanted.

Gisela, wearing an apron and a dishtowel over her right shoulder, came in and pointed to the front door. Susanne motioned to her that she didn't understand, and Gisela tried to talk over the loud vacuum without any success. Finally, Gisela came over to her and switched off the vacuum. What she told Susanne came out in a whisper.

"There is someone at the door for you." Her mother-law's face was hard to read, but at least Gisela was talking to her again.

"Who is it?" Susanne asked, wondering who knew she was home today. Georg would have just come in, and Diana had taken the babies, insisting that they needed some fresh air after their nap when in truth it was she who needed the fresh air after last night.

"You better go talk to him." Gisela sounded worried.

Who in the world could it be, Susanne wondered while she went to the front door, which stood slightly ajar. She opened it and fell back a step. Fleischer. What did he want? Why was he here? Then it hit her. Dieter's phone call. So they had listened. Susanne tried to swallow down the rising panic. She stared at the Stasi officer in front of her. He was not wearing his uniform but dark blue pants and a zipped-up gray jacket; nevertheless, he had the same official look about him.

"I need to talk to you, Frau Schmidt. Alone." Susanne glanced at Gisela, who had followed her to the front door.

"You may talk in the living room, dear," said Gisela, taking down the dishtowel from her shoulder and heading for the kitchen.

Susanne led Fleischer into the living room. Before he sat down on the couch, he looked around the room, his eyes stopping at the vacuum cleaner.

"You're not at the factory today, Frau Schmidt?" He looked up at her where she was standing.

"I took the day off. That is allowed, is it not?" She tried to keep not only her anxiety but also her cold annoyance out of her voice, unsure if it was really working. Fleischer was ruining her otherwise perfect day and she didn't like it that he showed up here unannounced. But then again, he had taken her by surprise before, when he had paid her a visit at the factory.

"It certainly is, Frau Schmidt." Fleischer's eyes moved in the direction of the basket full of empty bottles standing next to the stove in the corner.

"I see you're doing well. You seem to have reason to celebrate." He looked at her more directly now, his eyes searching her face.

"My children were christened yesterday," Susanne said, folding her arms in defiance. She was sure he had been informed about that, but she wanted to tell him anyway. She knew how it annoyed him that they were religious because people like him only found salvation in the ideals of communism. There was a hint of disdain in his gray eyes. She had gotten to him. For the first time, Susanne didn't feel helpless in front of this man and took a step forward. "So why did you come down here all the way from Berlin? I wasn't aware the Stasi made house calls." She felt confident standing up to this man. *Dangerously confident,* her voice of reason told her.

He looked up at her in surprise. He was clearly taken aback by her curtness, but then Susanne saw his gray eyes darken.

"I'm here for several reasons, Frau Schmidt." He went right on. "Herr Hoffmann received a phone call yesterday. I believe it was your husband?"

Susanne didn't respond.

"We have reason to believe that you will try again to defect," he said matter-of-factly, leaning back on the couch and watching her carefully.

Susanne swallowed hard. How did he –? Her mind was racing. She hadn't said anything to Dieter, had she? She tried to remember what exactly she or Dieter had said, but couldn't think of anything that could have given away her intentions. How did Fleischer know?

"I don't know where you got this information, but it's not true," Susanne said, trying hard to sound confident. "This is absurd. I would never leave my children. Never."

Fleischer searched her face for a moment. Then he said, "We'll make sure that won't happen, Frau Schmidt. Be assured."

Susanne's mind was still racing. How had Fleischer found out what she was planning to do?

"While I'm here, Frau Schmidt," Fleischer said, bringing her back abruptly, "I'm following up on your work as an informant for the Stasi. I hope this time you have something to report, or I don't see how we can still work together. You do have information for me, don't you?"

"There is nothing to report. No strangers in this village, Herr Fleischer. Nothing suspicious going on. Everyone is a law-abiding citizen. There is nothing happening around here," Susanne said frantically.

"There is always something or someone to report. As in your case. An informant notified us about your intentions to defect again. Again, Frau Schmidt?" He seemed to wait for her reaction. "What I don't understand is how you can be so ungrateful to your country. And your babies … Are you a good mother, Frau Schmidt? You are willing to put your children in such danger? We trusted you would take care of your children and do your part."

Susanne panicked. She stepped forward. "Herr Fleischer–"

"I think our deal is off, Frau Schmidt." Fleischer's voice grew louder now and Susanne wondered how much of all this Gisela was actually hearing. But that didn't matter now. She couldn't believe what Fleischer was saying. What did that mean? The children? They wouldn't take them away from her now, would they?

"I don't know what to do about you, Frau Schmidt. You're not cooperating. Your unwillingness to work with us leaves me no choice," Fleischer said, sounding final.

"No!" Susanne cried, stepping forward. "No, Herr Fleischer. I've tried. Believe me. I need more time for people to open up to me."

"You had enough time," he said coldly.

"Please, Herr Fleischer." She hated herself for begging him. "You must give me more time. I'm sure something of value to you will come up." She realized she was breathing hard, waiting for a response from him.

"You have until March. No longer." His tone was uncompromising.

She knew he meant what he said. He wouldn't give her any more leeway. That was certain.

She thought that they were done, but he opened the zipper of his jacket and motioned for her to sit down. She complied and silently walked over to the chair on the other side of the room to sit down. He looked at her and smiled. She couldn't believe he was smiling. It was a cold smile that matched the color of his eyes and the clothes he wore. He had her trapped. He controlled her life. And he knew it.

"Frau Schmidt. I want to help you. Do as I say and there will be something to report. Believe me," he said in a fatherly tone. She remembered hearing him talk to her like that before. In the hospital. She realized that nothing had changed. She was still at his mercy. More than ever. She looked down at her hands in her lap.

"You need to get out," he went on. Susanne looked up in surprise, but what he said next clarified that he wasn't about to help her to get out of the country. "I want you to get out more ... become friends with the people here. Mingle with them, get involved, participate. You might even want to dust off your violin and put it to good use."

Susanne just stared at him.

"We both know you won't be the concertmaster with your orchestra in Berlin any time soon – that job has been filled by your friend Diana."

Susanne couldn't hide her shock.

"Oh, I see. She hasn't told you." There was triumph in his eyes. Susanne's ears were ringing. His voice sounded far off. "You might want to consider putting on a little something for the people here. I'm sure they would appreciate a little concert. You might gain their trust."

Susanne felt numb. She only half heard how he was ordering her to come up to Berlin in March with something to report. She saw him zip up his jacket and leave without waiting for Susanne to show him to the door. Susanne stared after him, and only after a minute did she realize that she was still clenching her fists. She could scream. She only had until March. March. Less than four months. Would Dieter find a way for her and the babies to get to the West by then? Doubts clouded her mind as soon as she had the thought. Dieter had said he would get word to her. It had to happen soon, or she had to find a way out of this herself. There was no more time.

"Who was that man, Susanne?" Her mother-in-law's worried voice brought her back. She looked around, disoriented. She realized that she had not imagined Fleischer leaving. He was gone.

"Stasi," was all that Susanne could reply. She was certain Gisela had already come to that conclusion herself.

Gisela sank down on the couch across from her, sighing heavily. "I feared they might watch you." Susanne looked up, surprised by her mother-in-law's changed demeanor. Gisela was kneading her hands and staring out the window. "As if they haven't punished you enough already with that awful job at the factory and not letting you perform anymore. What kind of people are they, spying on those they've crushed?" Gisela said accusingly. Susanne didn't answer. She was glad for Gisela's compassion. Her motherly instinct for her had finally kicked back in. She seemed to be over yesterday's little argument.

"What did he want? Is it because of Dieter's phone call?" Gisela asked. Susanne had hoped that Gisela wouldn't bring up Dieter's phone call again. But her mother-in-law truly seemed distressed about Fleischer's visit. And after all, she was right in her assumption. "You need to be careful," Gisela went on. These people are dangerous. I've heard stories ..." She was pleading now. "I know Dieter plans to find a way for you to join him. Be careful. Don't trust anyone," Gisela said, her voice tired and full of sadness. "I've gotten used to the three of you. I wish Dieter would just return to us."

Susanne looked at her. "But he can't. Do you know what they would do to him?" "I just don't want to lose all of you," Gisela said in a tone that struck Susanne to the core. She looked at her mother-in-law, and a great rush of affection for this woman washed over her. She had no mother or grandmother left. But in the last few years, Gisela had been the mother figure in her life. Susanne knew that Gisela loved her, even though she had never said it out loud. Susanne hugged her, holding on to her mother-in-law longer than she would have felt comfortable in any other situation or at any other time.

Gisela patted her back and pulled free from her. Without another word, she left the room. An endless guilt wash over Susanne. She felt utterly selfish. She had hurt the only family she had left. It was all her fault, her fault alone. How could she hurt them again? But she, Dieter, and the children were a family, too. They needed to be together.

The next day, Susanne had to go back to work. The only time she got to spend with Diana was the few hours after work. But then they were never alone. Together they took care of the twins or spent time with Gisela and Georg, who had closed up his practice for most of those days, trying to keep Diana occupied in their quiet village while Susanne was at work. Susanne hadn't minded. She had welcomed it. She had avoided confronting Diana about the fact that she hadn't bothered to let her know that she had taken her position in the orchestra. It was good to have her friend around, so Susanne told herself that Diana must have chosen to keep silent only because she didn't want to hurt her feelings. Besides, what should Diana have done? Decline? Susanne wouldn't have declined if Diana had been the one trying to flee to the West, losing her position as concertmaster of not only Berlin's but also the country's best orchestra.

A few days later, Diana left for Berlin. Susanne walked her friend to the train station right before she had to go to work in the morning. It was cold. The fog hadn't yet lifted, and the ground was slightly frozen.

Gisela's house was only down the road from the train station but Susanne had put her friend's bag on the back of her bike so they wouldn't have to carry it. They walked quietly down the dark road, with Susanne pushing the bike. They were an odd pair. Her friend in dressy clothes, make-up, dark hair cascading down her back, and she in the blue work suit, no make-up, hair held back by a scarf. They looked like they were from two different worlds. And they were.

Diana had seemed shocked this morning when Susanne appeared in the kitchen for breakfast wearing her everyday work clothes. Like all musicians, Diana liked to sleep in. So the whole time her friend had spent with them, she had never been up to see Susanne leave for work. When Susanne returned home in her work overalls in the late afternoons, Diana hadn't seen her either because she had been out with Georg. By the time the two returned for dinner, Susanne had washed and changed her clothes.

Looking at Diana walking next to her, Susanne felt keenly how drastically her life had changed and what she had to give up. She repeatedly had to tell herself not to feel jealous of and resentful toward Diana. She was her friend and it was not Diana's fault that things had turned out the way they had. It was her own fault. It had been her decision to risk it all.

Even so, Susanne wished Diana had talked with her about Berlin, their friends, and the orchestra. She might have felt that it was still all there for her. But they both seemed to have avoided talking about friends they had in common, the orchestra, or the old times. Since Fleischer's visit, Susanne knew why.

Susanne and Diana walked on silently, both shivering slightly in the morning cold. The sun wouldn't be up for another half an hour, but there were already throngs of people heading for the train station to leave the village for work in the city. Susanne stopped at the last intersection before the train station would come into view and turned to her friend. She wouldn't have time to take her up to the platform. They had to say their goodbyes here.

"Thanks for bringing all that baby stuff down from Berlin with you. I really appreciate that. I had no idea how hard it is to come by. You're my only connection to all the privileges I used to enjoy," Susanne said, trying to sound light-hearted.

Her friend smiled. "Don't mention it. You'll just have to enjoy *my* privileges from now on –" Diana stopped herself, her smile fading from her face. She looked down at the tips of her black high heels. "I'm sorry, Susanne." Her friend didn't look up. Susanne saw Diana open her mouth again, but she hesitated.

"I heard," Susanne said. "It's all right."

Diana looked at her with big, rounded eyes, shame swimming in them. "I'm so sorry, Susanne. I'm so sorry. I didn't want –"

Susanne cut her off. "Don't be sorry. For what? You're a great violinist. You deserve it. Besides, someone has to do the job. And you're the best they've got." Susanne hugged her friend, who was sniffing back tears.

"If there is anything you ever need, you'll let me know, won't you?" Diana asked, wiping the tears off her cheek.

Susanne looked at her friend thoughtfully, not sure if this was really the right time or place to ask this of her friend. She wasn't even sure if she should ask her at all, but since Fleischer's visit, she knew that desperate measures were necessary.

"There is actually something you could do for me, Diana." Susanne said.

"Anything. Tell me," Diana replied, looking eager.

"You need to find something out for me. If there is any way for me to get into West Berlin."

"West Berlin? Susanne!" Diana looked around anxiously. Susanne did as well. A few people were walking on the other side of the road, but no one was within earshot of them. "You don't plan to try it again, do you? And how would I find something out like that? I don't know anyone who would know. You just don't ask around about stuff like that. I could get into major trouble, Susanne." Diana looked seriously worried. Panic turned her voice shrill.

Susanne instantly regretted that she had asked. Diana was right. One didn't just go around asking people. You had to have connections. And Diana was certainly not one who had such connections. "I'm sorry, Diana. I shouldn't ask something like that of you. I don't want to put you in any danger. But promise me, if you ever hear of anyone who might know people who know of ways to get into West Berlin, you will let me know." The words came tumbling out of her now.

Diana just stared at her anxiously. She was biting her lip and held her black leather purse in front of her as if to shield herself from Susanne.

"I have to do this. This is no life, Diana. I need to get out. I need to get to Dieter. There must be a way. Maybe sneaking into West Berlin somehow will be easier than trying to get across the border. We know how that turned out." Susanne forced a laugh.

Diana didn't join in Susanne's laughter. "But how? With the babies? How, Susanne?

"I don't know. I need you to find that out for me. Maybe I could get my hands on fake papers, or someone could smuggle us through a checkpoint along the wall. Something. There must be some way. There must be people in Berlin who know about these things." Susanne looked at Diana, who stood tight-lipped in front of her. She looked troubled and apprehensive, and Susanne couldn't blame her. Diana would lose everything if she were caught helping her defect to the West.

"All right. I'll help you. I'll see if I can find something out," Diana said suddenly.

Susanne looked at her in shock. "Are you sure? I know what that could mean for you."

Diana waved her off. "I don't want to see you like this anymore."

"Like what?" Susanne asked.

"Well... like this." Diana was pointing at Susanne's overalls and the scarf on her head. "Besides... you would do the same for me," she said. Now it was Susanne who had tears in her eyes. Diana took a handkerchief out of her purse and handed it to Susanne.

"Thanks," Susanne said feebly, wiped her tears, and handed the handkerchief back to Diana, who stuffed it back in her purse.

They hugged again. "Goodbye, Susanne. Please, come up to Berlin soon. "I'll take you to a concert. They can't forbid you to attend one. They can't." Then she added, "And maybe I'll find out something by then."

"I'll make sure I bring Georg for you." Susanne winked at her friend.

Diana blushed slightly. "Well, if you want to. He's always welcome. I told him that."

"You did?" Susanne smiled in surprise.

But then they heard the whistle of an oncoming train. "Do you have your pass?" Susanne asked hurriedly. Susanne knew that they wouldn't let anyone leave the Restricted Zone without that pass. Susanne had been surprised that Diana had actually gotten the permission to come to Wallhausen, to enter the Restricted Zone for the christening, and that she even had been allowed to stay for a few days. After all, Diana was her friend and not a relative. Relatives could usually get the permission to see family, but friends? She wasn't sure how Diana had pulled it off, but she was glad that it all had worked out.

Meanwhile, Diana had gotten out her pass and waved it in front of Susanne's face. "Got it." Pass in hand, she went over to Susanne and hugged her once more. Then she took her bag off the bike and waved over her shoulder. "Don't stop playing, Susanne. There'll be better times ahead. And watch over my godchildren," Diana called back to her before she disappeared around the corner.

For a moment, Susanne just stood there looking at the corner around which her friend had vanished. With a sigh, she turned her bike around, swung up on it, and started pedaling east where the sun was just barely starting to peek through the milky cloud cover.

Chapter 9

S usanne stretched and rubbed her aching back. She had been standing at the assembly line for the past seven hours. And it was Friday. At the end of the week, her back gave out from standing up and bending over all day, every day.

Susanne stretched once more, clenching her teeth. She glanced at the clock on the brick wall across from her. Another hour and it was the weekend. She thought of Henry and Jana. Oh, how she lived for the weekends. She was able to spend all day Saturday and Sunday with the children, a rare luxury in her mind. Not having to rush off to work after getting up in the morning, and not to have to hand over her children to her mother-in-law was what got her through the week. Not that she didn't appreciate what Gisela was doing for her and the babies, but she wanted to be the one to take care of them.

Susanne sighed and wiped a strand of hair off her forehead with the back of her gloved hand. She checked the clock again, the bigger arm moving across the dial in a slow but steady rhythm.

Susanne's thoughts turned once more to Jana and Henry. It seemed like the twins were reaching a milestone almost every day now. Henry was already sitting up by himself, and it would be only a matter of time until he was crawling. She could tell that he would have a lot of energy once he was walking. He would keep his grandmother up and chasing after him. Susanne chuckled at that thought. But then she reminded herself that this might not happen. She only had a few months left here. *Hopefully*, she thought, and sighed.

When she felt the woman next to her looking at her, Susanne wondered if she had thought out loud. She ignored her stare and put another folded box back on the conveyor belt.

Susanne worked for another hour until the signal finally sounded. She sighed in relief and dropped the half-folded box back on the conveyor belt. Following the stream of workers out of the hall, Susanne took her gloves off and pulled the scarf down from her hair.

As she went down the hallway to leave the building, she saw Hauser stepping out of his office. He immediately picked her out in the crowd of workers as if he had been waiting for her. But he didn't come toward her. He just waited there, by the door of his office.

When Susanne passed him, she thought she saw him smile at her. But he didn't say anything, no greeting, no well-wishes for the weekend. He had not spoken a word to her since Fleischer had paid the factory a visit. She hadn't minded. She mumbled a "Have a good weekend" when she had already passed him, just as those around her who were heading out the door and into their weekend, their hurried steps eager to leave the dreary factory behind until Monday.

As Susanne stepped outside and headed for her bike, the men who worked outside greeted her and other women leaving the factory with whistles. As usual, she ignored them as best as she could. But at times, this was difficult to accomplish. Such was the case today. When she reached her bike, one of the men had reached it as well.

"You need to come off your high horse, lady. And a fine lady you are," the man said as he exhaled smoke from a cigarette and looked her up and down before grinning at the other men across the yard.

Susanne tried to ignore him. He seemed to be her age and of a tall and slender build. One of his teeth was missing and the others looked stained. He wore soiled overalls with a dark coat over them.

Susanne bent down to open the lock. There was no need to reply to his comment. The man stepped around her and watched her provocatively, obviously interested in getting a good look at her backside. *Back off,* Susanne thought, teeth clenched. She got up, turned around, and wanted to leave the yard. To her dismay, the man stepped right in front of her, as if to prevent her from leaving. "Step aside," Susanne said, trying to sound calm. She was tired and couldn't wait to get home.

She was in no mood to be held up by this guy. He came closer and grabbed the bike's handlebar. Susanne tried to move her bike backward, but his grip was firm. "What do you want?" Susanne asked him, looking him square in the face.

He smirked at her. "Just a little of your–"

He stopped abruptly, looking past Susanne. She turned and saw Hauser approaching them.

"Everything all right, Fräulein Schmidt?" Her boss asked. Susanne just nodded; glad Hauser had shown up. "Off you go, Müller," Hauser said to the man. "Leave the woman alone. You're not her type."

The man left. The others had already scattered or left the vicinity of the factory. When the man had disappeared through the gates, Susanne found herself and Hauser alone in the yard.

"Don't mind these gawkies," Hauser said, motioning toward the now deserted gates.

"Thank you."

"No need to. I don't tolerate this kind of behavior. They know that. And one of these days they'll get it."

"I better get going then," Susanne said.

"Fräulein Schmidt..." Hauser started. Susanne flinched. Frau *Schmidt,* she thought angrily. Hauser came closer to her, his round belly touching the seat of her bike. "If there is anything I can assist you with..."

"Thank you, Herr Hauser. That's very kind of you, but I'm doing fine."

He brushed against her arm. "A woman like you shouldn't be alone."

Susanne looked around the deserted yard. With Hauser so close, there was no way she could just get on her bike and get away. "I'm not alone, Herr Hauser. If you will excuse me now, I need to head home." To her great relief, Hauser stepped aside so she could finally get on her bike. But Hauser looked rather offended and tight-lipped. Susanne swallowed and mumbled a goodbye, pedaling as fast as she could out of the yard, sure that Hauser was staring after her. First Fleischer's visit to the factory and now her rejection. She wouldn't be Hauser's favorite much longer. It only had to be for a little while longer, she reminded herself as she rode down Main Street. The cold air whipping her face felt surprisingly cleansing.

Chapter 10

"Sometimes it seems the bureaucracy is worse over here than over there," Dieter said in frustration, dropping down on the couch next to Anna. He had just spoken to the secretary of the Minister of Foreign Affairs. "No, I cannot tell you anything new, Herr Schmidt," Dieter said mockingly.

"You need to give this time, Dieter," Anna said. "I'm sure they're doing all they can." She looked scornfully at Dieter's feet on her coffee table.

Dieter didn't see her gaze but stared out the tall window into the large backyard with its immaculate landscaping. He had been living with Susanne's musician friends now for a year. A year. He couldn't believe it himself. Anna and Wolfgang Borowski insisted that he stay with them until Susanne and the children came. He didn't mind. Living alone would just worsen how he already felt. Maybe Georg had been right. Maybe he should go back. He missed Susanne terribly, as well as his mother. Most of all, he wanted to see his children. How he longed to hold them. He sighed and looked at Anna, who was flipping through a magazine. How he missed his old life. Especially on the days he was off work, Dieter found himself reeling with self-pity. So he was glad he had been able to secure a full-time job quickly to keep him occupied. He had found a position at the Hamburg Zoo. Not as a veterinarian, but as a zookeeper. It wasn't the same, but it was work. And with time, Dieter hoped, the West German government would recognize his degree and the work he had done at the East Berlin Zoo. "Where is Wolfgang?" Dieter asked, unfolding the newspaper. I haven't seen him since Wednesday."

"He moved out Wednesday, while you were at work," Anna said, her voice cold. "He did what?" Dieter took down his feet and stared at Anna in utter disbelief.

"He wanted to tell you himself tomorrow, when he picks up the rest of his stuff."

Dieter was shocked. He had no idea that Anna and Wolfgang were having problems. He hadn't witnessed any arguments or confrontations. What was going on? "Why? I had no idea –"

"We made that decision a long time ago. We were just room-mates for the last little while, but now that Wolfgang has found someone, he wants out."

"I'm so sorry, Anna."

She waved it off. "Care for some wine?"

"No, thanks," Dieter said, deep in thought. What would Anna and Wolfgang's split mean for him? Would he have to move out, too?

Anna got up and went to the kitchen. Only a minute later, she returned with a glass of red wine and sat back down next to Dieter. "Just pretend you didn't know yet when Wolfgang breaks the news to you tomorrow, would you?"

Dieter turned to her. "If you'd like me to move out, I understand."

"Dieter, no, this has nothing to do with you," Anna said, touching his arm lightly. "In fact, I don't want to be alone right now. Please stay, Dieter." She put her head on his shoulder.

"If you don't mind, I don't mind," Dieter said. "I don't feel like living alone either." Deep down, he hoped Susanne would understand. He liked Anna and would be forever grateful to her, but she was obsessed with cleaning and too high maintenance for his taste. He missed Susanne's charm and uncomplicated nature, the smell of her skin and her laugh. How he missed the sound of her laugh.

"So, what do you propose we do on this Friday night?" Anna inquired, interrupting his thoughts.

"I might just go to bed early tonight," Dieter said. He was in no mood for Anna's long Monopoly nights. "I'm exhausted and I have to get up early for work tomorrow."

"Oh, come on, Dieter. Let's play Monopoly." Anna paused for a moment. "No, forget it. Let's go out. What do you think?"

He knew Anna needed the diversion. He couldn't possibly leave her to herself on this Friday night. "All right then."

Anna clapped her hands. "Disco or pub?"

Chapter 11

The only place Susanne found a measure of solitude and felt somewhat close to Dieter was the hill overlooking the train tracks. From there, she could also see the village that bordered theirs. No man's land and the border fence separated it from Wallhausen. What fate had decided that the village over there was on the West side while theirs was fenced in the East? What fate, indeed, she asked herself. Fate had nothing to do with it.

America and Russia had swapped villages up and down the river. Gisela had once told her that Wallhausen had been occupied by the Americans first. While they had treated the villagers mostly with kindness, even sharing their rations with them, there had been only a few victims of the occupation. Young, beautiful women, mostly. Gisela had left it at that, and Susanne had wondered if Gisela had been one of those women.

Then the Americans left, and the Russians came in. This time, not only the beautiful women became victims of the occupation. Everything the villagers owned was ransacked. Retaliation and poverty in Russia were the reasons for this treatment, Gisela had explained to her. The last little bit of food was taken from the villagers. So Wallhausen had ended up in the Soviet-occupied zone. The village on the other side of the border fence, American-occupied. The West.

Susanne sat down with a sigh. The ground was moist but still somewhat warm from the pale sun. The first few days of December had been surprisingly mild. She hadn't minded, because riding her bike in snow and cold would make it even harder to get to the factory.

Susanne stared at the houses on the West side with their puffing chimneys. Their red roofs shone in the late afternoon sun. It looked as if the houses had been whitewashed and the roads tarred just yesterday. It all looked so new to her. Susanne looked over her shoulder at the road below, and Gisela's house at the far end of it. All roads in Wallhausen were cobblestoned, and Gisela's house looked as if it had needed a fresh coat of paint twenty years ago. But paint was hard to come by. Houses everywhere, even in Berlin, bore witness to that.

Susanne looked back at the village across the border. Cars were driving up and down the main road. Her mind drifted off to Dieter. She knew he wasn't living in the village across the line, but if she were over there, she could just hop on a train to Hamburg and see him within hours. He was so close, yet so far. It felt as if he were on the other side of the world.

The scattered leaves rustled behind her. Someone was coming. Susanne turned and was relieved to see that it was Georg who came her way. Rudi was by her side before Georg. The German shepherd jumped on her and licked her face as she tried to fend him off. Georg whistled, and the dog sat down next to her, wagging his tail so hard in excitement that she had to scoot to the side not to get lashed by it. Georg waved in greeting, and she returned a smile.

"I thought I'd find you here," Georg said. Susanne stared straight ahead. No reply was necessary. He knew she was up here a lot. Georg stared in the same direction as she. "May I?"

She looked up at him. "It's not my hill. Of course, you can."

Georg sat down beside her. "One might think you own it, though. You spend a lot of time up here." He grinned at her now. "And if it *were* your hill? Would you invite me to sit down?"

"'Course I would." She nudged him in the side, and he laughed. It felt good to have Georg here. She appreciated him interrupting her brooding thoughts. Rudi was jumping around in the leaves. "Will you come to my concert?" Susanne asked casually, still staring straight ahead at the village on the other side of the fence.

Out of the corner of her eye, she saw Georg's jaw drop. But he composed himself quickly. "I'm glad you're performing again." He sounded just as casual.

"The concert is at the church," Susanne added, still looking at the village in the West. "Nothing fancy. A few Christmas favorites."

He grinned at her. "Well, I'll make an exception for you." They sat there in silence for a few moments. Rudi was off, chasing after what Susanne assumed was a rabbit. Georg spoke first. "In return, you can take me to Berlin with you."

Berlin? Then it dawned on her. She had promised Diana a visit and Georg to take him along. Susanne smiled at him. "I promised someone I would. And I will." They shook hands on it as if they had just worked out a deal.

"What about next month?" Georg asked.

"What about next weekend? I don't want to make you wait any longer," she said teasingly. But in truth, it was Susanne who couldn't wait any longer. She had to talk to Diana and see if her friend had found out anything for her. She couldn't wait another month.

"I won't have time, though, until next month. I'm supposed to make my run through the village's collectivized farms and take inventory of the livestock. Sorry."

"Well, we'll go in January, then." Susanne wondered how she would handle waiting another month to speak to Diana privately.

She was so sick of waiting. Months were passing by, and nothing was happening.

"Will you take Henry and Jana?" Georg asked.

Susanne looked at him in surprise. "Of course, I will. Diana would never forgive me if I wouldn't bring them along. Besides, I have you to help me, right?" She slapped his arm and got up, wiping the dirt and leaves off her pants. "I better get back. It's almost dinner time. Henry is probably starving by now."

"Yeah, the boy seems to eat as much as I do," Georg said, and got up as well. He looked around for Rudi, who was nowhere to be seen. Georg whistled, and Rudi came into view instantly.

"Care to join us for dinner?" Susanne asked Georg as she started to make her way down the hill.

"You know me, I'd love to," he said with Rudi trailing after him.

Susanne stood by the window, her violin and bow in one hand. The music stand in front of her held loose pages of sheet music. With her right hand, she penciled in little marks or numbers above the notes and stuck the pencil back behind her right ear. She hummed the melody and with another look at the notes before her, she started to play. Her gaze was fixed on the notes, and she played with well-controlled strokes and precise rhythm.

Even after all this time of only occasionally taking out her violin, playing was still second nature to her. And she knew the piece well. Susanne lifted her eyes off the page and looked out the window while she kept playing. The house was quiet and so was the street below. She thought of Henry and Jana. Gisela had taken them with her to Uncle Heinrich's house, insisting that Susanne needed the time to prepare for the concert. Susanne knew Henry and Jana would get all the attention they could possibly want there, but this was Saturday. She only had the weekends to spend all day with her children. Susanne sighed and turned her eyes back to the sheet music. This was a sacrifice, but she had to admit to herself that she was glad to have the opportunity to play again. And after all, it served the purpose of following Fleischer's orders and to make him believe she was cooperating.

When Susanne had finished playing the piece in front of her, she took the page and put it aside. Another page was now in its place. Susanne looked at it and smiled. Putting her violin gently to the side of her chin, she closed her eyes and started to play. Light entertainment, exultant music would have a better chance of changing the villagers' disposition toward the stranger in their midst. Most people would be able to recognize this piece from Handel's *Messiah*.

The late afternoon sunlight fell through the window. It gave the dark wood of Susanne's violin a warm glow. The instrument lay on Susanne's bed while she anchored the bow to the lid of the case sitting on the floor next to her feet. She retrieved a cloth from a small compartment of the case, took the violin gently by its neck and started cleaning each string. The squeaky sound this procedure made had long ceased to affect her. Dieter, however, had never gotten used to it and he had cringed every time she had to clean her instrument.

After Susanne finished cleaning the violin, it too went back into the case. She massaged her aching shoulder. And only her shoulder told her she had played all day. Time had flown by. She had been used to long hours of concentrated practice. It had been her job. Performing was only part of it. It was the preparation that perfected the violinist. But she was no longer used to long practice hours.

Checking her watch, Susanne got up and reluctantly started to change. She had no choice. Fleischer had made it all too clear that she needed to keep her part of the bargain and gain the trust of the people in this village. Remembering the kind face of the pastor and his excitement when she had asked him for permission to hold a Christmas concert at the church, she felt instantly better. This wouldn't be so bad. She was able to perform. At the same time, she would give Fleischer the impression that she was fully cooperating now. And maybe the villagers would change their disposition toward her after today. Maybe this night really was what she needed.

With some enthusiasm, Susanne grabbed the long black silk dress that hung over the back of the chair next to her. She had worn it numerous times for her performances. While on one of her trips to West Germany, she had bought the lavish dress at a fancy department store. Such dresses couldn't be found in the East, not even in Berlin. One would have to hire a seamstress to get a dress like this. But Susanne knew that there was no seamstress in this village who would come even close to being able to make such a dress as this.

Susanne zipped up the dress and looked at herself in the mirror. It was tight around her hips, but she was grateful that it fit. She hadn't gained too much weight during her pregnancy. *Thanks to prison*, she thought grimly. She turned around to look at her back and then smoothed the silk down. This was far better than the clothes she wore to her new line of work. She sighed. It had been too long since she had worn this dress. She was probably slightly overdressed for tonight, but it might impress the right people. She combed through her brown curls with her fingers and decided to add more lipstick to her pale-looking mouth. She took another look at herself and nodded in satisfaction. She hadn't felt beautiful in a long time but tonight she did. *Just like I used to look,* she thought with a sigh, but couldn't deny the tiredness and fine lines around her eyes. After a last look she went over to her bed to get her violin and sheet music.

———

Georg was waiting by the front door in Gisela's house, looking out into the cold night through the nearby window. It was already dark outside. No one passed by in the dim light of the street lantern. He swallowed hard and loosened the tie around his neck. *As long as people show up tonight, everything will be fine*, he thought.

Just as Georg checked his watch, Susanne came down the stairs. He swallowed again. She looked stunning in her form-fitting dress and matching black pumps. Realizing he was staring at her, he cleared his throat and went to the wardrobe to get her coat. He had seen her perform before in Berlin when Dieter had invited him to come to a concert with him so Georg, as his best friend, could check out the girl he had fallen in love with. And tonight Georg could see what had made Dieter fall in love with Susanne. She looked beautiful and radiant. She had tamed her usually wild brown curls, and they fell loose just below her shoulders. Georg realized that she wore make-up, giving her usually pale complexion a soft glow. But it wasn't the make-up, hair, or even the dress that had turned her into the old Susanne. *She is happy*, he thought. The Susanne that had been introduced to him by Dieter after that concert a few years back. This night was good for her. She needed this. Georg turned around to Susanne, her coat in hand. "Do you want me to carry that for you?" He reached for her violin case.

"Thanks, but I'll carry it." She smiled at him. Her old confidence seemed to have returned.

He helped her into her coat. "Too bad Gisela isn't coming too," he said.

Susanne's smile faded and she said, "Frau Friedrich down the street bent over backward to babysit tonight, but Gisela refused.

She insists the twins are still too little to have someone outside the family watch them. I tried to convince her otherwise, believe me."

"Well, tonight my company has to do, then." With that, Georg opened the front door for Susanne, and they went out into the cold night, pulling their coats tighter around their shoulders as they made their way down the dark road to the village's church, Susanne's high-heels clicking loudly on the cobblestone.

Georg constantly checked his surroundings while he was walking. He couldn't resist. He had to get some idea of how many people would show up. There were only a few souls on the street heading in the same direction as they were. *It is still too early*, he reminded himself.

"Do you think anyone will show up?" Susanne asked suddenly, as if she had read his mind.

"Oh, no worries. They might not like church, but they still appreciate anything that puts them in the Christmas spirit." Susanne didn't answer. She looked worried.

Georg checked his watch again. "We should get there half an hour before it starts. That's plenty of time for you to set up, isn't it?" Susanne nodded. Then she put her arm through his. Whether it was because of the cold or because she was seeking comfort, he didn't know or care. He guided her along the dark road, glad to be close to her.

They reached the dimly lit church a few minutes later. There were two men outside, smoking. No one else seemed to be around yet. As Georg and Susanne passed them, the men simply nodded a greeting at Susanne, but greeted Georg by name.

Georg led Susanne inside, where they were welcomed by an eager pastor who immediately showed Susanne to the front. The church was cold. Only a few candles gave the hall a hint of warmth. The wooden benches would certainly not make things any more comfortable. He had avoided setting a foot inside a church for as long as he could remember, and not only because of the hard wooden benches.

Georg looked around and also scanned the balconies above him. There was no one here yet except himself, the pastor, and Susanne, who was tuning her violin. He could tell Susanne was just as worried about people showing up as he was because she was constantly glancing at the heavy wooden doors. Their eyes met, and he smiled encouragingly at her. She returned a grateful smile and waved him to the first-row bench. With a side-glance at the Biblical stories depicted on the old church walls, he sighed and started to make his way to the front. Each Christmas Eve, while he was growing up, his mother had insisted they all go to church. His father had grudgingly come along, only to get drunk after they had returned home. By the time Georg had opened his last present, his father would be in a mood that erased every bit of Christmas spirit they had felt before at church. Since his mother's death, Georg hadn't set a foot inside a church and had watched his father slowly drink himself to death. He lifted his eyes toward the altar, in front of which Susanne stood, adjusting the height of the music stand. He found a seat in the first row and sat down, the cold and quietness of the church engulfing him.

Susanne wasn't sure what made her shake so much. It could have been the cold church, which seemed to be impossible to heat up, or her nerves. She had never been nervous like this before, not even when she had to play a solo in front of Brezhnev, the Soviet leader.

Tonight was different for her, in many respects. She would face another kind of audience, her repertoire would be toned down, and she wouldn't have the full orchestra behind her. She wouldn't play for money, fame, or praise, or even because Fleischer had suggested it. Tonight, she would play for herself and for Dieter. Dieter, who had never taken his eyes off her when she played, who had brought her a little snack and something to drink during long hours of practice, and who had never grown tired of listening to her playing even when he was exhausted from a long day at the zoo. For him alone, she would play.

Susanne looked up as the church door creaked open and a few people, including the two who had been smoking outside, made their way in and sat down on one of the last rows as if to keep a safe distance between themselves and her.

A few more people came in. When it was time to start, only half of the benches in the little church were filled, Susanne noticed. But that was enough for her. She only needed a few people to warm up to in order to gain their trust.

The pastor stepped forward and welcomed everyone present. Susanne was certain that perhaps only ten of the people actually belonged to his congregation. The rest of the villagers had probably come out of plain curiosity or to get into the Christmas spirit. And this is what she had wanted. What Fleischer wanted – that she would become acceptable to and integrated into the village community. There was no doubt that one of them here was with the Stasi and certainly reporting this event back to Fleischer. *All the better,* she thought, and turned her attention back to the pastor who had started to introduce her.

When he finished, she positioned herself in front of the music stand and started to play. The people in front of her and the dark, cold church walls melted away, and she was lost in the beauty and lightness of the music. Dieter was there and looking at her, transfixed by the music or her, she couldn't tell. She didn't care. She was playing for him once again.

The applause after the first piece echoed through the little church. Susanne looked up at the people. "Jesu, Joy of Man's Desiring" had been a good choice. The well-known piece by Bach had gotten the attention of the villagers. They seemed to be enjoying themselves. *It's working,* she thought. She looked at Georg and saw he looked relieved as well. For the rest of the time, her nervousness subsided.

The other Christmas carols and hymns were just as well received as the first, and here and there people actually smiled at her while applauding loudly. Of course, she had chosen pieces that even the least religiously inclined member of her audience would recognize. When she played "Silent Night," some members of the audience even joined in and sang along.

Just before Susanne was about to announce her last piece, the big wooden doors of the church creaked open. A cold wind blew in that even Susanne, standing at the opposite end of the church, could feel. Everyone turned to see who had shown up so far into the concert.

Susanne didn't move but stared at the man who had come in and who was now closing the door behind him. He took off his hat and sat down in the last row, rubbing his hands together as if to warm them. He looked straight at Susanne and indicated with a nod for her to proceed.

Fleischer had come himself. Susanne couldn't say she was surprised. Someone from the village had informed the Stasi, just as she had hoped. But why had he come all the way down from Berlin to actually see her perform? Or was he here to put more pressure on her? Whatever the reason for coming, Susanne wished he hadn't. His penetrating gaze and self-congratulating demeanor unnerved her.

Susanne cleared her throat and announced her last piece. "I Know That My Redeemer Liveth." Susanne thought she saw Fleischer shift slightly in his seat. Or had she imagined it? She had saved this piece from Handel's Messiah for last. While she played the soft and slow melody, Handel's words came to her mind and she wished that someone was there to sing them. Thoughts of her first

Christmas without Dieter or music suddenly came to her mind. She had been in prison, cut off from everyone, completely hopeless and full of despair. Susanne tried to push the dark thoughts aside as she played the last notes. But the memory returned and with it the feeling of hopelessness and despair.

When she finished, she looked straight into the audience, who started clapping. She bowed and the pastor stepped forward, applauding as well. He thanked everyone for coming, and people slowly started to exit. The pastor came over to her, smiling, and shook her hand. It was done, Susanne thought and sighed in relief. Everyone who came out tonight seemed to have liked her little performance. Their faces and the applause had indicated that. She knew from experience when an audience was pleased or when the concert hadn't been to their taste.

Susanne looked toward the last row. There stood Fleischer, still clapping, his eyes resting on her. He certainly would want to talk to her. But he had to wait. She walked over to Georg. He had to leave before Fleischer approached her. She didn't want him to see her talking with the Stasi.

Like everyone else, Georg had turned around when someone had come in during the concert. He was shocked to see the Stasi officer who had paid him a visit in November. What did Fleischer want here? Slightly alarmed, Georg turned back around to listen to Susanne announcing her last piece for the night. When she started playing, she suddenly looked gloomy; her eyes seemed to be fixed on the man in the back. Georg wondered if Susanne knew Fleischer. Was she aware that the Stasi shadowed her? Georg again felt the knot in his stomach that had been developing since he so hastily agreed to inform the Stasi if Susanne were to plan another defection. Not that Susanne had revealed anything to him. Georg had no clue if Susanne was indeed planning something. He hoped with all his heart she wasn't.

Before the Stasi officer had appeared, Georg had enjoyed the concert. Susanne had played beautifully. It seemed as if the people had liked it as well. Why did she look so sad now that it was over? She had every reason to be happy. *Is it Dieter's absence? Or the presence of the Stasi officer,* Georg thought grimly.

Most people had already left when Susanne came over to him. She spoke first. "So, did you enjoy it?"

"It was great. You're great," he said and gave her a peck on the cheek to congratulate her.

"Thanks," she said and looked at the exit.

"Ready to go?" Georg asked, assuming she wanted to get home.

"Not quite. I need to pack up first and I want to talk to the pastor."

Susanne seemed flustered and there was still a sadness in her eyes. "Need some help?" he asked casually.

"No," she said rather hastily.

"Are you all right, Susanne?" He was concerned.

"I'm fine, Georg. Really."

"I don't think you are," he said, while she started to gather her things. Georg looked on silently, not sure what to say. It was obvious she didn't want to talk about it. "I'll wait outside," he said and left. He wasn't sure what had gotten into her. Maybe she would open up on their way home. When Georg passed Fleischer, their eyes met, but they didn't acknowledge each other.

After Georg had gone, Susanne sank down on a nearby chair.

"Well done, Frau Schmidt," an all too familiar voice said.

How had he come up to her so quickly? Susanne glanced at the door. Good, Georg was gone. "I didn't expect you to come all the way down from Berlin for this," she said to Fleischer as she got up to finish packing her things.

"How could I have missed this? You did very well, Frau Schmidt. From what I overheard the villagers say, you seem to have found some favor with them. Exactly what you need."

"I doubt they will trust me and tell me all their dark secrets now, Herr Fleischer."

"But this is a start. You can build on your success tonight. Make friends and believe me, by March there will be something to report."

March. March. *I have to be gone by March*, Susanne thought.

"Well, as I said, very enjoyable, Frau Schmidt, even if I didn't agree with your choice of repertoire."

Susanne looked at him with furrowed eyebrows. "You heard only the last piece." "Enough to get a clear understanding of where your loyalties lie, Frau Schmidt."

He looked up and down at her dress.

"This was a Christmas concert. This is a church. I think it was very appropriate," she countered, her arms folded in front of her chest.

He stepped closer to her. The tone in his voice could not be mistaken. "You tempt your fate, Frau Schmidt. I advise you to be more careful. You certainly don't want to make this worse, do you?" He stepped back and put his hat and gloves on. "I'll see you in March, Frau Schmidt." Without another word, he turned and walked away, his steps echoing in the empty church.

Susanne wrapped her arms around herself. The church seemed even colder now. She put on her coat and finished packing up her things as the pastor came back into the church and strode toward her.

The pastor's face was hard to read as he stood in front of her and watched her getting ready to leave. She felt a hand on her shoulder. "I'll put in a word for you," he said.

Susanne looked up at him, not sure what he had meant, but he raised his hand and pointed heavenward. "Oh.... Oh, thank you, pastor." Of course, that was what he meant.

"I enjoyed it," the old man said, smiling kindly at her now.

She returned the smile. "Thank you for letting me do this."

"Anytime, child. Anytime." Then he seemed to remember something. "Oh, your friend outside will be frozen solid soon if you don't hurry."

Susanne looked toward the door. She had completely forgotten about Georg, waiting outside in the cold for her. She took her violin case, hurriedly shook the pastor's hand, and left the church.

Georg was leaning against the old church wall, the collar of his coat turned up and his hands buried in his pockets. Susanne joined him. "I'm sorry it took so long. You must be freezing to death." Georg mumbled something Susanne couldn't understand. He simply started walking. Susanne hurried after him. "Everything all right? she asked.

"I'm fine, Susanne, but what about you? Why aren't you happy about how things went tonight?"

"I'm happy about tonight. I just miss Dieter, you know."

"I understand," was all Georg said. For the rest of their way home, neither of them spoke much, and when they said their goodbyes in front of Gisela's house, Susanne thought Georg's eyes looked colder than she felt.

Chapter 12

C hristmas came. Hauser had given Susanne a few days off. She was grateful for the extra time she could spend with the twins, even though she couldn't explain why she had gotten more days off than she should have. Maybe word about the concert had softened Hauser's disposition toward her again.

He had called her to his office, inquiring after her well-being and the children's. He gave her a woolen scarf for Christmas. It seemed as if Hauser had either forgiven her or forgotten about Fleischer's visit to the factory back in summer and her rejection in the factory yard. Hauser's newfound friendliness made work somewhat tolerable. To her own surprise, Susanne had even caught herself looking forward to work on occasion.

Not only Hauser was friendlier toward her. The women she worked with also opened up to her, and they happily chatted away the day while standing at the conveyor belt. They proudly talked about their children and their new accomplishments and how to get their hands on toys for Christmas. While no one from work had attended her concert, everyone seemed to have heard about it. This was the only way Susanne could understand the change of attitude toward her.

Susanne decided not to tell Dieter about any of it when he called at Christmas. Besides the fact that it was Henry and Jana's first Christmas, hearing Dieter's voice had been the highlight of the holidays for her. There had been no letters from him, so when he called on the first day of the Christmas holidays, they had talked for over two hours on Georg's phone without the call being disconnected. That had been a great surprise.

Would a little cooperation with the Stasi really make a difference like that? Susanne had the feeling it did.

Dieter and Susanne had mostly talked about the twins, the family, and people they both knew. Only after the phone call had Susanne realized that neither of them had shared details about the lives they were now leading separately. This shocked her more than anything. Were they growing apart?

When Dieter started to say his goodbyes on the phone that day, Susanne had cut him off. Dieter hadn't hinted about any plans for her and the babies to join him in the West. There were no hints about how he would get word to her. Susanne knew they had to be careful on the phone, but not even the slightest hint? Susanne couldn't stand it any longer. She needed to know. "How will you get word to me, Dieter? How? When? What are you going to do?" The questions came tumbling out.

At first, Dieter didn't reply. Then he spoke softly and carefully. "You need to trust me, Susanne. I'm working on it."

"Do you even have a plan, Dieter?" Susanne tried to keep the rising anger out of her voice. Her patience had come to an end. It had been too long. It was supposed to be only months. It had been over a year. Dieter was silent for a moment. "Are you still there, Dieter?" Susanne regretted her outburst.

"I am, love. I am." He drew in his breath. "I was finally able to get through to someone at the office of the Minister of Foreign Affairs. There is a program.

"What kind of program?" Susanne asked. They had both thrown all caution to the wind. The Stasi were certainly hearing this. Hopefully they wouldn't cut the line.

"They have talked to the East German authorities. I think they're already negotiating the price."

"The price?" Susanne didn't understand.

"The price for your and the children's freedom, Susanne," Dieter said.

"So the West German government has to pay a ransom for us?" She couldn't believe what she was hearing.

"That's how it's done. You have a good chance. They know you and your talent. They want to help us."

Susanne felt exhilarated. This sounded too good to be true. And it sounded as if they were close to securing her and the children's freedom.

"Susanne. You have to be more careful from now on. Now that they are fully aware of our plans, they will make life more difficult for you."

"More difficult?" Susanne was laughing now. Dieter wasn't. "I don't think they could make life any more difficult for me. Trust me, Dieter." Dieter was silent. "I'm sorry." Susanne knew that this had made him feel guiltier. So she changed the topic and a few minutes later they were saying their final goodbyes. Dieter ensured her that he would get word to her about any progress, and when Susanne hung up the phone, she felt jubilant. *Soon,* she thought. The only difficulty now was that she couldn't share the news with either Georg or Gisela.

Chapter 13

In January, Susanne, Georg and the babies went up to Berlin as they had planned. On a Friday evening, they all got on a train to spend the weekend with Diana. Susanne was glad to have Georg by her side. And not only because he kept Henry entertained. Her son had taken quite a liking to tall dark-haired Georg with his glasses. Nothing kept Henry occupied like grabbing Georg's glasses and pulling them off. He never grew tired of it. And neither did Georg.

Georg had been distant since the concert. They had seen each other almost every day, but something stood between them that Susanne had difficulty pinpointing. She even had feared he wouldn't come to Berlin with her. She had decided to use the train ride to find out what exactly had been bothering Georg.

"I'm glad you came," Susanne said, not looking at Georg across from her, but at the scenery that flew by the window. The sky already grew dark and the lights in their compartment flickered.

"I promised I would," was all Georg said.

The train entered a tunnel and Susanne looked Georg straight in the face. "What is it, Georg? What's been bothering you?" She stroked Jana's hair as she sat nestled against her chest.

Georg pulled his glasses gently from Henry's grasp and looked up at Susanne.

"Do you really want to hear it? Let's talk about it when we get back. I don't want to ruin this weekend for you."

"For me?" Susanne had stopped stroking Jana's head. "You'll ruin it if you don't tell me what's going on. You've been so quiet lately. Around me. Something's been bothering you. I know it."

"Let's talk about it later. Really," Georg insisted.

Susanne fell quiet. She kept staring out the window into the dark void, biting her lip. But then she turned back to Georg, her gaze determined.

Georg met Susanne's eyes and sighed heavily. "Do you really want to know what's been bothering me?" Georg put his glasses back on and looked at the compartment's sliding door. People were standing by the window right outside their compartment. He leaned forward and his words came out as a hiss. "That you would even ponder another attempt."

Susanne was taken aback. How had Georg gotten wind of this?

Georg studied her face. "You told me after Dieter's call on the day of the babies' christening. You said you would find a way to join him if he didn't."

"That is none of your business, Georg," Susanne hissed back. What did he expect her to do?

"I told you I didn't want to ruin your weekend," Georg said simply. "Do you expect me to sit back and do nothing?"

"Things will play out, Susanne. You should be happy with how things went at the concert. People are starting to accept you."

"I don't care about these people. What do I care if they accept me? I'm sick and tired of village politics."

"I thought that's what you wanted? For people to accept you." Georg's brows furrowed.

Susanne felt trapped. Even if she wanted to, she couldn't possibly share with Georg the real reason for the concert. He was partially right, though. She wanted the villagers to trust her, but only to find someone to report, to give Fleischer what he wanted.

"You're right. Let's not talk about it now. Let's just enjoy this weekend. As you said, things will play out," Susanne said, her tone final.

Georg was quiet. She felt his eyes on her as she watched the night cast her cloak outside their compartment window. It didn't matter anymore, at any rate. Dieter was getting her out. If the West German government secured her and the babies' freedom in the next two months, she wouldn't have to worry about pleasing the people of Wallhausen or Fleischer ever again.

Diana picked them up from the train station. After her never-ending hugs for Susanne and kisses for Henry and Jana, she turned to Georg and shook his hand. Both grinned at each other. *Perfect*, Susanne thought. They would pick up where they had left off. Diana would keep Georg's mind off her business. She didn't need Georg's patronizing speeches this weekend. Susanne had come to Berlin for different reasons. Of course, she was looking forward to spending time with her friend. After all, she was her children's godmother. But she was also hoping to accomplish something else this weekend. Hopefully Diana had found something out for her. She had to have a back-up plan, in case Dieter's didn't play out.

They took the tram to Diana's apartment, which was located on the tenth floor in one of the tall concrete buildings erected after the war. First, they put down the twins for the night and then they spent the rest of the evening talking. Georg treated her politely, but his attention was definitely directed toward Diana. Susanne didn't mind.

———

Before Diana or Georg had even stirred the next morning, Susanne took the babies and made her way to the zoo to see Dieter's gorillas. She was sure he appreciated her checking on them for him. She could only imagine how he missed his work and these monkeys. *Apes*, as Dieter had always corrected her in mock frustration.

She wasn't alone on this Saturday morning. A few mothers and elderly people entered the zoo with her, right when it opened. She ignored the giraffes on her right and the elephants to her left. She knew the way.

The apes were just eating their breakfast when she got to their enclosure. They were munching on leaves, ignoring the first visitors of the day. Susanne took Henry out of the buggy and held him up-close to the glass. As usual, his arms flailed, but he didn't look at the apes. His little hands excitedly hit his own reflection in the glass. Had the apes moved, Susanne was certain little Henry's attention would have been drawn to them. After Henry's turn, Susanne held Jana for a while, but she wasn't interested, either.

After she put Jana back in the buggy, Susanne sighed and pressed her forehead against the glass. The coolness of it provided a soothing compression. She felt so close to Dieter here. She stared at the animals, wondering if they missed him just as much as she did. *They're animals*, she chided herself. They had forgotten Dieter by now, she was certain. She had come here because she was beginning to forget things about him: the smell of his skin, how it felt to be in his embrace, and his throaty, infectious laughter. She had come here in hopes of feeling close to Dieter, of remembering his smell, embrace, and laughter. The apes' sanctuary had become hers. But now Susanne missed Dieter even more, and she left the zoo, wondering if it had been worth coming.

———

"I think I know where she went," Diana said between bites. She was sitting across from Georg in her small kitchen. Butter, jam, honey, cheese, ham, and fresh rolls were in front of them. Diana had been surprised to find the table set and Georg returning from the bakery carrying the smell of freshly baked rolls. She could surely get used to that.

"Where to?" Georg asked.

"The zoo, I'm sure." Diana had no doubt that was where she'd gone.

"But she's always hated the zoo," Georg said, looking up from his cup. Shrugging his shoulders, he added, "I guess kids change everything, don't they?"

"Yeah, maybe you're right," Diana said thoughtfully, looking out the small kitchen window at the row of high-rise concrete buildings. She sighed and turned back to Georg. "What would you like to do today?"

He ran his hand through his hair. "I never cared much for the city. What about visiting Sanssouci?"

Diana cocked her head and smiled. "Sightseeing?" That was the last thing she had expected.

"Why not? I heard the gardens are beautiful."

"It's January," Diana said.

"Gardens make for great long walks. And I heard the ones at Sanssouci are extensive."

"You've never been?" Diana was surprised to hear that. Hadn't Georg lived and studied in Berlin?

"I've never made it there, believe it or not."

"Well then. Sanssouci it shall be. You'll be impressed." Diana got up to take the dishes to the sink, but Georg grabbed her hand.

"I'll do that," he said, smiling at her. "You go get ready and as soon as I'm done with the dishes, we'll head out."

"Shouldn't we wait for Susanne to get back?" Diana felt guilty about sleeping in this morning. She wouldn't see her friend or Henry and Jana until tonight.

"She wanted to run errands today. I'm sure she'll do that right after the zoo."

"We should help her to do all this shopping. Imagine standing in line with the twins."

"It was her choice. She wanted us to spend the day together," Georg said as he cleared the table.

Diana knew Georg was right, but she still felt guilty. She knew the guilt she felt was not only about not getting up with her friend this morning. She sighed. "You're right. I'll get ready then."

Diana swung open the kitchen door and left Georg to the dishwashing. His taking charge like that had definitely impressed her. She began to feel excited about spending the day with Georg. Until tonight, she would push the guilt aside and enjoy herself. And maybe it was Georg who was the answer to all her troubles.

———

Susanne looked across the vast public square. Alexander Square, named after the Russian tsar Alexander I., was the central district in East Berlin and shopping heaven for East Germans or, rather, for those who could afford it. Susanne stared at the line of people in front of the department store and sighed. She had no choice but to get in another line if she expected to get her hands on some baby clothes and toys. Standing in line on the right day and at the right time to get what one not wanted, but needed, had always been part of life in the German Democratic Republic. Susanne hadn't expected anything different today. And Berlin was far better off than the rest of the country. She wanted to seize the moment while in the capital and get the things she couldn't get in Wallhausen or the nearby city.

When Susanne had made her way to the end of the line, the middle-aged woman in front of her turned around and looked at the buggy in which Henry and Jana were sleeping peacefully side by side.

"You can't get in line with the buggy," the woman said.

Susanne's brows furrowed. "And why is that?"

"You can't go in there with a buggy. This is a department store."

"What do you expect me to do?" She couldn't believe this woman. Why did she think this was any of her business?

"Let the father watch the children. And besides, who would want to put the children through standing in line all day? Don't you see that they're tired?"

Susanne couldn't believe what she was hearing. "I don't think this is any of your business," Susanne said, clenching the handle of the buggy even tighter.

The woman's face turned sulky and she whipped around, turning her back on Susanne and the babies.

After an hour in line, Susanne's turn at the counter had finally come. After the woman in front of her had paid and packed her goods, she shot Susanne a withering glance and left.

Jana and Henry were awake now and starting to get fussy. It was almost time for them to eat.

"Yes?" the clerk asked with an annoyed look at the buggy as Susanne managed to step up to the counter, pulling the buggy with her.

Susanne ran down the list of items she needed.

"Size?"

Susanne gave her the sizes.

"Boy or girl?"

"Both."

The woman glanced at the buggy again. "Twins?"

Susanne nodded. She thought she saw a hint of a smile on the otherwise sour face of the salesclerk.

After what seemed like an eternity, the salesclerk returned with an armful of baby clothes. Susanne looked at every piece. At times she held one up to either Jana or Henry to see if it would fit them.

"Do you carry any summer clothes?" Susanne asked.

The clerk looked at her as if she had gone mad. "It's January. We don't get any in until May."

Susanne only nodded, regretting she had even asked. Why had she bothered? In the summer, she would just go into a department store in Hamburg. Dieter would be by her side, and there wouldn't be any lines. And salespeople were so much friendlier in the West. Less cranky. Happier.

"Which ones are you taking?" the woman asked impatiently.

"The stack over here. Thank you," Susanne said, pointing to a pile of almost all white baby clothes.

The woman's grumpy reply was inaudible. Susanne didn't care. The thought of summer and finally being with Dieter had put her back in good spirits. Long lines, rude people, and grumpy salesclerks wouldn't get to her anymore, she decided resolutely as she left the department store.

When Susanne returned to Diana's apartment in the afternoon, her friends were still gone. She didn't mind. She was happy that Georg and Diana got along. Besides, she had been the one who had set them up. She put the twins down for a nap and lay down on the couch herself. She was exhausted and her legs were tired. A short nap in the now quiet apartment sounded very good.

———

Susanne heard voices and turned onto her side. *A few more minutes*, she thought.

"She's sleeping," Susanne heard Diana say.

"I'm sure she's exhausted," Georg whispered.

"I had fun today," Diana said in a soft voice.

They thought she was sleeping and that she couldn't hear them. Susanne was wide awake now, but she kept her eyes shut. She strained her ears. Were they kissing? Susanne smiled to herself, hoping they ignored her.

"I should be coming up more often," she heard Georg say. "There is so much to see in Berlin."

Susanne heard Diana chuckle. "Next weekend then?"

Georg didn't answer, but what Susanne heard were certainly kissing sounds.

Susanne started to feel awkward and decided to move. She yawned loudly to give them some warning, and then opened her eyes. She sat up and saw Diana and Georg busying themselves with hanging up their coats.

"How was your day?" Diana came over and sat down on the couch beside her.

"Well, you know. Standing in line takes its toll, but luckily the babies were in good spirits." Susanne decided not to tell them about her visit to the zoo. "What have you two been up to all day?"

"Sanssouci," Georg said, coming from the kitchen with three glasses and a bottle of seltzer. "Quite the palace. Have you been there?"

"Yes, once. For a concert."

Georg nodded knowingly.

Diana checked her watch. "Let's eat dinner so we can get going."

Susanne stretched and got up. She put a hand on Georg's shoulder. "You sure you can handle this all by yourself?"

Georg looked offended. "Henry loves me. And Jana is a doll. What's to handle?"

"Fine," Susanne said, smiling now.

"You ladies enjoy your night. I'll be fine. If not, I'll just turn on the news. I'm sure that will put the twins to sleep in no time," Georg said.

Diana chuckled, and Susanne rolled her eyes. These days, it seemed as if her friend found everything Georg said amusing. It was only a matter of time until Diana fell in love with him, if she had not already. Susanne knew her friend well.

Susanne had agreed only reluctantly to let Diana take her to the concert hall while Georg babysat. But there was no way Susanne could refuse. Diana had taken the night off just for her. Someone else would be the concertmaster tonight while they would be part of the audience. Only in this new world in which she was now living was this possible. Her life had truly turned on its head.

On the one hand, Susanne felt drawn to her former workplace. On the other, she felt repulsion. Susanne knew it would sting her to see her orchestra perform without her leading it as their concertmaster. At least she was spared seeing Diana sit in her chair. Besides, she only had agreed to this outing to be alone with Diana. She couldn't wait to find out if Diana had some worthwhile information for her.

A taxi picked them up to take them to the concert hall. Susanne's patience wore thin. The taxi driver's eyes were constantly resting on the both of them through the rear mirror. She couldn't possibly talk to Diana while this guy was looking on, for whatever reason. So she asked the driver to let them out two blocks short of the hall. Diana started to object, but stopped at Susanne's knowing look.

When they got out of the taxi, Susanne handed a few marks to the driver and he sped off, leaving the smell of exhaust fumes hanging in the air.

"You're my guest. I don't want you to pay for anything this weekend," Diana protested.

Susanne simply waved it off, looking after the taxi until it turned a corner and the rumbling ceased. When it was gone, she linked arms with her friend, and they started walking.

"Do you have any information for me?" Susanne asked, waiting until a couple passed them on the sidewalk. There was no time to waste. The concert hall was only two streets over. Diana seemed to hesitate. Had she understood her? Did she remember? "Do you remember? Diana, please talk to me. I've waited all this time to talk to you. Just say something."

Diana stopped walking and turned to face her. Judging by the expression on her friend's face, Diana had understood. "Susanne. There is no way you can make it across with the babies." Diana's words were uncompromising.

"What have you found out?" Susanne tried to sound patient. It wasn't easy.

"You alone. Maybe. With false papers. But not with the babies, Susanne."

Susanne took a deep breath and exhaled, her breath showing in the dimly lit street.

She looked up at the dark sky and then at her friend. "If I can get false papers, don't you think I could get them for the twins, too?"

"The three of you would raise suspicion. Don't you see, Susanne? This is way too dangerous. Imagine what would happen to you and the babies. You could be separated. And that is not the worst that could happen. Look what happened to Dieter and you." Diana was beside herself now. She stepped closer and hugged Susanne tightly. Her voice was a whisper. "Susanne. Please. Don't make this worse than it is. I wouldn't forgive myself if something were to happen to the three of you."

Susanne hugged her friend back. Diana wouldn't help her. And she couldn't even blame her for it. If she were in Diana's place, she would have reacted the exact same way. She understood her friend completely.

"Dieter will find a way for you and the children to get to the West. A safe way. You have to be patient," Diana added, still hugging Susanne tightly and stroking her back.

In Susanne's head, the thoughts were swirling. False papers. The twins. Dieter. Wait? Have to be patient. Where would she get those papers? Did Diana know? Wait. Be patient. Dieter would get them over there soon. His way. A less dangerous way. "Maybe you could tell me where to get those false papers in case –" Diana let go of Susanne and stepped back. Susanne quickly added, "In case things don't work out as Dieter has planned."

Diana exhaled in exasperation. "You have to be patient, Susanne. Give it some time. Please."

"It has been so long already," Susanne said quietly.

"I know this is hard, but for the sake of the children. You need to be strong for them."

"I am thinking of the children."

"I know you are. I know." Diana touched her arm lightly.

"I was just hoping you could help me." Susanne turned and started walking again.

Diana was at her side instantly and linked arms with her. "If there was a safe way, Susanne, I would help you. You know that, right?" Susanne didn't answer. She had put all her hope in Diana, but nothing had come of it. There wouldn't be a back-up plan. The disappointment she felt was overwhelming her. She swallowed hard. She knew Diana was right. It was too dangerous. If something were to happen to the twins ... And Dieter's plan would play out. It had to.

Diana had to practically pull her the rest of the way to the concert hall. They didn't talk. Susanne felt numb. When they came to the brightly lit building, Diana simply said, "Let's have a good time tonight. Forget all our troubles. This is our night out. Just like the good old times."

Just like the good old times, Susanne thought grimly as they entered the hall. When they tried to find their seats, Susanne had the feeling people were staring. Did they recognize her or Diana? The regulars certainly would. Would they know what had happened? But how? Were they wondering why she was here, sitting in the audience? She knew it was all in her head, and she felt ridiculous.

Susanne turned to Diana when she heard the first few notes of the overture. "Beethoven's Ninth?" she whispered to Diana.

"Thought you might like it."

Diana knew that it was one of her favorite symphonies. As well as the government's. Susanne had been taught about solidarity toward all nations and peoples since pre-school. Now she knew it was meant only toward those who embraced communism.

When the symphony concluded and the audience was still applauding and calling out their "bravos," Susanne leaned over to Diana. "Should we go?" Susanne wanted to leave as quickly as possible. Diana barely reacted. She nodded, but kept clapping. "Let's go," Susanne urged, nudging her friend in the side.

Diana seemed to give in. She stopped clapping and started to move down the aisle. "The orchestra wanted to say hello," Diana said, when they picked up their coats.

"I'm sure some do, but most will be glad I spared them the embarrassment."

"They might not agree with your desire to defect to the West, but they still care about you, Susanne."

Susanne pulled a face. "You know as well as I, to save their own face and reputation, they would never openly associate with me again." She pulled Diana with her out into the cold winter night.

"The night is still young. What would you like to do?" Diana asked. "We have a babysitter, and you should seize the moment and stay out late. What do you think?"

Susanne didn't feel like it. While the concert had lifted her spirits somewhat, she was still trying to accept that she would have to wait for Dieter's plan to work out.

"We could go to the disco?" Diana suggested.

"I'm getting too old for that," Susanne said, looking incredulous.

"What about visiting a few old friends? I know there are some who'd love to see you," Diana tried again. Susanne looked doubtful. "Really. Let's just go and see if they're home." Diana was already walking over to a nearby taxi.

Maybe it wasn't such a bad idea to touch base with old friends again. She had missed them. They got in the taxi and drove off.

At the first apartment, no one answered, even though they could see light inside. Susanne felt Diana's hand on her shoulder as they went down the stairs, back to the waiting taxi.

"Seems they are more loyal to their government than to their friends," Susanne said as they got into the taxi. Susanne tried to sound indifferent, not sure if it was working. She stared out the window into the dark night and swallowed down the lump in her throat.

"They might just be afraid," said Diana, touching Susanne's arm.

"You don't need to make excuses for them, Diana. You're still my friend, and look, it hasn't interfered with your life or your career." Diana withdrew her hand. She looked offended, but Susanne did not take back what she had said. They drove on silently for a while until they got to another friend's apartment.

Shortly after ringing the bell, a voice crackled on the intercom. "Yes?" the woman asked.

"It's me. Susanne." There was silence. But then Susanne could hear the buzz of the door opener and pushed against the door. It opened and they climbed up two flights of stairs. How often had she come up these stairs, alone or with Diana? How many wonderful evenings they had spent together with their friend Barbara, hanging out and listening to the newest records. They had met her at the university. While Diana and Susanne had studied music, Barbara had pursued engineering. They had always teased her about being the smartest one. The memories pained her. Why had Dieter and she even decided to leave? For a moment Susanne wasn't sure she remembered. When they had reached the door of her friend's apartment, she remembered again. It was not their friends, family, and jobs they wanted to leave. They had longed for freedom. To work and live wherever they wanted. To travel. To speak their minds freely. Not to be watched by the government. To read and watch whatever they pleased. Most of all, they had wanted their children to grow up without having their lives planned and restricted by the government. Ironically, she had not only lost her friends and job, but the government restricted and controlled her life more than ever before.

Barbara, a tall redhead, greeted them at the door. But it wasn't the greeting Susanne had expected. Her friend was rather cool and did not ask them in.

"Why did you bring her here?" Barbara asked Diana, pretending Susanne wasn't there.

Diana's brows furrowed. "Now listen, Barbara. This is no way to —"

"I wanted to see you," Susanne cut in.

"I heard what happened," her friend said. "What were you thinking?" Now Barbara finally acknowledged her presence.

"Don't you want to ask me in first and then we can talk about it," Susanne said with some impatience. She wasn't in the mood to be treated like that.

"I don't think we have anything to talk about," Barbara said, her voice cold.

"That's all you have to say?" Diana was furious.

Susanne grabbed Diana's arm to pull her with her. "It's fine. Let her be."

Diana tried to pull free. "The hell I will. Who do you think you are, Barbara?" But Barbara wasn't listening anymore. She turned and just simply shut her door in their faces without uttering another syllable.

"Unbelievable. That woman." Diana was beside herself.

"Let her be," Susanne repeated.

"You're right," Diana said to Susanne's surprise, but then Diana turned to the door. "She's always been pigheaded and will always be pigheaded," she yelled. Someone from farther down the stairs yelled at her to shut up.

Susanne snickered and pulled Diana with her once more. When they reached the bottom of the stairs, she turned to a still furious Diana with a smile. "Thanks."

"What for?" Diana asked, fists still clenched.

"Standing up for me like that."

"Well, forget them all."

"Who needs friends, when I've got you," Susanne said, nudging Diana, who finally cracked a smile.

"I'm sorry, Susanne. I wish I hadn't suggested this." Diana was gazing up the stairs.

"No worries. Let's just go home. Georg will be happy to see you." She winked at Diana whose smile broadened. They left the building and got back into the waiting taxi. Diana gave the driver her home address, and they settled down in the backseat. They were silent most of the ride home. Susanne didn't mind. She looked out the window as the city she had once so loved flew by, looking in the dark like a prison of concrete.

Chapter 14

S usanne enjoyed the few rays of sunshine that fell on her face as she walked past the last houses of Wallhausen toward a group of trees beyond which the village's playground was located. It was February. The air was cold, but not unpleasant. The babies were too big now for both of them to fit in the buggy, and Susanne had only been able to purchase one stroller. So, as with every time she was able to take a walk with the children, she carried Jana on her hip while she pushed Henry in the buggy. Holding him for a longer period of time was now impossible. He was quite chunky, and carrying him would have strained her back even more. Jana, with her delicate build, was much easier to carry around for a while. Jana was holding on to her hair with one hand, while Henry looked around happily from the stroller. Susanne smiled to herself. Henry was always so content when he was outside. Just like Dieter was. *A few more weeks*, she thought. In only a few weeks she would go up to Berlin to meet with Fleischer. But it wouldn't only be Fleischer who she would meet.

Dieter had sent her a letter. It had been opened, of course. As if in passing, he had mentioned that a mutual friend called A. would come to Berlin to visit another mutual friend, D. In an instant, Susanne had known what that meant. Anna would travel into East Berlin to visit Diana, who had also befriended her back at a concert in Hamburg. West Germans were allowed to travel into the East for visits. This was how Dieter would get word to her. Through Anna. She would be the messenger. Susanne would go up to Berlin next month, give Fleischer a fake report to keep him occupied and distracted, and meet up with Anna at Diana's apartment to hear the news about when she would join Dieter in the West. And now the only thing left for her to do was wait.

Susanne stopped and shifted Jana to her other hip. She now stood in front of a park-like playground that Dieter had said his grandfather built. A meadow stretched out before her, with a small forest on the left and fields, which now lay bare, to the right of it.

One big slide and a couple of sand boxes were the only activities a child would find at this playground. But it was the many trees, a gurgling stream, and the woods close by that would make this a paradise for children. Henry and Jana couldn't yet enjoy the playground, but still Susanne loved to come here. It was a place of solitude and around this time of year, there was rarely someone out here.

Susanne looked beyond the long slide toward a bench. It was cold, but the sun was warm enough to be able to sit down for a few minutes.

The bench felt cold when she sat down. With Jana in her lap, Susanne bent forward to pull Henry's hat back over his ears. He flapped his arms happily. It would only be a matter of minutes before he became restless, and she would have to get up and start pushing the stroller again.

Then out of the corner of her eye she saw someone rush by on a bike. Georg. Susanne called after him. He was almost out of her view when he turned his head slightly and then stopped. He had seen her.

Georg heard someone call his name and turned around to see who in the world would be out here on a Saturday morning. He saw Susanne wearing a long winter coat and a hat, sitting on the bench behind the slide. Jana was on her lap, and he assumed Henry was in the stroller next to her.

He stopped and got off his bike. He turned it around and headed toward where Susanne sat.

"I see you don't mind the cold," he said in greeting, taking off his scarf.

"It's beautiful today. The sun is shining for once," she said, looking up at him.

Georg went over to the stroller. Henry was flapping his arms happily, glad for the attention.

"What are you doing out on a Saturday morning?" Susanne asked, sounding somewhat amused.

Georg realized she was looking at his hair and right away tried to smooth down his tousled dark strands. "It's just from the wind. Riding my bike. You know ..." Georg tried to explain.

"And I thought you had just gotten up." Susanne grinned at him and bounced Jana on her legs. To keep her warm, Georg assumed.

"Actually, I had to attend to a patient this morning. Believe it or not, I sometimes have to work Saturdays," Georg gave back teasingly as he sat down on the bench next to Susanne. She glanced briefly at his bag on the rear rack of his bike. "The mayor's dog in the next village had puppies. All were stillborn," Georg went on.

From the look on Susanne's face, he could tell that it was better to spare her the rest of the details. He leaned over and stroked Jana's cheek, which was pink from the cold. Georg decided to change the topic. "How have you been? I didn't see you all week," Georg said.

"You know, work and changing diapers. And then the weather wasn't really inviting. Up until today," she explained, squinting up into the blue but cold sky.

Georg nodded knowingly.

Now it was Susanne who changed the topic. "Diana is looking forward to March.

You're still coming, right?"

"You bet." Georg winked at her. Diana was an interesting woman, and she was beautiful. That much, Georg knew. He hoped to get to know her better in March when they visited her again. Maybe something would come of it. He would definitely give it a try.

"I decided I needed to get out more," Susanne said suddenly. "The carnival festivities would be the perfect opportunity, don't you think?"

Georg shook his head, not believing what he was hearing. Susanne suggested getting out more? And above all, the carnival?

"You told me to get out more," Susanne said defensively.

"But to the carnival? You?" Georg said, not trying to hide his astonishment at Susanne's announcement.

"What's wrong with that? Tell me," said Susanne, interrupting him.

"People just get drunk. All year they're uptight–"

"You're calling me uptight?" Susanne had stopped bouncing Jana on her legs and looked at him with furrowed eyebrows.

Georg went on quickly. "Not you. People in general. With enough alcohol in their system ... even the butcher lightens up."

"I don't want to go there to lighten up, Georg. It was you who told me to mingle with the villagers so they warm up to me ..." Susanne said defiantly.

Georg didn't know how to respond to that. He had told her to mingle with the people here. But on the train trip up to Berlin last month, she had made it clear that she wasn't interested in village politics, as she had called it. The carnival? Georg couldn't imagine a worse kind of occasion to celebrate with the villagers. On the other hand, Susanne was right. They might consider her less of a stranger if she joined their bacchanal celebrations.

Susanne interrupted his thoughts. "So, you're coming with me then?"

"Me? I couldn't. Never have. Promised myself I never will. Not the carnival."

"So, you'd have me go there all by myself?" Susanne asked, with some disappointment in her voice.

Georg knew he couldn't possibly have her go alone. She needed him. There was no one else she could go with. Gisela certainly wouldn't. Dieter's mother hated the carnival just as much as he did. He had to admit that he was glad to see a change of attitude in Susanne. Maybe she was starting to get over all of it and accepting her life now. Maybe she was getting over Dieter. Georg swallowed hard. Guilt was not on his agenda today, and he pushed the dark thoughts aside.

"You don't expect me to dress up, do you?" Georg asked suddenly.

Susanne grinned brightly at him. "Of course, you need to dress up. You can't show up there without a costume of some sort. You'll be the object of ridicule if you come as you are. I don't recommend it."

"Well then," Georg said grudgingly. "But you owe me." He got up. What had he gotten himself into? He hated those days in February when everyone all of a sudden turned loose only to fall back into a state of stupor by Ash Wednesday, but for Susanne's sake he would go along.

Georg checked his watch. "Well, I better get going," he said. "I need to get to the store before it closes, or I won't have anything to eat this weekend."

"Good luck," Susanne said, "I'm sure by now they're out of almost everything." Georg swung up on his bike. "I'll just come over to visit you guys then," he said with a smile. "See you tomorrow?"

Susanne smiled. "And don't forget to let me know what you're going to wear."

Georg rolled his eyes. "I really have to think about this."

"Make it a good one," Susanne said and got up as well. "I better get going, too. It's cold."

They said their goodbyes. When Georg had left the park behind, he checked his watch again. Only thirty minutes until closing. He started pedaling a little harder, his eyes tearing up from the cold winter wind.

———

Susanne was still in her room when she heard Gisela squeal in delight downstairs. Georg must have arrived. She tried to imagine what he was wearing. He had given her no clues about his costume, even though she had nagged him for a week to tell her. Georg had insisted on keeping it a secret. Now he was downstairs, and judging by Gisela's reaction, it was quite the outfit.

Susanne took a deep-red lipstick and applied it generously. She smacked her lips, checked her teeth for stains, and then nodded in satisfaction at her reflection in the mirror. She ran her hands down her sides as she looked at her costume. This would definitely be uncomfortable, but hopefully worth all the effort she had put into it. It would certainly have an effect on half of the village. If it all worked out tonight, she would have someone to report to Fleischer next month. Susanne was fairly certain that at the carnival, under the influence of alcohol, someone would let slip some useful information. She would be able to get Fleischer what he wanted and keep him occupied and his attention away from her.

———

Georg felt surprisingly comfortable in his costume. He almost wished he could wear the wide flowing robe every day, but of course that was impossible. Unless he would ... He pushed that thought aside, grinning.

Gisela seemed delighted with his costume. Why, he couldn't determine for sure. As he sat there on Gisela's couch, he wondered if Susanne wouldn't make fun of him all night. Dieter would have. *Maybe it wasn't such a great idea after all*, he thought, biting his lip.

Susanne came in, and as she caught sight of him, instantly fell into laughter. She visibly tried to compose herself and then came over and fell on the couch next to him. As she crossed her legs, Georg finally realized that he was staring at her in a way he didn't want to stare.

"Interesting choice of costume," Susanne said, grinning.

Georg was still not able to get a word out. A tight corset hugged Susanne's body. In her hand she held one end of the long ruffled skirt, offering a glimpse of her long legs. Her hair was pulled back in a bun with a huge flower as red as her lips fastened to it.

"Well, should we go then?" Susanne asked, visibly amused by his reaction.

She got up and held her coat out to him. Georg swallowed hard and took it. He got up and helped her into her coat. Susanne's bare white shoulders were right in front of him and when she had slipped into her coat and turned around to face him, he had to close his eyes at what he saw right in front of him.

Susanne laughed at his reaction. "We're quite the pair tonight. You're a chaste monk, and I'm a Flamenco dancer." She crooked her head and smiled at him. "You're not going to act like one tonight, are you?" she asked.

He looked at her in surprise. "Act like what?"

"Well, like a monk, Georg. You behave like you've never seen someone dressed like this."

138

"I haven't," Georg said simply. Susanne couldn't possibly go out like this. If Dieter saw her like this ... he would ... Georg wasn't sure what his best friend would do.

"Gisela helped me sew it," Susanne said.

"She did?" Georg was shocked. *What was going on with the women?* Not in a million years had he imagined ever seeing Susanne like this. The dress was so revealing, it showed sides of Susanne he now wished he had never discovered. To his dismay, he had to admit that her costume had an effect.

"You can't go out like this," Georg said.

"Like what, Georg? It's the carnival. This is the perfect occasion to dress up like this. Come on, now," she said, pulling him with her.

Georg followed her silently. And he had worried about his costume. It seemed silly to him now. If he could only figure out what had gotten into Susanne. Maybe this was the night to find out, Georg decided as he followed Susanne out into the cold night.

There were only a few seats at some of the tables left when Georg and Susanne entered the big hall the villagers used for celebrations, concerts, weddings, and such. The hall had been decorated lavishly and a colorful array of people in costumes lined the tables across the hall. Clowns, policemen, Indians and cowboys, geishas and samurais were seen throughout, linking arms with each other and swaying left and right in unison to the rhythm of the music.

Georg and Susanne went over to the closest table. Georg was greeted with some surprise. People were shocked to see him here. A few, obviously already drunk, teased him about his costume. He had expected no less. When Susanne took off her coat, there were whistles all around them. The men at their table stared at her admiringly. Georg ignored the display of testosterone and made a point in introducing Susanne to everyone. Friendly nods were exchanged.

"I never thought you'd end up liking the carnival," Susanne said as loudly as she could into Georg's ear a few hours and drinks later. "You never struck me as a guy that likes to get incredibly drunk and pretend the world's a cheerful place, as these people do." She motioned with her chin at the people around them. They were visibly more drunk than when she and Georg had arrived. Their off-key singing drowned out most of the music.

"I still don't like the carnival. And the world actually is a happy and cheerful place, Susanne. Don't you see? You don't need to be drunk to realize that," Georg said, and took another sip from his glass.

Susanne looked at him with furrowed brows. Georg had to be drunk after that many beers. His eyes were glazed, and he looked flushed. But to her surprise, he was still able to control his speech and movements.

Susanne looked around. She grew increasingly impatient. Besides Georg, no one had really talked to her all night. She had made an attempt and gone to the bar after she saw one of her coworkers flirt with two men there. The woman had greeted her, but had obviously been more interested in hooking up with the men. But Susanne wasn't ready to give up yet.

On her way back to her seat, she made the effort and greeted a few people. She even started small talk with an older woman who lived on the same street as Gisela, but nothing came of it. Coming here had been a waste of time. When she finally made it back to her table, Georg was in a somewhat heated exchange with the man next to him. Susanne sat down on her chair but really only wanted to go home.

"Just stay out of my business, Rolf," Georg said to the man and turned his back on him.

"What was that all about?" Susanne asked, curious.

Georg just waved it off and rolled his eyes. "Village politics, you know," he said, and winked at Susanne.

She nodded knowingly, grinning at him. Georg and she had a couple more beers and just talked. Susanne didn't mind. She was done trying to connect with the villagers.

An hour later, Susanne asked Georg about the ladies' room. When she got up, she had to steady herself, not realizing how tipsy she was.

Georg pointed to the exit and yelled, "It's down the stairs toward the back of the building."

Susanne made her way through the throngs of people, annoyed that the restrooms weren't closer. She had to hang on to the banister to make it down the stairs.

In the lobby, she looked around. A poorly lit hallway led to the back of the building. *This is where the restrooms must be*, Susanne thought. She passed two teenagers leaning against the wall and making out in the narrow hallway. She squeezed by the undeterred couple and looked for a door. There were two at the end of the hallway.

One of the doors opened and two women came out, dressed as if they belonged in a harem. They were giggling and holding on to each other, almost bumping into Susanne when they passed her.

Susanne opened the door and instantly had to cover her nose and mouth with her hand. The smell of vomit, beer, and urine seemed to hang like a cloud in the tiny restroom. As fast as she could, Susanne took care of business and left. She didn't even bother to look at herself in the dirty mirrors.

Susanne decided she needed to catch some fresh air. Nauseated, she looked around and saw a backdoor slightly ajar to her right.

She breathed in deeply when she exited the building. The air was very cold, and she was surprised she wasn't freezing in her costume. She drew in another deep breath, trying to clear her head.

A few cars were parked at the backside of the building and by the fog that had built up on the windows of some cars, she could guess what was going on inside. She walked a little off to the side, leaving the cars and the building a few meters behind her. She hugged herself. The cold air was getting to her now. She decided to go back in and see if Georg was ready to go home. She hadn't gotten any useful information, but she didn't care anymore.

As she turned around to walk back to the door through which she had exited, a man came her way. When he was closer, she saw that it was Hauser. He was here? He was dressed as an American cowboy, his fat belly hanging over his belt and the buttons of his plaid shirt seemed ready to burst at any moment. Sweat stains lined his armpits and the front of his shirt.

"Fräulein Schmidt!" Hauser slurred.

Susanne knew there was no use correcting him. He was obviously drunk. "Good evening, Herr Hauser."

He made his way to her, his mountainous body blocking her view of the backdoor. "You make a fine Flamenco dancer." He wiped the back of his hand across his mouth while his eyes rested on her cleavage.

"I have to go inside," Susanne said. She felt uncomfortable, tired, and in no mood to deal with a drunk boss.

Hauser came closer. Susanne backed up a bit and found herself against the cold brick wall. She shivered slightly. What did he want? *Get out of my way*, she thought angrily. "You must know," Hauser went on, "that you're a pretty thing, Fräulein Schmidt." His belly was now touching her and she could smell the alcohol on his breath.

"Herr Hauser. I need to –"

Hauser pressed his body fully against her. His weight and the smell of alcohol and sweat made her struggle for air. His left hand was now fumbling with her skirt.

"Herr Hauser!" Susanne was yelling at him now, trying to push him away. He didn't budge. She tried to lift her knee, but he pushed it down, touching her. *This can't be happening,* she thought, fighting harder to free herself. Her mind was racing. She had to get away.

Hauser attempted to kiss her, his fleshy lips trying to find her mouth. She pulled back and hit her head on the brick wall. She was disoriented for a split-second but came back to her senses when Hauser was breathing faster and heavily into her ear. "I know you want it, too. Come, don't be so coy," he said between breaths, fumbling at his belt.

Susanne felt panic rise in her. Was there no one that saw what Hauser was trying to do? "Help!" She screamed at the top of her lungs while again and again trying to push Hauser off. She fought him vehemently now, but Hauser suddenly grabbed her jaw hard with his right hand and pushed her head against the wall. What she saw in his eyes scared her.

But then, all of a sudden, Hauser's weight was lifted off her and she could breathe freely. Someone had pulled him off her. A man was pushing him around, hitting him, and cursing at him. Susanne was wiping at her eyes. She hadn't realized she was crying.

She saw Hauser stumble away, holding his nose after the man had let go of him. He came over to her. The man wore a monk costume. Georg. He didn't say anything, just took her into his arms and held her. She didn't know how long she sobbed. She later only remembered that Georg took her home. The rest was a blur.

———

When Susanne awoke the next morning, she found Georg at her bedside.

"How are you?" He looked concerned.

143

"Fine, I think," Susanne said, trying to sort her thoughts. Her head was hammering.

"Did he do anything to you?" Georg asked carefully. "If he did–"

"No. You stopped him. Thank you, Georg. How did you know where I was?"

"When you didn't come back, I went downstairs to look for you. Someone told me she saw you leave through the backdoor. And when I saw Hauser harass you like that–" He stopped himself and took a deep breath. "I didn't think anymore. That pig …"

Susanne put her hand on Georg's arm. "Thank you for always being there for me."

"You don't need to thank me. I promised Dieter I would take care of you and the twins." His eyes locked with hers, and he added. "I'm just glad I could be there. I don't know what I would have done to him if he had hurt you."

Susanne smiled at him. "You're a great friend, Georg Hoffmann. What would I do without you? You tell me that."

"And you're a tough woman, Susanne. It's amazing how you've handled everything …" He trailed off. There was no need for him to say it. They both knew what he was referring to.

Susanne fell back onto her pillow and sighed heavily. "The truth is, Georg, I'm not handling it very well at all. I can't live like this anymore. This is not the life I wanted."

Georg handed her a cup of coffee, and Susanne sat back up. She felt so utterly exhausted. Mentally, physically, emotionally. All she wanted was sleep.

They didn't speak for a while. Susanne welcomed the silence. She was so grateful to Georg, but in no mood to talk any more about last night. All she wanted was to forget it as quickly as possible. *Was* it possible? She wasn't sure.

"I can't go back to work," she said into the silence of Dieter's room. How could she ever face Hauser again?

"You should go to the police," Georg said. To her surprise, Susanne realized that she hadn't even thought of it. "And you don't need to go back to work. I don't want you to ever have to see him again," Georg said, interrupting her thoughts.

"But I need the job. I can't see how I can't go back. I need the money. For the children. Besides, that's where I'm supposed to work and be a productive and contributing member of society," Susanne said sarcastically.

"I'll take care of you and Henry and Jana until you find a different job," Georg said simply.

Susanne stared at him. She couldn't believe what she was hearing. He would do that for her? "I can't let you do that, Georg. I need to go back. For several reasons."

Should she tell Georg about Fleischer? Maybe this was the moment to tell him about her deal with Fleischer and about Dieter's plans. She needed to tell someone. She couldn't keep it to herself any longer. Would Georg understand?

"I work for the Stasi," Susanne said abruptly, not looking at Georg but inside her now almost empty coffee cup.

"What?" Georg looked dumbfounded.

Susanne told him about Fleischer and the deal she had been forced to make with him. The words just poured out of her. She felt so glad to finally be able to share what she had kept to herself for so long. "That's why I have to go back to the factory. I need to play along. Besides, Fleischer will insist on it," she said breathlessly, finishing her account.

"I can't believe they've blackmailed you like that," Georg said absentmindedly.

He folded his arms and leaned back against the footboard.

"I have to report something or someone to Fleischer next month," Susanne said, biting her lip until it hurt. "He gave me until March."

Georg looked at her, his eyes narrow. Then he leaned forward. "What about Hauser?" His voice was only a whisper.

Susanne looked up from her cup. "Hauser? What about him?"

"Why not report him?" Georg asked intently.

"I don't think Fleischer is looking for a report of sexual assault, Georg. That's within the jurisdiction of the police."

"Then make something up. Something that the Stasi would be happy to know. If you report him to the Stasi, he's gone. He'll get what he deserves, and you'll be able to go back to work. And you satisfy Fleischer's demands. He'll leave you alone then."

Susanne looked at Georg. His plan sounded too good to be true. "But what should I report him for? And what should I do until March? I can't face him ever again." She couldn't stop herself.

"I'll talk to Dr. Waldenberg. I'll convince him that you have a bad case of tonsillitis." Georg winked at her. "That should put you out of commission for a good three weeks. He'll write you an excuse for work. You just have to lay low."

"That shouldn't be a problem. I'd love to stay home with Henry and Jana." And Susanne wanted to take some of the load off Gisela. Henry was already crawling, and it would only be a matter of time before Jana did. It was getting harder and harder for Gisela to keep up lately.

"Do you really think this would work?" Susanne asked, interrupting her own thoughts. "Any ideas what we could denounce Hauser for?" *Denounce*. It was such a strong word. Could she really do that to him? Lie like that? To her great dismay, her thoughts turned again to last night. Yes, she could. She could put that man in a Stasi prison for what he had tried to do to her. For what he had done to her, she corrected herself. That would be her revenge. Hauser would get what he deserved. Georg's plan had to work. She felt better already.

"He is the director of the factory, right?" Georg interrupted her thoughts once more.

"Hauser? Yes," Susanne answered, not knowing where Georg was going with this.

"Have you seen him take something from the factory?"

"You mean, has he stolen something? I don't think he has," Susanne said.

"Well, he has." Georg looked at her imploringly.

"He actually didn't steal only for himself. He stole and resold the goods to various people," Susanne said matter-of-factly, winking at Georg.

Georg seemed impressed. "Ahhh, the black market is booming. Hauser gets rich and the state poorer. The Stasi won't like that."

"Exactly," Susanne said, folding her arms resolutely.

"That should work. We'll work out the details so he buys the story. Then we only need to think of something to tell Fleischer once he finds out you led him on."

"I'll be gone by then," Susanne said.

Georg looked at her, his brows furrowed. "What do you mean? Susanne, you're not planning to -"

"The West German government will pay a ransom for us," Susanne said, interrupting Georg. She knew too well what he wanted to say.

"They're what?" Georg looked incredulous. "How do you know that?"

"Dieter told me on the phone back in December." Susanne told Georg about the program and about how Anna would visit Diana in March and that she believed that it meant that Dieter was sending her word when they could finally join him.

"Are you sure that's what it meant in his letter?"

"Of course, that's what it means. Why can't you be happy for me, Georg? You were the one that said it would all play out." Susanne folded her arms in front of her chest. She never had a doubt in her mind about what Dieter had meant in his letter. Now Georg had to be all negative.

"I am happy for you. I just don't want you to get hurt even more if something goes wrong."

"Georg. It will work out. Don't you see? It will finally work out. And it's safe," Susanne retorted impatiently.

Georg got up. "I really do hope it will all work out for you, Susanne. I'll leave you now. Get some rest." When he had reached the door, he turned around to her. His face was hard to read. "I really do hope you'll be happy again." With that, he left the room.

Susanne was staring at the closed door. *He just doesn't want us to leave*, she thought, and fell once more back into her pillow. Susanne knew that it would hurt Georg when they left. He had been such a good friend, and he loved Jana and Henry, especially Henry. And Gisela? She had spent so much time with Henry and Jana. Susanne didn't want to hurt them again. If she could turn back time, she would.

———

Leaving Susanne to get some more rest, Georg carefully closed the door of the room, which had once belonged to his best friend. For a moment, he stared down the dark hallway and wondered why things were so different now. Dieter was gone, and Susanne lived in his room. Soon, she and the kids would be gone, too.

It isn't right to leave family and friends behind like that, Georg thought as he went down the squeaky old stairs. He couldn't remember if they had squeaked when he was a child, but then again, he and Dieter had always run down the stairs. He smiled at the memories of one flaxen- and one dark-haired boy racing down the stairs, trying to beat each other to the front door. Georg couldn't remember when they hadn't played together growing up. They had mostly played at Dieter's since he didn't have a drunken father beating up on his mother. Georg shook off the memories as he entered Gisela's kitchen, which looked the same as it did fifteen years ago. Gisela was feeding the twins. *She looks tired*, Georg thought.

"How are those two this morning?" Georg asked, walking over to Henry, who reached up to him. Georg gave in and took him out of the highchair.

"How is Susanne?" Gisela asked, ignoring his question.

Gisela's worried, Georg thought. How much does she know? He only had told her that Susanne wasn't feeling very well when he had carried her in the night before.

"She's fine. All she needs is rest, I think."

"I'm glad to hear that," Gisela said, wiping her hands on her apron.

"Why don't I take the twins on a walk? What do you think?" Georg asked. He wanted to get out. He had a slight hangover from last night and wanted to clear his head. And it was obvious that Gisela needed a rest.

"All right then," Gisela said.

Georg was amazed that it had taken no persuasion to convince Gisela, as was usually the case. "You're all right with that?"

"Yes, Georg. Just go and take those two out. They need some fresh air, and it looks like so do you," Gisela said, taking off her apron.

"We'll be back for lunch," he said while putting Henry on his shoulders.

"Wait. You can't go out like that. It's freezing. Here, put on their coats and hats and use this," Gisela was handing him a thick blanket. "The stroller is in the back." With that, she practically pushed him out the door.

Georg was a little overwhelmed getting the babies dressed up warmly. After what seemed like an eternity, he headed out the back. Next to the stroller stood a wooden sled. It had snowed very early in the morning, but would it be enough to use the sled? He figured it was worth a try and packed them both on the sled, covering them up with the blanket. They both looked at him with curiosity from beyond their thick layers of clothing. "Off we go," Georg said, and pulled. Both kids fell back against the back support. He looked at them, worried, but they didn't seem to mind. "Just hang on," Georg said, realizing that Jana had actually grabbed on to a rail even though she was wearing mittens.

There was a nice blanket of snow on the ground. Georg's leather boots made a crunching sound. He loved that sound. It reminded him of his childhood. It seemed they had always had more snowy winters back then. Now it seemed that they had less snow every winter and that they got warmer. He remembered that the river had been frozen over when he was a child but couldn't recall when it had iced over in recent years.

Georg treaded on, staying on the sidewalks and avoiding the roads where traffic had already turned the snow into a gray mush. Snow was falling softly from the linden trees overhead, leaving a dust of powder on the babies' hats. The twins seemed to enjoy the ride. *Every child loves snow*, he thought, glad he had taken the sled. This would have been so much harder with the stroller. Impossible, really.

Then his thoughts turned back to his conversation with Susanne. He still had trouble comprehending the game Fleischer was playing. He had played them both off against each other. Georg shook his head and glanced over his shoulder to see if the twins were still comfortably sitting on the sled. Huddled together, they both sat motionless, with Jana's little hand still tightly wrapped around one of the rails. Their cheeks and noses were rosy from the cold, and their eyes were watering a little. He would miss them terribly. He wiped angrily at the corners of his eyes which had started to water as well. *Maybe the wind is too icy*, he thought, and looked at the twins. *They must be cold. I better head back.*

He turned the sled around and walked back until his own and Gisela's houses came into view. Susanne and the children would leave. The cold reality hit him now. Susanne had sounded pretty confident. How could she leave them so easily? Did she love Dieter that much? Georg knew the answer to that question and sighed. But then a thought came to him. Back in November he had told Fleischer of Susanne's plan to try to find another way into the West. In return, Georg had asked Fleischer to let Dieter back into the country. Fleischer had laughed at him. His laugh had seemed cold and calculated. "We don't want people like him in our country. We have expelled dissidents from this country before," he had said. So why not expel Susanne and the children? Fleischer had leaned back and crooked his head. "Frau Schmidt is an asset to this country." Fleischer had left it at that. When Fleischer wanted to dismiss him, Georg had gotten desperate and suggested that if they would offer not to persecute Dieter and get him his old job back, he would surely consider returning. Again Fleischer laughed his cold, hard laugh. But then he turned serious and made it clear that if Georg were to provide him information that was truly valuable to him, he would maybe consider such a preposterous plan.

That had been over two months ago. More than ever, he needed something of substance to report to Fleischer. Maybe then he would finally help him. And then he remembered what Susanne had told him this morning. If he told Fleischer that–Georg instantly shook his head. How could he betray Susanne's confidence like that? But Georg knew he was running out of time. *I have to at least try,* he thought as he stomped through the snow. When they went up to Berlin in March, he would meet with Fleischer, hopefully before Susanne went to see him.

Georg was surprised to find he had already arrived at Gisela's house. He took the twins back inside and undressed them. He found Gisela asleep on the couch and decided to take the children to their room and play with them. When he passed Susanne's room, he had made his decision. He wouldn't just let them leave. Dieter had to come back. It was as simple as that.

Chapter 15

The last few weeks had been the best weeks since Susanne had come to Wallhausen. She was so grateful to Georg for getting her a doctor's note from Dr. Waldenberg. She was thankful not to come across Hauser but also for all the time she got to spend with the children. She owed Georg. He had been such a great friend through everything. He was always there for her.

She looked at Georg sitting across from her. He was looking out the window at the people hastening up and down the platform. Their train to Berlin would be leaving in less than two minutes. "Are you excited to see Diana again?" she asked.

"Huh?" Georg turned to her. "Did you say something?"

"Diana. I'm sure you're excited to see her again." Was he even listening?

"Oh, yes." He seemed absentminded.

Susanne had expected a little more enthusiasm from Georg. He and Diana had gotten along so well when they had visited her in January. She knew Diana was looking forward to finally seeing Georg again. "Everything all right?"

"Yes. Everything's fine." He changed the topic. "How did Henry and Jana take it when you left them today?"

Susanne grimaced. "Not so well." She thought of how clingy Jana had been this morning, and how Henry had cried when she had handed him over to Gisela. After spending all this time with them these past few weeks, they had gotten so attached to her. She had to admit that she liked it, even though it had broken her heart this morning when she had to leave them.

It had been her idea not to take the twins along. Georg understood why, and Gisela was grateful to have the children again. They would only be in Berlin for one night and two days. That was enough time for her. What she had to take care of while in Berlin was better done without the babies around. Diana would be disappointed, she feared. She hadn't told her friend that the twins weren't coming along.

"How is Gisela?" Georg asked, interrupting her thoughts.

"She's fine, I think. Why?"

"She just seemed so tired over the winter, but then last week I saw her getting the yard ready for spring," Georg said.

"Yes, she did seem rather tired, didn't she? I think it helped that I was home these past few weeks." Gisela appeared less tired lately. She had probably been burned out. Since Henry and then Jana had started to walk, keeping up with them had even brought Susanne to the point of utter exhaustion.

"It has been good for them to have you home," Georg said. "All of them."

"I believe so."

"You should make that permanent."

Susanne looked at him with furrowed brows. He knew that she had no choice. Her current situation was certainly not what she could call "permanent." Once Hauser was in Stasi prison, she would have to return to work until … She didn't have to finish that thought. It cheered her up immediately.

"You're smiling. I thought it was a great idea," Georg said.

"You know I can't. Once Hauser is gone, I have to return. To make Fleischer believe I'm cooperating. I told you." Susanne tried to hide the impatience in her voice.

They were interrupted by the conductor's whistle. The doors slammed shut loudly and the train started to roll out of the station. Georg was quiet again, staring out the window. What was it with him? He seemed so different. So quiet.

Susanne made a few more attempts to get Georg to pay attention to her. But he wouldn't talk much. Susanne didn't understand. It was as if ... as if he didn't want to go to Berlin.

"Diana is really looking forward to your visit," Susanne said in another attempt to get Georg's attention and to penetrate his gloominess.

"Is she?" he said with disinterest in his voice.

"I thought you liked her. You guys were getting along so well." She didn't give up.

Georg sighed. "We were."

Susanne couldn't believe it. Why was he so preoccupied?

As their train rolled into Berlin's main station, both of them looked out the window. The train slowed down considerably. And when it reached the platform, Susanne could see Diana waiting for them. The brakes screeched, and the train came to a stop. Outside, Diana was scanning the windows, looking for them. When she saw them, Diana waved. To Susanne's great dismay, it was only she that waved back. Georg busied himself with getting the suitcases off the rack.

Susanne ignored him. What had gotten into him? Why had he gotten her friend's hopes up back in January? Diana certainly was a great catch. Susanne hoped that Georg wouldn't break her friend's heart this weekend. *Not this weekend of all weekends*, she thought as they got off the train to greet a smiling Diana.

"What's with Georg?" Diana asked when they finally were alone in Diana's kitchen. Georg had gone to see an old friend from when he had studied at the university, and they were waiting for Anna to arrive.

Susanne shrugged casually. She didn't want to talk about Georg right now. All her thoughts were directed toward Anna's visit. Susanne checked the clock on Diana's kitchen wall but answered Diana anyway. Talking about Georg would pass the time more quickly. "Who knows? Georg can be like that. Maybe he has to warm up again. You guys shouldn't have waited until March to see each other again."

"Yeah, two months was a little long. But I had suggested to him ..." Diana waved it off, not finishing her sentence.

Susanne put an arm around Diana's shoulder. "He'll be back soon." She smiled encouragingly at her. And with a twinkle in her eye, she added, "Let me tell you something. Georg can be an ass. Believe me. I've seen it numerous times."

Diana chuckled. "I agree with you. Especially after that reception at the train station. Here I was, getting my hopes up for a kiss ..."

Susanne grinned at her. "I think you really like him."

Diana pretended to straighten out the tablecloth on her kitchen table. "Well, he isn't half bad." And with a glance at Susanne, she added, "But who knows. He seems to have lost interest."

"But he came, didn't he?" Susanne offered.

"Maybe he just wanted to meet his friend."

Susanne wanted to protest, but the doorbell rang. She grabbed Diana's arm. "It's her."

Diana checked the clock herself and nodded. "This must be her."

They went to the door together. Diana peered through the peephole and gave Susanne a distinct nod.

Susanne swallowed hard as Diana opened the door. This was it. She could hardly contain the mixture of anxiety and excitement she was feeling to the point of making her sick.

Anna stood there in a fine long black coat, a large red leather purse dangling from her arm. Her brown hair was in a bun. She smiled coolly at them.

"Come in, come in," Diana said hastily, and pulled Anna inside her apartment.

Susanne felt Anna stiffen slightly when she hugged her. Or was it her imagination? Maybe she had been hugging her too tightly. *Get a grip*, Susanne told herself as Diana took Anna's coat and hung it up.

Diana offered Anna the couch, but she chose a chair across from it. So Susanne and Diana fell on the couch, Diana eyeing their friend with curiosity and Susanne with anticipation.

Anna rummaged in her purse and pulled out an envelope. Susanne flew over to her, ripped it out of her hand, and disappeared into the kitchen.

"You're welcome," Susanne heard Anna say as the kitchen door swung shut. Susanne ignored her. She was interested in one thing and one thing only.

She tore open the envelope and pulled out the pages. Dieter's handwriting.

Georg folded the collar of his coat up. It was March, but the wind was still icy. *Time for spring to arrive*, he thought grimly as he waited near the exit of the city park. He checked his watch and rubbed his hands together while regretting not taking his gloves with him up to Berlin. Ten more minutes until their rendezvous. He would be frozen solid by then.

He could hear the bells of a nearby church starting to toll. It was almost time. Where was Fleischer? At that moment, a black Lada pulled up and Fleischer got out. He came striding toward him, a briefcase in hand.

"Herr Hoffmann." Fleischer tipped his hat to him.

Georg acknowledged the greeting with a nod. There was no need for small talk.

"Do you have something for me, Herr Hoffmann?" Fleischer made no attempt to hide his curiosity.

Georg swallowed. *Here we go*, he thought, hoping that this wouldn't come back to haunt him. "I do. Regarding Susanne Schmidt."

"Let's hear it then."

"Not before we discuss our deal." Georg knew he had to play it smart.

"What deal?"

Fleischer is playing dumb, Georg thought angrily. He had to remember their deal. "The deal where I give you valuable information in exchange for your help to get Dieter Schmidt back over here." He added, "Without punishment and with his old job back."

Fleischer feigned a cough, which echoed in the empty city park. Some crows left the tree overhead, cawing loudly as they took off. "Oh, *that* deal," Fleischer finally said, his eyes mocking Georg.

Georg swallowed hard. He had to play his card. He had no choice. "What I tell you will certainly change your mind." He had to try. "Frau Schmidt will go to West Germany with her children and –"

"And how will she accomplish that, Herr Hoffmann?" Fleischer interrupting him.

"With the help of the West German government," Georg said, trying to read Fleischer's face to see if he had caught on.

Fleischer motioned to him to come closer. Georg complied.

"We know," Fleischer said, hissing the words with a mocking smile.

Georg's brows furrowed. What was going on? What game was Fleischer playing?

"Herr Hoffmann," Fleischer started condescendingly, "We're the ones negotiating with the enemy. The case of Susanne Schmidt is closed for us. An agreement has been reached. Which means ... we have no need of your services anymore. At least for now."

Georg felt as if Fleischer had slapped him. That was it? "But –"

"No buts, Herr Hoffmann. We don't want people like the Schmidts in our country."

The park was swimming around Georg. An agreement had been reached. Did that mean Susanne and the twins were leaving? He had put all his hopes into this meeting. But now... He felt like a fool.

"I have to leave. Work is calling," Fleischer said, leaving Georg staring after him.

How he had made it to the nearby bench, Georg couldn't remember. He didn't feel the cold anymore. His pulse was racing, and so was his mind. He would lose them. He felt childish now. How could he have hoped to–? He shook his head. Susanne had been right. Dieter's letter would bring her the good news. He checked his watch. Anna had to be there by now.

Georg got up. Time to visit an old friend. He was in no mood to witness Susanne's happiness after reading Dieter's letter. They wouldn't miss him anyway.

Susanne stared at the familiar handwriting and her heart skipped a beat. This was it. She would find out. Her eyes flew across the lines until they locked in place on the bottom of the first page. Her breathing stopped. Could it be?

She swung open the kitchen door. Diana and Anna stared at her. "In May. The twins' birthday is in May," she said, her voice hoarse and tears of happiness streaming down her cheeks.

She fell down on the couch next to Diana, who hugged her tightly. The letter was still in Susanne's hand. "Finally," Susanne said between sobs.

When she let go of her friend, she saw tears in Diana's eyes. With a sudden realization, she knew how it would hurt them both to say goodbye to each other.

Susanne noticed that she hadn't exchanged more than a greeting with Anna, who sat silently across from them. Her legs were crossed and her hands lay folded in her lap. Her face was unreadable. Susanne had so much to ask her friend.

"Isn't that great, Anna?" Susanne asked.

Anna smiled. "It's about time."

"How is Dieter?"

"He's great. Now that you and the babies will join him," Anna said. "He's been a mess without you."

Susanne felt a knot in her chest. She could only imagine how it had been for him.

"Thank goodness he had you and Wolfgang. I don't know how I can ever make it up to you."

"Wolfgang and I separated," Anna said suddenly, not looking at them.

Susanne just stared at her, taken aback by the unexpected revelation. She cleared her throat after she had somewhat recovered. "You did? I had no idea ..." Susanne didn't know what to make of this. Did Dieter live there with Anna alone?

"We both agreed that it wasn't working anymore. We both moved on," Anna said, sighing. "It's for the better, really."

"I'm so sorry, Anna." Susanne walked over to her and put an arm around her.

"It's all right, really. I'm over it now. Dieter helped me through this difficult time. It has been so good to have him around," Anna said. Susanne felt a sudden sting. "I know now why you fell for him," Anna added, looking at Susanne, her face still unreadable.

"And that's why Susanne married him. He's a great guy." Diana joined in. "And in only two months they'll be together again." She got up and walked toward the kitchen. "Susanne, will you stay in Hamburg?" Diana asked casually in Susanne's direction.

"I haven't thought about that yet," Susanne gave back, wondering where Diana's question had come from.

"Would anyone else like something to drink?" Diana asked as she swung open the kitchen door. "I'm parched."

"Sure," Anna and Susanne replied in unison. They smiled at each other.

Susanne didn't like the thought of Dieter and Anna living alone under one roof, but she was so grateful to her friend. She would forever be grateful to her. She trusted her, and above all, she trusted Dieter. She knew he still loved her, and the separation might have even made their love stronger. After all they had been through, they would appreciate every minute they would get to spend together. Two months. Susanne couldn't believe it. She could scream, she felt so happy. She felt Anna's hand on her arm and looked at her friend. "I've talked to the conductor. He says there might be an opening by the end of the year," Anna said.

"You mean it?" That was more than Susanne had hoped for. The Hamburg orchestra. Finally doing what she loved.

"They can't wait to have you, Susanne."

"But I'm really rusty. I didn't have much time to play, with the job I have and the twins."

"That's right. I forgot. You have children now," Anna said, with what Susanne thought was a hint of disdain. "Well, I'm sure they'll work something out with you."

Now Susanne had no doubt that Anna was indeed condescending to her. She had experienced condescension every time she had toured in the West, but Anna and Wolfgang had been different. They had not treated her, Diana, the conductor, nor the rest of the orchestra members as second-class citizens. Anna and Wolfgang had become dear friends of hers, and they had written each other or talked on Georg's phone almost every time she and Dieter had visited Gisela. What had gotten into Anna?

Just as Susanne wanted to respond to Anna's aloofness, Diana came out of the kitchen and handed a glass of orange soda to each of them. Anna took a sip and grimaced. "I don't know how you guys can drink this stuff. It's horrible," she said, setting the glass down on the coffee table.

"I'm sure it doesn't compare to what you're used to," Diana snapped, her tone biting.

"Well, I should get going anyway. There might be a line at the checkpoint." Anna got up. "Do you have anything you'd like me to take to Dieter?" she asked.

Susanne went over to the clothes rack where her coat hung and pulled out a letter.

"There're also some pictures of the twins in there. Current ones," Susanne said as she handed the letter to Anna. It disappeared into the red leather purse. "Please give him all my love." Anna nodded and put on her coat. "Thanks again for everything, Anna. I owe you," Susanne said, putting her earlier feelings of anger aside.

Anna waved it off. She hugged Susanne and then Diana, who didn't seem to be too happy about it. They said their goodbyes and Anna left.

"Can you believe her?" Diana asked after the door had closed behind Anna.

"You have to admit that our soda doesn't compare to anything you can buy in the West. You said yourself that it's awful. You've been to the West and tasted their stuff," Susanne said simply. She didn't feel like defending Anna's condescending tone, but she was so grateful to Anna and so elated that she would see Dieter in only two months.

"I don't mean the soda, Susanne," Diana said.

Susanne looked at her, oblivious to what Diana was referring to.

"The way she spoke of Dieter. She has a thing for him, I'm telling you."

"Oh, come on, Diana. You can't be serious," Susanne said.

"Don't tell me you didn't see it," Diana said.

"I really don't know what you mean." It was childish to assume something was going on between Dieter and Anna. No, she didn't like that Wolfgang had moved out, but Dieter loved her and he had done everything in his power to get her and the children to West Germany.

"She lives with Dieter under one roof. Alone. And she doesn't mind," Diana said accusingly.

"That doesn't mean anything." Or did it? No, it didn't. Anna had done so much for Dieter and her. And today, she had even come all the way from Hamburg to deliver the good news. How easy it was for West Germans to visit someone in the East. How unfair that they could come visit them on a whim. Of course, the harsh controls were frustrating, but at least they could come over. *We're prisoners in our own country,* Susanne thought grimly.

"I know you're grateful to her. I'm just telling you to be a little bit more wary and not so trusting," Diana said.

"I trust Dieter. That's all that matters." She didn't want to feel like she had to defend herself or Dieter. It was ridiculous to even talk about it.

Diana raised her hands in defense. "I'm just saying."

"I'll be over there soon. Dieter is waiting for me. If Anna feels something for him, I'm sure he doesn't return the same feelings."

"I hope you're right," Diana said simply, slouching down on the couch. She sighed. "When did Georg say he'd be back?"

Susanne smiled and sat down next to her friend. She patted her arm. "He'll be here soon."

"I hope you're right. You guys are leaving tomorrow, and I haven't even had the chance to talk to him, let alone spend some time with him."

"You really like him, don't you?" Susanne asked, wishing Diana could feel the same happiness she was feeling right now.

"He's not bad," Diana muttered.

"I'm certain he likes you, too," Susanne said, winking at her friend.

Diana didn't react as Susanne had hoped. "I'm not so sure he likes me the way I like him," Diana said cautiously.

"What do you mean? You guys were kissing." Diana's eyebrows rose, and she stared at Susanne. "Well, I didn't see anything. I only heard you–"

"You weren't sleeping?" Diana asked, interrupting her.

Susanne grinned at her. "Nope. Didn't want to disturb you two."

Diana hit her playfully. "I can't believe you, Susanne Schmidt." But then Diana turned somber. "I fear he likes someone else."

"Oh, he doesn't. Let me assure you, Diana. I live next to him," Susanne said. Diana stared blankly at her. "You don't even see it, do you?"

"See what?" Now Susanne felt utterly lost.

"He likes you, Susanne," Diana said, her voice grave.

Susanne was confused for a moment, but recovered quickly. "I know he likes me. I like him, too. We've become best friends. He's been there for me all this time."

"Not like a friend, Susanne. I think he likes you more than that."

"Don't be silly, Diana." What had gotten into Diana today? First, she had accused Anna and now Georg, of feelings she herself hadn't witnessed. "What makes you think that?" Susanne was truly curious. She hadn't seen anything that would tell her that Georg liked her in any way other than as a friend.

"The way he looks at you."

"Oh, come on, Diana. You can't be serious."

"Forget it." Diana waved it off.

Susanne didn't know what to make of all this. What in the world was going on with Diana today? She'd never seen her friend like this. So beside herself. Her assumptions were so ridiculous. Dieter didn't love Anna, and Georg didn't love her. She would know.

Susanne got up and pulled her friend up with her. "Let's go. I can't bear to see you like this any longer. If Georg isn't here, it's his loss. We're not wasting this day. Come on." She pulled Diana with her to the front door and threw her coat at her.

Diana protested. "What if he comes back, and we're not here?"

"You still have tomorrow. Now put on that coat. We're leaving." Susanne practically had to pull Diana out of her apartment. Susanne was determined that Diana would not spend the day waiting around for Georg.

———

"You're drunk," Susanne said angrily. She'd never seen Georg like that. What time was it? He had been gone all day. It was almost midnight. Diana looked on tightlipped as Susanne pulled Georg inside.

"That is ... none of your businessss, ladiesss." Georg stumbled his way to the couch and fell down on it.

"My old man knew ... how to solve ... his problemsss," he drew out, trying to hit the pillow into position.

Susanne walked over to him. Diana stood rooted to the ground, her arms folded across her chest. "What problems do you have, Georg?" Susanne said. She felt as though she was talking to a child. Even at the carnival, Georg didn't get drunk like this. What had gotten into him? He was behaving so... immature. Very unlike Georg indeed.

"You," he mumbled. He seemed to doze off.

Susanne stared at him. Had she heard right? She looked over to Diana, who just shrugged with an expression that seemed to say, "I told you so," and then came over to them. She pulled Georg's shoes off and threw a blanket over him. "Let's go to bed, too," Diana said with a look at the now snoring Georg who drooled on her pillow. She sighed.

Susanne shook her head. Why was she his problem? What did he mean? Then it dawned on her. He hadn't heard the news yet. That she would be able to leave in May. Georg no longer would have to worry about her and the twins. She wouldn't cause him sleepless nights anymore. Georg would be sad that they would leave, but his problems would be solved. He had taken care of her, as he had promised Dieter. Her problems were solved, and so were Georg's. She would tell him the good news first thing in the morning. He wouldn't have a reason to get drunk again. At least not over her.

When Susanne looked up, she realized that Diana had already gone to bed. With a last look at Georg, she decided to do the same. She had a tough day ahead of her.

When Georg woke up, he had no idea what time it was. He looked around and was surprised to find himself on the couch. How had he gotten here? When he stood up, his head was throbbing, and he felt slightly nauseated. His back and shoulders ached from sleeping on the couch. He cracked his neck and rubbed his shoulders, but there was no relief.

Georg made his way to the tiny bathroom, feeling the worst he'd ever felt. Luckily, he ran into no one. He needed to clear his head first, before he could talk to anyone.

When Georg looked in the mirror, he almost fell back. He was a mess. He looked a ghostly pale, dark shadows graced his eyes, which were bloodshot. His dark hair was matted and an utter mess. The dark stubble on his chin and above his upper lip made him look even paler. His shirt was wrinkled and soiled in places. He smelled it and shrunk back. The smell of cigarettes, beer, and what he thought was vomit made him gag. He breathed heavily but couldn't keep down the bile that rose up. He turned around to the toilet and was able to lift the lid just in time.

Utterly exhausted, Georg hoped some cold water would make him feel better. Repeatedly, he splashed handfuls in his face and rinsed his mouth. When he looked up, water was dripping from his face and hair. The image he saw in front of him was all too familiar, even after all these years. *It has come down to this,* he thought. *I'll end up like my father after all.* He shook his head at the image in front of him and grabbed the nearest towel.

Georg pressed his forehead against the cool glass of the mirror, his breath fogging the lower part of the glass. He thought of Susanne. Soon she'd be gone. He felt a new wave of nausea roll in and began to breathe slowly, in and out. Why was it so difficult to let her go? What was wrong with him? He thought of last night. He had behaved like his old man. All his life, Georg had tried very hard not to become his father. But his behavior last night was very much like the man he so abhorred. He remembered seeing Diana and Susanne and their disapproving scowls.

He tried to shake the image from his head and proceeded with his morning bathroom routine. When he was done, Georg felt somewhat better. A glance in the mirror told him that he looked somewhat back to normal. All he had to do now was face the women. He didn't know if he could bear seeing Susanne's over-joyed face when she shared the news with him. *You have to be happy for her,* he told himself. *So why can't I,* he wondered as he left the bathroom.

He found Diana in the kitchen. She sat at the table, sipping a cup of coffee and reading some sort of music magazine. West German, Georg realized. Diana seemed to ignore him. Where was Susanne? A look at the clock told him where she was. The meeting with Fleischer. It was already early afternoon. Their train would leave in about three hours. He looked at Diana and bit his lip. "Mind if I sit down?"

Diana gestured for him to sit, her lips pressed together.

"I'm so sorry about last night," Georg said.

Diana looked up, her eyes sad. "I had no idea you had a drinking problem."

"I don't," Georg said. Who was he trying to convince? "I just had too much to drink. I got some bad news yesterday."

"What bad news?" Diana seemed curious. "From the friend you were meeting?" Georg nodded. Diana got up and went over to the coffee pot. She came back and handed him a cup. "Here. That will help. Hungry?"

He shook his head, breathing in deeply. Then he took a sip. "I'm sorry about it all. I hope I can make it up to you some time," Georg said, taking another sip.

"What is it that you want, Georg?" Diana was now fully facing him, her face questioning.

"I don't know what you mean." Why was he stalling? *Just tell her you're not interested.*

"We had a good time back in January, I thought."

"We did." He couldn't deny that. "It's complicated."

"You have my undivided attention." Diana wouldn't let it go. He knew that. He had to tell her that he couldn't get involved with her.

She wasn't the one he wanted, he realized at that moment. "There is someone else, isn't there," she said. He looked at her in surprise. "So I'm right." Diana leaned back and folded her arms across her chest. "You know that she'll be gone soon. There is no hope for you to –"

"What? Hold on there." Georg was holding up his hands. "Who are you talking about?"

"You know who I mean. There is no denying it. I've seen the way you look at her." Georg just stared at her. He was in love with Susanne and Diana had figured it out before he did. He swallowed hard. "Don't worry. She's oblivious." Diana's face was hard. "How could you lead me on like that, Georg?"

He looked at her. "I didn't know ... I wasn't ... I had no idea I was–" He broke off and reached for her hand. If he had led her on, it was unintentionally. He had been so blind about his own feelings. He had slowly and steadily fallen in love with his best friend's wife. "I really wanted to give it a try. You're lovely. Any man would be an idiot if he didn't want to be with you..." He trailed off. "Under any other circumstances, I would have fallen for you. Who wouldn't?" He had said the last few words more to himself than to Diana.

"But she'll be gone. For good. There is no hope for you and her," Diana said, her voice imploring.

He had to pretend not to know Susanne and the kids were leaving for sure. Luckily, Diana went on without waiting for a reaction from him.

"She's leaving in May. Anna brought a letter from Dieter," Diana said, her eyes scrutinizing him.

May? So soon? Two months. And they would be gone. Susanne, Henry, and Jana. He would probably never see them again. So, that was it. He would lose her. The twins. But they weren't his children and Susanne was his best friend's wife. How could his feelings betray him like that, betray *them* like that? He had to let her go.

Georg got up and looked at Diana apologetically. She was right. He had led her on. How could he have played with her feelings like that? Who had he become? His hand reached out to touch her dark hair running down her back, but he dropped it. "I'm sorry, Diana. You don't deserve this."

She opened her mouth as if to say something but seemed to decide against it. As the kitchen door swung shut, he heard her. "Goodbye, Georg." He sighed and left the apartment.

———

Susanne looked at the gray office building in front of her and sighed. She was not looking forward to this meeting. She hated the man. He was a symbol of the horrible life she had to live since that fateful day in November. How long it had been. She sighed again. Not much longer.

It was true that she was less anxious to meet Fleischer since she had learned that she would leave in May, but she nevertheless had to face the man and pretend she was cooperating with him. But did she have to pretend? Wouldn't he be aware of what was happening?

Susanne went inside and up the stairs. People in uniform passed her. They didn't seem to notice her. She looked at the little note in her hand. Fleischer's office had to be on the next floor. She found the right hallway and searched for Fleischer's door. Her steps echoed in the empty linoleum hallway.

Susanne stopped when she saw the number on the door. Her hand rose, but she couldn't bring herself to knock. How she dreaded seeing him again. Someone appeared in the hallway, walking in her direction. Susanne didn't want to appear to be eavesdropping, especially not here, in the Stasi headquarters, so she quickly knocked. At first, softly.

There was no response. She knocked louder. It sounded too loud. When Fleischer's voice called her in, she involuntarily shuddered. With a deep breath, she opened the door and stepped across the threshold.

Fleischer pretended not to have seen or heard her come in and just kept on writing. She closed the door and looked around the small office, waiting for a sign from him. He appeared to be undisturbed by her presence. She cleared her throat. Fleischer didn't look up, but motioned for her to sit. "I'm glad you still came to see me," he said. So he knew a deal had been reached with the West Germans. He knew she would leave this country. Maybe she didn't have to denounce Hauser after all, even though he deserved it. Truly deserved it. She sighed and sat down for a last meeting with Fleischer.

Walter Fleischer looked up when he was finished with his report. There was no need to hurry. She could wait. She would have to wait. He put his pen aside and looked at her. She seemed to have her old confidence back.

"As I said before, I'm pleased to see you've honored your commitment, even though things have changed. For you." He eyed her, waiting for a reaction, but she just looked at him, her face expressionless. "Is there anything you wish to report, Frau Schmidt?" She stared at him. "I know you will leave us soon," he said, noticing her reaction, "but until then you're still considered an informant. I must ask you again, is there anything you wish to report?"

She seemed to hesitate and shift in her seat. He could tell she was uncomfortable.

"I have witnessed something that might be of interest to you," she said hesitantly.

"Go on." He motioned for her to proceed. Did she really have something to report? After all this time, had she finally fallen in line, or did it have to do with the fact that nothing mattered to her now that she was leaving?

"You know Herr Hauser," she said, looking at him intently.

"Wilhelm Hauser? Your boss?" What was she saying?

"He's stolen from the factory."

"Has he." It wasn't a question.

"He's also been selling what he stole."

"Is that true." Again, this wasn't a question, but to his surprise, she answered it anyway.

"It is," she said, folding her arms, her eyes showing a confusing mixture of relief and self-confidence.

He knew she was lying. He could tell an honest report from a fabricated one. And what Susanne Schmidt was telling him was certainly a fabrication. He decided to play her game for a while. *Only for a while,* he thought grimly, angry that he had believed she had finally come around.

"So tell me, Frau Schmidt. What has Herr Hauser been stealing?"

"Tools, mainly, and supplies, I think."

"When did these..." He was searching for the right word. "... this treachery occur?"

"Mostly after work," she said.

She had prepared her answers. It was almost amusing. "And you'll be able to defend your accusations in court, will you?" he asked her.

She shifted again in her seat, and he saw the hesitation in her eyes. "Yes," she said. She looked determined now. He wondered what Hauser had done to her to deserve this denouncement.

"I liked working under Herr Hauser, but he has done wrong," she went on.

Had she read his thoughts? "We'll look into the matter, be assured, Frau Schmidt.

We thank you for this report. It's a shame we have to let go of an asset such as yourself."

An asset. He had to smile at his own word choice.

"Is there anything else?" she asked.

If she thought she would get off that easily, she was mistaken. He wasn't done with her. "Well, there will be formalities concerning your expulsion from the country that need to be taken care of." He looked at the papers on his desk.

"Expulsion?" She looked at him, her eyes furious. "The West Germans had to buy my freedom. My children's freedom. You're selling us." She was almost shouting now.

"Your identification papers will be voided," Fleischer went on as if he hadn't heard her. "Once expelled, you are no longer a citizen of this country." She would get what she wanted, and he had to admit that it bothered him greatly, but he wouldn't let her go in triumph. He had the last word. From the torture he read in her eyes, he could tell that what he had said had gotten to her. She had to see how momentous her decision to go to the West was.

"Is that all?" she asked, her face expressionless.

She still felt she was someone better. The work in the factory hadn't changed that. He had tried to break her. He sighed. It hadn't done anything for her. She refused to be subordinate. "Not quite, Frau Schmidt. You'll have to sell your property –"

"I don't own any property."

"Ah, that's right. Then all we need to do is void your I.D., and you'll be able to leave with your few belongings."

"And my children."

"Of course, your children." He looked at her and felt only disgust for someone like her. Privileged and ungrateful. She had used the state and was now turning her back on it. "You can go, Frau Schmidt." There was nothing else he could do or say to her. She would slip through his fingers.

She got up and walked to the door. "I hope I'll never have the pleasure again," she said over her shoulder before exiting.

He got up too fast and his chair fell over. How dare she... But she was gone. He only had his clenched fists to hit the paper stack on his desk.

Susanne finally appeared on the platform. Georg saw her search for him among the few people waiting for the train to arrive. He waved. She didn't smile when she saw him.

Susanne strode toward him, her face drawn. He wondered if she had had the guts to denounce Hauser. But what did it matter now? She would leave.

As she approached him, Georg decided to talk first. "How was your visit with Fleischer?" he asked.

"Fine," was all she said, her voice as cold as the wind that blew across the platform. She checked her watch and Georg looked for the big clock farther down the platform. They had fifteen minutes until their train would leave East Berlin's main train station.

"I heard the news," he said, trying to pacify her.

"Which news do you mean?" She looked at him, her eyes searching his face.

"You're leaving. In May." He choked out the words.

"Yes," she said simply.

He couldn't detect any excitement in her voice. Just resentment. Resentment toward him. Georg knew what was bothering Susanne, why she didn't share her joy with him. She had to be so happy now that she would finally be able to go to the West. Diana must have told her. *She knows why I can't be with Diana.*

"You hurt my friend," Susanne said.

"Diana and I talked it over."

"Why, Georg? She's great. You seemed to like her. You got her hopes up back in January." Susanne was mad now. He was waiting for her to slap him with her purse. But she didn't.

"I like her, don't get me wrong."

"So, what's the problem, Georg?"

"She's not my type," he said flatly. What was he supposed to tell her? That he was in love with her, his best friend's wife? That he didn't want her to leave? He couldn't. Especially not now that she was leaving for sure. He had to get over her. Somehow. He swallowed and ran his hand through his hair.

"Why wouldn't she be your type?" Susanne asked, more of herself than him.

He didn't answer her.

"I didn't think you could be such an–" A voice was blaring from the speakers, announcing an oncoming train. When the train had come to a screeching halt at the neighboring platform, Susanne added, "You hurt her pretty badly. She likes you." She paused. "Well, she *liked* you."

There was nothing Georg could say to make this right and to make Susanne understand. Diana hadn't told Susanne how he truly felt. He was glad. But he felt terrible.

"And Diana told me you weren't interested because you liked me," Susanne said, her eyes searching his. Georg stared at her. "I know. It's ridiculous. She's been a little beside herself. Well, no wonder." Susanne shot an angry glance at him.

Georg didn't know what to say. Susanne hadn't believed Diana. That was good news. Or was it? For a brief second, he wondered if it would be better for Susanne to see that he loved her. Maybe she would ... Impossible. She wouldn't. She had always loved Dieter.

175

Together, they waited for their train to roll in. They didn't speak, just stared down the tracks, hoping for the train to come into view and shorten the time.

When their train was leaving the station ten minutes later, Susanne turned to him, her face somber. "I think this was the last time we'll go to Berlin together."

Georg swallowed. He knew she was right. They'd never visit Diana together again. But it had nothing to do with Diana. Susanne was leaving them. He had two months with her and the twins, and then they would probably never see each other again. He stared out the window, trying to focus in on the countryside that flew by. There was no reason for Susanne to see the anguish in his eyes.

Chapter 16

S usanne knocked on Gisela's bedroom door, but there was no answer. She had wanted to talk to Gisela since her return from Berlin a week ago. Gisela needed to know that they were leaving. Her mother-in-law would need some time to get used to the fact. Susanne knew that it would be hard on Dieter's mother. Very hard. And not only on her. Susanne had become so close to her mother-in-law. She loved Gisela almost as much as she had loved her own mother. But what made the thought of leaving Gisela even more unbearable was the fact that she would take Henry and Jana away from their grandmother. If it had only been her, the two of them would be able to handle the goodbye. But Henry and Jana? *It will break her heart,* Susanne thought, trying to swallow down the guilt that was rising up in her like acid.

Susanne knocked again. She had to talk to Gisela. Now. Before she lost the little bit of courage she had mustered. Susanne pressed her ear against the door and listened. Was Gisela even in her bedroom? Her mother-in-law had said that she wanted to take a nap, but there was no sound. Where had Gisela gone?

Gisela came home two hours later. Susanne jumped up from the floor where she had been playing with Jana and Henry once her mother-in-law came in through the door.

"You're jumpy," Gisela said with a tired smile. She pulled her scarf off and hung up her jacket.

"Not jumpy, only worried. Where have you been? I thought you were taking a nap," Susanne said, wondering why her mother-in-law had lied to her.

"I had an appointment."

"With whom? Why didn't you tell me?"

"I didn't want to trouble you."

"Trouble me?" Susanne was confused. What was going on with Gisela?

"I need to talk to you," Gisela said suddenly. She dropped down on the couch and put up her feet on the old armchair. When Henry realized his grandma had returned, he came waddling over to her. Gisela smiled and reached for him. She planted a kiss on his cheek and hugged him close, but Henry pulled free after only a few seconds and went back to where his sister was happily playing with the blocks in front of her.

"I need to talk to you, too. It's important," Susanne remembered, at the same time wondering what Gisela wanted to share with her.

Gisela looked up at her. Her eyes wide with surprise. "You do? What is it, Susanne?"

"No, you first."

Gisela only nodded and patted the empty couch space next to her. Susanne went over and sat down next to her mother-in-law, curious about what Gisela had to tell her but at the same time keenly aware of the horrible knot in her stomach. She would tell Gisela that they were leaving her. But not yet. Gisela had to share something first. She looked at her mother-in-law in anticipation.

Susanne saw Gisela hesitate. Her eyes hung on Henry and Jana. She swallowed and turned to Susanne. "What I have to tell you might be hard to take," Gisela said, taking Susanne's hand.

Susanne could only stare at Gisela. What was going on? This didn't sound good.

"I went to see Dr. Waldenberg today. Again."

Susanne's brows furrowed. Dr. Waldenberg? Again? She had no idea Gisela had been seeing the physician.

Gisela looked down at Susanne's hand now, stroking it. "I have cancer, Susanne," she said quietly.

Susanne didn't know if she had heard right. "What?" She had heard the words, but they weren't making any sense.

"Dr. Waldenberg said I have cancer. That's why I've been so tired," Gisela said, sighing.

"I'm... I'm so sorry," Susanne said, her voice hollow. This couldn't be happening. Cancer. Gisela had cancer. An all too familiar panic rose up in her, engulfing her, threatening to cut off the air. Susanne tried to concentrate on her breathing. She grabbed her mother-in-law by the shoulders and hugged her tightly. She didn't let go. She didn't want to let go. *Oh, Gisela,* she thought. *Gisela. Not you, too.* The memory of her own mother stung her fiercely. Her mother's hollow eyes and pain-stricken face, her frail body and morphine-induced blank stare came back to her mind with full force. Susanne felt dizzy. Heaviness pressed down on her. Gisela.

Gisela suddenly pulled free, and Susanne realized that she had hugged her mother-in-law too tightly.

"I know this is terrible. I'm trying to come to grips with it myself. I haven't, but I'll get there. The doctor says if I respond well to treatment, I will have a few good years left." Susanne knew Gisela tried to sound cheerful. "I know your mother died of cancer. I know how this must be for you. But Dr. Waldenberg is hopeful. I'm hopeful," Gisela said.

Susanne felt the tears coming. She didn't know what to say. She felt numb with fear. She refused to accept that she should lose another loved one. It was then that it hit her. Dieter! The realization took her breath away. She gasped for air. She was leaving. In two months. Gisela wouldn't be well enough in two months. Susanne stared at her mother-in-law.

"I won't be of much help to you," Gisela continued. "Useless, really. I'll have to go to the hospital to receive the treatment. At least six weeks, Dr. Waldenberg said. I'm sorry, Susanne." Gisela glanced at Henry, who was trying to pull a block out of his sister's hands. Jana screamed in protest, and Henry let go.

Susanne realized that Gisela might have taken her silence the wrong way. "You don't need to worry about us, Gisela. It's our turn to take care of you–" Susanne stopped herself, realizing what she had just said. She had to take care of Gisela. But that would mean–

"I can't ask that of you, Susanne," Gisela protested, shaking her head.

Susanne hesitated in her response, as if that which she was about to say would seal her fate. But then she realized that she had no choice. Her eyes filled with tears. The room started swimming in front of her and she realized she wasn't breathing. She took a deep breath, unaware of the tears that rolled down her face. She couldn't leave Gisela. Not now. She had to stay. *Dieter!* Her mind screamed his name. *Dieter, your mother has cancer. I can't come, Dieter. I can't.* How could she? Susanne tried to keep the despair out of her voice and forced a smile. "The twins are old enough now to go to childcare," she said without emotion, her voice hoarse. Susanne cringed at the thought of the caretakers in white clinical smocks taking care of Henry and Jana, indoctrinating them with the ideals of communism.

"Susanne, child, are you well?" Gisela asked, sounding worried.

Susanne stared at her and then threw herself into her arms, sobbing. "Oh, Gisela. I'm so sorry, so sorry." But the words she spoke were not only meant for her mother-in-law.

Gisela patted her back and from the tears that were wetting her shoulder, Susanne could tell that Gisela was crying as well.

Susanne didn't know how long they had been holding each other, but it had seemed a long while. Henry was tugging at her, trying to get her attention, and Jana had come over to her grandma, looking at her curiously and probably wondering why the grown-ups were crying.

Gisela pulled free. She took a handkerchief out of her purse and wiped her face. "What did you want to talk about?" Gisela asked suddenly, her voice hoarse.

Susanne looked at her. She felt her mouth move. She made it stop. She had to stop it. She couldn't tell Gisela. She wouldn't tell her. Gisela would want her to leave. But she wouldn't. Not now. They were all Gisela had. "It's nothing that can't wait," Susanne said, her voice sounding forlorn.

"But you said it was important, dear," Gisela protested.

"Your health is most important now. You'll be well again, Gisela. We'll get you well."

Gisela didn't protest this time. Susanne felt a new determination, but the fear wasn't gone. It was still there, only transformed into an all too familiar one. She had to tell Dieter. Not about his mother's cancer. She wouldn't. She couldn't. Dieter would go crazy and do something stupid. She knew he would try to find a way to return. And if he were to find a way into the country, what would the Stasi do to him if they caught him? She shuddered at the thought. She had to convince him that she decided not to join him in the West. But why? He would demand an explanation. She would have to tell him that she no longer loved him. The thought alone caused her so much pain, Susanne struggled for air. What else could she tell him? He would think that she gave up on them. How could she have him believe that? But she couldn't leave Gisela all by herself. For the first time in months, Susanne could clearly visualize Dieter's face. It seemed so real. She wanted to put her hand on his cheek. The tears welled up again as she realized he would never forgive her for this, for not leaving and for not telling him about Gisela's cancer if he ever found out.

That night Susanne couldn't find any sleep. She lay awake all night, staring at the ceiling she couldn't make out in the dark. She had cried for hours, desperation overwhelming her. She'd never felt this torn in her life. She had to give up Dieter for his mother. Her children would never meet their father. That was the cruel reality. It was too great of a sacrifice. There had to be another solution. There had to be. But was there? She had to talk to Georg. In the morning. As soon as there was light out. "He might think of something that I haven't thought of," Susanne whispered into the dark room. Something that included Gisela and Dieter. She strained her ears trying to listen for the first morning train leaving Wallhausen.

After what seemed like hours, she heard the train's whistle. *Morning*, she thought, got up and threw on her bathrobe.

Georg turned over. He blinked and saw that morning was just breaking outside. There it was again. Was that the doorbell? "Please, not today. It's too early," he mumbled and buried his face in the pillow. But whoever rang the doorbell was insistent. He had to get up. Georg peeled himself out of bed. Rudi was at his side in no time. He fumbled for his glasses and put them on. The doorbell rang again. "I'm coming," he grumbled, stumbling out of his bedroom.

Rudi already gave a low soft bark from the front door. *Someone we know*, Georg thought. Before he opened the door, he looked down at himself, regretting that he hadn't thrown his bathrobe over the undershirt and pajama bottoms he was wearing. He quickly ran his hand through the tousled black mess on his head and opened the door.

Georg was adjusting his glasses, his hand rubbing the stubble on his jaw. "Susanne?" She wore a bathrobe and no make-up. Her hair was in complete disarray. She looked as if she had just rolled out of bed. He saw her serious demeanor and opened the door wide. "Come in."

Susanne looked at his old couch but didn't sit down. She started pacing up and down. Georg watched her, waiting for her to begin.

"I need your help." Susanne stopped pacing and looked at him, her face anguished.

"Have you been crying?" Her eyes were red, and her voice was hoarse. What happened?

"All night," she said matter-of-factly.

"What's wrong?"

"I can't leave. I can't leave, Georg. I can't now."

The panic in her voice frightened him. Something had happened. "What do you mean?"

"I can't leave and go to the West, Georg. Not anymore."

Had he heard right? What was going on? He thought his heart jumped slightly. He had to keep his composure. There was no reason to get excited. Yet.

"Gisela. She has cancer. I can't just leave her. Without the cancer, it would have broken her heart. The twins. To leave her. But now? I can't just leave her," Susanne said, her voice frantic.

"Gisela has cancer?" Georg fell onto his couch, horrified by the news. "How bad is it?"

"I don't know." Susanne looked as if she hadn't thought about that. "She has to go in for treatment. At least six weeks. She might die, Georg." Susanne was pacing again, wringing her hands and biting her lip.

"Let's hope she'll respond to the treatment," Georg said quietly. Gisela had cancer and Susanne didn't want to leave her. Only rightly so. "I understand that you don't want to leave her."

"But what about Dieter? Look at how long we've been separated. And now I'm finally allowed to leave. What can I do, Georg? Help me. Tell me, what I can do."

Georg sighed heavily, his eyes on Susanne, who was still pacing. He was glad she considered staying. But how could he be happy when Gisela had cancer? Even if it was the reason Susanne would want to stay. "I don't know—"

"I can't take Gisela with me. They won't allow it," Susanne said, her face contorted from concentrating too hard.

"You can't tell Dieter she has cancer."

"I agree. I can't. He couldn't bear it."

Georg was glad they agreed. Susanne was right. Considering that Dieter would either worry or try to return without the sanction of the Stasi, they had to keep it from him. Gisela would do the same. He knew her well. She would want to keep it from him. She wouldn't want to worry her son, especially because he had no way to come see her. Dieter coming back? Georg wouldn't suggest it again. The Stasi didn't want to hear of it last time he tried.

"Maybe they'll let me leave once Gisela is better," Susanne suggested.

"I don't know how this is handled. You should ask someone. There might be a way around it," Georg said, picturing Fleischer. How would they handle him? Would they let Susanne stay as long as she wanted and then let her leave? He doubted that.

"You're right. I need to ask someone. The person who handles my case." Susanne stopped to turn to him. "Do you really think they'll let me stay a little while longer and then let me leave?" Her voice was doubtful.

"I don't know, Susanne." Georg didn't feel like destroying her hopes. "You can try."

"But what if they don't let me?" She stared out the window and then suddenly turned to him. "I think you've been right all along. Dieter has to come back." Georg looked at her, stunned. Did she mean it? "It's the only way we can be together. He has to come back if they don't let me stay and leave when Gisela is better again."

"But they'll put him in jail. If they even let him back in." Georg had heard the stories. Musicians, poets who had spoken out against the government. Expelled and never allowed to return. Not even for a visit. Fleischer had told him so himself. The state didn't want back traitors and defectors.

Susanne's face twitched. She looked as if she would start crying again. Georg went over to her. "We'll try. Talk to the person in charge to see how this is handled and then we'll reevaluate. What do you think?"

Susanne looked up at him and nodded. "But how am I supposed to tell Dieter?"

Her eyes started to fill with tears again. "How am I supposed to tell him I'm not coming?"

He took her into his arms and held her. His mind was racing, weighing the possibilities and savoring the thought that Susanne would stay. And if it turned out to be only for a while... He sighed, resting his cheek on her head and smelling her hair. He closed his eyes and held her just a tiny bit closer, letting her tears wet his white undergarment.

When Susanne phoned Fleischer in Berlin, he was certainly surprised to hear from her. To Susanne's great relief, he agreed to see her the following day. Now she regretted the things she had said to him when she had seen him last, thinking she would never have to deal with him again. But things had changed. Her life had taken another cruel turn.

All her hopes lay now with Fleischer. He had to have compassion for her situation. She would appeal to his human side. He had to have a mother who he loved.

"What brings you to me, Frau Schmidt," Fleischer asked when she was finally sitting across from him. His face was unreadable. She couldn't detect any curiosity.

"I need your help," Susanne said without hesitation. Fleischer's eyebrows rose. Susanne didn't wait for him to speak. She had to move in now. "Do you have a mother, Herr Fleischer?"

His eyes narrowed. "Of course, I do, Frau Schmidt, but I don't see what this has to do with you."

"My mother died of cancer eleven years ago."

"I'm sorry to hear that."

Susanne knew that he had knowledge of her mother's death. "Gisela Schmidt is my mother-in-law. She has cancer."

Fleischer nodded knowingly, and Susanne wondered for a split-second if he had been informed about that. "Again. I'm sorry to hear that."

"I can't leave her, Herr Fleischer. Not now. She needs me."

"I see," Fleischer said.

"I need to stay for a little while longer."

"You want to stay?" Fleischer asked, genuinely surprised.

"I need to stay," Susanne said firmly, but she couldn't stand his gaze and looked down at her hands. She sighed and looked back up at the man that she so despised. "Please let me stay until she is better and then you can ..." she swallowed. "... expel me."

Fleischer leaned back and folded his hands as if to pray. His mouth twisted into a smile. "We can't do that, Frau Schmidt."

"Why?" Susanne tried to keep the desperation out of her voice, but that was no use. He knew she was desperate.

"We can't let you stay. The deal has been finalized. You need to leave –"

"You could tell them that I don't want to leave anymore." What was she saying?

She wanted to leave, but not right away. All she needed was time. But they wouldn't give her the time she needed. "You could tell them ... that I've realized my mistake and that I don't want to be a citizen of an ... imperialist country."

Fleischer was laughing now. Susanne knew she sounded ridiculous. He knew her.

He knew her well. Fleischer knew she didn't feel that way, and he knew she never would.

"Then let my husband return." Susanne was pleading with him now.

"He doesn't want to return."

"How do you know that?" She looked into Fleischer's eyes and realized that he wasn't bluffing. Fleischer knew Dieter wouldn't want to come back. Somehow, he knew. She fell silent. What else was there to say? She felt numb. It was all hopeless.

"Do you still wish to stay?" His voice was ringing in her ears. "Frau Schmidt? I'm asking, do you wish to stay?"

She looked at him and slowly started to nod. They had won. She had to give up. The sharp pain she felt started to strangle her. Dieter. She would lose him. Susanne tried to picture his face and couldn't. It had been too long. It was over. She would lose him.

Fleischer didn't seem to notice her agony and went on relentlessly. "I can't promise you anything. You might still be expelled. However, you could write a letter, explaining your position to the West Germans. Make mention of your support for communism and your reasons for staying, of course."

Susanne looked up at him. He would use her for propaganda. And then another thought came to her. "Will my husband read this letter?"

"That's in the hands of the West Germans."

Susanne had never felt so utterly defeated in her life, not even when she had sat across from Fleischer for the first time. Back then, she still had hope. But now? It was over. She had to accept that.

"I promise I'll do everything in my power to help you stay in your native country." He looked at her thoughtfully. "Write a convincing letter, Frau Schmidt, and you'll be able to stay and care for your mother-in-law."

She nodded and got up. She left his office without another word. There was no need. It had all been said.

She couldn't leave Gisela alone. In return, she'd lose her only chance to get to Dieter in the West, to have her children grow up in a free country with their father. This was too great a sacrifice. How could she sacrifice Dieter's, her children's, and her own future for Gisela? Right away she felt guilty she had even thought it. Gisela had cancer. Just like her mother. She wouldn't miss another goodbye.

Georg was waiting at the platform for Susanne's train to arrive. He was anxious.

There were only a handful of people waiting on the only platform the Wallhausen train station had. This would be the final stop for Susanne's train or any train rolling into the village. The border was a dead end. No train would ever pass through. They would always stop here and turn back.

Georg couldn't wait to hear what Susanne had found out in Berlin. He had thought of something else after Susanne left his house yesterday morning. He had heard of people applying for exit visas to leave the country. The applications were denied all the time, but a few times, after a long wait, a few here and there had been approved. It could take years, if not a decade. And the persecution by the state would be intolerable. But it would be another way to have Susanne stay and not lose hope.

The train was announced and came into view within a minute. Georg decided to wait by the stairs that led off the platform. When he saw Susanne getting off the train, he couldn't stay there any longer and strode toward her. When she finally stood in front of him, he couldn't hold back the question any longer. "What did you find out?"

"Hello to you, too, Georg," Susanne said with a bite in her voice. It hadn't gone well. Georg bit his lip. She walked on and he followed her, waiting for her to tell him all.

"I can't stay and leave later. They won't allow it. Dieter doesn't want to return," she said, her voice hollow.

Georg remembered Dieter's words when they had talked on the day of the babies' christening. It had shocked him that his friend had been so opposed to the idea of returning.

"They'll let me stay if I explain myself to the West German government. But it will be indefinitely. They won't offer me another chance to leave." She stopped and looked at him. "I can't do that, Georg. I will leave. I have to explain it to Gisela. She'll understand."

"Of course, she'll understand. She loves you." Georg couldn't believe what he was hearing. "But would it be the right thing to do?"

"I can't sacrifice my family for Gisela. She wouldn't want that. She won't want it." Susanne started walking again and Georg took her arm. She stopped and looked at him, her brows furrowed.

"When you left yesterday, I remembered something," Georg said in a hushed voice, so people who passed them wouldn't hear. "There are people who apply for exit visas to leave the country. It's completely legal."

"People getting permission to leave? A visa?"

"Yes. It takes a while for them to be approved –"

"How long?"

Georg had to be truthful. "It can take years."

Susanne sighed. "Years. I've waited almost two years already. I can't wait anymore, Georg."

"Think about it. This might be the solution you've been looking for."

He could tell Susanne was deep in thought as they walked home. Absentmindedly, she waved her goodbye and disappeared into Gisela's house. All Georg could do now was wait and hope Susanne made the right decision.

When Susanne had put the kids down for the night and helped Gisela pack her bags for the hospital, she went into her own room that had once belonged to her husband. She leaned her forehead against the cold window glass and stared into the dark. *What should I do, Dieter?* How she longed to hear his voice, hear his advice. But she couldn't get his advice. Her eyes fell on the violin case next to her bed.

Susanne took out her instrument and walked over to the music stand by the window. She looked through her stack of sheet music and finally found what she had been looking for. Dieter's favorite piece. She took up her bow and started playing. Softly at first and then more vigorously. The familiar notes let her forget everything around her. The room dipped into a dark blue, and Dieter appeared in front of her, wearing the suit he had worn at their wedding. He smiled at her, nodding in encouragement. She played on, furiously. Dieter kept bobbing his head to the rhythm. He kept on smiling encouragingly, as if she needed encouragement.

Susanne stopped abruptly, and the room around her came back into view. She knew what to do. With a last look at the sheet music in front of her, she took her violin and bow and stored it away. Then she walked over to Dieter's small desk where he had done his homework as a youth. Susanne found a piece of paper in one of the drawers and started writing just as furiously as she had played her violin.

———

The day before she would drop off Gisela at the hospital to start her therapy, Susanne went downstairs to talk to her mother-in-law, but Gisela was nowhere to be found. She decided to go out and see if she was there and found her down the steps outside the backdoor, smoking.

As Susanne sat down, she took the cigarette from Gisela, put it out, and flung it in the bushes. Gisela only mildly protested.

"That was supposed to be my last one," Gisela said, her eyes fixed on the white Trabant parked in the carport.

Susanne followed her eyes and knew what Gisela was thinking about. "Those six weeks will go by fast. You'll be racing down Main Street again in no time. I'll watch over your baby." Gisela smiled at her weakly. "Do you have everything ready for tomorrow?" Susanne asked.

"As ready as one can be for this."

Susanne put her hand on her mother-in-law's arm. "Let us take care of you for a change."

"I don't want to be a burden."

"A burden? Who is the burden here?"

Gisela's smile was gone. "You're no burden, Susanne. You and the babies have been such a blessing. I wouldn't know what to do without you."

Susanne swallowed hard, trying to keep the oncoming tears out of her voice. Gisela could never know. Ever. That she and the kids had almost left her. "And we wouldn't know what to do without you. So, get better, will you?" Susanne choked out.

Gisela's smile returned. "I promise to do my best."

"What do you want me to tell Dieter when he calls?" Susanne asked carefully. She had to ask. He would ask to speak to his mother. And Gisela would be gone. Susanne knew Dieter would call. Soon. Once he found out. She swallowed down the nausea.

Gisela whipped around to her. "We can't tell him. No matter what. He would be worried sick."

Susanne nodded, and Gisela seemed to relax. "I'll think of something to tell him,"

Susanne said, knowing that it would be the most painful phone call of her life.

"I should go to bed. Who knows how much sleep they will let me get in that hospital," Gisela said suddenly and got up.

Susanne got up as well, and to her surprise, her mother-in-law hugged her tightly.

"I could have gotten no better daughter-in-law," Gisela whispered in her ear.

Susanne hugged her back, no longer trying to hold back the tears. "Good night, Gisela," Susanne sniffed.

When Georg came running over to her a week later, Susanne knew in an instant that Dieter was calling. She only nodded at Georg and made her way out the door. It seemed that every step she took toward the phone was harder to take. Susanne tried to slow herself down to catch her breath and gain the composure she so desperately needed for this phone call. When she took up the phone, she realized Georg was right behind her, breathing heavily. Sweat was glistening on his forehead. His face looked pained.

Dieter didn't spend any time on a greeting or inquiry after her well-being. His voice was thick with emotion. Susanne could tell he tried to restrain himself. "They showed me the letter, Susanne.

They put you up to this, didn't they? Why, Susanne? I don't understand."

"It's more than that, Dieter." So much more, she added in her head.

"Explain it to me, Susanne. Why? Why won't you come?" Dieter sounded as desperate as she felt.

"I can't hurt them again," she said, trying to sound firm.

"Them?"

"Your mother and... Georg. I can't, Dieter. I have to stay." She had to be strong.

"My mother will be fine without us. And what about Georg?"

"It's not like that." Dieter was getting the wrong idea.

"I'm your husband, Susanne. Henry and Jana's father. Susanne! Put Georg on the phone, Susanne. Put him on!" Dieter was beside himself now.

Susanne hesitated. This was between Dieter and her. There was no need for Dieter to talk to Georg. Susanne reluctantly handed the phone to Georg. She saw her hand shaking.

"Georg! You bastard!" Susanne could hear Dieter scream at Georg. *This isn't Georg's doing,* Susanne thought angrily. How could Dieter think that this had anything to do with him?

Georg didn't say anything. Susanne could hear Dieter go from yelling at Georg to pleading with him. She could tell it was torturing Georg. They had been best friends all their lives. But Georg continued to listen silently. He didn't respond to any of Dieter's accusations.

Susanne took the phone from Georg. "There is nothing going on between Georg and me. There never will be. Why don't you believe me? He is your friend and mine, Dieter. Nothing more." She looked at Georg and was startled by what she read in his eyes. All of a sudden it dawned on her. Diana's words rang in her memory. Her friend had been right. Georg had feelings for her.

She was still staring at Georg, who had turned away from her, when Dieter called her back to the painful reality of their phone call. "Susanne, I really don't understand. We've been waiting for this for so long. How can you not want to come, now that you can finally leave ... unless ... unless you don't love me anymore." Dieter's voice was breaking.

Susanne felt dizzy. She had a hard time sorting her thoughts, trying to remember why she was about to hurt her husband like this. And then she remembered. She pushed the thought of Georg aside. Dieter wouldn't easily accept her decision. She had expected no less. She had hoped it wouldn't have to come to this. But she saw now that she didn't have a choice anymore. "It has been so long. I have a life here, Dieter." These were the words of a stranger. She hated herself for saying them.

There was silence at the other end. Susanne held her breath. She didn't dare to breathe. Her eyes closed, and she tried to picture Dieter at the other end of the line.

"Susanne, is this really how you feel?" he asked quietly into the silence.

Susanne nodded, tears starting to trickle down her cheeks. She realized that he couldn't see her nod. "Don't you feel the same?"

"No!" He shouted it.

His last word took her breath away, and she had to steady herself. Her tears were flowing freely now. There was no use. This was too painful for them to endure any longer. She had to be strong. "It was my decision, my decision alone, Dieter. Don't blame them. If there is anyone to blame, it's me. For everything, Dieter. For everything." The tears choked her voice. She cleared her throat, but it came out feebly. "I'm so sorry, Dieter. Everything is my fault. I should have never –" She sobbed into the phone, her tears falling onto the mouthpiece. "I need to... let you go, Dieter. It's for the best. Hopefully, someday you'll feel the same... as I do." Someday he would understand why she had chosen to stay.

Someday, she hoped, he would be grateful that she had been there for his mother. But would he forgive her for not telling him that his mother had cancer?

She could still hear Dieter's voice scream out in desperation when she hung up the phone. This time it wasn't the Stasi that had ended the call. Her hands were shaking when she sat down next to the phone. She stared at the wall across from her. The yellowish wallpaper started to peel off along the cutting line. Susanne felt sick to the stomach. It had been the most difficult decision of her life. She had given up on them. For now. In time, she would find the strength to explain it all to Dieter. It would be a long letter, but she had to wait before she could write it.

Georg handed her a handkerchief. Out of the corner of her eye, through the blurred vision the tears were causing, she thought she saw him cry as well. She had never seen Georg cry before. It cut her to the core. He had lost his best friend for good. And it was her fault.

Susanne got up slowly. Without a word, she went over to Georg and put her arms around his neck, pulling his head onto her shoulder. Only after what seemed like an eternity did he put his arms around her. They stood there, holding on to each other, Georg wetting her shoulder and Susanne too keenly aware of all the pain she had caused.

Part II

1988

Chapter 17

Henry Schmidt felt the adrenaline pump through his veins. His eyes were fixed on the cinder track below, every muscle in his body as tight as a bowstring. He glanced at the competitor next to him and saw him breathing heavily. *Slow your breathing*, he reminded himself, and concentrated on every single breath.

Someone from the sideline yelled, "Set!" Henry got in position and waited for the gun signal. There it was. They shot out of their starting blocks like stones out of slings.

It was over faster than Henry could think. His body lunged forward and threw himself across the finish line. An experienced look to the left and right told him he had won the final heat. He bent forward and tried to catch his breath. Someone patted him enthusiastically on the back. "A new best time, my boy." His coach gave a satisfied grunt. "If you keep going like this, you'll be at Nationals next year."

Henry gave a half-hearted smile and shook his coach's hand while searching the crowd of people sidelining the track. He found who he was looking for. He took his spike-shoes off and handed them to the coach to walk barefooted to the dark-haired man with the black rimmed glasses who was now coming toward him with his duffle bag.

As Georg handed him his bag, Henry heard the coach call after him. "Don't be late for the medal ceremony again." Henry ignored him and took a pair of shoes and gray sweatpants out of his bag. He put them on quickly and grinned at Georg. "Told you this would be an easy one. These guys are no competition for me."

"Well, congrats anyway. A little less arrogance would suit you well." They both grinned at each other.

"Let's get out of here," Henry said, running his hand through his blond curls.

"Don't you have another event? Long jump?"

Henry waved it off. "Not in the mood."

Georg shrugged his shoulders. "It's your life. The coach won't let you get away with that."

Henry laughed it off. He knew his coach would make a big fuss and threaten him to never let him start again, but he wasn't in the mood to please anyone today.

They left the stadium and made their way to the train station.

"Thanks for coming today," Henry said after a while.

"No problem. I like track-and-field meets. I was pretty good myself when I was young. If I may say so. Ask the coach."

"He was your coach back then? How old is he?" Henry couldn't believe how long the coach had been around.

"Stop gaping. I'm not that old," Georg said in exasperation. He pushed the button on the traffic light, and they waited for the little green man to appear on the pedestrian light.

"What events did you do?" Henry asked.

"I wasn't fast like you. I was more of an endurance kind of guy. The longer the race, the better. The 10,000-meter race really was my specialty. Without bragging or anything, I was the District Champion in 1965."

Henry was truly impressed. He had never heard anything about Georg being a runner. His mother had told him how his father had been a sprinter, just like him, as a youth, but no one had said anything about Georg. He looked at Georg and realized that his father would never see him compete. But Georg had always been at his competitions since he began competing in fifth grade.

"Your father and I went to practice together. Three times a week. We always warmed up together, but we had to work on different things," Georg said, his eyes far off.

The traffic light started blinking. They crossed the street and held their breath in the cloud of exhaust fumes. Henry now wondered why Georg had never told him this before. He had never mentioned his own sporting past, or his father's, for that matter.

"We were pretty good back then. I have a few medals of my own," Georg continued.

"Who cares about medals," Henry said. "They're just a piece of metal. They're not even real. Of course, if they were real, I would only be interested in the gold." He grinned at Georg, who rolled his eyes.

"Well, if you work hard enough, you could get all the way to the top. You're definitely fast. You just need to work harder, and the Olympics wouldn't be out of the question."

"The Olympics," Henry snorted and pulled a face.

"Isn't that any athlete's dream? Why do you race then?"

"I just like the way it feels when I win."

"Then just imagine what it would feel like racing at the Olympics and maybe even winning," Georg said.

"I don't think they would let someone like me go to the Olympics."

"Why not? You're very good."

Henry knew that Georg knew exactly why not. "Let *me* travel abroad for the Olympics? *Me*, the son of a dissident? And they have noticed I don't fall in line easily, as you know." Henry decided to change the topic. "So, when we get back to Wallhausen, will you have dinner with us tonight?"

"If your mama lets me."

"Of course, she will. You know that. By the way, I'm glad that woman dumped you."

"Excuse me?" Georg looked irritated. "Irene didn't dump me, we agreed to separate."

"Whatever. I'm just glad you can come over for dinner more often now." The train station came into view. Henry checked his watch and then glanced at Georg, who was still brooding. "There's still time for an ice cream cone." Georg's face lightened up, and he grinned.

"Any time. My treat today."

———

When Henry walked onto the school grounds the following Monday, everyone looked at him. He knew why. They had heard of his win. He passed a group of girls who burst into giggles. Henry rolled his eyes and sighed. It would pass. Two days, and they would forget and leave him alone.

When he entered his classroom, his teacher stepped toward him and shook his hand. "Well done, Henry." Henry just nodded. He felt the burning eyes of his classmates and took his hand from the teacher, who couldn't stop shaking it. On the way to his desk, he glanced at his sister, who looked genuinely annoyed. When he sat down next to his friend, Christian gave him thumbs up while the teacher started writing Russian verbs on the board.

When Herr Ronwitzki turned around to them, he raised his arms and led them all in the chorus of Russian verb conjugations. Henry stared out the window into the overcast sky. Fall was here, and another dreary winter lay ahead. Henry felt his lips move to the monotonous rhythm of the verb conjugations, but his mind was somewhere else.

———

"We can't possibly award her with that." Sylvia Müller, biology teacher at the only secondary school in Wallhausen, was furious. "Her mother tried to defect to the West and keeps trying to leave. And her father. And not to mention her brother. Think of it. What example would that set?"

The principal rubbed her forehead. "Sit down, Sylvia. Compose yourself."

Sylvia Müller fell into the old armchair and stared at the principal, who was a tall, slim woman with a stern demeanor. But she wasn't as stern as she looked, and as Sylvia Müller had hoped. She looked at the principal in frustration. Even behind her desk she looked long and wiry. In the presence of that woman, she felt even more petite than she already was.

Sylvia Müller listened apprehensively as the principal went on about Jana Schmidt and how she had earned the highest decoration the school bestowed. She couldn't believe what she was hearing. In her day and time, this wouldn't have happened. This girl didn't deserve it.

"She's our best student..." the principal went on. "... and besides, I haven't seen someone pass the exam with such bravura in years. That girl deserves it. You can't pick your family, Sylvia. She's living proof," the principal said while scribbling her signature onto what looked like a certificate.

Sylvia Müller opened her mouth in protest, but the principal raised her hand. "The decision is final. She seems to be a very loyal girl. Maybe she will instill pride in her mother."

Sylvia Müller got up, tight-lipped. She doubted that Susanne Schmidt would feel any pride in her daughter's accomplishment. "You are to inform her this instant," Sylvia heard the principal say as she walked to the door. "We'll award her at this week's assembly."

Sylvia turned around. "But she has geography right now."

"I am sure Helga won't mind you interrupting for a bit." The principal got up and nodded a brief goodbye. Without another word, Sylvia Müller left the principal's office that she once thought to be the only refuge in this school. She headed up the stairs and stopped in front of a door. Knocking wouldn't be necessary. She went inside the classroom where maps of the GDR and the USSR adorned the walls. The students were reciting the Soviet republics with their capitals and did not stop until the geography teacher raised her hand when she saw Sylvia standing in the front of her class.

"I need to speak to Jana Schmidt, if I may?" Sylvia said to the teacher.

The geography teacher only nodded, and Sylvia proceeded toward Jana who looked at her with her big brown eyes. With her curly brown hair, she was the spitting image of her mother. That girl couldn't possibly think she was in trouble. Miss Perfect always did as she was asked.

"Will you accept the gold decoration for great knowledge in Marxism-Leninism?" Sylvia Müller asked coolly. Jana just stared at her. The girl had no idea what she was talking about, and someone like that would receive this kind of honor. It was just ridiculous. "What's your answer, girl?" Sylvia Müller tried to keep the annoyance out of her voice, but she knew she failed to do so. It didn't matter. She was sure Jana Schmidt knew she had always disliked her and her family.

"Okay," Jana said feebly.

"Does that mean yes?" Sylvia Müller was sure the girl had gotten that kind of language from illegally watching West German TV.

"Yes, Frau Müller," Jana said, no less feebly than before. She still looked confused.

"Well, then … It will be awarded at the assembly. This Friday." With that, Sylvia Müller turned her back on Jana and stalked off. There was no need for further talk.

"She doesn't seem to be very happy about it, does she?" Jana's friend Bianca said, following Jana's eyes, which stared at Frau Müller, talking quietly to the geography teacher now. Both teachers looked at her.

Jana turned to Bianca, sitting next to her. "Gold?"

"You must have aced that exam. You're quite the communist, you know. I had no idea," Bianca teased, dodging Jana's hand as she tried to slap her arm.

"But I'm sure more people than I did well on that exam."

"Gold rarely gets awarded. And it's not just for that. You must have made an impression on someone. To receive gold is actually a great honor. Really," Bianca said, trying to keep her voice to a whisper. She had realized that those around them were listening intently while the two teachers at the front of the classroom conversed quietly and weren't paying any attention to them at the moment.

"I wonder what my mother will think. She won't think it a great honor, I am sure," Jana said, biting her lip and looking at the teacher who had to be talking about something else now because they were chatting away happily.

When the school bell rang, Frau Müller left first. Classmates filed out after her. Jana and Bianca also made their way out of the classroom, but Jana was held back by the geography teacher. "It's a great honor, Jana. Congratulations. You deserve it. You did an outstanding job on the exam."

Henry came walking over to them. Jana hadn't realized he was still there. "You've always been a red sock, and you always will be." His tone was sarcastic, and Jana found her hands in fists. Henry seemed to have noticed her reaction. "Take it easy, sis, I'm just kidding." He tugged his blond curls behind his ear and gave her a little friendly shove.

Jana saw the geography teacher turn away from them to pack her bag. "Yeah, sure you are," she gave back in sarcasm of her own. "You're just jealous."

"Yes, I am," Henry said and grinned. They both laughed and headed for the door. When they walked down the stairs, Henry whispered, "You're not going to accept that, are you?" He was serious now.

"I'll give it some thought," Jana said, knowing she would. Who wouldn't? She had to think ahead. If she wanted to get into the university of her choice and study medicine, she needed the state on her side.

She saw Henry's lips tighten and changed the topic. "So, you still need some help with your physics homework?"

"I've actually done it already," Henry said.

Jana doubted that he had. Well, it was his problem. If he was out to get bad grades, there was nothing she could do to prevent that.

"Your coach and the principal were here today while you were in school." Henry looked up at his mother and stopped spooning his lunch. "They are insisting you go to that sports school." His mother had her arms folded. Her eyes were scrutinizing him.

"I told them last year I didn't want to."

"And why is that, Henry? They're being very generous, considering... considering I'm your mother. You don't know the opportunities you'll have. The training you will receive there. You could travel abroad for competitions." Susanne Schmidt was leaning forward now.

Henry could hardly bear her hard look, but there was nothing to discuss. "And then come back to this? No thanks. Besides, who wants to be ordered around all day? Do you know how much training they get at that school? Six hours every day. In addition to school work. That's not for me."

"Then what is for you, Henry? What do you want to do with your life?"

"I don't know yet." He stared down at the soup in front of him as if it would yield an answer.

"Well, your grades will decide that for you. They won't let you go on with school.

They'll make you do an apprenticeship at the local LPG. Clean up after cows and pigs? Is that what you want out of life? Look at your sister. Did you hear what they want to award her with?"

"I'm not my sister. I don't care about these things." Henry dropped the spoon and got up. He didn't feel like fighting with his mother today.

"I know you don't care about these things. Neither do I. But just think about it, Henry. You could do so much better."

He knew she tried to pacify him. Henry sighed. "I don't want to go there. They can't make me."

"No, they can't, and I won't either."

Her answer didn't surprise him. He knew how she felt about living in this country. How she felt about the government. He understood her completely. And she knew that he understood her and that he felt the same.

"I told them to stop asking," she said.

"Thank you."

"They weren't happy." Henry hadn't expected any less. "But you still should think about what to do with your life."

"I know." Henry knew she was right.

His mother got up as well. She looked at his soup. "Now go on and finish that soup. It's not that bad, is it?" He shook his head and grinned at her. "Sit down already."

He sat back down and resumed spooning his soup. His mother turned and went over to the stove. Henry looked out the kitchen window and observed the sky. It was overcast. *Perfect,* he thought, and then smiled thankfully at his mother, who dished up more soup for him.

Henry cursed at the stairs that squeaked as he made his way down. There was no moonlight falling through the tall windows, so he had to find his way by touch only. He made it safely to the back door, even though he was sure someone must have heard him. With another look back toward the pitch-black foyer, he grasped the old key and, with his own body weight against the door, turned it. It had always been hard to turn that key, but tonight it unlocked the door easily and Henry slipped out into the moonless night.

They didn't live far from the school. Henry tried to stay in the shadows of the old linden trees and when he got to the street corner, he looked anxiously to the south. Would he come?

"I'm here," someone said from behind the hedges along the fence that lined the school grounds.

Henry whipped around. "Shh. How come you've never learned how to whisper?"

"I know how to whisper."

"No, you don't. Believe me."

A boy stepped out from behind the hedges. It was Christian. Henry's classmate and best friend since kindergarten. "What if we get caught?" Christian asked.

Henry could tell that Christian was nervous. For a moment he wished he hadn't involved his friend. He could have done this alone. But it was more fun like this. They always had hatched up plans for new pranks and carried them out together. Like when they had opened all the gates of the pigsties at the local LPG and let out all the animals. It had taken the workers days to find all the pigs that had scattered throughout the village and its surrounding fields and forests. No one had caught the culprits. And so it would be tonight. It had to be because this could really get them in trouble. His thoughts turned momentarily to his mother and the conversation they had had over lunch. He shook his head and turned to Christian. "Let's go."

They crouched forward along the hedges until the main school building came into view. The gate in the fence stood open as usual.

"Could they find out who it was?" Christian asked in a hushed voice.

Henry shrugged. "How?"

"Handwriting?"

"Nah," Henry waved it off. "Anyone could have written these block letters."

Christian seemed to buy his explanation. "Let's get to the stairs now," Henry said, motioning with his chin to the stone steps that led to the main entrance of the school building.

He went first. Christian followed him. They entered the school grounds through the open gate. They took their steps carefully on the noisy gravel, ducking their heads low. If someone were to be out, he or she would be able to spot them. But then there was no moon out tonight. The street lantern from around the corner wouldn't be enough to reveal them.

Suddenly Henry saw something move across the stairs. He held his breath and stretched out his arm to stop Christian, who had come up beside him. They listened intently, and then Henry saw what had caught his attention. "Just a cat," he whispered, and started moving again.

When they reached the stairs, they went around them. They crouched down and carefully lifted the heavy crate off the basement window well next to the stairs. Henry reached in and drew out a roll of fabric. He handed it to Christian and then replaced the crate. Together they went up the stairs and unfurled the fabric. With pins they had brought, they fastened the fabric to the old wooden school door, pushing the pins in with all their might. Then they stepped back and looked at their work. They grinned at each other in satisfaction and left, knowing school tomorrow would be quite different.

Jana wondered what the commotion was on the steps that led inside the school building. It was almost eight and school would start in only a few minutes. Yet, it seemed as if almost all students were still outside, gathering around the entrance, seemingly waiting to be let in. Students were pushing past her, brushing along her freshly ironed black pants and blue blouse. Jana was one of the few who were already wearing the uniform blouse of the Free German Youth. Most stuffed it in their schoolbags and threw it on right before assembly. But today's assembly would be special, and she needed to look immaculate. Her brown curls were pulled back into a neat ponytail and she even had put on a little of her mother's lipstick.

Henry walked up next to her. He had still been asleep when she had left only ten minutes ago and had probably only rolled out of bed and thrown on his clothes. And of course, he wasn't wearing his blue shirt yet. He probably hadn't even brought it. His blond hair that reached almost down to his chin was a tousled mess.

"I wonder what's going on there. Come on, sis, let's check it out," he said and pulled her with him.

Jana didn't resist. She was curious herself and if no one was in class yet, she couldn't get in trouble for being late.

Jana stared at the letters on the banner that was pinned to the door. She couldn't believe what she was reading. She didn't care anymore about the people who elbowed their way past her.

"Quite the statement, isn't it," Henry said.

Jana felt that Henry was watching her, waiting for her reaction. "Who would write such a thing?"

"It could have been anyone, really. Could have been me, you know."

Jana slapped his arm. "Shush it, Henry. People might take you seriously." She nervously looked around, but no one was paying any attention to them. Everyone was talking excitingly, even though in hushed voices. "Why hasn't anyone removed it?" Jana tried to crane her neck to see if any teachers were around. She saw the math and physics teachers guarding the door. But why?

The answer came when two men in long gray coats pushed their way through the crowd of students, eventually making their way up the steps to where the banner was flapping lightly against one side of the wooden door in the morning breeze. Everyone knew they were Stasi, or at least all of the older students did. They talked to the teachers and one of them disappeared into the building. The other cupped his hands and started to yell at everyone to move inside quickly. They all obeyed. Students started to file inside, casting down their eyes when they passed the Stasi man and the banner.

When Jana and Henry had made it to their classroom, Bianca greeted them at the door. "Did you see that?" she asked unnecessarily.

"I just wonder why they left it up for all to see. The teachers are here early. Why didn't they take it down? No one would have known," Jana thought aloud.

"They didn't touch anything because they had to wait for the Stasi to secure the crime scene. They don't want to get in trouble. Or worse, be accused of tampering with evidence," Henry said matter-of-factly.

Just then, their teacher, Herr Ronwitzki, came in, his face grim. He didn't greet them. Everyone hurried to his or her seats and he instantly started to throw questions about the new vocabulary at them.

Jana thought about the words that had been written on the banner with bright red paint. Peace to the Volk, War on the Communists! Down with the GDR! Not anyone could have written it. She felt Bianca's elbow in her side and looked up into Herr Ronwitzki's impatient face. "вольность," she said, glad she had reviewed the vocabulary last night.

———

When Jana stepped out of English class a few hours later, Bianca, who had been taking another class, came toward her. "Assembly is cancelled today," she said.

"Why?" Jana asked, knowing the answer already.

"Because of what happened today. I think this is serious. If they called out the Stasi to investigate, whoever has done this will be in major trouble," Bianca said, scanning the crowd around her.

"I'm just glad we get to go home early," Jana pretended. She had been looking forward to getting that decoration today.

"It would even be better if it were a Saturday and not a Friday."

"I agree," Jana said. She had always hated going to school on Saturdays.

"Do you want to do homework together today?" Bianca asked.

"Sure. Let's go to my house. What's due tomorrow?"

"Only Math. Russian and Chemistry are not until Monday."

They left the school grounds and made their short way home to Jana's house. They were greeted by Susanne, who had already heard what had happened at school. News like that spread quickly through a village.

"Did they find out who did it?" Susanne asked the girls over lunch.

"No, they haven't yet, Frau Schmidt," Bianca said eagerly. "But the Stasi is investigating. I'm sure they'll find the culprit soon."

"I see," Susanne replied.

Jana looked at her mother, who seemed deep in thought. "Assembly was cancelled today," she said, trying to get her mother's attention.

"Really?" Susanne asked absentmindedly and got up.

Jana's eyes narrowed. Did her mother even care that she would have been awarded the gold decoration? Or had she simply forgotten about it?

"I have to go," Susanne said suddenly. "You girls can manage without me, right? Jana, could you please do the dishes?"

Before Jana could answer, her mother had left the kitchen. She wondered what had gotten into her.

Susanne had felt sick when she had learned what had happened at school from the grocer this morning. She had heard the women, gathered around the cases of yogurt and milk, gossip frantically. Usually she didn't care, but as more and more women and even some men began to gather and listen to what was being discussed, she knew something extraordinary had happened. She went over to the grocer stacking cases of fresh cabbage and asked him about it. When he had finished his account, Susanne understood why everyone was talking. She had left the store in a haze, repeating the grocer's account over and over again in her head.

The sick feeling didn't subside when Susanne got home, and not even when she had questioned Jana and Bianca about it over lunch. She had the terrible feeling that Henry had something to do with it. Was it the red paint stains she had found on the floor of the carport? She had to talk this through with Georg. She might just be imagining things that weren't really there. After all, Henry wouldn't be so stupid to do something like that. He knew better. Or did he?

Susanne knocked on Georg's front door. Her eyes lingered on the sign next to his doorbell. She was grateful that Georg had decided to run his practice out of the back of his house and to hire her as his assistant, even though she had no experience at all.

She had never returned to the factory. That had been the upside of those terrible years of Gisela's battle with cancer. She had been allowed to care for her mother-in-law, and the state had supported her financially. Money had been tight during those five years, but she had managed until she had put in her first application to leave the country only a month after Gisela's death. That was when things changed. The state no longer supported her, and Georg had suggested employing her. She had refused at first, but Georg and her desperate situation had convinced her. She had to think of her kids, and even though Gisela had left everything to her, Susanne had understood that she needed a steady income.

Even though she had been reluctant to work with Georg, it had turned out to be the best solution. Georg had been generous. Whenever the kids had been sick, Susanne had been able to take time off. In the beginning, she hadn't been of much help to Georg, but he had patiently taught her to care for the animals and assist him when he had to operate. To her great surprise, she had been able to tolerate the smell, blood, and even the constant feeling of the pity she felt toward the animals. They worked well together, and above all, Georg had been nothing but professional.

Georg had never openly admitted or even suggested he had feelings for her since that dark day when she had told Dieter she wouldn't go to the West. Susanne had even begun to think that she had imagined what she saw in Georg's eyes that day. Although Georg had been distant for the first few weeks after, their friendship was as strong as ever, even when Georg got serious with other women. Unfortunately, none of them stuck around. Georg blamed it on the women's refusal to move to the Restricted Zone and his lack of commitment. In Wallhausen, he had long been known as the stout bachelor, which explained the female population's lack of interest in the vet in their midst. The few single women in their village were seeking relationships resulting in marriage. Susanne had long thought that Georg had missed the boat, feeling almost sorry for him. But he always insisted that marriage was not for him. While he never said so, Susanne assumed that it had to do with his parents' relationship, which he had described to her as abusive.

Susanne knocked again, but still no one answered. *Georg must still be working,* she thought, growing increasingly more anxious about Henry. She needed to talk to Georg. He always saw things more clearly. She made her way around to the back of the house and the small annex that housed Georg's practice. She knocked and found him inside, taping the beak of a beautiful parakeet.

"Whose is that? He's beautiful," Susanne said, stunned about the beauty of the colorful bird. The only time she had seen one had been at the zoo.

"She's beautiful, isn't she?"

Susanne walked over to Georg and lightly touched the feathers of the bird. It was shaking, and she withdrew her hand. "It's the dentist's," Georg explained. "The beak got infected. Some fungus, I think." He turned to her. "What brings you over here? It's your day off."

Susanne was glad Georg decided to skip the small talk. She was anxious to hear his opinion. "It's Henry. I think he has something to do with what happened at the school today. Have you heard?" Georg only nodded, his eyes concerned. "I found traces of red paint outside. In the carport. The grocer told me the writing on the banner was red. He didn't say anything about paint, though." Susanne looked at Georg, waiting for a reaction from him. She couldn't tell what he was thinking, so she went on. "It could be nothing, but I think I ought to talk to Henry."

To her great dismay, Susanne realized that Georg looked more concerned by the minute.

"Is he home?" he asked.

"He wasn't when I left. Maybe he is now."

"Let me talk to him," Georg offered. He took the parakeet and put it into a cage.

"Would you? I know he listens to you more than to me," Susanne said, glad Georg had offered to talk to Henry.

"I don't know about that, Susanne."

"But he might be more honest with you." She started for the door, but then turned around. "Georg, what if it *was* him? What are we going to do? If they found out it was him –" She shuddered at that thought.

"I'll come with you," Georg said, taking off his white lab coat. "If he's not there, we'll be there when he gets home."

"Thank you."

They left Georg's practice and the parakeet behind and together headed over to Susanne's. The sickening feeling increased with every step Susanne was taking. There was no longer a question in her mind whether it had been Henry. Everything pointed to him. The only question was how they could get Henry out of this mess.

—————

Henry came home whistling. He was in a good mood. Assembly had been cancelled, and even more important, the banner had the effect he had hoped for. He stopped whistling when he saw his mother and Georg on the couch, staring straight at him as if they had been waiting for him.

"Sit down, Henry," his mother said.

He could tell she tried to restrain her emotions. He sat down and looked them straight in the eye. They knew. His mother would be on his side, understand his actions. She felt as he did. But Georg?

214

Georg always lived by the rules, and his mother held his opinions in high regard. His mother wouldn't excuse his actions, but she would understand them.

"We have to ask you a few questions, and I want you to be as honest as you can, all right?" Georg said.

"Fair enough," Henry said. *They aren't sure it was me,* he thought.

"Your mother found traces of red paint in the carport. Did you write and put up that banner on the school doors, Henry?" Georg asked, his voice low and eerily quiet.

Henry knew in an instant that he should have cleaned up more carefully after himself. "Yes," he said simply, bracing himself for their reactions.

His mother's hands flew to her mouth and Georg looked at him. He looked resigned and disappointed. He had never seen Georg look at him that way.

"How could you –" Georg began, but Susanne put a hand on his arm and stopped him.

"This has gone too far, Henry." She got up, her eyes blazing at him. "You will clean the carport. And you will bury the leftover paint in the forest somewhere." His mother looked at him, her eyes full of determination. He knew that she would mean what she said next. "And you will go to that sports school." She left and Henry stared at the door through which she had disappeared.

"If they find out, Henry ..." Georg didn't need to finish his sentence.

"They won't."

"Then you better go and do what your mother told you to do," Georg said.

Henry knew there was no use in arguing, but door in hand, he turned around to look at Georg. "I won't go to that school. I swear to you."

Chapter 18

The air was cold and moist. Susanne shivered as she made her way through the cemetery, which looked more like a park. Tall birch trees stood throughout like a protective roof for those laid to rest there. The pathways that wound through the cemetery were lined with heaps of leaves the gardener had piled up.

Despite the lousy weather, the cemetery was bustling. The villagers were preparing the graves for winter and tomorrow's holiday. It was the last Sunday of November and the day set aside to commemorate the dead. Everyone was expected to have the graves ready by the holiday. The gravesites were tidied up and brushwood was put on the graves to protect the plants from cold, frost, and snow.

Susanne made her way through the rows of graves and looked for the gray tombstone at the end of the last row. She sighed when she stood in front of it. She dropped the bundle of brushwood she had brought, pulled out the garden tools, and crouched down to weed and rake.

Two older women greeted Susanne as they passed her. She only acknowledged them with a nod. She didn't want to give them any chance for small talk. She didn't feel like it. The holiday tomorrow was always a somber day for her. It was the day she was reminded of all the loved ones she had lost. Her mother. Her grandmother. Susanne involuntarily glanced up at the gray tombstone with its golden lettering. Gisela.

Her mother-in-law had died about five years after she had told her that she had cancer. Gisela had struggled on for those years, and at the end she had succumbed. Susanne had been at her side at the hospital when she died. It had been a heartrending experience. Gisela had suffered from excruciating pain, and it had cost Susanne all to see her like that. At the end, Susanne had wondered if it had truly been better to see her mother-in-law in that state. In so much pain. Only a fraction of her former self. But Susanne had been there for her until the end, and for that she was glad.

Susanne got up with a sigh, gathered up the weeds, and carried them over to the compost. When she got back to the grave, she wiped her hands clean on her pants and then leaned forward to rub traces of a spider web off the golden letters embossed on the marble stonework. The tombstone felt ice cold to the touch, and Susanne shuddered involuntarily. Gisela had been dead for years, but Susanne still found it difficult to visit the grave and take care of it. She missed her terribly and coming here not only reminded her of losing her mother-in-law, but also her husband. Until the end, Gisela had insisted she not tell Dieter that she was dying of cancer. And Susanne had obeyed her wishes, agreeing that it was better not to worry him. There would have been nothing he could have done for her.

Susanne stared at the golden letters. The memory of calling Dieter and telling him that his mother had died was forever engraved in her memory. Susanne was sure Dieter had hated her since that day. And who could blame him? She certainly didn't. First, she had broken his heart when she didn't join him in the West, and then she had kept Gisela's illness from him. Dieter's reaction to the news had been utter silence. She told him that it had been for the best not to tell him about Gisela's cancer and that she had only obeyed his mother's wishes. He didn't accept her explanation and had hung up. That had been the last day she had spoken to him. He never called her again. The only time she heard from him was when he sent packages for the kids' birthday. The letters accompanying the gifts always included a greeting for her. Nothing more, nothing less. With every birthday, she was reminded that he had not forgiven her.

Susanne wiped at the hot tears that were rolling down her cold cheeks. She took the brushwood and pulled it apart to spread it out over the grave, covering up all plants and perennials. *That should do it,* she thought, and collected her things to leave. She glanced once more at the tombstone that was as gray as the November sky above. She wouldn't lose Henry, too. It was his face and his blond curls that reminded her of Dieter daily. If anything were to happen to him ... She would protect what she had left. By all means necessary.

Susanne fell onto the couch next to Jana, holding an envelope in her hand.

"What's this?" Jana asked.

"Another denial." Susanne tried to keep the resignation out of her voice.

"I don't know why you keep trying, Mama. This is our home." Jana got up. "It doesn't really help that you keep applying to leave the country. Half the teachers hate me."

"There is nothing wrong with you."

"I know that," Jana said.

Susanne felt the sting. She really hadn't made life any easier for the kids. On the contrary. But she wanted to get them out of here. Give them a future. Have them meet their father.

"If I want to go on with school and get into university, I need you to stop this. They'll never let me go if you keep applying. They'll deny it anyway. What's the use?"

Susanne knew Jana was right. Since Gisela's death, she had applied for visas to leave the country. With today's letter, it made three denials. Should she keep trying? The answer came to her instantly. She had to. They wouldn't deny her request many more times. Eventually, they would approve her application and issue an exit visa for them. It had to happen by next year. For Jana's sake. And Henry's. It had to.

Jana finally received her gold decoration at the assembly the following week. As they stood at attention in their blue shirts in a u-shape formation across from the principal and a party official, Jana was called forward. She tried to stride confidently across the schoolyard but felt insecure and embarrassed. When she arrived in front of the principal, she saluted her and the government official. They shook her hand and congratulated her, and she was handed the small decoration and a certificate. Out of the corner of her eye she saw Frau Müller step forward toward her, arm extended. Jana turned to her and shook her hand. Jana felt the hard, bony hand grasp hers. Frau Müller's grip was strong, but still she seemed apprehensive to shake her hand. Jana was glad when she let go of her. Frau Müller had offered no congratulatory remarks. Going back to her spot among her classmates, Jana tried to avoid Henry's gaze. She was sure he would only roll his eyes at her. But she wouldn't let him ruin this for her. She had worked hard for it, and it would serve her well later.

That had been the last assembly before the Christmas holidays. Henry was talking about nothing else these days, glad to get out of school and homework. It had always been his favorite holiday and so it was for Jana, not because of getting out of school and homework, but because of the time she was able to spend with her family. This year Georg would probably join them again, now that he was no longer with Irene. He wouldn't go to church with them on Christmas Eve, but he would join them later for dinner, Christmas carols, and presents. And he would certainly come the next two Christmas holidays for the great feasts her mama would prepare for them and everyone else that would join them, such as old Uncle Heinrich and his wife.

Jana could still remember her grandmother at Christmas, even though she had been only six when she died. Her homemade cookies had been the best, and Jana had always helped her cut out the cookie shapes. It was the smell of freshly baked Christmas cookies throughout the house she remembered most about her grandmother.

Today was the last day of school and light snow drizzled down as Jana made her way to school. As usual, Henry was still asleep when she left. They hadn't walked to school together in at least three years. She didn't mind, since her walk was short and sometimes Bianca swung by her house to pick her up and they walked to school together.

As Jana walked onto the school grounds, some kids were already forming snowballs and throwing them at each other. The elated mood of the approaching holidays showed in their careless laughter and silly behavior. She dodged a few snowballs and then waited by the door to be let in. There wouldn't be much happening today. All tests had been taken and no new homework had been assigned. They would sing Christmas carols, read stories, and hear again about how the Soviets celebrated the New Year with Father Frost. Some teachers might even bring cookies or some other treats. She rubbed her gloved hands together to warm them and looked up as the creaking wooden door fell open and students started to file inside. She joined the crowd and pulled off her hat as soon as she entered the warm but stuffy school building.

They only had four hours of school today and Jana was already bored out of her mind by the second hour. Nothing was happening. Mostly they sat around and talked, or the teacher told a lame story they had heard numerous times. The highlight of the day was the Russian confection Herr Ronwitzki had brought. It was gooey chocolate truffles wrapped in shiny paper. Henry had let Jana eat his. He had never cared much for chocolate.

Henry's disinterest was even more profound today. His head rested on his arms most of the time, and as soon as the teacher wasn't looking in his direction, he closed his eyes. He had been called on three times already, but the teachers were lenient on their last day of school, and Henry took advantage of it.

When the bell rang, they put on their warm coats, hats, scarves, and gloves and headed out for much needed fresh air and a well-deserved break from the slow passing of the day. Jana huddled together with Bianca and some other girls, and talked excitedly about the upcoming holidays. Jana wouldn't see much of her friend, and she enjoyed spending today gossiping with Bianca and making plans for the new year.

When the bell rang again, they grudgingly made their way back into the stuffy building through the gray mush the snow in the schoolyard had turned into. Bianca was ahead of her, and Jana followed her, stepping into her friend's footsteps to avoid getting her pants wet. Her new ankle-high boots were already soaked, and she could feel the wetness creeping in. Suddenly everything happened all at once. Bianca whipped around and called out her brother's name, her eyes frantic. Jana stared at her friend, not comprehending. She felt people around her staring at her when she saw two men dragging someone from the school building. They wore no uniform, but they looked like Stasi. Her eyes moved to the person wedged in between them. Her breathing stopped. Henry. What ...?

She ran toward the stairs, no longer caring about the snowy mush splashing up on all sides. Bianca was right beside her. She couldn't get through to Henry. A crowd of students surrounded her brother and the Stasi men. She saw the principal following them down the stairs toward a car that was parked right outside the fence that lined the schoolyard.

Jana tried to push herself forward, but couldn't get through fast enough. Bianca had fallen back. Jana opened her mouth to call out to Henry but closed it again quickly. There was no use. She saw one of the Stasi men open the back door of the black Lada. They pushed Henry inside. She heard teachers behind her call everyone inside. The crowd of students started to disperse, but Jana didn't move away from the fence and stared at her brother, who stared back at her from behind the car's window glass. His face was unreadable, but she saw a hint of defiance in his eyes. *Oh, Henry*, she thought. *What have you done?*

Then the car drove off. Jana stared after it, long after it had disappeared. She looked down at her hands and realized that she still had a tight grip around the fence post.

She let go and turned around to find the principal standing behind her. Her face was expressionless, and so was her voice. "You better go home and inform your mother."

———

Henry found himself still tied to the chair in the same cell the next morning. He was surprised that he had actually fallen asleep. His head was throbbing from the beating he had received, and he could barely see through the small slits that his swollen eyes had become. The green metal door before him seemed oddly out of focus. He heard boots coming down the hallway and he braced himself for whatever was coming. They couldn't possibly leave him like this forever. This wasn't the Third Reich. He swallowed hard when the door was noisily unlocked and then thrown open. The same Stasi officer as yesterday appeared, smirking at Henry as he entered.

"Slept well? Gathered new strength? You'll need it." Henry didn't react, his heart was pounding horribly against his chest. He couldn't go through something like yesterday again. "So, do you want to give me the names of the others today then?"

"I told you I acted alone. There are no others." Henry swallowed. "When will you get that?"

It happened so fast. He had expected it, but the shock of it hit him faster than the fist. He winced, trying to breathe through the blinding pain. *I can't, I can't anymore. Oh, please, God* ... The fist came down on his head again. This time he screamed. He could feel the blood trickling down from his eyebrow. A wave of nausea washed over him, and he puked right onto the guard's boots. He received a slap for that, but barely felt it. His face was numb.

"You will tell us who else was involved, you scum. Was it your mother, scum? Was it?"

"No!" Henry screamed, both in pain and horror.

"Well, it seems that's where you got your attitude, boy."

"No one was involved, I told you." It came out feebly. It was no surprise that the fist came down on him again. This time, his pain turned to anger. He wanted it to stop. "Fascists! Fascists!" He screamed at the top of his lungs, again and again. Fists were pounding down on him now until everything went black.

Georg knocked on the door and waited for a reply. It came, and he went in. The man behind the desk looked familiar. Too familiar. He had gotten quite old and wore glasses now. His hair had turned completely gray. Georg stepped closer to the desk. "I'm here to talk about the release of Henry Schmidt." There was no need to draw out what he had come for.

Fleischer looked up at him and Georg knew the man had instantly recognized him.

"Are you Henry Schmidt's father?"

Georg knew that Fleischer was very well aware that he was not and that his question was only supposed to question the credibility of his request. "Not exactly," Georg said. "But I've taken on that role since ... over the past fifteen years."

"I see." Fleischer's eyes seemed to penetrate him. "How is Frau Schmidt?"

"She's doing all right. Considering the circumstances."

"Why didn't she come? She's the mother, isn't she?"

Georg chose to be blunt with Fleischer. "She couldn't bring herself to come back to this ... facility."

"I see," Fleischer said, his tone mocking.

"When will you release Henry Schmidt?" Georg didn't want Fleischer to sidetrack him. He hadn't come to talk about Susanne's past. "He's just a boy."

"Who has insulted our republic and caused a public disturbance among our citizens by calling for nothing short of a revolution."

"He's young. He had no idea what he was doing."

"I think he very well knew what he was doing."

Georg nervously ran his hand through his hair. This wasn't going well. "What can we do to make this right, Herr Fleischer? What can Henry do?"

"He will have to do time in a correctional facility for his – "

"How long?" Georg asked, interrupting Fleischer. He had thrown all caution to the wind. Henry was going to prison.

"A year, if he behaves himself."

Georg was shocked. A year. That would kill Susanne. Georg felt panic rise up in him. There had to be something he could do or say to keep Henry out of prison. "He didn't know what he was doing." There was a knock on the door, but Georg didn't hear it. "He is just a stupid boy –"

Georg felt that someone had come into the room. He turned. A guard had led in Henry. He was handcuffed. Georg drew in a sharp breath. Henry's face was a purplish blue and swollen. But it was Henry's eyes that shocked him the most. They were full of hatred. A hatred that was locked on him, not on Fleischer, not on the guard. On him. Henry stared him down, and Georg realized that he must have heard what he had told Fleischer. Georg felt instantly ashamed. *But Henry must know I didn't mean it*, Georg thought frantically, and hoped Henry would read that in his eyes. But Henry didn't seem to have noticed. He walked past Georg and declared. "This man is not my father. I have nothing to do with him."

Susanne sat on her bed and stared at the violin case in front of her, then back at the clock on the wall. It would be another three hours before Georg would get back from Berlin on the evening train. She couldn't just sit here and wait. She was going crazy. How she hoped and prayed that Georg would accomplish something. She certainly couldn't. There was nothing she could give the Stasi for Henry's release. And who would listen to her? Her file with the Stasi was probably as thick as the Berlin phonebook.

Her eyes fell again on the case that rested on her knees. Susanne zipped it open and stared at the wooden instrument. She had hardly played in the last few years. The violin represented everything she had lost. Dieter, her career ... She sighed and, with a swift movement, took out the instrument. She placed it on her shoulder and put her chin in the rest. It felt cold against her skin and she shuddered slightly. Holding the instrument felt foreign and awkward. Susanne knew she was badly out of practice. She let her fingers slide across the strings and decided to take out the bow. She struck a note. It was horribly out of tune.

For the next ten minutes, Susanne tried to tune her violin. She struggled to do so, but she wanted to play. She had to play. Today, she had to. She thought of Henry. How had they found out that it had been him who had painted and hung the banner? He had done what she had asked him to do. All traces had been wiped clean or covered up. She had no idea how the Stasi had found out. And it was almost Christmas. She was horrified by the thought of Henry in a Stasi prison, let alone on Christmas.

When she found the violin to be in tune, she tried to strike up a melody, but she couldn't remember the notes. Frustrated, she put down the instrument and went over to a bookcase where she kept her sheet music in a handful of folders. She rummaged through them and decided on a practice piece rather than a concerto.

She bit her lip as she played the first notes, concentrating hard to get it right. Her fingers felt stiff and her arm tired easily. She tried harder, correcting herself along the way. Suddenly, the door opened and Jana stuck her head in. She smiled and Susanne beckoned her in.

"You're playing?" Jana asked, her eyes resting on the violin.

"More like trying."

"I remember you playing often when I was little."

"You do?"

"I heard you practice all the time," Jana said, touching the instrument as if it were something precious. "And one Christmas, you played carols and Grandma sang along."

Susanne didn't remember that, but if Jana said so, it must have happened. How had she forgotten so much from her past? Susanne realized that she remembered the bad things more vividly and that she had forgotten many of the pleasant things.

"Can you play on Christmas Eve? For us?" Jana asked suddenly.

That took Susanne by surprise. "I'm dreadfully rusty. I don't know if I can."

"You could practice."

Susanne realized that Jana wasn't giving up easily. "Christmas Eve is in three days."

"You could practice now. You have your violin out."

Susanne smiled at her daughter. Jana was already such a strong young woman. She could easily persuade anyone. And then a thought so terrible entered Susanne's mind that she looked at Jana in horror.

"What is it?" Jana asked, looking concerned. Susanne hesitated. She couldn't possibly ask Jana to do this. "What is it, Mama? What's wrong?" Why did children always sense when something was wrong? Parents weren't really good at hiding things from them. Susanne looked at her daughter. She decided she would ask and leave it up to Jana to decide if she would be willing to do this for her brother in case Georg was unsuccessful.

———

On the train ride home, Georg repeated what had happened over and over again in his head. But there was no use. He couldn't change what happened. He hadn't accomplished anything. Nothing at all. How could he come back to Susanne with that? He would certainly not tell her how Henry looked. It would break her heart to know he had been beaten. She might even do something irrational, and Georg would certainly not let that happen.

Georg sighed loudly in the almost empty train car. He stared out the window at the endless white. Christmas Eve was around the corner, and Henry would be in prison. But worst of all, Henry hated him now. They had always had such a good relationship. Georg had been more than just a father to him. He had been a big brother, a friend. They trusted each other. *Not anymore,* Georg thought grimly. *What was I thinking?*

Susanne wasn't waiting for him at the train station. He was surprised. He was sure she was eager to hear any news he would bring. Reluctantly, he made his way to her house. He felt defeated and worthless. When Susanne needed his help most, he failed. He had always failed to give her what she wanted.

She opened her front door with her violin in hand. Again, he was surprised. He hadn't heard her play in a while. Why today?

Georg looked into her expectant eyes and followed her in. He took his time to take off his coat and scarf while she watched him silently. She must be sensing what was coming. He turned and looked at her and simply shook his head. Her face fell, but she looked as if she had expected it.

"How long," she asked.

"Probably a year."

She drew in her breath, and he went over to her and hugged her. Georg held her for a long time. He could feel she was crying. Eventually she let go of him and he followed her into the living room. Susanne put down her violin, and they sat. She didn't offer him anything. He was parched, but didn't say so. He could see her thinking hard, and he chose not to interrupt her thoughts. She stared at her instrument. After a while, he couldn't bear the silence. They had to talk this through. "I'm glad you're playing again," he said, sounding more casual than he felt.

She didn't react, but tore her eyes away from her violin to look at him. "Thank you for going up to Berlin for me," she said mechanically.

"I think Henry is upset with me."

"Why?" She fully turned to him, looking confused.

"He overheard me talking about his stupidity."

"Georg is right," Jana said. She had suddenly appeared in the doorway. Georg wondered if she had eavesdropped. "It was stupid of Henry. Very stupid," Jana went on. "He not only ruins his own life, but mine as well. That's not fair."

Susanne motioned for Jana to sit down. Georg couldn't remember a time when Jana had been this upset. He didn't know how to react to it, but Susanne seemed to know. She put an arm around her daughter's shoulder. "There is a way to get Henry out of this mess and to get you what you want," Susanne said to Jana.

Georg perked up. What was Susanne up to?

Jana had perked up as well. She looked at her mother. "What do you mean?"

"If you help the government, they'll help you," Susanne said. Her back was now turned toward Georg, her full attention directed toward Jana, whose eyes were fixed on her mother's lips.

"We can offer them a deal to get Henry out of prison," Susanne went on. "There are young, loyal people such as you who help the government and in return they are rewarded for their loyalty."

Georg started to feel uneasy. He couldn't believe what he thought Susanne was about to propose to Jana.

"How?" Jana asked. Georg read nothing but confusion in her face.

"They let the government, the Stasi, know what people are up to," Susanne explained.

"You mean they spy on people?"

"I wouldn't put it that way. They just keep the government ... informed."

Susanne had probably forgotten that he was still there. He'd never thought Susanne would go that far. But she did. And she did it with such stride that it scared Georg.

Susanne went on relentlessly. "If you let the Stasi know what your friends are up to, they will make sure you get into the university of your choice ... and you'll help your brother. He needs you, Jana. There is nothing that Georg or I can do for him." She paused and he felt that she remembered that he was still there and that he had heard everything she said. But she didn't look at him. She looked at Jana, waiting for a response.

It came quicker than Georg had anticipated. Too quickly. "I'll do it," Jana said with determination. Georg knew that look. She looked so much like her mother. "On one condition," Jana added.

"What is it, *Schatz?*" Susanne sounded surprised.

"That you stop applying for an exit visa."

There was silence, the heavy kind that presses down on one. Georg heard Susanne swallow. He knew that this would be hard for her to agree to.

"Fine. I won't anymore." There was a hint of defeat in her voice.

"You mean it?" Jana asked incredulously. Susanne's head bobbed. Jana looked satisfied and leaned back, her arms folded. "So how are we going to offer the Stasi my ... services?"

———

Susanne knew that Georg was not happy with her using Jana like that. He had called her unscrupulous after Jana had gone off to bed. But she knew that he was also aware of how desperate she was. He wanted Henry out of prison just as much as she did. And luckily for Henry, so did Jana.

The next morning, Susanne phoned the Stasi headquarters and asked for Fleischer. The secretary refused to put her through to him, so Susanne left a message for him. To her surprise, he not only called her right back before she had even left Georg's house, but he had also agreed to see Jana and her the very same day. He seemed intrigued, but Susanne could not deny the coldness of his voice that still made her shiver, even after all these years.

Only a few hours later, Susanne and Jana got on the early afternoon train to Berlin. It was bitterly cold and the heaters on the train had a hard time keeping the cars warm. There was hardly anyone on board. Christmas was approaching, and most people were already off work. School was out as well. So close to Christmas, everyone was home cooking, baking, wrapping presents, or spending time with family. The last thing Susanne wanted to do right before Christmas, or any other time really, was face Fleischer again, but she had no choice. If she wanted to get Henry out, she had to suffer the man. But she found strength and comfort in the fact that Jana was with her and that she finally had someone who understood what needed to be done. Susanne had been surprised to see Jana drive such a hard bargain. But Susanne also knew that she should have known better. After all, Jana was taking after her in so many ways. Unlike Henry, Jana knew what she wanted, and she was willing to sacrifice and do whatever she needed to do to accomplish her goal. Susanne admired her for it, but it also scared her. She only hoped that Jana would drive just as hard a bargain with Fleischer today as she had done with her yesterday.

"We're usually the ones seeking out deserving, loyal youth to ... work for us. But your daughter's record speaks for itself. Eventually we would have contacted her anyway," Walter Fleischer said, eyeing the two women across from him. Susanne Schmidt's daughter was a spitting image of her mother, who had aged considerably. But he hadn't seen Susanne Schmidt in years, and she was no longer twenty-six.

By what he had found out, Jana Schmidt had turned out to be the polar opposite of her mother. The girl was an excellent student, obedient, law-abiding, and willing to follow her leaders. It pleased him that the system had worked and turned an otherwise hopeless offspring of a dissident into a promising defender of communism.

And he couldn't believe he had the luck and pleasure to see Susanne Schmidt again. And a pleasure it was, indeed. He scrutinized the girl and her mother. They had only one concern. And he would be the one they had to deal with. He felt a sudden surge of satisfaction. His job had provided him with numerous opportunities to single out and punish those rebelling against the government, but nothing had been more to his liking than the case of Susanne Schmidt.

"I take it you're offering your daughter's services to negotiate your son's precarious situation," Fleischer said directly to Susanne.

"And my acceptance to the university of my choice ... when the time comes," Jana butted in. "With the field of study being my choice as well."

"I see," Fleischer said, not knowing if he should be annoyed or impressed by the girl's attitude.

"Will you release my son, then?" Susanne Schmidt asked.

"You know how these things work, Frau Schmidt. First there needs to be proof that your daughter is truly willing to work for us as an informant." He saw some recognition in her eyes and how her face fell. He turned to Jana now. "I cannot release your brother until you have something to report that shows me you're of value to us." Jana Schmidt opened her mouth and he quickly added, "Or to guarantee you a place at the university of your choice."

He saw the girl nodding in acknowledgment. Susanne Schmidt, however, looked at him with cold eyes.

"You will leave my son in prison. On Christmas," she said, her voice as cold as her eyes.

"So it seems, Frau Schmidt." He matched her cold stare. He remembered that they were religious people. People who would observe Christmas for what they believed it was. Fleischer felt the same feeling of satisfaction he had felt earlier. In the end, people like Susanne Schmidt would always get what they deserved. Even if it happened years later.

He extended his hand across the table toward Jana. "We have an agreement then." It wasn't a question.

Without hesitation, the girl took his hand and shook it. Her mother looked on, her face unreadable.

"Merry Christmas, then," Fleischer said, dismissing them. He thought he saw Susanne Schmidt flinch, and he had to quickly swallow a satisfied grunt.

Chapter 19

Jana didn't try to stifle another yawn. Everyone around her looked just as bored by this meeting as she was. They weren't making any progress. They had been sitting here in the cold classroom for two hours now, trying to organize the May Day demonstrations. They still had two months, but the way things were going, they would need the time to get their act together. The leading members of their council couldn't agree on anything and she, as their president, had trouble keeping the meeting from constantly getting sidetracked.

Jana raised her hand, but it was a while before everyone stopped talking and turned to her. "The meeting is adjourned. We're not getting anywhere today. Let's meet again next week. Any old ideas and suggestions are out. Come up with something new, please," Jana said, getting up.

A few nodded in agreement and got up to leave.

"But we only have a few weeks left. We should at least decide how many flowers we'll need. They need to be ordered," Bianca said loudly.

Jana put a hand on her friend's shoulder. "Next week. It can wait one more week."

Bianca eyed her contemptuously. Jana knew her friend didn't appreciate being patronized in front of everyone. Jana also knew that Bianca harbored some resentment toward her since she had been made president of the Council of the Free German Youth at their school. Bianca had wanted that position as it had been occupied by her older sister before.

"We'll never get this done," Bianca said, packing her bag more furiously than necessary. "It is the fortieth anniversary of our republic coming up later this year, for crying out loud."

Jana sighed. There was no use arguing with Bianca. She herself feared that they wouldn't get it all done. And this year, it had to be something special and momentous. This was her first year as the president of the council, and she had to prove that she was up to the task. The added pressure only contributed to her fears of failing to free Henry. She hadn't been able to produce any worthwhile info she could share with Fleischer. Denouncing kids from school for watching West German TV wouldn't do it. Fleischer would want something of substance. He was waiting, and so was her mother. Her brother was still in jail. They were all counting on her and so far, she was failing everyone miserably.

Jana looked around and saw Bianca disappear through the door. Three others still lingered in one corner of the classroom, whispering quietly. She walked over to them, and they stopped talking instantly. They looked at her as if she had caught them whispering about her.

"What's going on?" Jana asked, trying to pretend she wasn't really interested. They eyed her suspiciously. One of them, Tom, a tall boy in her grade with dark eyes and even darker hair opened his mouth, but he was shushed immediately by the other two, a boy and a girl a year older than them.

Now Jana was curious. What had they been talking about? If it had been about her, they might have offered a lame excuse, but they hadn't.

"Her brother's in jail. He put up that banner. She'll be interested in this," Tom said to the other two.

"What would I be interested in?" Jana asked, no longer hiding her curiosity. The other two looked at Tom nervously. "Have you heard about these meetings?" Tom asked her.

"What meetings?" Jana hadn't heard a thing. What was going on?

"Random meetings." Tom leaned in closer to her, his voice a whisper. Jana's brows furrowed. Random meetings? What did he mean? Couldn't he be clearer? She was getting frustrated. *Just spit it out,* she thought. Stop beating around the bush. "Don't you watch the news?" Tom asked, waiting for her reply. It didn't come, so he added, "West German news. They're reporting that people in our country are getting fed up with the government. That people in our country want reform."

Jana realized the other two started to look more scared than nervous. Their eyes were darting back and forth between the door and Tom. She hadn't watched the news in a week, but her mother had. But her mother hadn't said a thing. Why hadn't she shared that with her?

"You said something about meetings. Here in the village. Where're they being held? Who's going?" Jana asked, no longer trying to hide her impatience.

Now it was Tom who looked at her nervously. She saw that he hesitated, so she encouraged them. "My mother and my brother would surely love to hear about all this." She tried to sound conspiratorial.

"People meet at the church," Tom said.

"What are they meeting about?" Jana still didn't understand.

"Well.." Tom hesitated. "You have to go yourself and find out. There's a meeting tonight at nineteen-hundred hours. Everyone is going."

"*Everyone?* Who do you mean?" What was he saying? Why hadn't she heard anything about this?

"Everyone." Tom left it at that. "Just come and see," he said, heading for the door, followed by the others.

Jana was the one left behind, staring after them. Everyone was going to this meeting? What meeting? She racked her brain. Why at the church? This was strange. There were never any public gatherings that weren't announced beforehand. And there never had been public meetings at the church before. What was going on? Something was happening. She could feel it. She had to find out what and use it to her advantage.

Jana walked home slowly, still deep in thought about everything she had learned. Her thoughts turned to Henry, and she sighed. How she missed him, even his annoying attitude and habits that drove her mad. They couldn't be any more different, but they had always been there for each other. She had never been separated from him for longer than a week, and now she felt something crucial was missing from her life. She would be going to that meeting. That was for sure. There might be something said there she could report back to Fleischer. Would her mother be interested in coming? Had she heard about this? She hastened her step. The only way to find out was to talk to her.

Susanne was feeding a litter of guinea pigs that someone had dropped off at Georg's practice when Jana walked in. Georg had left to make a house call, so she was startled when someone came through the door and even more surprised that it was Jana. She had allergies and rarely set a foot in the practice. "What's going on, Jana? Has something happened?" A look on her daughter's face told her that something was indeed on Jana's mind. She looked troubled, and she was biting her lip.

"Have you watched the news, lately? On the West German channels?" Jana asked without hesitation.

"I have, of course." So that's what was on her mind.

"So you have heard about what's going on."

"I have," Susanne said, trying to busy herself with the guinea pigs.

"Why didn't you tell me that all of this is happening?"

Susanne hesitated. "I haven't had the chance to talk to you about it." It was a lame excuse, and they both knew it.

Jana's brows furrowed. "Will you tell me now what's happening?"

"Quite frankly, I don't really know what's happening." She saw that Jana wanted to protest, so she went on. "It seems as if there are some opposition groups forming."

"Opposition groups? What do you mean?"

"Groups opposing the government. They're meeting to discuss the change that needs to come to this country. They're meeting in churches. They want to do this peacefully."

"Peacefully? Do what?"

"I don't know. They want reforms, I guess."

"There's a meeting tonight," Jana said suddenly. "Will you go with me?"

"No!" Susanne was almost shouting. What was Jana thinking? "I don't want to have anything to do with it. And neither will you. Your brother is already in jail. We stay out of it. It's too dangerous." Who knew what would happen at the meeting. Stasi would certainly be present, and if it got out of hand, those men would break the meeting up violently.

"But the meeting is at the church. They won't do anything there." Jana was adamant.

"They would. Believe me. They don't care if this meeting is in a church or at Sanssouci."

"I need to go," Jana said. Her voice was firm.

"You can't, Jana. Please understand. Give in this once."

"You forget that I'm an informant for the Stasi. I have an obligation to go and find out what's going on. I need something to report to Fleischer," Jana said, all business now. Then she added, more gently, "I need to go ... for Henry."

Susanne felt defeated. She knew Jana was right, but what if this turned out to be violent? She felt a hand on her arm and looked up into Jana's eyes.

"It's time for Henry to come home. Let me go ... please."

Susanne didn't answer. She embraced Jana in a big hug. Her daughter was now as tall as herself. Her kids were almost grown-ups. For a moment, Susanne felt ancient.

———

When Jana reached the church, it was almost time for the meeting to start. People were still entering the small old village church where Henry and she had been christened, confirmed, and where they went for every Christmas and Easter service.

Jana was surprised by the number of people entering. And there were still some on the road behind her. *It must be packed already,* Jana thought as she climbed the stairs. Her thoughts were confirmed when she walked in. She had never seen the church that full. There were no seats left, and people were already standing up against the walls. She saw the pastor sitting in the first row. Jana wondered how active his role would be in such a meeting.

Jana found a spot near the chancel. Leaning against the wall and feeling slightly out of place, she looked around in anticipation. She saw Tom and some other kids from her school, along with their parents. Tom waved at her, and she shyly waved back at him. How she wished her mother had come. The church was bursting with people, but she felt utterly alone.

A hush fell on the crowd when someone in the fifth row stood up. It was the photographer, who had a little studio on Main Street.

"We all know why we're here, again," he said. Again? There had been a meeting before? And was the photographer the ringleader? Was he conducting the meeting? He didn't seem to be, or he would have sat up front and stood up in front of everyone. The meeting was not very organized. No one wanted to take responsibility. "We need to make our voices heard. The government needs to know they can't go on like this," the photographer went on. There were grunts of approval from the people.

"Their planned-economy isn't working anymore," the village baker yelled.

"It has never worked," someone else shouted. Some people laughed.

"Last winter, I wasn't even able to buy boots for my children. They just didn't have any," a woman Jana had seen at church said.

"We should protest," someone shouted. Jana looked at who had said that. It was Tom's father.

"We need to demonstrate," two people shouted at once.

Jana realized the meeting was getting louder. People seemed to use this opportunity to let off steam, but would it accomplish anything? She doubted that.

"*We* are the people," someone said suddenly loud enough over all the squabbling that was going on. The church fell silent. Everyone looked around to see who had said it.

There in the door stood Jana's mother, Georg by her side. "We are the people," Susanne said again and again, looking into the crowd. Georg joined in the chanting. Jana followed. People around her looked at her, but then everyone put their fists up in the air and shouted, "We are the people." The church was trembling from the unified chorus of their voices. Jana had chills run up and down her spine. People were shouting louder and louder, their chorus penetrating bone and marrow. As Jana was shouting along with everyone else, it hit her. *We are the people*, she thought. We are the people. It was that simple but yet profound. She loved school and learning, but she had never dared to speak up or question what they taught in school. So much was propaganda. Henry had never accepted anything they tried to drill into their heads. But she had. Blindly. And now Henry was in jail for a prank. Would he be in jail in West Germany? Her thoughts turned to her father, who she had never met. When she was eight, her mother had told her the whole story about their tragic separation. At first, Jana had not fully comprehended the story and its implications, but over the years, she had come to understand the details and her mother's opposition. But instead of accepting her mother's sacrifice and desire to leave, Jana had grown up naturally accepting the way things were in their country. She had ignored, or rather accepted feeling intimidated and controlled. Her mother's opposition had only brought them grief and had erased any misgivings and dissatisfactions.

She looked at her mother and for the first time in her life, Jana felt supportive of her and tried to understand what she had suffered at the hands of the regime that didn't care about the people, but only its own agenda. She wouldn't denounce any of the people who had spoken here tonight. How could she now? Henry would never want it. And neither did she.

The pastor rose up and held up both arms. Slowly, fewer and fewer people chanted their new motto, until it was quiet in the church. "Let's do this peacefully," the old pastor said. "Let's pray together. For reform. For democracy. For freedom." He bowed his head and led them in prayer. Out of the corner of her eye, Jana saw that even Georg had bowed his head.

Chapter 20

When school was out on Friday and Jana was about to leave the school grounds, Tom stepped in her way. She was surprised.

"I have an idea about the May Day demonstrations," he said.

Jana realized he was almost bursting. It seemed as if he had waited a long time to talk to her. "We have a meeting tomorrow. I'm sure everyone would like to hear it," she said, even though she wanted to hear now what Tom had in mind.

"I wanted to run it by you first," he said, stepping closer to her.

"Go ahead then. I won't pretend I'm not interested in your idea. We all know we need one."

"It's better we walk then," he said, starting to move.

Jana stayed rooted in place. Why didn't he just come out with it? Why was Tom always so secretive? It drove her insane. "Why not tell me right here?"

He stopped walking and turned around to her. "It's not for every ear." Jana's brows furrowed, but she didn't say anything and walked up to him. He started talking as soon as she was by his side. They walked closely and Jana felt herself bump into his side every few steps. "We should use this year's May Day demonstrations to protest the government," Tom said quietly. Jana stopped walking instantly and stared at him, but Tom just pulled her with him again. "Keep walking," he said, scanning their surroundings.

"You're out of your mind, Tom," Jana said. She still couldn't believe what Tom had proposed. They were on the council and in charge of making the May Day demonstrations go smoothly. These demonstrations were held every May to celebrate the workers. Party officials would be present. And this year had to be special. The republic had a big birthday coming up. They couldn't possibly hijack May Day like that.

"The word out on the street is that other villages and towns plan to do the same," Tom said.

"That's what they say, but will they go through with it?" Tom didn't answer. Jana assumed he had doubts of his own.

They had reached her house, and Jana wanted to leave it at that. "I doubt you can raise the idea at tomorrow's meeting. Others will be there who haven't attended any meetings at the church."

"It's time that we take the next step," Tom said. He stood resolutely at the gate, his arms folded, and gazed at Jana's house.

"I think you're getting too careless. It's true the Stasi hasn't done anything about the meetings at the church, but that doesn't mean that we're not reported if we talk about it at our own meeting. It's hardly the right venue, don't you think?" Jana reached for the handle to open the gate, but Tom grabbed her hand. For a moment, they looked into each other's eyes, until Tom cleared his throat and stepped back to let Jana pass.

"Just think about it," he said, and left.

Jana went inside. Her mother was gone. Probably still at Georg's practice. She headed for her room, which was located just next to Henry's room, which her mother had told her had belonged to their father. She fell down on her bed. A nap would be good right now. Maybe her thoughts would sort themselves out in her sleep as they sometimes did. She was certainly not looking forward to tomorrow's meeting. They had to finalize everything. And there was Tom's idea, which she thought was out of the question. On the other hand, she wished to see everyone's reaction, but she was right. They had gotten too careless. She didn't want to end up like Henry.

———

Jana was dismayed when she found their supervising teacher present at their meeting. He said he wanted to make sure they got everything lined up for May Day, but Jana suspected that Bianca had a hand in it. She caught Tom's eye when she sat down, and she saw that he was just as annoyed as she was by the teacher's presence. In theory, he always had to be present, but he rarely had shown up, for which they had all been grateful. She shot Bianca an angry look when she opened the meeting and another when they were all reciting their motto. She wanted her friend to know how she felt about her going behind her back. Bianca didn't meet her eyes. She was staring at the teacher the whole time, avoiding her. Jana was sad about what had become of their friendship. They had been friends since they were small.

The meeting went as planned. May Day demonstrations would go on as they had always done. The only difference was that they would have more carnations. Nothing out of the ordinary would happen, even if it did in other towns. Wallhausen would follow tradition. The teacher looked pleased, and Jana ended the meeting.

Jana saw Bianca shake the teacher's hand when the meeting was over. After the teacher had left, Jana cornered her friend. "What is going on with you?"

"I don't know what you mean," Bianca said, still avoiding looking at her.

"We used to be such good friends. Why are you like this?"

"Like what? You're the one who's changing and becoming this ... this ... like your brother," Bianca burst out, looking directly at Jana now.

People around them stopped talking and looked at them, but Jana didn't care. She was stunned Bianca thought of her that way.

"Change is good," Tom said to Bianca, coming up on Jana's side. "We need change in this country, don't you realize that?"

Bianca didn't know what to answer to that. She just stared at Tom and then again at Jana. She obviously hadn't expected a united front and such open rebellion. "You'll be sorry for what you said," Bianca said defiantly. "I'll report you."

People around them drew in their breath. Jana was shocked into silence. This wasn't her friend talking. Tears came to her eyes. Their friendship was over, and she knew it.

"Go right ahead, Bianca," Jana heard Tom say. Through her tears, Jana saw her friend leave, and then she felt an arm around her shoulders. Tom was holding out a handkerchief to her, and she burst into giggles. It had gnomes and toadstools on it. Tom blushed. "My mother always puts one in my bag. Comes in handy, you know." He looked embarrassed.

Jana couldn't stop giggling. She felt close to hysteria. The stress and pressure from the last months seemed to finally want a release.

"Come. I'll take you home." Tom put on his jean jacket, took Jana by the arm, and led her out of the classroom. Jana felt embarrassed to have been so hysterical in front of him, but he seemed to understand.

"I don't want to go in," Jana said when they reached her house.

Tom looked confused. "What do you want to do?"

"I don't know. Go somewhere." Jana had no idea. She just didn't want to spend the rest of the day at home.

"We could go and get some ice cream in Heimroda," Tom suggested.

Ice cream sounded good to her. It always sounded good to her. And the village was only two kilometers away. "Do you think they're already open? It's only April, you know."

"Almost May," he said with a twinkle in his dark brown eyes. "Besides, I heard they're already open for business. It's been a warm spring."

"Sounds good. I'll get my bike, then," Jana said. The old green bike was actually her mother's, but they both used it whenever one of them needed it.

When she came back with the bike, Tom was leaning on the fence, smoking. With the cigarette in his hand and his strong jawline clenched, he looked so much older than he was. "You smoke?" Jana asked.

"Want one?" Tom held out his pack.

"No, thanks. My mother told me my father always smoked and kissing him was like kissing an ashtray."

Tom stepped closer but blew out the smoke in the opposite direction. "I think she just told you that so you'd never start smoking."

"I think she told me that so I would never kiss boys. Boys who smoke," Jana teased, tucking a brown curl behind her ear.

Tom broke into a grin and put out his cigarette. "Well, how do you feel about kissing ... an ashtray?"

Jana didn't try to hide her disgust and pulled a face.

Tom laughed. "Well, I guess I'd have to give up smoking then if I ever want to kiss you."

Chapter 21

The weather fully cooperated on May Day. Susanne was sitting on the garden canopy swing with her feet up and reading a book. The air was warm and the blossoms from the fruit trees around her were scattered on the ground in a white sea of petals. From far off, she could hear the marching drums and the chorus of voices. Susanne looked up when someone was approaching. It was Georg. He wore an old t-shirt and a pair of black pants. His feet were in a pair of sandals. She put her book face down on her chest and looked up at him. His graying sideburns shimmered in the sun. "Has she delivered yet?" Susanne asked, not surprised to see Georg come over. She hadn't expected him to attend the May Day demonstrations.

"Yes, she has." Georg sat down on a bench across from her. "Want to see them?"

Susanne shook her head. She loved kittens when they started their first attempts at walking. However, newborn kittens were rather disgusting to look at. They were naked, their dark eyeballs shone through the still-closed eyelids, and their little squeals were heart-wrenching.

"Do you want to come along?" Georg asked, motioning toward the far-off sounds of the May Day celebrations.

Susanne sat up. So he did want to attend, after all. Susanne knew that Georg was fully aware of how she felt about it. "I never went and I never will. You know that very well."

Georg got up. "Well, I'll leave you to your book then," he said tersely.

Susanne instantly felt a pang of guilt. *Be nice, Susanne,* she told herself. *Georg doesn't deserve rudeness.* He was her boss and neighbor, but foremost, he was her friend. A friend she could always count on and who had always been there for her and the kids. So she got up. "If it makes you happy, I'll come with you," she said with a sigh.

"No need to," Georg said, and started to walk away.

Susanne ran after him in frustration. When she caught up with him, she held him back by his arm. "Don't be like that, Georg."

"Be like what, Susanne?"

"You've been so ... so distant, since you came back from Berlin when you tried to get Henry out of prison."

Georg looked at her thoughtfully, but didn't say anything. "What is it, Georg?"

He turned around to face her. "I think Jana would appreciate if you were there today."

Susanne was taken aback. So that was what this was about. "I've been going to the meetings at the church with her, haven't I?"

"That's not the same," Georg said.

Susanne thought that Georg was unnecessarily severe with her. "And how is that not the same, Georg?"

"You approve of going to the meetings at the church because they're in opposition of the government, but you don't approve of the May Day demonstrations because they celebrate communism. But your daughter is involved, even in charge this year. It doesn't matter whose side she's on. You should support her, no matter what. As her mother."

"She knows I can't stand for it. She understands that it is against my principles," Susanne snapped angrily.

"Yet you'd have her spy for the government," Georg said defiantly, and then walked away.

Susanne was speechless. Georg had pointed out her hypocrisy and it hurt. It mostly hurt because he should understand her. He knew why she had been so desperate to ask Jana to work for the Stasi. They had to do something to get Henry out. She hated herself for it. And she hated Georg for rubbing it in her face. She missed Henry so much and she was so worried about him. He was just a boy and he was in prison. Every day since the day Jana had come home and told her that Henry had been arrested, she had woken up to the thought of Henry being in prison. Every day.

———

Susanne never looked forward to going down to the cellar. It was dark, cold, and reeked like rotten potatoes. It was a grubby place due to the downtrodden dirt that was the floor and the dust from the coals. Spider webs were hanging around the wooden door frames and in the corners of the low ceiling.

She avoided coming down here as much as possible, even sending Henry or Georg to fetch coals, potatoes, or apples. But since Henry was in prison and Jana and Georg were at the May Day celebrations, she had no choice but to come down here herself. But she wouldn't have sent them down here for what she needed anyway.

Susanne made her way to the last cellar room in the far back. The door was ajar. Inside, the walls were lined with wooden shelves on which bottles and jars of all kinds stood. Some looked so old and dusty, Susanne knew she would never open them for fear of what they might be harboring inside. She went to the shelf on her left and looked at the hand-written labels of some bottles.

She decided on a bottle of Gisela's home-brewed black currant liquor. Susanne grabbed it, blew off the dust, and made her way quickly upstairs. When she closed the old wooden door that led to the cellar, she shivered lightly. She bolted the door and went to the living room.

When the sun was setting outside, Susanne was in such good spirits, she felt like dancing. For a moment, she even thought about joining Jana and Georg, but then she remembered Georg's words and downed another shot of Gisela's liquor. She got up and felt the room spinning around her. Somehow she made it over to the radio. She tried the dial to get the West German channel but couldn't keep her hand steady enough to succeed. Fortunately, the radio also had a cassette deck. She decided on a tape and put it in. After three attempts to hit the play button, the music finally started playing and Susanne began swaying around in the living room, the bottle in one hand, and the shot glass in the other.

Susanne hadn't felt that light in a while. She was alone, but today she didn't mind.

She liked it. She closed her eyes to the music and almost fell over. Catching herself, she started laughing. Her head was spinning, and so was her mind. Susanne felt so free, her troubles a distant memory. She fell down on the couch and had another shot. The door opened and someone stepped inside. She assumed the silhouette of a man was Georg, the slowly darkening room obscuring her vision. The man reached for the light switch, but Susanne raised her arm to stop him. "Don'ttt. I ... likkke ... yes, likkkke ... to be in the dark," she blabbered, and then broke out in a hysterical giggle when she realized what she had said.

Georg came toward her and took the bottle and the glass from her. "You've been drinking, I see."

"Woulddd ... yooouuu like .... sommme? It's Gisssela's famous blackkk ... what's the berry ... it'sss black ... schnaps," Susanne tried to say but felt her tongue was too numb and slow to keep up with her spinning mind.

She fell against Georg's chest and looked up into the familiar face.

"I should take you to bed. You're drunk," she heard Georg say.

She felt she was being led out of the living room, but bumped into the doorframe. It didn't hurt. Georg swept her up and carried her to her bedroom. When he tried unsuccessfully to open the door, Susanne broke out into hysterical giggles again. He finally managed to open the door, dropped her on the bed, and started to remove her shoes. She tried to control the hysterical giggles, but found she couldn't stop them. Georg pulled the blanket over her, and she threw her arms around his neck. He tried to free himself, but she planted a kiss on his mouth. Georg froze, but Susanne didn't care. She kissed him again. At first his lips didn't move, but then he started kissing her back.

Georg woke up and found himself grinning. When he looked in his bathroom mirror, he saw himself still grinning. He tried hard to give his reflection a somber expression, but it didn't work. He felt silly and started brushing his teeth.

He wondered how Susanne would feel this morning. She had been pretty drunk last night, but he was sure she still had been aware of what was going on. Would he have stopped if he had thought she hadn't been in the right state of mind? Probably not, he had to admit. He had loved her all these years and finally they had gotten together.

When Georg left his house, he wondered if Susanne would already be awake. He doubted it. It was too early after such a night. He had left after she had fallen asleep. He didn't want her to wake up next to him and give her the shock of a lifetime, in case she didn't remember anything about last night.

He took his bike and made his way to the bakery to get some freshly-baked rolls and danishes for breakfast. He would brew a strong coffee, and then they could talk about last night and where to go from here. He felt slightly nervous at that thought. Would she feel the same? She had to after last night.

When Georg knocked on Susanne's front door, he didn't wait for her to open it. He went straight to the kitchen that had once belonged to Gisela. He found Jana there, wrapped in a bathrobe, sipping tea. She looked up in surprise when he walked in.

"I brought breakfast," Georg said.

"Oh. That's nice of you." Jana got up and looked at what he had brought.

"The rolls are still warm. Would you mind getting your mama? I'm making you two breakfast today." Jana peered at him, her mouth twitching in amusement. Had she heard them last night? He cleared his throat and busied himself with filling up the kettle with water.

"I think you should go and get her," Jana said. He looked up. Jana had folded her arms and looked straight at him. "It's about time, you know."

Georg broke into a grin. "Well, it had never been up to me."

"I know," Jana said, and sat back down.

"Would you mind?" he pointed at the kettle as he was about to leave the kitchen. "Of course." Jana waved him out the door.

He went to the other end of the hallway and knocked on Susanne's door.

The bedroom with all its furnishings had once belonged to Gisela, and Georg had felt slightly awkward last night when they had made love in her bed. He heard a sound coming from inside and opened the door. Susanne was in bed, her blanket pulled all the way up to her face. Her clothes were scattered across the floor where he had dropped them last night. "Good morning," he said, and picked up a few pieces of clothing on his way over to her bed. He sat down on the edge, and Susanne groaned.

"How do you feel," he asked carefully.

"Horrible."

"I'm sure you have quite the headache after last night." Susanne didn't respond. "I brought breakfast."

"I'm not hungry," came the short reply.

"I'll mix something up that will make you feel better."

"There's nothing that can make me feel better," Susanne said, emerging from underneath her blanket and looking at him for the first time. "Georg ... whatever happened last night ... I don't want you –"

Georg kissed her. He put enough longing into it to make sure she knew how he felt. She didn't kiss him back, but she didn't push him away either. He took that as a good sign. When he let go of her, he had to catch his breath. "I love you, Susanne. You know I always have."

She looked at him. There were tears in her eyes. "I can't, Georg," she said feebly.

For a moment, he just stared at her. The only thing he could get out was a one-word question. "Why?"

"I don't love you the same way you love me," Susanne said. "You deserve better than that."

"I know you'll never love me as much as Dieter. I can live with that." He had to live with that.

"That wouldn't be fair to you."

He looked at her. "The only person you haven't been fair to is yourself, Susanne."

She looked taken aback by the sudden turn their talk had taken. But he went on relentlessly. "It's time to let go of the past. You need to live your life. Stop waiting and start living, Susanne." He scooted closer to her and took her face in his hands. "Be with me, Susanne."

She put her hand on one of his. "No expectations, no commitments," she said, scrutinizing him. "Can you live with that?"

"For now..."

She slapped his arm playfully. "Do us both a favor and don't get your hopes up, Georg Hoffmann."

Georg smiled and pulled her up. "Let's eat. I'm famished."

New local government elections for May were announced over the village loudspeakers which were used by the government for public announcements. At the last meeting at the church, it had been decided that everyone would turn out and void every single candidate on the ballot to show their dissatisfaction with the government and protest the way elections were held. Since the candidates' party affiliation was not listed on the ballot, they had no other choice but to cross out every single one to avoid voting for the candidate of the communist party.

Jana had wanted to vote more than anything this year, but she was too young, of course. But she accompanied her mother and Georg to the village's town hall on election day. When they arrived, a long line led up to the only election booth that had been put up. Voting was usually done in the open. It had always been considered a cause for suspicion and an act of rebellion to use the booth. Only a very few had dared cast their ballot in secrecy in the election booth in years past, but this election was different. Many of those who came to vote ignored the intimidating looks of the election workers and waited for their turn to use the booth.

It had taken hours for Georg and her mother to vote, but Jana hadn't minded. The elections this year would turn out quite differently, unlike May Day, which to Jana's great dismay had been celebrated as if nothing was wrong. They had marched. They had carried the flags. They had sung the same communist songs as every year.

Bianca hadn't spoken to her since the day Jana had confronted her at their planning meeting. Jana missed her, but there was no way she would speak to Bianca until her friend came to her senses. Jana couldn't understand why she didn't see what was going on around them.

At recess, Jana started to spend time with Tom. She liked him. He seemed mature beyond his years, and she admired him for his straightforward courage to point out mismanagement within their government to anyone who would lend him an ear. Jana was sure that the Stasi was watching him.

"You've come a long way," Tom noted one Monday morning when they were standing by the fence during recess. She looked up from the sandwich she was eating and gave him a puzzled look. "Or maybe I misread you all these years," he continued.

Jana swallowed her bite. "What do you mean?"

"You were always so ambitious and no-nonsense, doing what the teachers told you, following ... you know ... living the exemplary life of a youth in the GDR."

Jana chuckled. "I was, wasn't I?"

"In some sense you still are."

"As you are," Jana shot back. "You're getting perfect grades. And you're on the Council of the Free German Youth. Who are you trying to fool?"

Tom didn't look pleased by her little jab. "It was my father's idea."

Jana knew that Tom's father was very vocal about his opposition to the government, so it seemed contradictive of him to encourage his son to show model behavior. The bell rang and Jana quickly finished up her sandwich. She felt Tom's eyes on her. "What?"

"I can't figure you out, Jana Schmidt," he said. "It is as if you were hiding something."

Jana was shocked. What was Tom getting at? "What makes you think that?"

"It's almost as if you wanted to please both sides."

Jana swallowed and tried to recover from her shock. Did Tom suspect something? The best defense was a good offense. "So, is that what you're doing? Pleasing both sides?" Jana asked. Without waiting for a response, she stalked off. She would give Tom the cold shoulder until he stopped being so confrontational. If her cover were blown, they would have nothing that could help Henry. And she needed to report something or someone to Fleischer. Soon. Henry had been in prison long enough. Tom's father? She pushed the thought away as soon as it had come. She couldn't. Even if she didn't like Tom as much as she did.

Henry had been waiting for over half an hour, he guessed. What was taking so long? He looked around the small holding room. There were no windows, just a couple of chairs and a small table. Nothing else. Finally, the door was unlocked from the outside and a guard led them in. They rushed over to him while the guard positioned himself by the door. He would be able to hear anything they said during the visit.

Henry stood up, and his mother threw her arms around him. He hugged her back, comforted by the familiar smell of her perfume. She held him for a long time. He let her. He could only imagine how his mother had been feeling these past months. They had never had the chance to talk about what had happened. Henry knew they probably never would. There was nothing to discuss about his situation. It was what it was. He had been caught and was now suffering the consequences. But he also knew that he would do it again. If he had the chance.

His mother finally let go of him. Jana was next. He had never heard that whole families were allowed to visit, only one person at a time, usually the parent. Why was he allowed more visitors? He didn't care. They were here. Jana squeezed him so hard it almost hurt. He pulled free of her with a throaty laugh. Jana stepped aside and Georg appeared. His hand was outstretched to him. He had no choice. He had to shake it. Georg seemed relieved. Henry regretted instantly that he had given in so easily. He wanted to make sure that Georg knew how he felt about his betrayal.

His mother had brought a bag, which she was unpacking now. She placed toothpaste, socks, and a couple of books on the table. At last she pulled out what he thought was a cake.

"I'm sorry you have to spend your birthday in jail, sis," Henry joked, his eyes on the cake. Jana didn't laugh. He knew it pained them to see him here in jail. On his birthday. His mother cut the cake and, with a look in the guard's direction, she handed him a piece. He bit into it eagerly. His eyes closed automatically, and he savored the taste of the homemade marble cake. Together with the cake, he swallowed the lump in his throat. He looked at his mother and realized she had tears in her eyes. She mouthed a happy birthday and proceeded to cut off another piece of cake.

While Jana and Georg were eating, his mother stepped closer to him. She motioned for him to sit with her. "Georg and I ..." she began. Henry furrowed his brows at Georg's name. "Georg and I are together now," she continued.

Henry didn't know what to say. All these years, he had hoped for Georg to become his father. But not anymore. Did his mother know what Georg had said about him? What Georg really thought of him? All these years he had believed Georg was his friend, but he had been mistaken. "Georg is not the man you think he is," Henry whispered with a side-glance at Georg.

His mother stared at him in disbelief. "What do you mean?"

"He pretends to be someone he's not."

A knowing look appeared on his mother's face. "Georg told me about what he had to say in Fleischer's office." She leaned forward and put her hand on his arm. "He wanted to help you."

"He didn't have to say what he said, nor did it help me. I'm still here, am I not?" Henry couldn't believe what he was hearing. Obviously, Georg had told his mother his side of the story. "You and Jana would have never said that about me, no matter what the circumstances." He looked his mother in the eyes. "No matter how stupid I acted."

He saw his mother bite her lip. She knew he was right.

They sat there for a while, and she got up when Jana came over to them. "I'm sorry you feel that way," his mother said and let Jana sit down in her place.

"Feel sorry about what?" Jana asked as she pulled the chair closer up to him.

Henry waved it off. Jana seemed to accept that it wasn't up for further discussion because she immediately started to tell him everything that had happened in the past months in so rapid a flow of words that he had difficulty keeping up. His sister told him everything. From how awful it had been without him at Christmas, the May Day celebrations, and the meetings at the church. At times, she glanced at the guard and tried to lower her voice.

Henry couldn't help smiling. He didn't recognize her. Jana had changed. And for the better. She had finally come around. But when she started to talk about Tom, he raised his hand and stopped her. "Tom Bauer?" Jana nodded, and he detected something in her eyes that concerned him. Did she like the guy? "Tom Bauer is not the guy you think he is."

"Oh, I know who he is."

He didn't like what she was saying. "Do you really? What do you know about him?"

"He's on the council with me, gets good grades, but has the courage to voice his opinion about the government."

"Does he?"

"And he goes to the meetings at the church just as I do. I know who he is, Henry."

"No, you don't. He's an informant for the Stasi." That shocked her into silence. She stared at him in disbelief. "He's attending these meetings so he can report what's being said back to the Stasi."

"But... his father... he's always been opposed to the government."

"Has he?" Henry could tell Jana was thinking hard. She was biting her lip. The concentration showed on her face.

"How do you know?" she finally asked.

Henry looked at her. "I just know."

He could tell Jana wasn't satisfied with his answer. "You need to tell me how you know," she insisted. "You can't simply claim –"

"Five minutes," the guard announced loudly.

"It's time for him to come home. Prison has changed him," Henry heard Georg say. How dare Georg talk about him like that? He had no right to –

"It has, hasn't it," his mother said, and Henry felt his stomach tighten.

He restrained himself from looking at them, so he focused on his sister's face. He saw that she had heard them as well. Jana got up and hugged him. He had to swallow. They would say their goodbyes now. He felt that Jana was crying and had to swallow again. How he longed to go with them. How he had missed them. For the rest of his existence, he would make those who had wronged him pay for what they had done to him, to his family.

"Can you tell she missed you?" His mother came over to them. Jana let go of him and wiped at her tears.

"And I missed her," Henry said. "I'm glad to see she's finally come around though," he said with a smile in Jana's direction.

"She has." His mother's somber look didn't match what she was saying. Henry didn't understand her subdued reaction. Susanne Schmidt of all people had to be happy that her daughter had finally realized how oppressive their government was.

The guard cleared his throat. His mother hugged him. "Hold out a little while longer," she whispered in his ear.

He let go of her and again Jana came to give him a last hug. "Happy birthday, Henry. I promise you'll be out soon."

"Don't do anything stupid, sister," he joked. But then he realized how serious Jana had sounded. Was she up to something? It worried him instantly.

But Jana just grinned at him and motioned over to where Georg stood. "Yeah, we all do or say stupid things at times." Jana winked at him.

Henry felt his face harden. Jana didn't understand. Nor did his mother.

When they returned home that night, Tom was waiting at the gate for Jana. Her mother winked at her, and they left her alone with Tom.

As soon as they were gone, he stepped closer and pulled out a small bouquet of flowers from behind his back. "Happy birthday," he said, and held the flowers out to her.

Jana was taken aback. But she had no time to sort her thoughts. Tom stepped even closer and he kissed her. It was a gentle kiss, but Jana thought it lasted an eternity.

Henry's words came back, and her head was spinning. Was Henry right about Tom? She pulled back. Tom stepped back and looked at her. "Did you stop smoking?" she asked.

Tom looked surprised by the question, but then shook his head. "It's not that easy, you know." He grinned at her. "Want to go somewhere?" he asked.

"Where?" Where would they go? Everything in the village was now closed.

"We could go to my house."

"To do what?"

"Celebrate." Tom's brows started to furrow. "Your birthday," he added.

Jana looked up at her house. She felt drained after the emotional day she had, but she didn't feel like joining her mother and Georg for the rest of the night either. And maybe she could find out if Tom really was an informant, as Henry had suggested. "Let me make sure my mother allows it. She likes to have me all to herself on my birthday." Tom nodded, and Jana went inside. She felt so confused. She liked Tom, but she was no longer sure about him. How well did she really know him?

When she came in, she found Georg in the kitchen preparing tea. Leftover cake stood on the table. Jana put her flowers down to take a piece.

"Where is Mama?" Jana asked him between bites.

"In the cellar, getting some wine."

"In the cellar? She actually goes down there now?"

"Yeah. It seems she finally believes me that the undead don't live down there." Georg laughed at his own words.

Just then, her mother came in. She put two bottles on the table and turned to Jana.

"Let's celebrate some more."

"I was just wondering if I could go over to Tom's for the rest of the evening."

"On your birthday? He's certainly welcome to join us," her mother said.

"He invited me over to his house."

"To do what exactly?"

She had no idea. "I don't know. Maybe it's a birthday surprise or something."

Her mother looked genuinely annoyed. "He's a boy, Jana. Why would he invite you over to his house?"

Jana blushed. "He's not like that." She started to feel irritated by her mother's interrogation. What was she thinking she'd do?

Georg butted in. "She's sixteen, Susanne. She doesn't want to hang out with old people on her birthday. Let her have some fun with her friends."

Her mother mumbled something, but she didn't seem to object any longer. Jana kissed first her mother and then Georg on the cheek and left. Her mother had to get used to not always having her around on her birthdays. She was no longer a child.

Tom was waiting where Jana had left him. He looked pleased when she told him she could come. Together they started to walk to the other end of the village where Tom lived. Just as the sun went down, Tom took her hand. Again, it caught her off guard. She didn't object, but it felt awkward holding his hand. What did the kissing and holding hands mean? She hoped Tom wouldn't ask her the dreaded question. She'd never had a boyfriend, and going steady with a boy wasn't on her agenda. And what would Henry say? He obviously disliked Tom because he assumed he was an informant. But what would Henry think of her if he found out she was one herself, even if she had done it to get him out of prison? She thought of Georg and how Henry still hadn't forgiven him. Would her brother forgive her?

When they got to Tom's house, he turned to her. And again, for the third time this night, he surprised her. He pulled her close and hugged her. When he let go of her, he kissed her again. This time, she was surprised to find herself kissing him back. He wouldn't need to ask the question now. They were a pair, whether Henry approved or not.

Jana looked around in Tom's room. It was plain. The kind of room a boy would have. It reminded her of her brother's. There were a few clothes strewn across the floor, it smelled a bit like the gym, and there were no pictures or posters on the walls, no dolls or stuffed animals sitting on the bed.

Tom gestured for her to sit down on the bed next to him. The only chair in the room was an uncomfortable looking wooden chair at his desk, so Jana sat down next to him and looked around. "Would you like to listen to some music?" Tom asked. Jana nodded, glad Tom had interrupted the awkward silence. He got up and went to a cassette player that stood on a shelf. He pushed play and immediately the music filled the room. He sat back down next to her. "It's yours if you want," he said.

Jana didn't understand. "What do you mean?" she asked over the rather loud music.

"The cassette."

"Oh ... I see ... thanks." She didn't know what else to say.

"I listened to the West German radio station and recorded a few songs." He looked her straight in the eyes. "Songs that remind me of you."

Jana swallowed. "Thank you," she said. Realizing it came out hoarsely, she cleared her throat.

"I'll get us something to drink," Tom said suddenly and got up. "Are you hungry?" Jana shook her head. Tom left, and Jana found herself alone in his room. She got up and walked around. First over to the shelf on which the cassette player stood. She found a cassette case next to it and looked at the label. Songs for Jana, it said. She quickly put it down.

Jana walked over to the window. She briefly glanced at his desk when she passed it. She saw a stack of papers and a folder next to it. Henry's words came to her mind once more. She looked at the door and then back at the papers on the desk. She could take a quick peek. But what was she expecting to find? And if he *were* an informant? So what? She was too. How could she condemn him for something she was doing herself? The door opened, and she whipped around, feeling guilty.

Tom came in carrying a bottle of beer, two glasses, and something to snack on. He put the stuff he'd brought on the desk where she stood and started pouring the beer. "I should have cleaned my room some more," he said.

"It ... it looks fine," Jana said, trying to recover. She felt caught, although she hadn't really been prying.

He offered her a glass, and she took it, knowing she wouldn't drink the beer. She already had a bitter taste in her mouth. They clinked glasses. Tom toasted to her health and then he downed the beer. Out of politeness, she took a sip and quickly put down the glass. Tom did the same and then turned to her. "We have a birthday tradition in my family," he said, holding up the now empty beer bottle to her. Jana looked at the bottle and then back at Tom. What was he talking about? Drinking beer on one's birthday was as ordinary as a roasted goose on Christmas. Tom took a piece of paper out of one of the desk's drawers. "On birthdays, we write our birthday wish on a piece of paper, roll it up and put it in a bottle to throw it in the river."

"What for?" Jana asked, taking the pen Tom held out to her.

"Sometimes the bottle is found by someone who makes sure the wish is fulfilled.

Most times, however, the bottle disappears. But a wish is a wish, right?" Tom winked at her and motioned for her to sit down. Jana did and looked at the empty piece of paper in front of her. A wish? This was silly. "Everyone has a wish or two. Don't you?" Tom said, moving over to the bed to sit down.

Jana turned around to look at him. "You're serious about this?" Tom grinned, nodding. All right, she couldn't get out of this silly Bauer family tradition. Why not play along? What wish could she put on there? She started scribbling. There was no magic in this, but it wouldn't hurt to write down what one wished for. Jana rolled up the paper and put it in the bottle.

Tom came over to her and sealed it. He held out his hand. "Let's go down to the river and throw it in, so we can send your wish on its way." Jana took his hand and he pulled her up.

It was completely dark out now when they made their short walk to the river. Jana knew where Tom was taking her. There was a spot by the cemetery where steps led down into the water. It was a great spot for fishing. Georg had taken Henry and her with him a few years ago.

When they reached the spot, Tom took her hand to lead her down the steps. The dark water was rushing by, and Jana felt a chill.

"Throw it in far, so it doesn't get caught in any branches." Jana took aim and threw. There was a splash. "You know, all rivers eventually flow into the ocean," Tom said, putting his arm around her shoulder.

"They do, but I doubt it will get there," Jana said, staring at the dark waters only inches from the tip of her shoes.

"You never know. By the way, what did you wish for?"

"I thought it was a secret."

"It kind of is, but I thought maybe you'd tell me," Tom said.

Tom's head was very close to hers, and she could smell his aftershave. "No, I won't. I want my wish to come true."

"I see," Tom said, and pulled her against his chest. "Is there anything I can do to make it come true?"

"I doubt you'll be able to find that bottle. It probably already reached the West." "Well, then I will have to go to Hungary to get it," Tom said.

"What do you mean?" Why did she always have such a hard time comprehending what Tom was getting at? He didn't make sense half of the time.

Tom pulled free and he stared at her. "You haven't heard?" Jana shook her head in total confusion. "Hungary has opened its border to the West."

Chapter 22

On Sunday afternoon, Jana was going through a pile of letters in her room when she heard a knock on her door. "Come in," she called without looking up.

"What are you doing inside? It's beautiful out," Tom said.

Jana looked up and turned around to him. "I was just going through my father's letters. He always sends a package and a letter for our birthday. I wanted to put it in the box but then I felt like reading through some old ones.

"What does he write about?" Tom asked, sitting down on her bed.

"Not much, really. He wishes us a happy birthday, inquires after our health, and tells us that he longs to meet us. That's pretty much it." Jana put the letters in a pile and placed them in the box. "Oh, and he always ends his letters with a greeting for my mother. That's really all." Jana sighed and placed the lid on the box. She came over to Tom and sat down on the bed beside him.

"Do you ever write back?" Tom asked.

"Of course. I have to thank him for his gift, don't I? I usually do it for both Henry and me. My father never writes back after that. Only the package with the letter. Every May."

"What does he send you?"

"When we were little, mostly toys. Now it's clothes, chocolate, music tapes. I got a Walkman last year. And three years ago, Henry and I both got a nice calculator. You know, the ones you can't get here."

"Sounds like you're pretty privileged. I wish I could get my hands on a Walkman."

Tom seemed genuinely impressed, but Jana didn't care about such things. She liked the Walkman and was glad she had that calculator, but those things also reminded her of the father she didn't have or didn't even know and who didn't know her or Henry. Her family rarely spoke of him. To her, he was a phantom. She didn't know if he really existed. Anyone could have sent these packages or written these letters. He never called. Jana was glad. What would they talk about? He was a stranger to them and they to him. "You know, he doesn't even know Henry is in jail." Tom looked at her in surprise. Jana swallowed. "I can't believe he's still in jail, Tom. Poor Henry."

Tom took her hand. His was warm and moist. She didn't mind. "He'll be out soon, won't he?" Tom asked carefully.

"Not for months. Not if I can't help it."

"What do you mean?" Tom sounded surprised.

Jana turned to him. She trusted Tom. They'd become so close. He was her only true friend. So why not tell him? "I made a deal." Jana felt nervous. What would Tom think of her? Had she acted too rash? He only looked at her, puzzled. So she continued. If he wanted to be her boyfriend, he had to accept her and whatever she had to do to get Henry out. "I made a deal," she began again, "with the Stasi. If I have something worthwhile to report, they'll let Henry out." Tom was silent. He just stared at her. Jana swallowed. He would hate her. Why did she tell him now? *I'm so stupid*, she thought.

"You're an informant?" Tom looked incredulous.

"I guess so." She shrugged. "If that's what you want to call it."
Tom got up. Jana also got up, feeling she had to explain. Informant
sounded so harsh. That wasn't her. "I have to help Henry. He
would do the same for me," she said hastily.

"I see," Tom said, his brows furrowed. He looked concerned.
"Well, I have to go," Tom said suddenly. "Homework."

Jana was too stunned by his abruptness to utter a response. He
was already at the door when she found her voice. "All right. I –"

He cut her off. "See you in school tomorrow."

Jana stared at the closed door. She felt tears well up and swallowed them down.

Tom ...

Jana felt reluctant to go to school on Monday morning. Tom had
left her so suddenly and she knew that could mean only one thing.
He didn't approve and would probably break up with her today.
He was so outspoken against the government. Like his father. He
would never be with someone who worked for the Stasi. But she
wasn't *really* working for the Stasi. She looked up into the overcast
sky and shivered from the cool breeze that brushed against her
skin. She only wore a t-shirt and regretted not taking her cardigan
along. It had been such a nice and warm weekend. Why was it so
cool today?

Jana hugged herself against the morning chill as she walked
the sidewalk underneath the linden trees toward the school. She
looked up when she heard someone approach from the opposite
direction. It was Tom, who strode toward her, the expression on
his face stoic but determined. She swallowed.

When he had reached her, he took her by the arms and pressed
her against the trunk of a linden tree. Without warning, he kissed
her. It was a passionate, demanding kiss. Jana was too bewildered

to kiss him back, but she let him continue, her mind racing to find a reason for Tom's demeanor. When he proceeded down her neck, she gently pushed him away. Tom was out of breath. His eyes almost scorching. "What's going on, Tom?"

He pulled away from her and paced up and down in front of her. He suddenly stopped and looked at her. "I'll help you," he said breathlessly. When Jana didn't answer, he added, "To get your brother out."

—

Georg looked at Susanne as she sterilized the instruments for surgery. "You've been so quiet today," he said, trying to hide the worry in his voice. Susanne looked up at him but didn't respond. "It wouldn't have anything to do with what they announced on the news?" This time Susanne lowered her eyes. So that was what was on her mind. Georg decided not to give up. "Pretty crazy, huh? Hungarians now able to travel to the West." Susanne still didn't say a word. Biting her lip, her eyes were fastened on the instruments she was arranging on a tray. Georg went over to her and put his arm around her. "What is it, Susanne?"

"It's nothing," she said, pulling free and taking the tray with the surgical instruments over to the operating table. "Everything is ready. Do you want me to go ahead and get the cat?"

Georg simply nodded, ready to give up. It was obvious Susanne didn't want to talk about Hungary opening its borders. From the bottom of his heart he hoped that she wasn't considering going there to get to the West. The West German news had reported that hundreds and hundreds of East Germans were now traveling to Hungary to seek asylum in the West German embassy in Budapest. Some had even attempted to flee across the border into Austria – the promised West – illegally, not waiting for any papers from the West Germans.

270

Georg began the operation and only spoke when he asked Susanne to hand him this instrument or that. She was still quiet and did not once look at him. He began to grow more worried, trying hard to think of what to say to her so she would open up to him. But he knew now wasn't the time. The kitten on the table in front of them was breathing evenly, but surgery required not only a steady hand but also a focused mind. He had done this numerous times, but he had to clear his head. Spaying cats had been his steady income. People didn't bring their male cats to him to neuter them, but they had no issues with spaying the females even if it was more invasive and difficult on the animal.

The surgery went well and after Georg finished up, Susanne put the sleeping cat in a crate. The animal would be out for another hour before waking up to excruciating pain. He would give the cat the lowest dose of pain medication. It had been harder and harder to get the amounts he requested. It was as if the country had stopped producing anything and was going broke.

They cleaned up together, but still neither of them spoke. Georg decided to wait to talk to Susanne until after dinner. But this time he wouldn't give up until he knew what was going on, why she was so distant.

———

Susanne was glad when Jana and Tom walked into the practice. The awkward silence between her and Georg had gotten unbearable now that the surgery was over. She had felt cornered when Georg had asked why she was being so quiet. Apparently, Georg was aware that something was going on with her, but she couldn't tell him. When she had heard the announcement on the news about Hungary opening its borders, it had instantly hit her that this presented them with the opportunity to leave the country. But how could they? Henry was still in jail. She knew Jana would

271

come. But Georg? He would never leave Wallhausen. But she couldn't just break up with him and leave him like that. She felt so comfortable around him, but did she really love him? Was what she felt for him enough to stay? She had wanted to leave all these years, and now there was a chance she could. Who knew how long the borders would stay open?

Susanne sighed, took off her lab coat, and went to greet Jana and Tom. She still hadn't gotten used to the sight of them together. In her opinion, Jana was still too young to have a steady boyfriend. They were spending all their free time together. It annoyed her. She wasn't sure what to make of Tom. He seemed too mature for Jana, even if he was in the same grade as she. Weren't boys usually less mature than girls at that age? Susanne was still wondering about it when Jana spoke.

"We have a proposal," Jana said, flushed with excitement. She was holding hands with Tom, who looked confident about what Jana was saying. Susanne's eyebrows furrowed at Jana's announcement. It seemed important to them. Georg looked up curiously.

"Tom and I've been thinking about what to do this summer," Jana continued. "Why?" Susanne asked, confused.

"I know we usually go up to the coast. You, Henry, me..." Jana said.

"And we will." Susanne folded her arms in front of her chest. She didn't like any of this.

"Tom and I decided to go to Hungary once school's out."

"We'll be camping at Lake Balaton," Tom chimed in.

Susanne held up her hands, and Tom stopped speaking immediately. Had she heard them correctly? Hungary?

"I'm sixteen now," Jana continued, ignoring the gesture that Tom had understood so well.

"Exactly. You're *only* sixteen. And Hungary? Why Hungary? I can't let you travel to a foreign country all by yourself. Where did you kids get the idea?" What were they thinking?

"No one goes on vacation with their parents anymore when they're sixteen," Jana said defiantly.

"I did. With my grandmother."

Jana bit her lip. She looked angry, but she had stopped talking. Susanne took that as a sign that she was winning the battle.

"It's five of us who are going," Tom said suddenly. "A group of friends. All our age."

"Who are they?" Susanne asked.

Tom told her the names. Susanne realized they were all good kids she knew. But she couldn't possibly let them go to Hungary all by themselves. And what about their own vacation to the coast? She had planned to take Georg along with them for the first time. But it started to look as if it might be just her and Georg, with Henry in prison and Jana unwilling to join them.

Jana stepped forward. "If you hear why Tom and I really want to go, you'll let us."

Susanne felt her heart stop. And then Jana told her what Tom and she had been planning. When Jana was finished, Susanne knew she had no choice. She had to let Jana go.

Jana was glad Georg had come with her. He didn't agree with her being an informant for the Stasi, but he had volunteered to accompany her. She could never have gotten up the courage to go see Fleischer all by herself. Thoughts of the man sent chills up and down her spine. If their plan failed ...

Jana understood why her mother was so reluctant to meet the Stasi officer. He was cruel, unbending, and he had no compassion for them. Indeed, he seemed to relish their fate. Jana only hoped that what she would tell him today would finally set Henry free. Her brother had missed most of the school year. He would have to repeat the grade, and she knew how he would hate that.

She no longer cared about going on with school and being able to study at a university. She started to understand her mother and her feelings toward the government. What she had to endure throughout the years. Her mother had lost her husband, and Henry and she had lost their father. As long as one conformed and complied, things went well. But if one didn't ... Jana understood that now.

Georg looked at the duffle bag next to her. "Got everything?"

"Tom has the rest," she said. Tom and the three others would come up to Berlin on a later train, bringing what they needed for their camping trip in Hungary. But it wasn't really a camping trip. Jana could still remember how she had felt her heart plummet when Tom told her that cool Monday morning under the linden tree that he and his friends wanted to go to Hungary, to flee to the West. She had been so shocked that she hadn't heard Tom ask her to come with them. He had to repeat the question two more times before she comprehended what he was asking. She had vehemently protested and cried. How could he ask that of her, and how could he leave like that? Tom managed to stop her hysteria only when he told her that this would offer her the opportunity to free Henry. She could report them to Fleischer for desertion. This time, she was shocked into utter silence. Tom had taken her hands in his and explained how they would pull it off. At the end of the day, she was convinced that it would work, and that it was exactly what she needed to get Henry out. He was her brother, and for him she would do anything, even give up everything, even Tom.

So she had helped Tom with the planning. She found that she compared him to Henry who also would have had no second thoughts about a risky undertaking such as this. They planned every detail and considered every eventuality. They had to. Jana would go to Fleischer and inform him of the boys from Wallhausen who planned to desert. While she was at the meeting, Tom and his friends would come up to Berlin and wait for her at the train station to take the first train to Czechoslovakia. From there they would go on to Hungary. They would be out of the country by the time the Stasi discovered that they had already left. Jana could just stay behind, but she had insisted on going with them to Hungary. It was the only time she would have with Tom. Only after he and her mother had agreed to let her come, had she consented to denounce Tom and his friends. But it was important that Jana's absence could be explained with various summer activities if Fleischer tried to contact her while she was gone. Her mother and Georg would string him along until she returned from Hungary. If something didn't go according to their plan, all of them would be exposed and suffer the consequences. But Jana knew she couldn't allow herself to think of any of that. It just had to work.

When Jana and Georg entered Fleischer's office, the Stasi officer was leaning over his filing cabinet. Without turning around to them, he bade them to sit. This was the second time Jana was in his office, but she felt just as uneasy as the first time she had been here. She only hoped that this was the last time. All she wanted was to get it over with as fast as possible.

When Fleischer was finally seated, Jana told him she had something significant to report to him. Fleischer nodded in encouragement with such a pleased satisfaction playing around his mouth that Jana felt instantly nauseated. She breathed in deeply to calm herself and reported. Fleischer listened eagerly. He jotted down notes. And he didn't interrupt her. His face was unmovable throughout her report.

"Names of your friends?" he asked when she was finished.

She gave them to him. What she didn't tell Fleischer was that the same people were waiting at the train station for her. She checked the clock on the wall. By the time Fleischer checked up on her report, they would already be in Hungary. The Stasi officer wouldn't have a chance of catching up with them. She looked at Georg from the corner of her eye and felt unbelievably grateful to the man who had been like a father to her all these years. He hadn't liked her plan, but he was going along with it. She was sure it was also because of Henry. Georg wanted him out of prison at least as much as her mother and she, and he wanted to be the one there when Henry was released from prison. There was nothing more Georg wished for than to reconcile with Henry. On their train ride home, there would be plenty of time for the both of them to make up. This detail of their plan had been another motivating factor for Jana to go through with it.

Fleischer looked at her, his eyes scrutinizing her. Did he suspect anything? She kneaded her hands nervously, but tried to look calm.

"This is indeed some useful information. You've shown that you're up to the task. Well done, Fräulein Schmidt. Well done."

"What about my brother then?" Jana thought she saw Georg shift nervously in his seat. She knew this was the crucial moment. Would Fleischer stand by their deal?

"He shall be released as promised."

"When will you release him?"

"Tomorrow."

"Will it be all right if you released him into Georg Hoffmann's care?" Jana asked, trying to sound nonchalant.

"Of course," he said condescendingly. Jana tried to stifle a sigh of relief. "Will you not be there as well?" Fleischer asked suddenly.

Jana thought her heart stopped, but she recovered quickly. She had prepared for this. "No. I have other plans."

"What other plans, if I may ask?"

Jana had known that it had to be something extraordinary to explain why she wouldn't be there when her brother got out of jail. Something that Fleischer would buy and see as a worthy excuse. "I'll be visiting the Minister of Culture with members of the Free German Youth from Wallhausen." Fleischer eyed her suspiciously. Would he believe her? She shifted nervously in her seat. Fleischer's penetrating gaze made her swallow. He wouldn't be easily fooled.

Jana was right. He reached for the phone on his desk. She swallowed again. He dialed.

"The office of the Minister of Culture, please," he said, not taking his eyes off her. "Do you have a group of Free German Youth coming to see the minister in the morning?"

Jana could hear the woman on the other end of the line say something to Fleischer. "Yes," Fleischer said. Jana glanced at Georg next to her. His eyes were fixed on Fleischer's phone. He didn't seem to breathe. "Yes," Fleischer said again. "From Wallhausen?" There was a pause. "Thank you," Fleischer said and put down the phone. He leaned back in his chair, smiling. "I think I now completely understand you, Fräulein Schmidt. I consider it also more important to visit the minister than to be at the gate when your criminal brother reemerges from prison. I understand, indeed. Herr Hoffmann here may pick your brother up while you have more important things to attend to."

"Thank you," Jana said, surprised she had summoned the words. It wasn't meant for Fleischer, but for Diana, her godmother, who with her many contacts had arranged their visit with the minister. However, they would never show up at the office of the Minister of Culture. Jana had purposely neglected to tell her godmother that. The fewer people that knew of their plans, the better. It simply provided another distraction from what they were really doing. It was all going well, all according to their plan. Jana checked the clock again. It was time to leave.

"If you need any further information, please let me know," Jana said, and got up. She felt confident. Georg got up as well and looked at her with slight astonishment.

"Oh, Fräulein Schmidt," Fleischer said suddenly.

Jana stopped short. What else could he want? It had gone so well. "Yes, Herr Fleischer?" She tried to keep her voice steady.

"Aren't you still interested in getting into the university of your choice?" he asked, his eyes scrutinizing her once more.

How could she have neglected that? Fleischer knew that it had been of importance to her. Was he suspecting her change of heart? "I didn't want to stretch my luck. It was my first priority to get my brother out. I didn't dare ask for more ... today." Would Fleischer buy it? Jana looked at him firmly and was relieved to see that he had indeed accepted her reply.

When they left the building, Jana felt jubilant. She saw that Georg looked rather worried. "Don't worry," she said. "Everything went to plan." Jana checked her watch. "But we'll have to hurry. The train will leave in thirty minutes."

Georg didn't move. "Just camping in Hungary? You'll be back, right?"

Jana turned to him. "Of course. I could never leave my mother, Henry ... and you like that," Jana said. She was glad she hadn't mentioned to her mother or Georg that Tom wanted her to come with him to the West. If they had known, they would have never let her go to Hungary with him. She couldn't deny that she hadn't pondered deserting with Tom and his friends. She had thought of her father, even daydreamed about the moment they would meet for the first time. But when reality had set in, doubts had overcome her. What would her father think when she just came to his door one day? Would he want to see her? But Jana meant what she had just told Georg. She could never leave her family. But she would lose Tom. The thought made her dizzy. But maybe they wouldn't be separated forever. As soon as Jana had agreed to the plan, she had gone to her mother to encourage her to apply for another exit visa. She liked her life in Wallhausen but to be with Tom and so assure a better life for her mother and her brother, she was willing to leave her home behind. She looked up at Georg and swallowed. What about him?

"All right," Georg interrupted her thoughts, apparently relieved she wouldn't be so daring like the boys and escape across the border. "I'll take you to the train station then."

They took the bus and made it just in time. Tom and his friends were already waiting for them on the crowded platform. She could tell from fifty meters away that they were nervous. As soon as they spotted Georg and her, Tom came running up to them.

"How did it go?" he panted.

"As we had planned it." She grinned at him.

"So Henry will be out soon?"

"Tomorrow." Tom swept her up and she had to laugh. Their train was announced and Tom set her down.

"I'll see you in a week or so, right?" Georg asked while hugging her goodbye.

"Tell Henry I can't wait to see him." Jana thought she felt Georg start.

He let go of her. "You kids have a good summer vacation." He looked at Tom. "Good luck. And be safe."

"We will be, Herr Hoffmann." Tom shook Georg's hand.

When Georg had walked away, Tom turned to her. "Let's get out of here." Together they walked over to the others and they all boarded an already full train.

Georg had gotten up too early. It only seemed to make the time go by even slower until he was able to go to the prison to pick up Henry. He decided on a morning walk. The sun was out and it was already warm when he walked through the city that was just awakening to another bustling day. He was surprised to actually hear the birds sing in this concrete maze that was East Berlin. He couldn't remember ever having heard the birds sing as a student when he had lived in the city. He walked aimlessly for another hour and then took a bus to the prison.

After Georg had signed the papers, it took another hour before Henry was brought out. His hair was very short, and he looked older than his years. Georg wondered if he had grown. He seemed taller, but maybe he appeared so due to his skinnier frame.

When Henry recognized Georg, his lips tightened and his jaw clenched. Georg realized nothing had changed. Henry had not forgiven him. With a sigh, Georg ran his hand through his hair and made his way toward Henry.

"Where is my mother? Where's Jana?" Henry asked, without offering a greeting.

He looked angry. Georg had expected no less.

"Your mother is preparing your room and dinner. She wants your first day home to be special. Jana's gone camping in Hungary with some friends."

"She's where?" Henry seemed dumbfounded.

"At Lake Balaton. She felt she was old enough to go on vacation with her friends."

"And my mother let her?" Henry looked incredulous. He stared at him for a while and then turned without a word, giving the door a hard push to step outside the prison walls. Georg sighed deeply and followed him out. It would be just as difficult to get through to Henry as he had imagined. Even more so.

They walked silently to the train station. Henry's mouth was clamped shut, his face dark with anger.

They boarded the train to Wallhausen, found two empty benches facing each other, and sat down. More people boarded, and Georg was glad that no one sat down beside them. Georg had dreaded this moment, but he cleared his throat, knowing he only had so much time to straighten things out. "Henry, I regret what I said. Believe me, every single day I've regretted what I said. But I didn't mean it. You must know that." Henry didn't respond. He stared out the window, his jaws clenched. "I wanted to help you. Get you out," Georg continued.

"It didn't work, did it?" The bitterness in Henry's voice was like acid. "You're a coward, Georg. And who knows, maybe even one of those sleazy Stasi informants who spies on his own family and friends." Georg felt as if Henry had slapped him. "I have to use the bathroom." Henry got up and left.

Georg fell back in his seat. Only now did he realize that people around them had listened to their conversation. Of course, they had. It had been a heated exchange. Some looked at him out of the corner of their eyes. An old man shook his head in his direction. There were no friendly gestures or words. He sighed and ignored them.

Henry took a long time. When he finally came back, he sat back down across from Georg, not looking at him but out the window. However, people around them looked on with curiosity, probably hoping to get another show, but Georg wouldn't give it to them. Maybe he should let it go for now. Maybe Henry just needed some time. Time outside the prison walls to understand and to forgive.

They didn't speak for the rest of the tedious train ride. Georg was glad when he was able to release the brooding Henry into the care of Susanne, who was waiting for them at the train station. She was already in tears when they got to her. He knew they were tears of joy because Susanne couldn't stop hugging Henry. And Henry let her, his bitter face slowly turning softer and revealing glimpses of the old Henry.

They took him home. Susanne had prepared a feast. Henry eagerly wolfed down the food, and he seemed even more relaxed. When they cleared the table, Henry grew serious again. "Now tell me about Jana. What is she doing in Hungary? I can't believe you let her go. Who did she go with?"

Susanne laughed lightly when she saw Henry's concerned face. Georg felt glad to see her like that, even if he hadn't worked anything out with Henry. "Well, first of all..." Susanne began, "... you have to thank your sister for getting you out." Henry's eyebrows furrowed instantly, but he didn't say anything.

"Spending her summer vacation in Hungary was all part of the plan," Georg chimed in. Henry didn't look at him. His eyes were fastened on his mother as if he hadn't heard him.

"Jana volunteered to be an informant, waiting for an opportunity to report something worthwhile in exchange for your release from prison," Susanne said carefully.

"Jana? An informant?" Henry's expression had darkened. He got up and started pacing. "Jana, too?"

"It was just a set up. For Fleischer," Susanne got up as well.

"There is no one I can trust. No one," Henry said as if to himself, but he was staring at Georg.

Georg could no longer listen to this. He stepped toward Henry, ignoring the threatening stare. "There isn't only black and white, Henry. In this country, there is a lot of gray. Even your mother understands that." Georg saw Susanne flinch, but he didn't care. Henry had to wake up from his stupor and see how the world really worked. The sooner, the better. It would save him a lot of grief and pain in the future. "Jana volunteered to be an informant. She made a deal with Fleischer. Denounce someone to get you out. She put herself and the others in danger for you. It's time you showed a little gratitude." Henry stared at him. Georg could see the corners of his mouth twitch. For a moment, Henry's eyes flickered to his mother. Her face showed shock, but she nodded ever so slightly as if to encourage Henry to listen.

"Who are the others?" Henry asked suddenly.

Georg looked at him, not understanding.

Susanne answered for him. "It wasn't Jana's plan alone. Tom really came up with it."

"Tom Bauer?" Henry asked in a strained voice.

Susanne nodded. "He and two of his friends want to go West through Hungary. It was his idea to have Jana report him and his friends to the Stasi for attempted desertion."

"The coward's trying to get away."

"Many try to get away these days," Georg said, trying to avoid looking at Susanne.

"He's trying to get away from *me*," Henry said.

———

Only two days left, Jana thought anxiously as she watched Tom cook their lunch over the little cooker they had brought for their camping trip. This had been the best summer vacation of her life so far. And she knew it was due to Tom's presence. How could she let him go? Now they had no choice. He would be in trouble if he returned to Wallhausen and didn't go through with the rest of the plan.

She watched Tom try to cut a watermelon with the little knife they had brought. After a minute, she got tired of watching him. "I can ask someone to let us borrow a big knife," she said. She looked at the rows of tents to her right, where some people were preparing lunch as well.

"I can get it," Tom said, biting his lip in concentration or frustration. Jana couldn't tell which. She sighed and got up. She pulled a shirt from the makeshift clothesline they had put up between their tents and pulled it over the swimsuit she was wearing.

Without another look at Tom, she went over to the nearby tent and approached a young mother who was feeding her toddler. "Do you have a large knife we could borrow?" Jana asked the woman.

The young mother looked up at her in surprise. "Sure." She looked around, scanning her kitchen utensils until her eyes fell on a large knife. She handed it to Jana. "You can have all this stuff when we leave tomorrow," the woman said. Jana didn't comprehend. The woman must have read her expression correctly, because she stepped closer to her. Her voice was only a whisper. "We're trying to get into Austria tomorrow. We can only take one bag each." She motioned to the child.

Jana stared at her in horror. Why was this woman telling her this? She saw the excitement and anticipation in the woman's eyes and understood. She's seen it in Tom's eyes. But this woman had a small child. She would risk taking her little one across the border? Was she out of her mind? This was way too dangerous. What if –

"You can even have the tent," the woman interrupted her thoughts. "It's all yours tomorrow. We won't be sitting around any longer waiting for our papers. We'll leave before the sun is up."

Jana was stunned by the woman's naïveté. She mumbled a thank you and stumbled back to her own tent. Wordlessly, she handed Tom the knife.

Tom took the knife from her but stopped midway. "What's wrong? You look like you've seen a ghost."

"The woman over there ... she and her family will cross tomorrow. With a small child."

"They will?" Tom looked thoughtfully in their direction, but then seemed to remember something. He put the knife down and hugged Jana. "I know this is hard for you. I promise we'll be together again. Eventually your family's exit visa will be approved. It will." He stroked her hair soothingly, but Jana didn't feel comforted by Tom's words. Her mother and father had been separated, each living on a different side of the fence. And they never had been able to be together again. She and Tom wouldn't either.

She had to accept that. They would be separated, and as things were, it would be forever. Jana swallowed. She couldn't stop the sobs that were welling up in her. Tom took her face into his hands and started kissing away the salty tears that were running down her cheeks now. *Two days*, she thought, regretting with all her heart she had agreed to the plan, even if it had meant Henry's release.

———

They stood at the edge of the forest, their eyes fastened on the checkpoint. Jana had her fingers wrapped tightly around Tom's. The last days together had flown by, and here they were. Tom and his two friends were each carrying a backpack with the bare essentials they would need. Some food and drink and toiletries, and another set of clothes. Nothing else had fit into their backpacks. A meager start into a new life. While they stared at the checkpoint, Jana's mind turned to the boys' parents. She trembled at the thought of them finding out their sons would not return. They were still kids, not having reached the legal age. Would the Austrians or West Germans send them back? She doubted it. Foster care would await them. Jana doubted that Tom and the others had considered that. She hoped that they wouldn't have a rude awakening and regret their decision later.

"We should get moving," Tom whispered. Jana's attention turned back to the checkpoint. The only border guard was leaning lazily against the wall of the little building, smoking. His Kalashnikov was dangling to his side. The border was no longer fortified and guarded in the same way, since the Hungarians had cut down the barbed wire fences. Still, there were checkpoints, and crossing the border into Austria without proper papers was illegal. Tom and his friends didn't have such papers. Still, Tom had decided it would be best to go through a checkpoint. Jana had been furious when he had told her. It made no sense. But Tom was insistent that the guards would not shoot at them. He had heard from people at their campground that the Hungarian border guards showed solidarity and would let East Germans through, even if they didn't have papers. Jana knew that these were only rumors. But Tom wanted to go through a checkpoint to make sure he arrived on Austrian soil and not run across fields, rivers, or forests, not knowing where he was and get caught that way. Checkpoints were at all major roads that led west, and Tom wouldn't take any chances. He had heard stories from other campers about people trying to cross into Austria where the border was no longer patrolled, only to run into the arms of Hungarian patrols later and be taken into custody, not realizing they had never made it across. There was only one fate that awaited those that got caught. They were returned to the East German authorities. Hence, wanting to test the checkpoint first. Tom's plan was to run, should the border guard lack solidarity. They would then try their luck and cross the "green" border where nature and not border patrol stood guard. Jana only hoped that they wouldn't get arrested either way. It was a dangerous undertaking. For Jana, there were just too many variables and things that could go wrong.

Jana sighed and looked at the border guard. There was no way he would let the boys pass. True, these were different times, but he was there guarding the checkpoint for a reason. Jana now wished she had been able to convince Tom to forget the checkpoint and just cross the border at a less conspicuous point. But it was too late now. Tom breathed in deeply and stepped out of the forest. The others followed him. It took the guard only half a minute to see them. He was instantly alert, his face wary. Jana gasped quietly when she saw the guard raise his Kalashnikov. He yelled something in Hungarian at them, but Tom strode forward as if he hadn't heard what had certainly been a warning. The guard threw his cigarette to the ground and yelled at them again. This time there was no mistaking that what he yelled was a warning. His accented German was easy to decipher. Jana clasped Tom's hand tighter.

They were only about one hundred meters away from him when Tom stopped. They all came to a halt. Tom turned to her. She knew it was now time for their goodbyes. Jana looked nervously at the guard and swallowed. His Kalashnikov was still pointed at them. Tom looked at her calmly, as if the guard and the others weren't there. She could see anticipation, but also pain in his eyes. She swallowed again. She had known that this would be hard. Tom pulled her close, and she leaned against his chest and hugged him.

"There is something that I haven't told you that I need to tell you before I leave," he whispered. Jana looked at him, confused by the grave expression on his face. "It was me who reported Henry to the Stasi," Tom said quietly. Jana stepped back. She raised her hands as if she wanted to defend herself and shook her head vehemently. She had only imagined it. Tom hadn't told her what she thought he had told her. He hadn't. "Christian had told me about their prank. I had no choice. When the Stasi questioned me, I had to tell them. My father said it was the only way to stay under the Stasi's radar." Tom no longer met her eyes. Did Tom want to make their goodbye easier for her by saying these terrible things about himself? "I know I made a terrible mistake. That's why I wanted to help you to get Henry out. I owed him that much. I owed you that much." Then he suddenly grabbed her by her arms, his voice urgent. "Come with me, Jana. You can finally meet your father."

Jana pulled free and took another step back. "I'm glad I'll never see you again, Tom Bauer," Jana said. Her eyes were burning, but there were no tears. She turned around. She felt nothing. Certainly, the feelings of betrayal and hatred would come later. She was sure of it. But now she felt nothing. She started walking. Her legs were automatic and seemed strangely foreign to her, but they obeyed and did what she wanted them to do. Tom called after her, but she ignored him. There was nothing he could say that would make her turn back around. She never wanted to see him again. It was over. Henry had been right. He had played both sides. She swallowed hard, pulling all her strength together to keep the tears that blurred her vision from spilling over. Whatever happened to Tom Bauer was none of her concern anymore.

Henry stared at the house across the street from him. He sat loosely on his old bike, one leg dangling over the rail. The house lay still and quiet. It was too early. He assumed no one was up yet. It was overcast today. People tended to sleep longer when a good cloud cover hid the sun. He hadn't gotten used to sleeping in yet. Wake-up time had been before the break of dawn while he had been locked up.

How much time he had spent at that house across the street growing up? Christian had been his best friend since kindergarten. No longer. Henry had promised himself he'd get back at everyone who was responsible for the miserable months he had to endure. Christian would be among them. Tom Bauer had reported them both. That much Fleischer had told him in one of the numerous interrogations he had gone through. How Tom had found out that it had been the two of them who had put up the banner, Henry knew now. Christian had gone off bragging about it to Tom, assuming his anti-government father would mean their secret was safe with Tom. Not so. Tom had reported them. When Christian had been interrogated, he had broken down and had blamed it all on him. His former friend had gotten off easy. Probation, probably working for the Stasi, and a different school. In the city.

Henry had heard horror stories about these schools. Indoctrination, physical exertion, and mindless skills for future mindless jobs were taught. Subordination would be the order of the day. And Henry would go to the same school as Christian. He knew that this was another punishment. Whoever the state considered difficult or a criminal was deemed worthless until one complied. Their future would be ruined, designated to the lowest level of society.

There were only a few weeks of summer break left. He wouldn't go to that school to be indoctrinated and learn skills that would never afford him a better position than that of a factory worker. He had other plans. There was no sense in punching Christian in the face every day he would see him in school if he were to go. He would punch him one time, and one time only. Today.

Henry looked down at his hands on the handlebar. His knuckles were white. He loosened his grip. Someone inside the house flicked on a light. Henry pushed his bike forward to cross the street.

Out of the corner of his eye, he saw someone on a bike. Henry squinted. *Not him. Not now.* Unfortunately, Georg had seen him and came toward him. The man he had once considered somewhat of a father certainly looked surprised to see him. Henry still hadn't gotten used to the fact that Georg felt right at home in his house, as if he belonged there. He still lived next door in his own house, but he spent too much time at theirs. Henry had felt like a stranger in his own home since returning from prison. Georg came to a standstill in front of him.

"Are you following me now?" Henry asked through clenched teeth.

"Do I need to?" Georg asked coolly.

"You're not my father, you know," Henry said.

"I never pretended to be your father." Georg held his eyes, and Henry had to look away. "All I wanted to be was your friend. To be there for you when you needed me." Henry looked past him at Christian's house. "What are you doing here, anyway?" Georg asked, looking up at the house as well.

"Paying Christian a long overdue visit. What do you think?" *If you'll just leave,* Henry thought angrily.

"Christian will still be there tomorrow, I think." Georg looked at the house as if he doubted his own words. "I want to show you something. Come with me, will you?"

Henry stared at him. Was he serious? If he thought that he –

"Come on. It's going to be good," Georg said, getting in position on his bike.

Henry's eyes flitted back and forth between Georg and the house. Georg was right. He could still punch Christian in the face tomorrow. But if he went with Georg now, the man would believe he had forgiven him. The last thing he wanted was to give Georg that impression.

"It's not for the faint of heart," Georg said.

Henry looked at him, trying hard not to show the curiosity on his face. He sat up on his bike. "What are we waiting for, then?" Henry asked.

Georg grinned and started off. Henry followed him. He glanced at the house one more time. *I'll be back tomorrow,* he thought grimly.

When Georg turned into the local LPG, Henry fell back. No way, he thought, and came to a halt. Georg stopped, too. He seemed to have realized that Henry was no longer behind him. He looked over his shoulder at Henry.

"What are we doing here?" Henry looked at the barracks and the earthy courtyard. There were heaps of dung lining the sides. The stench was unbearable. He swallowed down the nausea that welled up in him. The only time he had set foot in here was when he and Christian had let out the pigs. He flinched at the memory.

"You're not afraid of pigs and cows, are you?" Georg mocked.

Henry could feel the anger rise up in him again, but he pushed his bike forward until he was at Georg's side. "As you know, I'm not afraid of pigs."

"That won't matter today. It's the cows we're paying a visit." Georg pushed his bike to the first barrack and leaned it against the wall. He took his bag off the back rack and looked expectantly at Henry.

"I'm not playing your assistant," Henry said. He didn't like the game Georg was playing. Why had he fallen for it? Why had he come? He swore under his breath, but loud enough for Georg to hear.

"I don't need an assistant. But if you think you can't stomach what I'm about to show you, you can leave."

Henry started to get really irritated. "Let's get this over with," he growled and parked his bike next to Georg's. He followed Georg to the next barrack, and they entered.

It smelled even worse inside. Rows of black-and-white marked cows were lined up on the left and right side of the barrack, munching on some brown, unidentifiable stuff from the troughs. Georg was striding to the end of the barrack where a worker was waiting for him. The man eyed Henry suspiciously. Georg was explaining something to the man, motioning in Henry's direction. At last the man seemed to reluctantly agree to whatever Georg had tried to talk him into.

Georg waved and Henry reluctantly went over to him. Together, they left the barrack through the door at the opposite end from which they had entered. As Henry passed the man, he shook a finger at him as if to warn him.

Henry breathed in deeply when they were outside again. The air was not great but so much better outside than in the warm, stuffy, and dung-reeking barrack. He followed Georg to what looked like a barn. They entered and walked to a corner where a cow lay on its side. The animal was moaning, and its eyes were rolling wildly around in their sockets.

"She should have given birth hours ago. Something's not right," Georg said as they stood looking down at the animal.

"You brought me here for this?" Henry couldn't believe it.

Georg looked at him, all business. "I told you, if you can't stomach it, you're free to leave."

Henry stared at the cow. Georg wanted him to see a calf being born? Why would he think that would interest him? He turned.

"I lied earlier. I might need your assistance," Georg said without looking at him. He was kneeling beside the animal now and put his hand on the cow's belly.

Henry turned back around. "I'm sure this isn't the only time you lied to me."

"Nope."

Henry was too shocked to respond.

"I lied to you all the time when you were little. Mostly about food though." Georg looked up at him and grinned. "You ate for two. We had to stop you somehow."

Henry tried really hard not to laugh.

"Would you hold up the tail for me?" Georg asked.

"Excuse me?"

"I need to check her. It would help if you held up the tail and kneeled on her hind legs, so she won't kick me in the head," Georg said while rummaging through his bag.

For a moment, Henry pictured Georg getting kicked in the head by the cow. He had to grin. "Sure, I'll help."

Henry kneeled down and lifted the cow's tail. It twitched in his hand for a moment, but then hung slack. He proceeded to kneel on the cow's legs. The animal shifted slightly, but then lay still.

"She's in a lot of pain," Georg said. "If we don't hurry..."

Henry couldn't believe what he saw. Georg had pulled on a long blue rubber glove and was now reaching inside the animal. Henry looked to the side and swallowed hard.

"The water already broke, but it's breech." What did that mean? What did Georg have to do? "I'll have to give her some medication. And then..." Georg was pulling out a huge injection needle from his bag. The cow didn't even react when Georg injected her. Within a couple of minutes, Henry could feel the animal relax under his knees.

"I will need to reach in with both arms and pull the calf out."

"You what?" Henry tried to get rid of the mental picture that sprang up in his mind.

Georg pulled another rubber glove over his other hand and forearm. Henry looked away. He didn't want to witness again how Georg reached inside the animal.

"When I say so, let go of the animal and bring me those scissors over there."

Henry looked at where Georg was pointing and nodded. When he saw Georg proceed to reach inside the animal, he quickly looked away. Henry felt the animal shift slightly as Georg tugged on what Henry thought was the calf. Georg muttered under his breath, and Henry hoped this would be over soon. Out of the corner of his eye, Henry saw something slide out of the cow to the floor.

"The scissors, Henry."

Henry let go of the cow, glad to get up. As he grabbed the scissors, he wondered if Georg would now get a kick to the head, but another look at the animal told him that wouldn't happen. The cow lay as still as if it were dead.

Henry handed Georg the scissors. "Did the cow make it?"

"Her heart's still beating strong. She's out though. I'll give her something to bring her back.

Henry's eyes for the first time fell on the calf, which lay shivering in the straw. Georg began rubbing it down, and Henry eyed the calf curiously. He couldn't believe that a perfect living creature had been inside that cow. Its little tail was already wagging, and his eyes were bulging at them.

"Is it all right?" Henry asked, unable to take his eyes off the black and white calf. "Seems to be in perfect health. Now we need to get the mother back to health, so she can take care of this little one.

While Georg worked on the mother, Henry's attention was still drawn to the young animal. It shivered less and less, but it now moaned softly.

"I think it's hungry," Henry said.

"The mother's just coming out of it," Georg said.

When Henry looked over to where Georg was, he saw the cow trying to stand up. He saw her legs shaking, but she managed. The calf next to Henry suddenly tried to get up as well. It staggered up, but its legs faltered. Henry helped to push it up again, and this time it stood for about thirty seconds before its legs gave way again.

"It takes them a few tries before they're up and walking," Georg said.

Henry shoved at the calf again. This time it got up even quicker and when it stood on its spread out legs, it seemed to hold itself up well enough. Walking was another matter. When it tried to take a few steps on its quivering legs, it stumbled and the legs gave way again. But it was up before Henry could even react. Slowly the calf staggered toward its mother, and when it had found her, he started sucking greedily.

"Mission accomplished, I think," Henry said.

Georg grinned. "Well done, Henry. You remind me of your father."

Henry felt himself tense. "What do you mean?"

"Your father and I once delivered a calf together as well."

Henry looked at Georg in surprise. He had never pictured Georg and his father working together, although he knew that his father and Georg had been best friends and had studied together. And that his father had been a veterinarian just like Georg, but he had never pictured them together like this. Working side by side. Just like he and Georg had.

"You would be a great veterinarian, Henry," Georg said suddenly. "The animals seem to relax under your hand."

"Tell that to the pigs that went missing."

Georg chuckled.

Henry had never considered becoming a veterinarian. Or becoming whatever. He had always felt too young to know what he wanted to do in life, unlike Jana, who had known since fifth grade that she wanted to become a doctor. When he was younger, he had often visited Georg at his practice. Georg had let him play with the instruments and he had helped him feed the animals. But that was years ago.

"I think our work is done here," Georg said, packing up.

Henry glanced at the cow and its calf one more time. Taking care of animals didn't seem so far-fetched now. That was something he could certainly imagine doing. But then Henry's face fell. He would never be allowed to attend the university now after all that happened. They wouldn't let him, even if he had the grades.

Henry followed Georg out of the barn and back to where they had left their bikes.

"Thanks for the assistance," Georg said as he secured his bag on the bike.

"Yeah, thanks for lying to me."

"Any time." Georg grinned. "And anytime you would like to... assist... feel free to come over."

"Yeah. Sure," Henry said. He got up on his bike, not sure if he should thank or hate Georg for making him come here today. As Henry pedaled away, he had to admit that his sister had been right about school all along. But he also knew that this realization came too late.

———

"Oh, Henry. It's so good to see you." Jana threw her duffle bag aside and hugged Henry so tightly it hurt.

"All right, all right. Let me live," Henry said and pulled free. He was just as happy to see his sister as she was to see him. She had always annoyed him, but he had missed her terribly. Henry assumed that had to do with the twin thing.

Jana grew solemn and looked at him. Was she crying? "You were right," Jana said suddenly, her face solemn.

"Right about what?"

"About Tom Bauer." Henry's lips tightened at the mention of the name. "He told me. That it was he who reported you." Jana cried now, but then wiped angrily at the tears. "Thank goodness he's gone, and we never have to see him again," she said indignantly. Henry hugged her. He would never forgive Tom Bauer for what he had done, but he would forgive Jana for falling for the guy. "I'm sorry, Henry. I'm sorry I didn't believe you."

"It's over now. He's gone," Henry said, letting go of Jana.

She looked at him, scrutinizing him. "You're not mad at me for working for the Stasi, are you?"

Henry realized he had forgotten about that. "Well, it got me out, didn't it? As long as you're done with them, I see no reason why I should be mad at you."

"It was Tom's idea, his plan, you know," Jana said carefully.

"So I heard. But that doesn't make it right."

"No, it doesn't. Not for me anyway," Jana said. "I just hope this doesn't come back to haunt me."

"About that ... Fleischer called twice while you were gone. The first time we told him you were at the store. The second time we told him you were spending some time at your godmother's. He called her, of course. Diana has been covering for you. But she's not happy about it. Not at all. I'm glad you're back. We're all glad." Henry didn't want to tell Jana that Diana had doubted that Jana was coming back from Hungary. He had thought so himself at times. If it had been him, he would certainly not have returned. His future in the GDR looked bleaker than ever.

"I should call Fleischer. I hope he doesn't suspect anything."

"That plan of yours was tight. After Diana found out that you didn't show up at the minister's office, she was furious and demanded to know what was going on. We told her then. She wasn't happy, but she promised to cover for you. We both know you're her favorite."

"It was all for you, Henry. I'm just sorry we couldn't get you out earlier. I'm sure it was hell in there."

Henry pushed the tormenting pictures aside that Jana had triggered. All he wanted was to forget. Forget the pain, the despair he had felt. He would never share with them what he had experienced inside that prison. Never. It was all a bad dream. A bad dream he would forget, eventually.

Chapter 23

"We shouldn't risk going to those meetings at the church anymore," Susanne said over dinner. For the first time in over a year, she finally had both of her children home again. Safe and sound. She wouldn't take chances anymore. "I'm sure they're keeping a close eye on Henry and possibly on Jana. We shouldn't give them a reason to ..." Susanne shuddered involuntarily. "Besides... what's the use? These meetings don't seem to accomplish anything. Nothing is changing."

But what she didn't say was that she didn't want to risk anything, now that she had applied for another exit visa. Susanne looked at Georg, sitting across the table from her. She hadn't told him yet that she had applied again. He wouldn't approve, or rather, he would feel betrayed. Of that, Susanne was certain. And she did feel as if she was betraying him. She didn't know where it would leave them when it was approved. If it ever was approved. She had to tell him. Soon. She owed him that much.

Susanne realized it had gotten quiet around the dinner table. She looked at Georg to see why he hadn't reacted to her announcement about no longer attending the church meetings. His eyes were glued to the TV. Henry and Jana had stopped eating and were also staring at the screen. Puzzled, Susanne also turned to the TV. The West German news anchor was talking about an influx of more East Germans – in the thousands now – seeking asylum at the West German embassy in Budapest.

The last time Susanne had thought about getting to West Germany via Hungary was when Henry was still in prison. Now that he was out ... It would be crazy. These people were crazy. Desperation made people do insane things. She knew how they felt. They just wanted to be free. She once had considered getting false papers for the kids and herself. How stupid she had been. How crazy. The video footage of people climbing the fence of the West German embassy in Budapest brought her back to her senses. It was too dangerous, too uncertain. They would have to leave everything behind. She would wait for the approval of her exit visa. Do this legally. "I'm just glad Jana came back from Hungary. If she had left us like that –"

"This isn't about Hungary, Susanne. This is Czechoslovakia. They also opened their borders. They're talking about the West German embassy in Prague, not Budapest," Georg said, his voice awed.

"They, too?" Susanne was stunned. What was happening?

She felt Georg looking at her. She pretended to watch the report.

"I think you're right. We shouldn't go to those meetings anymore. For Henry and Jana's sake," Georg said suddenly. He reached for her hand. His palms felt warm and rough. "We shouldn't give the Stasi any more reason to interfere with our lives." He kissed the palm of her hand.

Our lives, Susanne thought, and sighed. She felt Georg's eyes on her once again, but pretended not to notice.

Jana couldn't believe how easy it was to go back to school after a summer like that. As if nothing had happened. Bianca still wasn't talking to her. Of course, Tom wasn't there. Neither were his friends. A few families never had returned from Hungary either, so there were a few other kids missing.

While teachers and students went about their school day, Jana noticed a smoldering sense of unrest. Everyone was aware of the events of the previous months. People felt something looming on the horizon, but they couldn't say what it was. Neither could Jana. She thought that it was her that had changed, but it was more than that. Was it because people were starting to talk openly about what was happening in their country?

When she came home from school one day, Henry was already there. He was sitting in front of the TV, a plate with bread and cheese in his lap.

"You're home already?" Jana asked. Henry was never home before her. He had to take the train home from school, which was located in the nearby city.

Henry mumbled something that Jana couldn't understand. Henry had become too quiet since attending that school. Jana was worried.

"Everything all right, Henry?" For the first time since she came in, he looked at her. He didn't have to answer. It was in his eyes. She knew he hated the indoctrination and the military atmosphere of his new school. He had to cut his hair short again. Very short. One no longer could tell that his hair was naturally curly. Jana sighed and slumped down on the couch next to him. "Since you're home early..." Jana started. Henry looked at her again. "We could do something together. What do you think?" Jana was just as short on friends as Henry was. She feared Henry wouldn't be too keen to spend his afternoon with her, though.

"What do you have in mind, sis?" Henry asked.

"Homework?" Jana asked carefully. Henry looked at her as if to say, "Are you kidding me?" "Ice cream then?" Henry waved it off. Jana ran out of ideas. This was a village, after all. There was only so much to do.

Georg came in. "You're home already, Henry?" Again, Henry muttered something under his breath. "Excellent. You can help me out then," Georg said. He looked at Jana. "You, too."

"No, thanks. You know..."

"Allergies. I know," Georg said with a sigh. He turned to Henry and looked at him expectantly.

It seemed forever until Henry tore his eyes off the screen and looked up at Georg.

"What is it, Doctor?"

"Mice and bunnies," Georg said.

"All right then." Henry pulled himself up and switched off the TV. He turned to Jana. "Sorry, sis. Maybe some other time." He walked out with Georg.

Had she missed something? Henry was helping Georg at the practice? Jana knew they had been talking again for a while, but working together? Henry and animals? Jana couldn't fathom that. Henry wasn't of a particularly gentle nature. She shook her head again. And then she remembered that Henry had never answered her earlier question. Why was he home so early today? Well, she'd just have to find out then. There was nothing else to do. *I really need new friends. Or more homework.* She chuckled to herself as she left the living room.

Henry scanned the market square. Not too many people were out doing their shopping. But this was a city and at this time of day the center of it should be busy. It was the weather that kept most inside. The sky was a brooding gray, and it was drizzling. For the

301

first time, it really felt like fall. Most leaves were gone from the trees now and the air was chill with moisture.

This was the fifth day that Henry had skipped school. Not in a row, of course. It would have been too obvious. A day here and there. He wondered how much longer they would tolerate it. His excuse was always the same. A bad case of stomach flu. It was Georg who wrote him the excuses, and so far the school had accepted them and not asked questions.

His mother was oblivious. She knew how unbearable it was for him to be at the school, but he also knew she wouldn't be happy if she found out that he skipped school like that. She feared the Stasi could take him away for good. So he took the early morning train to the city, even on those days when he planned not to attend.

Henry looked at two men crossing the square. They were heading to the bakery on the north side by the church. He had heard meetings were also held there. Just like in their little village church. But tonight, something else would happen. On his way from the train station to the school, someone had put a flyer in his hand. The man in a tan overcoat had rushed by him without looking at him. Henry had followed him and watched him put flyers in the hands of startled passersby. The man did it in such haste that Henry had a hard time keeping up with him. At one point, he lost the man and Henry studied the flyer. It was as if the announcement on the flyer was meant just for him. Today he would take the last train home.

He looked up at the sky and felt the drizzle on his face. After a moment, he got up and walked over to a store that carried office supplies. There, he would hopefully find what he needed for tonight.

Henry pushed through the crowd. He wanted to be in the center of it, be a part of this. He had no fear of what could happen. He had left all fear behind in prison. If his mother knew what he was doing... Henry didn't finish that thought. He glanced warily at the police lining the square. They stood on guard. Henry was sure they would intervene as soon as the crowd started moving.

More and more people seemed to want to join them. There was a constant influx of people from the alleys that led into the square. It seemed as if everyone who lived in the city was either already here or on the way to join them. He had never seen or heard of anything like this. Not in this country.

It was still drizzling, as it had been at midday, but no one seemed to take notice. As Henry made his way to the church, a voice over a megaphone whipped the crowd into silence. Everyone turned toward the entrance of the church, in front of which a man stood facing the crowd.

"Today we march," the man's voice blared. "For justice! We have a voice, people!" He looked around, his face determined. "We are the people!"

"We are the people!" The crowd took up the slogan and the chorus echoed across the market square. Hundreds and hundreds of people started moving at once and swept Henry with them.

Around Henry determined faces were pushing forward. The police moved along with them as if they were herding them like sheep. With a defiant glance at them, Henry raised up high the poster he had written this afternoon. "Freedom" it said in big red capital letters. He looked at all the signs held up around him. The feeling of unity washed over him. He had always been the outsider, the troublemaker. But today he wasn't the only troublemaker. To-day, those that stood by and didn't participate were the outcasts.

"Peaceful demonstrations? The government is certainly not just going to stand back and watch. They'll send tanks. The Russians will come in and put a stop to it." Susanne couldn't disagree with Jana, who stared at the TV anxiously. It seemed as if tens of thousands of people moved across the screen. "These people don't even look afraid. This could end in a huge massacre," Jana continued.

"I know." Susanne was worried as well. The government leaders wouldn't let this go on forever. She had heard the police and army were on high alert. She thought back to a report she had seen on West German TV about the revolts by workers in East Berlin and other towns and villages on a June day in 1953. Food and supplies had been scarce back then, due to the Russian occupation that had left the East Germans with very little. Workers had been dissatisfied with working conditions and increasing and unfair demands for their labor. People had taken to the streets. But then the Russian tanks had rolled in. It had been a bloody day. Dozens had been killed and scores put on trial. A few had even been executed. The East German TV reports, of course, had portrayed it very differently. There was an advantage to living close to the border and being able to receive West German TV. Susanne had always appreciated that.

"How's this going to end?" Georg had come in. His eyes locked on the TV. He looked thoughtful.

"I can't believe people are actually demonstrating against the government," Susanne said. While they had attended the meetings at the church, they had always hoped for this next step. But now that it was taken, it was rather unsettling.

"This is the second week. It's nothing short of a revolution. I'm surprised they haven't stepped in yet." Georg sat down on the couch next to Susanne.

"It's too many. Maybe they simply can't because of the sheer number of people. It wouldn't look too good if they ... massacred that many people. Maybe there is strength in numbers after all," Jana mused.

"Maybe," Georg said.

"But the Russians ..." Susanne said.

"I'm not sure. Gorbachev seems rather lenient and preoccupied. I don't think he'll interfere.

Remember what he said?"

Susanne remembered. Gorbachev had met with the West German chancellor, Helmut Kohl, in June. New treaties had been signed. West and East would start to collaborate. Gorbachev had promised that the USSR would reduce its weapons to a bare minimum, enough to defend themselves, but not enough for an attack. The Soviets no longer planned on interfering. If it hadn't been for the Russian leader, Hungary and Czechoslovakia would probably not have dared to open their borders to the West. And besides, Gorbachev tried to push through reforms in his own country.

"Where's Henry tonight?" Georg asked suddenly.

Jana shrugged. "I haven't seen him yet today."

"He should have been on the 4 o'clock train." Susanne involuntarily checked her watch. It was almost dark out. The last train would arrive in about an hour. Henry would have some explaining to do.

"He's probably hanging out with some friends after school," Jana said.

Georg nodded in Jana's direction. "Probably."

Susanne stared at the TV. *Hopefully*, she thought.

"If Mama finds out, she'll be –"

"Furious. I know," Henry said, rolling his eyes at Jana. He dropped down onto her bed.

"You don't understand. You could get arrested. And then what?" Jana couldn't believe that Henry was still so reckless after all he had been through. *They* had been through. Why had Henry come to tell her? She now wished he hadn't. Sometimes it was better not to know what Henry was up to.

"These are peaceful demonstrations, sis."

"I heard people are getting arrested in Berlin."

"When it all started. They don't dare now. We're way too many. They can't arrest all of us. You really should come," Henry said, punching her pillow into form.

"Forget it." Jana was frustrated by Henry's attitude. He hadn't learned from the past at all. Here he was, annoying her once again. "They haven't talked some sense into you at your new school?"

Jana saw how Henry's face fell. He got up from her bed, his jaw clenched. "You don't know what you're talking about," he hissed. When he got to the door, he said, "I shouldn't have told you. I'll have to remember that in the future." He left and slammed the door behind him.

Jana fell onto her bed. It seemed that she and Henry hadn't changed all that much after all. Henry was still reckless, with no thought of the consequences of his actions, and Jana still felt like she was patronizing him and playing the moralizer. No wonder they still annoyed each other.

Georg wrapped his arms around Susanne. They were sitting on the couch, waiting for the nightly news. No one wanted to miss the news anymore. Georg pulled Susanne closer and buried his face in her curls. It felt as if they had always been together. They had been in some way over the past sixteen years as neighbors, friends, and then co-workers. He had spent most of his adult life in her presence, he realized. Susanne snuggled up against him and yawned. Jana came in to join them just as the news began.

"Where's Henry?" Georg asked.

Jana only shrugged, and he let it go. Henry never let them know where he was. Nevertheless, it had become a family event to watch the news every night. No matter what everyone was doing, they would all drop everything and gather in the living room to watch the news together on Gisela's old black-and-white TV. This was usually followed by a discussion about the developments of the current events. Over the past few days, the crowds of demonstrators have been swelling. Hundreds of thousands of people now took to the streets. And the government had not reacted. Everyone was waiting for them to do something. Anything. They could no longer ignore the masses.

The familiar face of the East German news anchor appeared, and a picture on the left of her face showed a picture of the Politburo's press conference.

Jana yawned. "Can we change the channel, please?"

Georg leaned forward and reached for the channel button on the TV set. He didn't want to be bored by the mundane press conference either. He switched around, waiting for a signal from Susanne or Jana to stop. There seemed to be nothing interesting on the few channels they received. He went through them again when Susanne grabbed his arm.

"Wait."

Georg looked at the screen. There was the same news anchor again, with the same picture next to her head.

"We report that Comrade Gunter Schabowski, head of the Politburo, just announced that travel restrictions have been lifted. After he was asked by a reporter, Schabowski confirmed that these new regulations are in effect immediately." They stared at the TV set.

"What does that mean?" Jana asked.

"I don't know," Susanne said. "That we can travel? Anywhere?" Susanne had gotten up, still staring at the TV.

"They opened the borders?" Georg was stunned. That was impossible. What would the Soviet leaders say to that? They were the last frontier of the West. If the GDR opened its borders ...

They waited. Waited for the news anchor to elaborate on what she had announced, but she had already moved on to other news items.

"What does that mean?" Jana asked again, interrupting the silence.

"I'm ... I'm not sure," Susanne said, shaking her head.

"What's happening?" Again, it was Jana who asked, clearly confused by the events, just as he and Susanne were.

"I don't know, but something is," Georg said, leaning forward again to switch channels. He marveled at the implications as they waited for the news coverage on the West German channels. They would surely elaborate on what was happening. But then the noise coming from the streets pulled them away from the TV and to the windows. Their neighbors were outside, talking excitedly. Some were shouting or hugging each other. With them was Henry. His face was jubilant. He saw them behind the window and motioned for them to come out. They almost ran. No one thought about putting on a coat, although it was November.

They had just picked up their temporary travel visas at the police station and left Wallhausen when suddenly Gisela's old Trabant sputtered. Susanne had expected no less.

"We better stop. I'll check what's going on," Georg said, and pulled over. They rarely used Gisela's old car. It was too unreliable. Susanne had always preferred the train over the car Gisela had left her, especially in the last years. She had wanted to sell it but had never gotten to it. Or maybe she was reluctant to sell it because she knew how much Gisela had loved that car.

After the news the night before, they had decided to go up to Berlin first thing. They could just have passed through the newly opened border at a checkpoint near Wallhausen, but Susanne had grown up in Berlin and she wanted to see with her own eyes that the wall had indeed fallen. They were at the train station before dawn, but after seeing the throng of people there, they turned around to take Gisela's old car that had been collecting dust in the carport. *Of course,* Susanne thought grimly, *we're finally going somewhere important in this car, and it breaks down.*

They all got out of the Trabant to wait on the side of the road. While it was chilly, the sky was unusually clear. They watched Georg open up the hood to check what was wrong. There was a constant stream of cars passing by them. Everyone was heading in the same direction-the border crossing ten miles upstream.

"Can you take off your tights?" Georg asked, looking up from underneath the hood at Susanne.

Susanne looked at him in shock. "Excuse me?"

Georg grinned at her. "If you take them off, I will be able to fix the car. It's the belt. I need to replace it. Since we don't have one, your tights will do."

"But... but these are the only ones I have without a hole in them. They're my best ones. I had to use all my charms for the clerk to sell them to me. Is there nothing else you could use? Your scarf?" She looked hopeful, but Georg just shook his head and motioned for her to hand over the tights.

Susanne wanted to protest further, but Georg shook his head and she knew there was no other way if they wanted to make it to Berlin today. She waved Henry and Jana away impatiently. Henry rolled his eyes and Jana, chuckling, pulled her brother with her a few meters away.

ReluctantlyReluctantly and murmuring to herself, Susanne crouched downbehind the car, hiked up her skirt and pulled down the tights while
looking nervously at the cars passing by. Georg busied himself
with checking the engine again until Susanne's tights were dangling in front of his face.

Georg took them from her with a grin. "Thanks. These will do.
We'll be back on the road in no time."

"I doubt that with all my heart!" Susanne stalked off and sat
down on a rock on the side of the road. Georg took out the old
belt, twisted the tights and tied the ends together. He leaned in
and put his new belt where the old one had been.

Minutes later they hammered down the cobbled-stoned road,
Georg looking smug and Susanne staring out the window with
folded arms. Henry and Jana tried in vain to stifle their chuckles.

"How do you know how to fix cars, anyway? You don't own one,"
Henry said, trying to keep a straight face.

"My dad showed me growing up. He had always hoped I would
become a mechanic like him."

"I'm glad you didn't. I don't think my mama could have assisted
you in that profession," Henry quipped.

"Who did just assist him, Henry?" Susanne asked with playful
mockery.

"She's right. We wouldn't be back on the road without those
tights," Georg jumped in.

"I'll be freezing today," Susanne said.

"Today, you can buy yourself ten pairs of the best West German
tights they have."

"I sure can, can't I?" Susanne looked out the window at the
scenery flying by.

They would be in West Berlin today. She couldn't fathom that.
The West. Without any warning, her thoughts turned to Dieter.
George's and the kids' voices grew distant, and it was as if time
had stopped. Dieter. How long it had been. He was a stranger to

310

her now. Every year when his packages arrived, Susanne checked the return address. It had been the same for fifteen years. He was still in Hamburg, living with Anna. They probably had gotten married and had children of their own. Who knew? He never mentioned anything about himself in his letters to the kids. Dieter. She wanted to see him, she realized. After all these years, she needed to see him. This desire had always been inside her, but she had smothered it, aware that it would take its toll if she let it consume her. She had moved on, and so had Dieter. But still, she could see him today if she wanted to. She turned to Georg, who announced that it was only a few short kilometers to Berlin. Today, they would be in Berlin. West Berlin.

East Berlin was packed. Susanne was shocked to see so many East German cars at once. And so many people. Everyone was out on the streets. And everyone seemed to be heading in the same direction. The checkpoints along the wall.

Georg steered the car through the chaos. He tried the first checkpoint and after seeing all the cars lined up, they decided to try one further north. It was the same there. It would be the same everywhere. Every East German was heading west. Who would stay home today?

They lined up behind other cars, the anticipation trying their patience as never before. Pedestrians and bikers passed the cars. Some people were running, too eager to just walk up to the checkpoint to be let through to the other side.

All around them, the jubilant and celebratory atmosphere was electrifying. Georg rolled down his window. Susanne, and Henry and Jana in the back seat, followed suit. It was hard to take it all in. People let out screams of joy, peace signs were handed out, hymns sung, and flags waved. It was infectious.

A couple on foot passed their car. Susanne thought she recognized them. She stretched out the window to see. "Diana!"

The woman turned and broke into a smile. She pulled her husband with her and came running to them.

"Susanne! Isn't this unreal?" Diana shouted as she hugged Susanne through the window, tears glistening in her eyes.

"It is," Susanne said, happy to have run into her long-time friend.

Diana nodded a greeting to Georg and then turned to Jana and Henry. "It's good to see you kids. I've missed you."

"Missed you, too," Jana said, squeezing her godmother's hand.

"You're welcome to stay at my place tonight. We're not sure when we'll be back, though." Diana gestured at the chaos around them. Her husband was impatiently tugging at her.

"I need to go. I'll see you over there?" She grinned and quickly kissed Susanne's cheek.

"Have fun," Susanne yelled after her friend. Diana waved as they rushed off.

It took three hours to make it through the line of cars. When it was finally their turn, they involuntarily stiffened when the border guard held up his hand for them to stop. His face was stern when he peeked inside the car. Georg handed him their IDs and, in what seemed like the slowest way possible, he inspected them. Henry wanted to say something, but Susanne shushed him before he could.

When he finally handed back the papers, Susanne thought he saw a hint of defeat in his eyes. His voice was monotone when he wished them a good day.

The old Trabant crept slowly forward. They had all fallen silent. Outside their now rolled-up car windows, the noise was escalating, washing up against them like a tidal wave. Georg was finally able to accelerate. Honking, loud singing, and yells rushed past them as they drove into West Berlin.

"We're here," Susanne whispered to herself.

They stood in line at the bank for two hours, but they had no choice. Their East German Mark wouldn't buy anything here in the West, and the West German government's welcome gift, handed out at the banks, consisted of one hundred Marks for each of their East German brothers and sisters.

When they came to the first grocery store, it was so overcrowded they decided to head farther into West Berlin. Susanne enjoyed just driving around the city and taking it all in. The clean house façades, the well-dressed people, the decked out shop windows, and the expensive-looking cars. It had been over seventeen years since she had last performed in West Germany and seen its splendor. She looked at Henry and Jana, who stared just as much as she did at the world outside their car windows. Only Georg didn't seem too impressed. His eyes were fixed on the street and the cars ahead of him. He rarely looked left or right.

"Would you like me to drive?" Susanne asked Georg.

"Why?"

"So you can look around and take it all in."

"I'm fine," was all Georg said.

On the far outskirts of West Berlin, they finally found a store that was less crowded. Susanne felt the stare of the West Germans as they entered. She knew their clothing and hairstyles gave them away. And probably their gawking. She didn't care. Jana and Henry were leading the way, oohing and ahhing at produce and the wide selection. There were a few other East Germans in the store as well. Moving slowly through the aisles, they stared at the products on the shelves, in awe of the sheer amount and variety of offerings. The shelves in East German grocery stores had never been fully stocked like that.

Susanne fell back, letting Georg keep up with Jana and Henry. She watched them, half amused, half irritated by their unguarded praise of the stuff on the shelves. Georg followed the kids quietly down an aisle, seemingly less enthusiastic.

Susanne sighed and turned to go down another aisle but froze mid-way. She stared at the man putting a six-pack of Coca-Cola in his shopping basket. Of all people, he would have been the last man she expected to see in a West German store. And he looked so different. Did he wear new clothes? New glasses? Even his hair looked different. Less gray, she thought. So, he wanted a piece of the pie. How quickly he had betrayed his ideology. Susanne could do nothing but stare at him. The utter shock and overwhelming disgust she felt for this man overpowered her.

Susanne quickly scanned around to see where Georg and the kids were. There was no sight of them. She stepped closer toward Fleischer, staring at the man who could now easily be mistaken for a West German. This all seemed so surreal. It was hard to imagine Fleischer with West German money in his wallet. But here he was. The Stasi officer, trying to fit in as nothing had happened. Moving on from the lives he had ruined.

He looked up and found her face. His eyes danced around wildly. He tried to hide his basket half-way behind his body. "Frau Schmidt," was all he said.

Susanne wasn't thinking now. She walked up closer to him and before she knew what she was doing, she slapped him across the face. His glasses hung askew on his nose, his right cheek a flaming red. He didn't move. Just stared at her. "You stole my life from me." Her voice was hoarse with anger. She turned to walk away.

"Go ahead. Blame me. You were the traitor. I only tried to protect the country from dissidents like you. You'd be surprised how many helpers I had, Frau Schmidt. Your friends, your pastor ... surprised I say."

Susanne didn't turn around but walked on, Fleischer's voice echoing in her head.

She had to get out of this store. Outside, she breathed in deeply and decided to wait by the car for Georg and the kids. She didn't care for anything that could be bought in this store.

Leaning against the car, the thoughts in her head were hammering relentlessly. She tried hard not to let Fleischer's words get to her, but they did. Mercilessly. Who had spied on her? Her pastor? She couldn't believe it. He had let them hold the meetings in his church. Had everyone played both sides? She shook her head vehemently. Her friends?

Georg? Diana? It couldn't be. Susanne started to feel sick, the rising suspicion overwhelming her. She had to steady herself. The chills she felt weren't caused by the stiff November breeze. She had to ask Georg. Now. She couldn't wait. She had to find out.

The sickening feeling increased.

When Georg and the kids appeared, she asked Jana and Henry to go and find a pharmacy to get her some medication for headaches. It was a lame excuse, but she needed to talk to Georg. She needed to find out.

She waited until Henry and Jana had disappeared around the corner. She looked at Georg, his eyes showed worry.

"Are you not well? You don't look so good," Georg said, coming over to her. Susanne held up her hand as if to stop him. "Do you know Walter Fleischer?"

It stopped Georg short. "Of course, I do," Georg said, looking surprised by the sudden interrogation and her blazing eyes. "I talked to him about Henry, and I went with Jana to see him. Remember? Why are you –"

"When you went to see him about Henry, was that the first time you met him?" Georg's face fell and he stared at her, but he didn't answer.

Susanne stared back, her hands balled up in fists. "Answer me, Georg. Was that the first time?"

"It wasn't," Georg said, his voice defeated.

"Did you work for the Stasi?"

Georg fell back a step as if she had slapped him.

"Did you, Georg? Are you?"

"I didn't work for the Stasi the way you think I did. I was approached by Fleischer when you had just moved to Wallhausen. He wanted me to keep an eye on you."

"And you willingly accepted. What did you get for it, Georg? What?"

"I didn't accept willingly. No one works for the Stasi willingly. Of all people, you should know that, Susanne. And there was nothing I got in return."

Susanne fell on the hood of Gisela's Trabant, staring at the ground in front of her.

Georg had spied on her. And she had trusted him and talked everything over with him. She stared at him. He looked somber, his eyes pleading with her. She ignored it.

Henry and Jana returned, and they immediately sensed that something had happened.

"What's going on?" Henry asked.

"We'll not be returning," Susanne said, shuddering at the coldness of her own voice.

"What do you mean?" Jana's eyes were dancing back and forth between Georg and her. "Because you had a fight with Georg?"

"No, Jana." Susanne breathed in deeply. She had to convince her children to leave everything and everyone behind in a spur-of-the-moment decision. "They certainly won't leave the borders open for long. We're finally here in the West. Safely and legally. We'll not be returning, living under that oppressive regime."

The kids stared at her, and so did Georg, but she completely ignored him.

"But what about our stuff, the house?" Jana asked. "School?"

Jana was clearly troubled, but Henry wasn't. "School?" he asked. He laughed coldly.

"It's now or never –" Susanne stopped short. Those had been the words Dieter had yelled at her from the other side of the border fence. Over and over again. He had made it, and she had still been struggling to climb up. The vividness of the memory took her breath away, but it also spurred her on. Dieter. She was in the West. She could finally see Dieter. She steadied herself against the car and turned to Jana. "What they did to your brother, to us as a family... we can't return. This is our chance. Don't you see?"

"It will be fine, sis," Henry said to Jana. "Mama's right. Now or never."

Susanne looked at her son. Now, more than ever, she saw Dieter in him.

"What about Georg?" Jana asked in his direction. Georg had been quiet the whole time, silenced by the shock of the earlier confrontation and her announcement not to return.

"He's returning," Susanne said quickly.

Georg cleared his throat. "I've lived in Wallhausen all my life. It's my home," Georg said quietly, running his hand through his hair. Then he checked his watch. "I'd better hurry. Who knows how late their trains are running over here."

Susanne's lips were pressed together. This was painful, but necessary. Jana went over to Georg and hugged him. Then Georg went to Henry and stretched out his hand. Henry took it, only to pull Georg closer to him and hug him as well. Susanne could tell both were choked up, so she busied herself with getting the car ready.

"Promise you'll visit?" Henry asked Georg.

"If the borders are still open..." Georg said, his voice thick with emotion. Susanne looked away, but Georg went over to her.

"Goodbye, Susanne. I hope you'll find what you've been looking for all these years."

Chapter 24

"Please list your skills here," the clerk said, and handed Susanne another form.

Susanne looked at the pile of forms in her hand and sighed. She nodded a thank you to the clerk and left the office to sit in the hallway. There were other people sitting on hard chairs with their backs to the bare wall and filling out forms. A line of people snaked down the hallway from the clerk's office. Susanne found a chair and sat down with a sigh. It would take her hours to fill out all the forms. And she had thought the bureaucracy in the GDR had been bad.

For weeks, Susanne had tried to find a job on her own with no success. The influx of East Germans had made jobs scarce, even in a big city like Hamburg. She had finally gotten herself to the unemployment office to seek their help. And here she was, feeling that she had come to another low point in her life. There had been times when she had wondered if her decision to stay in the West hadn't been a bit hasty after all, especially since the calls for uniting the two Germanys got louder and louder. The East German government was changing. Rumors of the GDR's insolvency were flying. If she had held out a bit longer... She bit her lip and started scribbling furiously.

After what seemed like an hour, Susanne was finally done filling out the forms. She looked at the line of people and knew it would be another hour before she sat in the clerk's office again. She got in line behind a middle-aged man.

"That will take until lunch," the man said to no one in particular, but Susanne assumed he wanted to start a conversation.

"How long before you hear back from them after you give them the forms?" Susanne asked.

The man turned to her. "Weeks." He scrutinized her. "Are you from the GDR?"

Susanne nodded, wondering what had given her away. Her clothes or her East German dialect, she wondered.

"There aren't enough jobs as it is. And then you people come and take those few away from us."

"I don't believe we're in the same field," Susanne said, trying to keep her anger in check.

"That doesn't matter." The man turned back around, and all Susanne could do was stare at his back. Susanne knew that most West Germans had been enthusiastic about the fall of the wall and the opening of the borders at first, but now it seemed as if some of them thought it hadn't been such a great idea after all.

Susanne checked her forms again. The line moved slowly, but the closer she got to her turn, the less hopeful she felt. When the man who had been in line in front of her exited the clerk's office, he looked just as hopeless as Susanne felt. With a sigh, she went in.

The clerk looked up from the forms. "You've been out of it for too long. I don't think we can still utilize your musical training and resurrect your former career."

Susanne had expected nothing less. "I could always teach private lessons at one of the local music schools," Susanne suggested.

The clerk looked at her with a doubtful expression. "You worked for a veterinarian?" Susanne nodded. "But no formal training?" Susanne shook her head. She knew this wasn't going well. "Will it be possible to get a letter of recommendation from the veterinarian?" The clerk asked. Susanne froze. *Georg.* He would probably write her one if she asked him. But she hadn't spoken to him since the day they parted. The last thing she wanted was for him to know how miserable she was. "It looks as if we need to retrain you."

"Retrain?"

"Office clerk or something like that." Susanne nodded in defeat. "You'll hear from us." The clerk's tone was dismissive. Susanne got up. "Next," the clerk called.

"How's our Ossi today," the boys mocked in the exaggerated East German dialect of Saxony as Henry passed them. He ignored them and scanned the school yard for his sister. "We're talking to you, Ossi," they called after him. Henry saw Jana in the far corner, under a tree. She was alone. Her nose was buried in a book, and she didn't look up as he approached. When he sat down next to her, he held out a chocolate bar to her.

She looked up in surprise. "Where did you get the money?"

"I had some left."

"You shouldn't spend it on stuff like that," Jana said, looking at the bar but not taking it. Suddenly she looked past him, her face showing concern.

"We'll take it if she doesn't want it, Ossi," a boy called, approaching them with two others. Henry got up. One of the boys walked up to him and, without warning, snatched the bar out of his hands. Henry didn't have to think. He punched the boy in the face. He heard Jana's scream and looked at the boy on the ground before him. The bar lay next to him in the dirt. How sick he was of their teasing. How sick he was of this school.

The boy scrambled to his feet, holding his nose. "You'll pay for this, Ossi," he hissed. He bent down and picked up the bar. He ripped open the paper and bit into it. Henry could feel Jana's hands around his arm, holding him back.

"He needs the help of a girl," one of the two other boys smirked.

"Ignore them," Jana hissed in his ears. "They're idiots."

The boy who Henry had punched stepped forward. "Watch it, cow."

Henry felt the hands around his arm squeeze tighter.

"We'll go to the principal and report you," one of the other boys said.

"Yeah." The boy who Henry had punched, threw the wrapper at him, but it didn't hit him and just sailed to the ground. "Pick up the trash, Ossi. That's the job you'll have."

He turned and walked off with the two others.

"Don't listen to those idiots," Jana said, releasing his arm.

"We need to change schools," Henry said.

"I think it will be the same wherever we go." Jana sat back down and picked up her book.

"Not in Wallhausen," Henry said, staring at the crowds of kids now entering the school building.

———

"The principal called. Do you know how embarrassing that is? There is no privacy in the barrack as it is. They called me to the phone. Now everyone thinks I have troubled children. Will it be the same at every school you attend, Henry? Can't you just be like your sister? She fits right in. She doesn't get in trouble like that."

"It wasn't Henry's fault. The boy tried to –"

"You stay out of this, Jana." Susanne was beside herself. Why was Henry always making trouble? What was wrong with him?

They were at the playground. It was empty. A light drizzle gave them the privacy they needed to have this conversation. She looked at Henry, who sat on top of the bench, his face grim. "I know this is hard," Susanne continued. "It's hard on all of us. We just got off to a rocky start. In time, it will all play out."

"Kids at school hate us," Jana said. Susanne looked at her, doubting it was that bad. "They tease us all the time because we're from the East," Jana continued. "You have no idea what we have to listen to every day."

"I know this is hard. You need to be strong for me. I don't want you to get expelled." Susanne looked at a still brooding Henry.

"Can't we switch schools?" Jana asked.

"I don't know."

"Please," Jana said.

Susanne looked at Henry. "I'll try. I don't know if they'll let you in the middle of the school year."

"Please try, Mama." Jana was pleading now.

"I'll try," Susanne said, making no attempt to keep the defeat out of her voice.

When Susanne returned to the former military barrack, where she, the kids, and other GDR defectors now lived, she felt exhausted and hopeless. She had spent another morning at the unemployment office without any success, and she was worried about Henry and Jana. They were so unhappy here. The uninviting gray of the building did nothing to lift her spirits. She was grateful for how the West Germans took care of them, housed them, and fed them. Even if it was just a former military barrack on the outskirts of the city they called home for now. However, the housing situation and her unemployment were only temporary. Susanne had to remind herself of that throughout the day. Every day.

They had been promised an apartment by the end of next month. And maybe she would begin her occupational retraining soon, too. Susanne sighed as her steps echoed in the linoleum-covered hallway. When she got to their sparsely furnished room, she threw her purse on Henry's cot and lay down on the lower bunk bed. The children wouldn't be back from school for another two hours, so she closed her eyes and drifted off to sleep.

"Frau Schmidt?" Susanne opened one eye and looked at one of the volunteers who peeked inside her room. "You have a visitor, Frau Schmidt."

"Thank you," was all Susanne said. She felt dazed by the announcement, sleep still clouding her mind. But the meaning of the words slowly became clear in her mind. A visitor. This could only mean... She lay there, frozen. There could only be one. They had been here in Hamburg for weeks now, and she had not yet mustered the courage to see him. Henry and Jana had asked her numerous times to go visit him, and she had promised them they would. Eventually. And now he had found them. He had come to see them.

Susanne got up hastily and straightened her clothes. She went over to the little mirror on the wall and checked her hair and make-up. She stared at her reflection. How old she looked. Her hair was shorter and it had lost its shine. Her skin lacked the youthful glow she had once been so proud of. Would he even recognize her? Would she recognize him? She wondered how much he had changed. She breathed in deeply and exhaled slowly as she walked down the hallway toward the lobby. The last time she had felt that nervous was when Dieter and she had tried to escape across the border. How long it had been since she saw him last. She kneaded her fingers. Did she have butterflies in her stomach? She brushed the thought aside, nervously clearing her throat as she stepped into the lobby.

Susanne stopped short, bewildered by the mixed emotions of joy and disappointment she was feeling. She recognized the man instantly. He broke out in a smile when he saw her. Susanne was still frozen in place, confused that it was not Dieter but Georg who had come to visit, and confused that she felt extraordinarily glad to see him. But her face must have also shown disappointment, because Georg's smile vanished as he approached her.

"You look as if you had expected someone else. Are you happy to see me?" he asked carefully. How had Georg found them, and why had he come here? Susanne still couldn't speak. "You forgot something." Georg handed her a violin case. Her violin. She took it without looking at it. "The East German government is returning everything they confiscated after you didn't come back."

"Everything?" Her tone was sarcastic. She had found her voice again. "I doubt that, Georg."

"Well, I thought you might like it back. That's why I picked it up for you."

"Why are you here, Georg?"

"They're talking about reunification."

"I heard."

"We will live in the same country then," Georg said lightly.

"Where people are still the same."

"People change, Susanne."

"Do they, Georg?" Her eyes were cold. "I guess you're right. They change according to which way the wind is blowing."

"I'm so sorry for everything, Susanne. All I ever wanted was for you to be happy again. I had made a promise to Dieter. To take care of you. To watch out for you and the kids. And that I did. By whatever means necessary."

Susanne swallowed. The meaning behind his words was clear to her. She had protected her children by whatever means necessary. She had worked for the Stasi. She had made Jana work for the Stasi. How could she condemn Georg for it?

"And that's why you're going to see him. Dieter. Today," Georg said suddenly. Susanne stared at him in disbelief. "He called me," Georg continued. "He has been looking for you. I told him you and the kids lived in Hamburg now. I think he was a bit offended you hadn't come to see him," Georg said, smiling now.

"You talked to him? He called you? How is he doing? He wants to see me? And the kids?" The questions were now tumbling out of her. She felt she had to catch her breath.

"I really think you should see him," Georg said soberly. "It's time."

"Why are you doing this, Georg?"

"All you ever wanted was to see Dieter again. I understand and accept that. He is the love of your life. The father of your children. And I want you to be happy. I'd rather be your friend than an unappreciated lover. And after all, don't forget that he is my friend, too." Georg ran his hand through his dark hair as he always did when he was feeling strongly about something. "So, let's go. We'll pick up the kids from school on the way to his house. He insisted you bring the kids." Georg took her by the hand and led her out of the building. "You still have the Trabant?"

"Of course," came Susanne's subdued reply.

———

Georg parked the car across the street from the house. The street lay quiet in the cold afternoon sun. Susanne stared past Georg at Anna's house, remembering how she had visited the home on one of her trips to West Germany many years ago. She turned to Georg, her face flushed with anticipation.

"I'll be right here waiting for you," he said, giving her an encouraging nod.

Susanne bit her lip and stared straight ahead. She recognized the trees lining the street, even without their foliage. Linden trees.

They reminded her of Wallhausen. She swallowed and turned around to Henry and Jana in the back seat. They looked just as nervous as she felt. Taking a deep breath, Susanne reluctantly opened the door and got out. They had agreed she would go alone first, without Henry and Jana. She needed to see Dieter alone first. There was too much that had stood between them all these years. More than just the border fence. How she had waited for this moment. How she had dreamed about seeing Dieter again, for the kids to meet their father, but she was frozen with fear. Afraid of what she might find, of who Dieter had become, and how he would receive her. Would he be happy to see her? He wanted to see her. After all, he had called Georg and inquired about her whereabouts.

As she went around the car to the driver's side, she had to steady herself by holding on to the hood. Georg reached out to her and squeezed her hand. "Good luck." His hand felt like hot coal against her cold clammy hands. She managed a faint smile. With another deep breath, she started for the door of the house across the street with the finely manicured garden. When she reached the wrought-iron gate, she placed her hand on the handle but couldn't bring herself to push it down. She looked at the door and then back at the car.

A car pulled up. Dieter recognized it instantly. His mother's Trabant. How old, small, and backward it looked. He wasn't used to seeing cars like that anymore. Slowly, he moved toward the window. He saw Georg behind the wheel and caught glimpses of Susanne, who was sitting in the passenger seat. Her name was on his lips, but it was Anna who appeared by his side and said her name.

She's here, he thought. She had come. He saw her getting out of the car. Susanne was still too far away to clearly see her face but he knew it was her. Even after all these years, he could easily recognize her shape, her hair, her walk. She looked older and her hair was shorter, but she was still beautiful. He realized he had stopped breathing and closed his eyes to order himself to be calm. He felt Anna's hand on his and shook it off.

Susanne reached the gate. He felt his heart jump as she started to open the gate, but didn't. Her hand rested on the handle. She seemed to hesitate. Should he be running out to her? And then what? Embrace her? He felt an overwhelming sadness sweep over him. It was at that moment that he saw her turn around toward the car and stride back with a steady pace, as if she knew, as if she was certain, that she had forgotten something. Midway, she suddenly stopped. She turned around and scanned the house. She found his face behind the window glass and raised a hand in greeting. She was smiling, but with a finality that pierced Dieter to the core. Slowly he raised his hand to wave back and mustered a faint smile. He gave a nod and her smile broadened. Then she turned back around, walked to the passenger side and simply got back into the car.

"What's wrong? Is the gate locked?" Georg looked at Susanne in confusion as she got back into to the car.

"Nothing's wrong," Susanne said, still smiling.

"You got cold feet. I can only imagine how hard this must be for you, but you've waited for such a long time. It will be alright," Georg said, still confused. Susanne turned to him with a big smile. Georg was taken aback by the joy he saw in her face. "I don't understand," he stammered. "What's going on?"

Susanne put her hand on his cheek. "I want to go home." He still didn't understand, so she kissed him, not caring that her kids looked on.

"It's about time, you two," Henry said, patting Georg's shoulder. He was grinning from ear to ear.

Susanne, still smiling, turned around to Henry and Jana. "Go and meet your father and we'll pick you up at the end of the weekend." Henry and Jana looked at each other and then at Georg and her. Without hesitation, they got out of the car. As they walked toward the house, they waved back at them, their faces showing excitement and anticipation. Susanne put her arm through Georg's. Leaning on him, she watched how Henry took Jana's hand and pulled her through the gate to the front door. When it opened, Susanne looked straight ahead down the street lined with leafless linden trees.

"So now that we have the weekend to ourselves, what do you suggest we do?" Georg asked, following her eyes.

"Let's go home," Susanne said, snuggling up against Georg's arm.

Epilogue

Susanne and Georg sat on their hill overlooking the neighboring village. There was no longer a border fence obscuring the view. Susanne had her head cradled against Georg's shoulder while he was stroking her arm. They both looked at the white houses with their red-tiled roofs and neat colorful front yards. Cars were going back and forth between the two villages.

"No dead-end anymore," Georg said. "All one country."

"Did you hear that they plan to build a public pool right where no man's land was?" Susanne pointed at the strip of barren field between the two villages.

"Really?"

Susanne snuggled up closer to him. "It feels good to feel the sun on one's back, doesn't it?"

"Maybe we should go somewhere when it gets cold. In November, when it gets all gray and rainy. Somewhere warm and sunny like Italy or Greece," Georg suggested.

Susanne looked up at him, amused. "You want to migrate south like birds or retired people?"

He looked offended. "I just thought it would be fun going somewhere. Now that we can. Explore the world, you know." Georg looked at the neighboring village and then at the sky above. "And escape the dreary weather for a few weeks, that's all."

"I'd rather stay home."

He smiled at her, cradled her face in his two hands and kissed her lips, which felt surprisingly cool for a hot summer's day.

Afterword

With the fall of the Berlin Wall and the opening of the border that had separated East and West, as well as the reunification of the two Germanys, the whole Eastern block of Europe eventually regained its freedom and a free democracy was established in the respective countries at last.

May no wall or fence longer divide a people!

About Author

C. K. McAdam writes historical fiction. Her debut novel *No Man's Land* was inspired by her family's history, her own upbringing, and the history of Cold War East Germany. A prequel, set during WWII, is planned for late 2023. Her current project is a Holocaust fiction novel, coming out Summer of 2023. She holds a Ph.D. in history and literary studies, and teaches college. Together with her family, she resides in Texas but hails originally from Germany where she grew up.

Subscribe to the author's newsletter by visiting

www.mcadambooks.com
for more info, news, and updates.

Connect with and follow the author on
Facebook @ckmcadam
Instagram @ckmcadam
Twitter @CK_McAdam!

Printed in Great Britain
by Amazon

40866018R00192